D1429392

HEROES AND SARACENS

In Memoriam
RUTH

who had so large a part in everything I ever wrote
with warm interest and cool judgement

who died before this book was finished
but was interested to the last

its faults are not hers

dying and in pain she said
come and kiss me now and let's be laughing

this was the spirit that the singers created
for the paladins of Charlemagne and the Saracens of Babylon

> Morte est Guibors, ma cortoise molliers
> Et mes lignages, dont jou sui mout iriés.
> Or ai por Dieu tout mon pais laissié.
>
> Moniage Guillaume (2) 2275–7

HEROES AND SARACENS

An Interpretation of the
Chansons de Geste

NORMAN DANIEL

Edinburgh University
Press

© Norman Daniel 1984
Edinburgh University Press
22 George Square, Edinburgh

Set in Monotype Barbou, 178 series
by Speedspools, Edinburgh and
printed in Great Britain by
Redwood Burn Limited, Trowbridge

British Library Cataloguing
    in Publication Data
Daniel, Norman
Heroes and saracens: an interpretation of the
Chansons de geste
1. Chansons de geste—History and criticism
I. Title
841.03   PQ201

ISBN 0 85224 430 4

CONTENTS

ACKNOWLEDGEMENTS

My first thanks are to my wife, for her criticism, interest and encouragement, and her example (which the dedication may help to explain); and also to Mademoiselle Marie-Thérèse d'Alverny and Sir Richard Southern, for encouraging me to go ahead, and to Mr A. R. Turnbull, Secretary to the Press, who is a stimulating as well as inventive publisher. Academic acknowledgements relating to particular issues are made in the course of the notes. I am most grateful to Dr Michael Rogers, Monsieur and Madame Jean-Yves Tadié, and Mr and Mrs J. R. Young, all of whom helped me in a number of ways, and in particular to get material at times when it was inaccessible to me, sometimes at considerable inconvenience to themselves; and to Mr Robert Anderson and Mr Peter Mackenzie Smith, who also helped me materially at moments of need. I am under a great debt to the Abbot and Community of St Benoit de Port Valais, and to the Sisters of Ste Marthe, for their hospitality, and in particular to the Prior, Père Michel de Ribeaupierre, for making me comfortable in his 'scriptorium', and to the Librarian, Père François Huot, for all the attentions that a librarian can give.

I am similarly obliged to the Prior and Community of the Institut dominicain d'études orientales, Abbasiah, Cairo, in whose grounds I live for most of my time, and in particular to the Director of Studies, Père G. C. Anawati, for making all their facilities always available. I am indebted for the quiet efficiency of the Students Room at the British Library, for the determination of the staff of the Reading Room to overcome their many difficulties, and for the efficiency and courtesy of the staff of Bodley. I am also greatly obliged to Madame J. le Monnier, conservateur en chef du service photographique de la bibliothèque nationale in Paris, for making photographs of a manuscript quickly available in special circumstances, and to the staff of the bibliothèque de l'Arsenal, who make it so easy and pleasant for a stranger to consult their manuscripts. I am most grateful to Dr Carole Hillenbrand, whose understanding of a tangled script made the preparation of the text possible.

INTRODUCTORY

A good deal of attention has been paid to what we might call the official Christian attitude to Islam in the Middle Ages; I am myself one of those who have done so. Much less has been said about ordinary and unofficial attitudes, and most of it relates to the origins of the idols imputed to the Saracens. Official attitudes were expressed by theologians whose function was to speak for the Christian Church of the West. Apart from its material privilege, the Church was privileged to speak for Christian society in a period when all overt opposition was successfully suppressed. The existence of official spokesmen and the absence of open opposition do not, of course, eliminate unofficial attitudes and ideas, and these are not necessarily part of a hidden opposition. Hypothetical secret organisations of opposition need to be fully substantiated to be plausible, and they rarely or never are. I am thinking more of instances of divergent thought or sentiment which were not meant to compete with, let alone harm or destroy, the official view. People may accept an established authority quite willingly, and still live their own lives and think their own thoughts.

This book is about *unofficial* attitudes to Islam and the Arabs. Exhaustive or even adequate source material is much harder to come by than is the case with expressions of theologically acceptable opinion, because unofficial attitudes were not encouraged, and received little explicit and formal expression; if they had done, they would no longer have been entirely unofficial. What material there is is much harder to interpret, because we often cannot take it at its face value. It is a question

1

of making the least improbable guess, when refusing to guess at all is to fall back on some uncalculated assumption without conscious reflection. Where conclusive proof is impossible, we naturally look for the explanation that best fits the known facts and, so far as we can manage, is least anachronistic.

It is probably safe to assume that, in any age, in the Middle Ages as now, most Europeans have had very little idea of Islam and very little interest in it. We cannot study here the ideas of the mass of the common people, who may or may not have heard about Saracens, and may or may not have believed what they heard. We shall never know the thoughts of those people who had no technique with which to express themselves, because they could neither write nor command an amanuensis, and because they did not have skills of oral composition and memorial retention. The subject is too flimsy to pursue; but there were people whose ideas bear upon Islam; who composed without needing to write; who were not spokesmen for the Church, though they did have to satisfy an audience; who were not philosophers, not theologians, not even propagandists – or, if propagandists, not necessarily propagandists for what ostensibly they supported. They made propaganda rather for the chivalry that often paid them and that provided their subject matter, than for the endless religious war in which they set their stories. Indeed, it is already to beg the question to speak of a religious war, before we have established that that is what it was. We should more safely say, war against people of another religion. If we are looking for an unofficial view, it is natural to turn to the poets of the *chansons de geste* and of the later romances that developed out of them, because these were not theologians. They composed for the benefit of laymen, primarily soldiers, but at all social levels of society interested to hear about courtly adventures.

The *chansons de geste*, historical fictions mostly set in the time of Charlemagne or his son Louis, appear several generations earlier than that other courtly literature that is concerned with the dalliance of lovers. Their lovers have little time to dally. The chansons appear in the twelfth century in manuscript, in the three forms of Old French, Francien, Picard and Anglo-Norman and they had a European influence throughout the Middle Ages, especially on Italian, but also on English and German literatures, as well as in Spain, and, of course, on Provençal. They certainly had eleventh century forebears, probably, as we shall shortly see, in oral form. We do not know how far they go back. They preserve a memory of a distant past, always incorrect, yet uncannily preserving authentic recollections, not only of events, but often of a forgotten atmosphere of defeat by alien armies. They were once supposed to derive from *cantilènes* contemporary with the events they describe, but this is just a hypothesis, and Joseph Bédier inferred written sources in monastic records instead; there is no agreement about their pre-history. They survived for several centuries, compromising with modish themes of love-making and surrendering assonance to the new taste for rhyme, but always preserving certain conventions that mark them out from all other medieval literature; these concern their treatment of the Saracens, and of religious themes connected with them. From the 'Benedictine centuries', through the Gregorian Reform, to the rise of papal temporal power and of canon law, and in the Conciliar age, there is still no important change in their peculiar view of the Saracens.

Many people, if asked what they think of as the medieval idea of Islam, will think first of the idolatry imputed to the Saracens by these songs of action. It is useful to remember that this absurdity became notorious in the last century, when these poems were rediscovered and many of them published; since then, our modern awareness that this is so gross an error makes us give an anachronistic emphasis to the importance we suppose the medieval poets must also have seen in it. Even so, the facts remain that these poems are concerned with the Saracen religion, and that they do commit this absurdity. What they say about the Saracens and their gods is the obvious place to look for an unofficial, unchurchmanlike, medieval view of Islam – if only we can interpret it correctly. I am therefore going to concentrate on these songs or poems, concerned with a war between Christians and Saracens, but composed by poets with ideas of their own, not so much original individual ideas, as ideas taking the form of a clear but complex convention within which the poets chose to work. It is this conventional framework which sets the literature apart. While I hope to offer some check on my conclusions, by comparison with other sources wholly or largely outside the convention, I will concentrate on the seventy and more works within it. I want at the same time to compare these songs of action with the official polemic, and with the legendary and libellous origins from which it developed. Finally, I want to compare what the poets say with whatever we can suggest may have been a possible source in Islam itself; it is *prima facie* improbable, yet conceivable, that Saracen religion in the songs relates to actual facts about Islam in the same way as a distorting mirror twists a real object into an unrecognisable travesty.

The origins of the poets' pantheon and of their concept of a Saracen have, of course, been studied before, but mainly from the point of view of literary criticism.[1] I do not propose to attempt literary criticism or literary history for which I am not qualified by training or experience. It will no doubt be impossible to write a whole book about a series of literary texts without expressing or implying some literary opinion, but such opinions are personal, and I hope not to obtrude them. I have no special experience in literature as an artefact, rather than as an historical source. Neither would I attempt to judge the history of texts or of manuscripts, their inter-relations and mutual influences. Although I trust to make full use of the work of editors, of critics and of commentators on the texts, I confine myself to the history of ideas. I want to discuss the ideas in the minds of the poets, without reference at all to the literary skill with which they speak. Because I am not concerned with the history of written texts, but with the content of a convention used and modified only slightly over a long period, I am able to use material from different dates throughout the period, often to illustrate the durability of the tradition. We are using texts that have reached us in a final form determined in many cases only when they were committed to writing; they are the fossils of a lengthy evolution which is largely homogeneous. Texts that are an exception to the rule only show some variation of ideas within a convention that remains unchanged in all its essentials.

Modern literary studies, and historical literary studies such as comprise the area of *sociocritique*, are exploring some lines of enquiry which, though they first appeared in the last century, and lay dormant for a time, are now approached with highly sophisticated techniques, and relate the content and form of a work to major social change, rather than just to the superficial details of social background in an author or an audience.[2] If we are to work on the convention as a whole, on the other hand, we must expect to single out those elements that do not change, even when they are understood in a new way. It is a fact that very different audiences may enjoy the same convention, though it may be for new reasons or with a different kind of appreciation. For the preliminary control of the material over the whole field it should be useful to eliminate the unchanging convention from new forms and purposes. I do not attempt more than that, and I do not attempt either to write the history of the convention, which would be too much for one book, and perhaps for one author. My own interest is a special one, not a general one.

I am concerned only to find out more about how the chansons represent Islam – and the Arabs – to their public. To examine, not only what they did, but what they thought they were doing, I am qualified by long experience of the problems of European and Christian apprehension of Arabs and Muslims in the Middle Ages, and also other periods, including our own. My experience is professional as well as lengthy. It is in this field that I believe I may usefully supplement, certainly not compete with, the literary specialists and the social historians.

I shall usually say 'poets' for the creators of the chansons, including those that created only a passage here and there, or just modified verse they had inherited from other singers,

perhaps varying a *laisse* with a different assonance, blending or
interpolating passages that others had composed. I say 'poets',
rather than 'singers' or *jongleurs*. 'Jongleur' has no adequate
English equivalent, and may anyway mean just buffoon or
trickster. I am using 'poet' to designate the jongleur as author
or adapter, and 'singer' when I refer to him as executant, without meaning to draw a line between these in practice, or only a
notional line. I rarely need to speak of the singer rather than of
the person whose ideas I am talking about. Rychner stresses
the wide range of jongleur professionalism, from singer to
manipulator of performing fleas, and Faral speaks of two kinds
of jongleurs, the respectable, needed to compose the lives of
saints, and the rest, those approved by the Church and those
disapproved; perhaps one man might at different times be
either.[3] Rychner shows how the text is fluid, an oral trans-
mission which the singer may modify as he goes along, and
which at some stage, determined by chance, may be committed
to writing. There is no correct text, no *'expression singulière et
originale'*. In his support he cites Milman Parry's work on
Homer, and his examples of songs of action in Herzogovina.[4]
The results of Muhsin Mahdi's revolutionary work on the
'Arabian Nights' (*alf layla wa layla*) are similar, except that
in this case a conglomeration of works in prose was committed
over five centuries to a progressively more classical written
form. It remains true that, in this case also, the text was constantly adapted or manipulated by the performer, that there
cannot be said to be any one original form, and that the authorship is both communal and gradual.[5] *'Mais tous les bons chan-
teurs sont encore des improvisateurs'*, says Rychner, *'ils créent eux-
mêmes leurs chants, et, quand ils ne créent pas à proprement parler,
ils savent combiner les chants entre eux, condenser plusieurs poèmes
en un, modifier, compléter, amplifier.'*[6] We cannot tell how many
lost poems there are, or how much each surviving author owes
to phrases and notions in general circulation. When I say 'the
poet says', I mean the author or authors of the line or the lines
or the passage I am quoting, no more; I imply nothing about
his literary quality; and I say 'poet' even if the passage in

question is like a patch of garden, worked over by many gardeners, one or two of whom may – or may not – have imposed a pattern individually conceived.

This literature is best conceived, not as a library of editions, but as a conglomeration of discrepant manuscripts behind which, and beyond our reach, loom the oral forms of what was once a living tradition, only partly caught and crystallised when they were written down. '*La chanson de geste n'est pas dans le manuscrit que nous ouvrons, nous n'en tenons là qu'un reflet; elle était ailleurs, dans le cercle au centre duquel chantait le jongleur.*'⁷ The case for a kind of communal authorship does not depend on Rychner's powerful arguments; he attributes *Roland* to a single author, and some poems were certainly the work of individuals, a Jean Bodel or a Jean Renart, for instance. But these too made use of communal forms and worked within the set tradition of a convention. As a garden may be more-or-less landscaped or designed, or just planted haphazard, so a poem may be built up from traditional fragments more or less neatly fitted together. Any text, however fragmentary, and whatever its literary quality, is good evidence for ideas. This vast literature, with its marked peculiarities, persisted for centuries; but, although the same formulae, ideals, words, phrases, must have acquired new meanings or shades of meaning as society developed, the convention as a whole remained the same. I am studying it as an episode – a long episode – in the history of ideas, as a vehicle for thought and feeling, stated and implied; often a bald statement implies much, sometimes the context alone does so. We recognise disjointed pieces, a mother's lament for her son, the dying warrior's farewell to his horse, a stereotype sometimes spatchcocked in a little carelessly; but there is an inference to be drawn just from where the poet has chosen to insert it.

There are cycles of poems, and sometimes the same characters appear in different works, with repetitions and inconsistencies in one story, or from one to another. From one song to the next, from one passage in it to another, there are marked differences of mood. In *Le Charroi de Nîmes* and *La Prise*

d'Orange, the hero Guillaume's light-hearted audacity over-
comes the Saracens; in *Le Couronnement de Louis* and *La
Chanson de Guillaume* he is fighting with his back to the wall.
The same characters occur in different stories and are often
consistently developed from story to story, in spite of multiple
authorship. Guillaume d'Orange is a good example. The old
man who becomes a hermit in *Le Moniage Guillaume* is quite
consistent with the eager young lover of *La Prise d'Orange*. It
is as though the author of the later poem had said, 'wouldn't it
be amusing to imagine this cheeky young man become a monk
in his old age?' – and he has succeeded. Another example is
Renoart in poems which overlap with the Guillaume poems and
in which he tends to overshadow Guillaume. His character is
developed in different songs a little differently, but consistently
with his first appearance in *La Chanson de Guillaume*. Versions
of the same story may vary considerably; the Saracen King
Desramé is killed in one version of *La Bataille Loquifer*, and in
another he survives an apparently fatal blow to appear again
in another song.[8] There are conscious links between songs;
in his *Moniage*, Guillaume wants to attract the attention of
robbers, and makes his reluctant servant sing, in one version
'an old song', but in another a song 'of lord Tibaut the Escler
and Guillaume the shortnosed marquis' and the capture of
Orange, in fact the song of his own youthful exploits.[9] Yet in
spite of all variations and divergences, the literature as a whole
has somehow managed to create stories homogeneous not only
in idea, mood and feeling, but in the framework and background within which they are composed; all these combine to
create the characteristic convention of behaviour and situation.

It is easier to define 'Saracen' than to define 'poet'. The word
Saracen came into use in late antiquity in both Greek and Latin,
and meant simply 'Arab'. After the rise of Islam and throughout
the Middle Ages, academic and historical writers used *Saracen*
to mean 'Arab' or 'Muslim', or both, according to context.
'Saracen' in the sense of 'Muslim' gave place to 'Turk' with the
rise of the Ottomans. Before that, 'Turk' had been used either
specifically for '(Seljuk) Turk' or in a vague way interchange-

ably with 'Saracen' or 'Persian'. 'Saracen' in the sense of 'Arab' began to be displaced by 'More' (Moor) in the fifteenth century: and, as the number of travellers increased, the word 'Arab' came to be used, especially in the pejorative sense of 'Beduin'. What the chansons de geste meant by 'Saracen' we have to determine; it is an important part of our enquiry to find out whether their Saracens are meant as a realistic portrait of Arabs in Spain, the Maghrib, Egypt and Syria. *Saracen* normally denoted all these Arabs, and the imaginary Saracens of fiction are certainly described as inhabitants of those areas, but we cannot assume that the two uses of *Saracen* carry the same meaning unless we know that the songs are meant to describe the Arabs actually living in those places. Fictions are inhabited by fictional people, who may or may not be intended as the real thing. In this book I shall say *Saracen* when I am citing a medieval source, and specifically *Saracen* as it is used in the songs when I am quoting from the songs; when I am speaking in my own person about Arabs, I shall use the word *Arab*.

The first part of my book is my attempt to understand what the poets meant by 'Saracen', and the second part is about their extraordinary imputation of false gods to the Saracens of their invention. I shall examine how these fictional and poetic gods are to be interpreted within the convention, and what is meant in it, and during the Middle Ages generally, by the word 'pagan'. The gods are, of course, doubly false, conceived by the poets in the first place as false gods in whom their imaginary Saracens erroneously believed, but falsely so conceived of Muslims, if these Saracens are Muslims – the same Muslims as suspected the purity of Christian monotheism. It has often been taken for granted that this misconception was a serious Christian error of judgement based on simple ignorance. We shall look closely at that assumption, because, if it is justified, we must also have reason to assume that the fictions of the songs are intended to be realistic; the two assumptions can only go together.

In speaking of the first and most often cited of these gods I shall always use the form 'Mahon' (and not the English equivalent, 'Mahound') because 'Mahon' is the form least like the name of the Prophet. We will only use the Prophet's name if propaganda hostile to him at least assumes that he put forward his claim to be a prophet; otherwise, we shall only use it correctly. Whatever explanation of this curious convention of a pantheon we finally adopt, we shall recognise that it is offensive to use the name of the Prophet to denote something that in no way at all resembles the historic Muhammad, whose name the poets borrowed for reasons that we shall look into closely. One well-known poet refers to *Mahom* and *Mahomés* as if they were separate. Avoidance of offence which gives pain is sufficient reason for this; but there is also the point that a special terminology serves to keep the distinction clear. *Saracen*, then, I use for the fictional people, and *Mahon* for the fictional god.

While we are thinking about a long series of much-loved stories, we must not forget that much other material was being written about Arabs and about Islam. A class of theologians concerned as official teachers and spokesmen of Christian religion had an interest in preparing serious polemic. One department of their effort was the collection of authentic information which, they supposed, would make their arguments more effective. Their work was at any rate serious. Between the polemists and the poets is an indeterminate class, largely chroniclers, prepared to make use of any material, offensive or authentic, that would make their work more interesting. The polemists, as representing what we began by calling the official attitude, must always be in our minds as a standard of comparison for the songs. At each point we must measure the distance between the songs and the polemic, but we shall hardly expect to find them agree, when their purposes were so different: the poets to amuse and the polemists to convert. We must in any case know what the polemists were saying.

They seem to have had the needs of missionaries in mind. Indeed, they seem to have conceived that there would be actual debates with Muslims who would be outargued and convinced publicly; perhaps it was thought they would become Christians when they had been brought to see reason. The polemists tried to adjust their matter to this vain hope, but debates hardly ever did take place under open conditions, and when they did, were inconclusive. Preaching to Muslims in Europe was a means of putting pressure on them to become Christians. Conquered Muslim communities were absorbed into expanding European Christendom, and the captive audiences could never say what they thought of the preachers' arguments. In the reverse situation, the polemic may have done something to fortify the convictions of Christians in Muslim countries, subject, not quite to the same pressures as their opposite numbers in Europe, but to the general pressure always exerted by the human wish to conform. Missionaries who went to Muslim countries and did not confine their attention to Christians were not allowed a hearing, and, if they publicly attacked Islam, often achieved a martyrdom which, being rashly incurred, was contrary to a Church Council;[10] the Muslim authorities saved Lull in spite of himself, until finally an angry crowd got him.[11] Self-deceived by the characteristic scholastic faith that rational argument would 'prove' every aspect of the Christian position, actual or notional missionaries had no idea of the differences of which any genuine communication between Christians and Muslims would have to take account.

Peter the Venerable is an honourable exception. In his book against Islam, which is the culmination of his work to gather information for public use in polemic, he began by addressing his supposed audience 'in the East and the South', as 'by function, abbot of those who are called monks'; and as 'a man very far away from you, speaking a different language, divided from you by vocation, alien in ways and life' he approaches 'those whom I have never seen and perhaps never shall see'.[12] Peter's sensitivity and rare awareness of cultural differences contrasts with his failure, so far as we know, to turn his moving and in many ways well-judged appeal to Muslims into Arabic, and also with the fact, if we take him literally, that he made an extended visit to Spain without meeting a Muslim. It is possible that he took his awareness of the nature of the problem a step further, and realised that what he had written could not be delivered or published in any way that would ensure its being given any attention, and so gave up the attempt. It is also possible that he never intended it to be anything but a warning to Christians about the best way to approach Muslims. Yet even if this book is no more than a rhetorical exercise, it contrasts with the assumptions of other writers. The rest of the Cluniac corpus follows the usual pattern of medieval polemic against Islam, and Peter's choice of new and different themes for this one book must be deliberate. It is unlike the short summary about Islamic error also attributed to him, and is not so free from familiar arguments. The headings prepared for him by his assistant, Peter of Poitiers, are a fair sample of ordinary Spanish polemic material. Peter the Venerable's principal book on the subject remains at worst a *tour de force*, and its argument frequently drives home the difficulty he recognises of obtaining a hearing across the cultural barrier.[13] We shall see just how far such a barrier was perceived by the poets.

Other writers, including all the scholastics, reverted to the traditional themes of Christian polemic in one combination or another, and are repetitious to the point of creating a canon of their belief about what Muslim belief consists of. When they show originality it is usually in refinement of method only. Yet they were anxious to use authentic Islamic material, and so by implication were aware that they ran the danger of being derided by any Muslim not too angry for scorn, if he heard the usual Christian libels against his religion and his Prophet. It is not clear whether they realised at all how counter-productive their arguments would have proved, could they have uttered them to a Muslim. Nevertheless, the fact that they thought it worth while looking for authenticity necessarily implies that they understood the need to adapt their matter to their suppositious audience. Ricoldo da Monte Croce, whose great polemic work is unoriginal,[14] recounts his astonishment in Baghdad at the Arabs' 'care for studies, devotion in prayer, their pity for the poor, their reverence for the name of God, the dignity of their manners, their friendliness towards foreigners, and their harmony and love for one another'. He admits that he reports this 'rather to confound the Christians than to praise the Muslims',[15] and some of what he reports seems exaggerated for his homiletic purpose. We cannot believe in such virtue and harmony, though they may well have compared favourably with Christian behaviour in the West. Whatever his motive, he makes the existence of cultural differences impossible for a reader to ignore.

The curious claim by Walter of Compiègne that when he wrote his highly imaginative, but very far from authentic, *Otia de Machomete*, he had his information about the Prophet direct from a Saracen, reminds us that in the twelfth century it was already fashionable to lay claim to authentic, first-hand information, although in this case it must surely have been a literary device.[16] No Arab could have provided the sort of misinformation that constitutes this text, unless conceivably a Christian Arab or a Jew, and even then more probably with malice than in innocence. One is reminded of the 'forty amirs and highly placed men' brought back to France converted by Louis IX; it would take only a venal *drugement* to impose on the King; perhaps these were Eastern Christians.[17] We may doubt whether stories of Arabs wandering or settled in Northern Europe were altogether authentic, without further evidence that we are unlikely to find, but it is quite clear that authenticity was in fashion among intellectuals. Could the tale of Louis' amirs even be an attempt to authenticate the chansons de geste ? It would be fanciful to suggest that it was so consciously; but fictions dressed up as history, as all the songs were, may easily become seen as history until current history is seen in the light of the fiction. May there not have been proto-Quixotes centuries before Cervantes ? We know that theologians sought authenticity, but it must rest an open question whether chivalry was looking in its own way for an authenicity of its own; and if so, whether that would have influenced the poets' concept of a Saracen pantheon. We might expect poets to take chivalry more seriously than theological nicety, and we have to consider separately whether they were trying to get their facts right about Arabs and about Islam; and I shall in any case try consistently to measure the distance between their ideas and those of the theologians.

Arab society and European society between the Christian tenth and fifteenth centuries were comparable but far from identical. We could hardly expect medieval European writers to analyse their own feudal institutions in modern terms, let alone to analyse land tenure and its obligations in different parts of the Arab world, to compare and contrast the results, note the resemblances and bring out the differences. We might expect those who knew anything of Spanish affairs to have observed the political and social changes when the minor courts of the taifas gave place to the unitary rule of the Almoravids and Almohads in turn. They noticed of course the change in military quality in their enemy, they knew something of Spanish Muslim politics, and some even took in something of the changes in religious observance.[18] But this is very superficial. It would be anachronistic to expect the same attention to have been given to the social sciences as to theology, philosophy and even the natural sciences. The extending use of the word *maurus, more* in French, suggests a widespread realisation of invasion from North Africa; the chansons speak of 'Africa' rather than of Moors, and this seems likely to mean Tunisia rather than Morocco.[19] There is little suggestion that Arab and Christian administrative institutions caused practical problems of assimilation; they were not prominent among the worries of rulers who recaptured parts of Arab Spain, and in the Latin States of the East a number of local Arab institutions were absorbed without difficulty.[20] When it came to making cultural comparisons, they were made in religious terms, as in the case of the commentator who noted the resemblance between the Caliph for Muslims and the Pope for Christians (in a rough way, correct enough) and between Christ crucified for Christians and Muhammad for Muslims (a basic misunderstanding) but even this sort of comparison was rare, and anything like it in social terms is barely conceivable.[21] There is some assimilation of *qādi* to *bishop*.[22]

The sort of differences between the two cultures which made an appreciable impact on anyone at all were in the field of learning. Western scholars in the twelfth century diagnosed without difficulty their loss of their own Hellenistic tradition in philosophy and science, and acknowledged their need to learn from translations from the Arabic.[23] They were even willing to learn from ibn Sina how to adjust Greek philosophy to revelation. On the other hand, comparisons in the moral field, though only too common, were almost always doctrinaire, based, not on observation of how Muslims behave, but on an inference from what their law allowed them (see Chapter 4, below). From the same source were inferred the circumstances in which Islam began: *luxuriosus autem fuit et bellicosus*,[24] a gross interpretation highly offensive to Muslims and sufficient to preclude all communication with them. The theologians and canon lawyers who claimed to control thought and behaviour were convinced that Islam was antinomian, a ludicrous error that derived from the assumption that there can be only one law. Another failure in comprehension was not to admit that Islam and Christianity had alike been revealed to pagan peoples, in the latter case by the Apostles; as the two cultures inherited Greek medicine, so they inherited the sophisticated astrology of the ancient world.[25] They had in fact shared the experience of imposing revelation on paganism, and had not drawn further apart since; in at least one respect the opposite happened, and the law of Crusade came to resemble in astonishing detail the law of *jihād* (see Chapter 5, below). This was another resemblance that no one seems to have noted at the time. To generalise, the intellectuals of Europe saw differences between Muslims and Christians that were not there, and missed resemblances that were. In our perspective to-day all this seems strange; even in their religion they look, at this distance, so alike, each with its strict laws governing behaviour, usually and in most places observed at least in public, each wholly devoted to the communal celebration of a revealed religion. If we compare them with the pagan world before Christianity or with our own world of conformist indulgence, they look as like as two peas. The greater change has been in the West, where there is another point of difference; the intellectual developments of the twelfth century were founded on the recovery of an old tradition, as those of the later twentieth derive from a loss of a classical tradition in language and literature. But it was the very closeness of the two cultures that formed the basis of war and rivalry. The translations of scientific texts were the fruit of Christian conquests in Spain, and in Syria and Sicily also; and the war that made so much possible was itself a result of the likeness of the two religions, each exclusive in its revelation, each with a divine commission to dominate (it does not affect this that the Muslim was the more tolerant).

We ought on the face of it to have little difficulty in fitting songs of action in which, in the well-known line, 'Christians are right and pagans are wrong',[26] into the pattern of religious war, but that line is a deceptively simple one. It does indeed mean that pagans have the wrong religion and that it is right to fight them, but it does not tell us how wrong the pagans are, whether they may be good, brave and virtuous, or how right the Christians; and it does not tell us whether the wrongness is the cause of the fighting or a justification for it when it happens. We shall see that the religious war in the chansons cannot be assumed without enquiry to conform to the clerical model for Crusade. We have seen the condemnation of Islam by some Christians to follow two chief categories, *luxuriosus* and *bellicosus*. To judge the degree of conformity of the songs to these two criticisms is one of the principal purposes of the first part of this book.

In interpreting what the poets mean by *Saracen* and *pagan* and 'god' and 'right' and 'wrong', one is always conscious of the danger of patronising them as naive or despising them as ignorant. Even ignorance is too easily taken for granted – it may be only a sign of lack of interest in anything that might distract attention from where the poet wants it to be; but naivety is the most dangerous accusation of all to make, for one man's sophistication is the next man's naivety. The variation from high seriousness to humour is really quite clear, but the transition is often fast and subtle, and then it is possible to mistake the level of seriousness. There are warning signs. When something looks silly and childish we may suspect a joke, particularly with hyperbole and exaggeration. It is some-times difficult to recognise a joke across the centuries; and especially when the author takes frivolously what our own age takes more seriously. The reverse also happens. The poets often make a joke of killing and torture, but hardly of loyalty; it is not a matter of approval or disapproval, but just of what we can laugh about. It is much like the way one nation thinks funny what another does not – 'the past is a foreign country'.[27] Some subjects, such as adultery, seem to be funny everywhere and in all ages; and other subjects seem to belong to their own age. Few or none of our songs are devoid of humour, but it seems as though the themes associated with Guillaume and *R*enoart, and in another way Maugis d'Aigremont, particularly attracted the joking mood, and yet something serious usually underlies the crudest joke, and no situation is so desperate but some absurdity enlivens it. The whole theme of *Le Voyage de Charlemagne* is itself a joke – the paladins, as tourists, in un-wonted relaxation, make absurd boasts that they must after-wards make good.

It is difficult to draw a hard and fast line round the poems of this convention, to define everything within it as belonging, and everything outside as alien to it. There are stories about Saracens which treat them as pagans, but which barely name the gods or name them not at all. There are *chansons de geste* and *romans d'aventure* which treat subjects without gods or Saracens. The aim of this book is to examine what the poets meant by the gods. Material that is about Saracens but lacks the gods is negative evidence, and on the whole I reserve it for my penultimate chapter. There are inevitable inconsistencies; the *Roman d'Auberon*, for example, by itself would belong clearly in this category, but it cannot be separated from the rest of the Huon cycle. It is Tervagant who is peculiar to the convention, although he is subsidiary to Mahon; *Mahon* may be used to refer to the Prophet, but Tervagant can only mean the god. There is no other Tervagant anywhere in literature and so I sometimes speak of the 'Tervagant conventions', to mean the convention of the entire Saracen pantheon, but that is only a convenience, not an assertion of his special importance. He may not be mentioned often or in any special way, but he exists nowhere else but in the pantheon of this convention, and therefore he can very suitably lend it his name.

War with the Saracens, or adventures among hostile Saracens always provide the framework. War is the principal theme, but, although the poems as a whole are candid about the horrors of war as it affects ordinary people, it often seems more like an extended tournament, with plenty of scope for star parts in single combats. Physical danger is the mainstay of the excitement, and battles are often long drawn-out. The poets show some courage in describing a soldier's life and work to what must often have been an audience of soldiers, and under the patronage of lords who command them in battle. Few of the poets can have excelled in the soldiers' skills. No doubt the ironic hyperbole and the physical improbabilities with which most encounters are described will have helped the poets here. Since the songs were successful we must conclude that the audiences did not miss the joke or mind that the technique of war should be frankly stylised or even burlesqued. We need some willing suspension of unbelief in the terms of the convention to enjoy it as the poets intended and as the contemporary audiences did. When the poets show a happy indifference to facts, we can take pleasure from it only by being happy and indifferent too. In a meaningless and recurring phrase like *Sarazins et Esclers*, *Esclers* adds nothing to the sense, but it is the sound of folk poetry.

I want to see the convention in relation to outside factors

which may or may not have affected it: the strongly held opinions and widespread libels about Islam of more literate and more official spokesmen for Christendom, from the local monastery to the Pope; and also the relevant facts about Islam. I want to consider the internal consistency of ideas within the convention; the first and most likely explanation of every problem, and the reason for every apparent absurdity, is that it improves the story, or seemed to the poet to do so. The songs were sung to entertain. I want to relate the outside and inside factors to each other, and especially to decide whether the hostility of the Church theologians to the Muslims is the same as that of the heroes of the songs to their kind of Saracen. I do not attempt an exhaustive series of references; my aim is to quote enough to illustrate each point. There is a thorough treatment in C. Meredith Jones' *The Conventional Saracen*; it is too concentrated to be more than occasionally interpretative, but there are usually further references to be found there.[28] At the end I hope to reach a conclusion about the purpose and function of the gods. I claim to make no new discovery, and much that I say agrees with the authorities on the subject; not all of it. What is different derives from the application of outside standards: the facts about Islam, the history of Christian apologetic, my long experience of cultural interaction. I recognise that we shall never assess the past with perfect accuracy, or even with enough sensitivity, but I try to approach each problem warily, remembering above all that the ignorance of the poem tells us nothing about the knowledge of the poet.

I have not always been consistent in choosing the form of names by which I refer to the characters in the poems, but mainly I have preferred a French form – *Guillaume*, even in the *Chanson* which calls him Willame. My references are to any printed text easily available to me, and where there was none, to unpublished manuscript. There are many of the songs, and they are confusing even to those who have read them. To help readers who are not familiar with them, the names of characters in the poems who are born Saracen are printed with an italic initial, and the names of those born Christian with a roman. They retain the mark of their origin if they change sides. At the end of this book will be found summaries of the plots of the songs chiefly quoted, with detail intended only to clarify episodes referred to in my text.

THE PEOPLE

CHIVALRY

Chivalry

The poets' view of Saracen society is several removes from the facts that were known in their own day, still more from anything we think now. We can compare it only with their estimate of their own society in the same poems, what they thought of themselves and projected on to others, a picture within a picture. The heroes mostly belong to the dominant class of feudal superiors and professional knights, a class the poets knew personally as patrons and employers. By what code do these characters act, and by what standards do their creators judge them? Is the society of their enemies, the Saracens, imagined as different, and are the standards by which they are judged the same?

Today we see chivalry, not only through the wrong end of a telescope, but through lenses that distort our vision. Since the original European experience, the Arthurian cycle has remodelled the European idea of chivalry. For English-speakers, Malory, writing when Saracen romances were still popular, has shaped our views, and so in due time did Tennyson. It was not only Arthur. Ariosto introduced his own taste into the legend of Roland, and Cervantes made a deep impression on the whole world; Rabelais too has influenced our modern view. New developments of the literary myth of chivalry in the twentieth century naturally continue to distort the old. It is difficult to recapture an age when the code of chivalry was a practical reaction to social needs, the rules of a trade compar-

23

able to the conventions of trade-unionism to-day; when a great lord was top management, and a tournament was as good a release for aggression as a picket-line. Managers and shop stewards may be the actors in romantic literature of the future, and, if so, it will be difficult for posterity to recover the practical, unglamorised impression of them we have to-day.

Tennyson, sceptical perhaps of his own rendering of chivalry, reflected on the death of Arthur that 'the old order changeth, yielding place to new', but new patterns of social life are not wholly different. There is more difference between a reality and its literary image, between patterns of social behaviour that correspond to actual need and these same patterns when they have been idealised. The ideals remained largely constant during several centuries of social change, while one nobility succeeded another. On the other hand, the literature about Saracens is not wholly unrealistic. The chivalry with which we have to do is not the chivalry 'baptised' by the church, with vigils and prayers and a liturgical office; it is not much concerned with defenceless maidens; or not, at any rate, with protecting the very sharp ladies whose initiative in our poems seems so often to dominate the prowess of their men; it is largely free from Celtic twilight, and only occasionally, and mildly, subject to magical interference. It is a practical code for soldiers, and as simple as the rules of football, though not written out like canon law, or even like the 'code' of courtly love as defined by Andreas Capellanus.

The literature with which we are concerned looks back to hard times for Christian arms, to the period when not only Saracens, but Vikings and Hungarians, in succession to Saxons and Lombards, laid Europe waste. Charlemagne's preferred 'Crusade' was against Saxons, not Arabs. Entirely new stories are set in the time of Charlemagne or his son Louis;[1] one (*Floovant*) is in a Merovingian setting. The poems were composed, in the state in which we have them, roughly during the period of greatest Christian aggression in the Mediterranean, a time when in Western Europe the royal admini-trations were extending their influence in conflict with the barons, a time when the European economy was expanding, the population growing, and many younger sons of lords and knights were landless.

The Crusade cycles proper are different in setting, the second cycle reflecting both the economic needs and the political situation of a later period, but even more fantastic and implausible, and the first cycle[2] carrying most of the conventions of the other poems into relatively sober contemporary history. The whole literature is chivalrous in that its themes reflect the interests of the knightly class and baronage as the poets apprehended it. The stories are set higher in the social scale than the poets could expect to see reflected regularly in their audiences, and no doubt they were gratifying to the lesser vassals who could 'identify' with the heroes, and even to camp-followers who could do so only with total fantasy. The words 'vassal' and 'ber/baron' are used in the general sense of 'gentleman' and we rarely hear of minor fiefs. The rank of *vavasour* is not more than respectable. All the fantasy is of men in very high places.

Because the vast majority of the poems claim to be historical accounts dating a long way back, it was easy for listeners to accept a rearrangement of the political scene known to them; and as the social framework was that of their own day, they had no difficulty in understanding what was going on. They even chose to isolate their heroes from much of the social background. The lords in the poems, most of whom we must assume are magnates, Roland, for example, are first and foremost heroes, an exalted and isolated rank unknown to the feudal economy, and extrapolated from real life. A great lord in the audience who identified himself in person or in his ancestor with one of the heroes forgot his position as the hub of a great household and the ruler of large, populous and profitable estates, to become a soldier, commanding only shadowy armies, but fighting with superhuman physical strength and courage.

From a technical point of view the wars described reflect those that were taking place when the poems were written, in

Spain, in Syria and Palestine and later in Egypt. Yet there is a certain authentic memory of the earlier days in which ostensibly the stories take place. In the days of Saracen raids on Europe, especially in the eighth to tenth centuries, the Christians could barely hold their own, just as they could barely do so against the Magyars, and not much better than they could against the Vikings. Some genuine memory of the days of hopelessness seems to survive, although it has been transformed by the exuberant morale of the new aristocracies. Chronicles of the ninth century describe just such single combats and town sieges as make the staple diet of the *chanson* audiences, with the difference that there is no triumph.[3] In the twelfth century, people were used to things going well for the Christians, but even in our poems the Saracens would have everything their own way, if it were not for the exploits of the heroes. It is this memory of a state of mind from the past, rather than the arguable substructure of historical fact, that links the poems to the Carolingian age.

There is a lively description of chivalry encamped in *Gaydon*. There are many tents, shields of shining gold, pennants of Almeria silk, many war-horses, many Syrian mules, knights and vassals, rogues and entertainers: 'so many jongleurs, so many wrinkled whores'. There is the sense of varied interests. The hangers-on belong to the same scene as the fluttering pennants, and the poets' trade goes with that of the prostitutes, because both need a full purse. The knights 'have no desire to make peace, they have always heard the war-cry, and they love war more than Nones or Compline. They would much rather one town burned than two cities surrendered without a struggle'.[4] Chivalry was the code of the cavalry, and nothing was allowed to stand in the way of the main purpose, which was to fight, or of the reward, which was often booty.

The eponymous hero of *Maugis d'Aigremont* makes an interesting remark. He is running away from the anger of the Saracen King *M*arsile, who found him in bed with his queen, and he says to his companion, 'Friend, things are going badly for us. I worked a lot for *M*arsile and did a good job, and in the end he made a poor return for it.' He adds that they have nothing, money, gold or silver, apart from their arms. His friend says: 'There is no better thief than you from here to the Orient . . . We will steal what we need and give away freely, take from the rich men and give to poor people.' Maugis says: 'You say well and speak with *cortoisie*' (*bel et cortoisement*). [5]However satirically, the sense of *cortois* seems to extend to any expedient favourable to a knight. Giving freely is aristocratic, and it is taking such an expedient brutally that makes it possible. Booty given or taken is one condition of a soldier's service and irresponsibility is another. We must suppose that the listeners imagined themselves in the ranks of privilege and impunity. *Roland* offers a different but comparable example. Roland himself looks at the Saracens proudly, and at the French humbly and gently, and he says in courtly fashion (*ad dit un mot curteisement*): 'We shall have fine, good booty to-day; no king of France ever had it so rich'.[6] We may say that what was courtly about this was to encourage his comrades, or to joke in the face of death, but, even so, the encouragement was booty, and the joke was booty too. *Cortois* is most often used as an indeterminate epithet in praise of someone, with no meaning more specific than 'civilised' (in an aristocratic way). We also meet *cortoisie* in the more familiar sense of generous and trusting behaviour between equal opponents fighting to the death with great mutual respect, but this is for special occasions.[7]

These privileged, courtly men are professionals. They suffer incredible deprivations and ghastly wounds in battle, but fighting is their business. *La Prise d'Orange*, at its beginning, and again at its end, sums up their lives. They are waiting impatiently for war at the beginning, and sighing for girls to pass the time till business begins. The happy ending, equivalent to 'they lived happily ever after' is: 'not a day passed without a summons to fight'.[8] The heroes are not always young. The most popular public favourites are given an exciting old age; but the typical hero and his friends are young, of marriageable age, and their *enfances* and old age are added later. Gui de Bourgogne is younger than most; he leads the sons of the paladins into Spain, and though they have a sense of obligation towards their fathers, the point of the story is that they manage better. Their war against the Saracens is fought across the generation gap. In this form it is not typical, but the war which gives ambition its chance against established authority is common.

The typical adventure in one kind of story is the expedition to seize lands for the landless (the well-born landless). Aymery and his sons have to carve fiefs for themselves from lands theoretically the emperor's to give away, but actually held by Saracen kings (corresponding roughly to the taifas of the eleventh century) – Narbonne for Aymery himself, Nîmes and Orange for Guillaume (these were thought of as in 'Spain'), Guibert at Andrena, Bueves at Barbastro and his son Bertrand at Cordova. The pattern hardly varies when the stakes are higher; the young Breton knight Anseis plays for all Spain (*Cartage*). Doon de Mayence forces Charlemagne to 'give' him a kingdom in 'pagan' (Saxon-Saracen) country; this gives him a title, if he can make it good, as well as some claim for help on the emperor, of whom he is however suspicious. Many of the stories describe the struggle to retain or regain lands filched by 'traitors'.

Then there are the individual adventurers, especially in the thirteenth century onwards, Fouke Fitz Warin in North Africa, and, in the East, Gui de Warewic, Bueves de Hamtoune, Blancandin, Simon de Pouille and, in Jean Renart's *L'Escoufle*, Richard de Montivilliers. These later French poems and their English translations reflect the life of the wandering mercenary of the thirteenth and fourteenth centuries. They do not, in the same way as the poems of the Reconquista, envisage the acquisition of family lands from the Saracens. There is also an intermediate group; the Roland of the Franco-Italian poem *L'Entrée d'Espagne* should probably be classed with the mercenaries, but Maugis lives for a time at a Spanish court, and the story of Charlemagne's education as 'Mainet' at the court of the Saracen *G*alafre, and his early marriage there, is in a class by itself.[9]

Of the earlier baronial group, the outstanding example is Guillaume d'Orange, *au cort nez*, himself: he expresses the economic necessity of the young lackland baron. 'God', says the count, '. . . what a long wait for a poor young man who has nothing to take and nothing to give', and, again, 'what a long wait for anyone so young', *com ci a longue atente | A bacheler qui est de ma jovente!* He does not like having to wait till someone else dies and the King can give him his lands and his wife.[10] This is the reasoning behind 'adventure' which, when it is at the expense of Saracens, will have the support of the church. The pattern is either of a single adventurer, with his friends and allies, or of a family alliance in a foray in force, supported ultimately by Charlemagne or Louis.

The role of the Saracen varies. In *Les Quatre Fils Aymon* the Saracen episodes are incidental to the story of a family in conflict with the emperor, which reminds us of Gerard de Rousillon, who has to suffer greatly for his wars with his rightful lord. *Aye d'Avignon* and *Gui de Nanteuil* reverse the pattern, when the good Saracen king (converted, of course) supports the persecuted family of Garnier, whose widow he has married, and saves their lands from the line of Ganelon, who enjoy the emperor's favour. The poems of the two Crusade cycles seem at first glance not to conform to the pattern, but that is wrong. The first cycle has a larger element of authentic contemporary history than other poems but the events of the First Crusade fit the requirements of the adventure convention; and the second cycle differs from the usual tales of conquest only in the greater liberties taken with known facts and with the illustrious names of the kings and the kingdom of Jerusalem, and the still more illustrious name of *S*aladin.[11] There is always a background of land grab.

The theme of a terrible invasion of Europe dominates some songs; those that come immediately to mind are *Aliscans*, *Chevalerie Vivien*, *Chanson de Guillaume*, *Aspremont*, *La Destruction de Rome*, the beginning of *Fierabras*, the early part

of *Ogier*, the last part of *Roland* and of the second redaction of
Le Moniage Guillaume, and *Le Couronnment de Louis*. There is
still room for the individual protagonist, the tragic Vivien, the
comic *Renoart*, Guillaume who is both. In such poems as these
it is the Saracens who are land-hungry, and sometimes looking
for revenge; they want *la douce France* and try to buy the aid of
Christian heroes by offering them a share of their conquests.[12]
In general outline this is a true though dim memory of the past
Arab invasions which found Christian allies, but naturally seen
from the side of the Europeans. The precise motivation of the
Saracen is missing; there is no *iuventus*[13] or mercenary. The
economic situation of the individual Saracen is indicated only
vaguely or not at all, and very few appear as clearly motivated
by a career. On the other hand, they share the knightly virtues.

The ideals of chivalry between the middle of the eleventh and
the middle of the thirteenth century when so many of the songs
took shape were not a golden, exotic, out-of-the-way ethic;
what the songs admire is the qualities of the successful soldier.
A conventional and deeply-rooted phrase is embedded for
example in the half-line, *Aymery au corage aduré* – 'with the
invincible spirit' or 'iron will' or 'tough morale'; or Guillaume
qu'a proesce adurée. Roland states the unacceptable qualities:
he 'never loved a coward, an arrogant man or a vicious one, or
a knight who was not a good vassal' – here a 'vassal' means a
good fighting man with virtues such as *corage* and loyalty.
Success is almost a moral virtue, and failure unredeemed by
death is a disgrace. Guillaume, seeking help in the great battle
(which ultimately is saved only because he fetches help) has
an orgy of self-abasement to *G*uibourg his wife: 'They said at
my lord's court that you were the wife of a notable, a bold
count and a hard hitter, now you are the wife of a miserable
fugitive, a coward count, a wretched refugee who does not
bring a single man back from the battle.' The poet is only partly
serious (he makes Guillaume excuse himself as 350 years old)
but he is laughing at him in a genial way: 'the pagans treated
me so foully, they would not run away from me or retreat'.[14]
The stories make the value of prudence clear enough; Guil-

laume's decisions proceed from common sense, and it is Roland's obstinacy that causes his death and that of his companions. But toughness is the top priority.

Proesce adurée is only a little more complex than *corage aduré*. Prowess includes skill at arms and physical strength as well as hardened sensitivity. It is the capacity to endure, not passively, but with soldierly initiative, which is the chief characteristic of all the heroes. They will not be put down, not by the numbers of the enemy, or by terrible wounds, by starvation or by years in filthy prisons: not by any odds, however impossible. In life and death they are indomitable. This is the best word to describe them. This is true in those songs where they die in true epic and Germanic fashion, facing fearful odds, and in the long tales of adventures, where they never seem discouraged.

There is something haunting, although it is absurd, in the conception of Vivien, Guillaume's nephew, in some versions also his foster son. He is not in a general way sympathetic, but he makes a covenant when he is still in our terms an adolescent boy, that he will never give way in battle with the Saracens. In detail the legend varies. In the final battle he is alone; he did not want to get Guillaume's help until it was too late. He does not give ground, but he fights his way ahead to shelter for the night; he has not broken the letter of his covenant, but it seems to him that he has evaded it. It must in any case have ensured his early death; it would not make for good soldiering. Guillaume is different, brave as needed, he has common sense and lives to fight another day, and into old age. When he does arrive, he finds the exhausted Vivien dying, and is in time to comfort him. Vivien, unlike Guillaume, is *démesuré*. Gerard dies in the same battle, but with *mesure*, also comforted by Guillaume at the last; and he too is indomitable. Wounded beyond cure, he asks to be set on his horse, so that he may die fighting; he asks for a drink of wine, or, failing that, muddy water. He actually dies with the effort of sitting up in the grass. This is a stereotype, but all the more, it reflects the importance of indomitability.[15]

In the same poem, in the same battle, two Saracen kings,

*D*esramé and *A*lderufe, die badly wounded, but thinking apparently only of the welfare of their horses. They are as indomitable as Vivien and Gerard, and it is the poet who makes them so, but his sympathies are not engaged in the same way. He does not hide their heroism, but he takes no personal interest in them; they are not his heroes, and so he does not notice the heroic behaviour he has given them. It is suggested as a general proposition that Saracens cannot endure like Frenchmen, *Sara\u0105ins ne porent sofrir ne andurer*, but it is taken curiously for granted that they can suffer and endure as well as anyone. It is more a question of boasting French toughness; a French defector says, 'I told you . . . that the French are tough people', *que Franceis sunt gent aduree*.[16]

Another word for indomitability is pigheadedness. It is for being irrational that inflexibility and foolhardiness are admired. *Mesure*, a sense of proportion, is admired too, but with less enthusiasm; and yet, as Oliver says, 'Soldiering with common sense is not foolishness and *mesure* is worth more than foolhardiness'. *Corage* also means having the right feeling at the right time, and when 100,000 knights weep for pity it is not unmanly.[17] Two important qualities related to each other are *fierté* and *orguil*; they may be weighted more towards the pejorative or more to the laudatory, and in any case stretch from the one to the other. Both Christians and Saracens may have them. *G*orham, the seneschal of the Saracen *A*golant in *Aspremont*, has reason to be proud of a whole list of accomplishments which include being proud to the proud, *fiers enviers les orgellos*.[18] *Fierté* means fierceness, even savagery, as well as pride; the two qualities are not mutually exclusive. *Orgoillois* leans to the sense of 'disdainful'. Both sides admire both qualities. The stronger the enemy, the greater the victory over him. Aggression is a moral aspect of prowess; good soldiers win battles, and pride is necessary to put down pride.

NOBILITY

The soldierly qualities of courtliness are fitted into a concept of nobility. *Blancandin et l'Orgueilleuse d'Amour*, in spite of its

name, is an adventure story more than a love story; it dates to
the first third of the thirteenth century and harks back to an
imaginary golden age of chivalry, when king and emperor
maintained firm justice without payment and 'chivalry was not
dead'. Now, there are no more great actions, ladies are deceit-
ful and make love to the manservants and the yokels, and lines
of descent are no longer pure. 'It comes to this, that there is
scarcely anyone left who is gently born.'[19] This seems a mixture
of satire and nostalgia for a time that never was. Roughly contemporary, a passage in Renart's *L'Escoufle* exclaims, 'Vilain!
And how could it be that a vilain was gentle and frank?' A rich
man, however, must be humble and (in the modern sense)
gentle, and strict in doing justice.[20] The word 'vilain' in Antoine
Oudin's collection of sayings is overwhelmingly contemptuous
in its use.[21] Vinaver says of Malory's Arthuriad that the story
'is largely based upon the distinction between noble and
churl',[22] and, with some differences, this was true also at a
much earlier date. 'A man must suffer great evils for his lord',
says *Roland*, 'and put up with hard cold and great heat'. In
Jourdain de Blaye Renier and his wife Eremborc give up their
baby son to be murdered in place of their lord's son, and in
Daurel and Beton Daurel and his wife do the same for the infant
Beton.[23] This was not very credible at the time, as the poet of
Jourdain realises, but it was more intelligible then than now. In
the fifteenth century burlesque, *Rauf Coilyear*, the collier meets
Charlemagne and is knighted, but the other knights would have
liked him to be hanged.[24] I do not want to labour the point, but
nobility and lordship are integral to the framework of the
songs.

Of course there is a relation between the qualities of a knight
and noble birth. *Franchise* and *largece*, openness and generosity,
are not confined to the rich, but they are not traditionally
bourgeois virtues, and in the period under discussion, neither
was *renomée*: all three come in the list of a hero's qualities,[25]
of which fame is the culmination. In *Moniage Guillaume* 11,
the new monk and ci-devant count is shocked when the monks
do not serve wine and meat and white wheat bread to an

important visitor, *uns haus hom*, but Guillaume also annoys the monks by giving food to the younger men.[26] A knight may be addressed as *franc*, or *cortois* or *ber* (nominative of baron). These seem indefinite in meaning, except that they recognise the class of a person.

Guillaume does not like it at all when he goes to Nîmes disguised as a merchant, seedy and down-at-heel, and is treated by the Saracens, King *O*trant and King *H*arpin, rudely and roughly, and has his beard pulled. 'You will pay dearly for this before evening', he thinks, and gets so angry that he kills *H*arpin at a blow. The surrounding pagans get angry because *H*arpin has been insulted and killed by an apparent merchant.[27] All this happens because a noble in disguise is not recognised for what he is. Yet arrogance with the low-born is not part of the code. *G*orham, who was 'proud with the proud', was humble and compassionate with the low-born.[28] When Guillaume becomes a monk and tries to be really *humle et dous*, he is called away to defend Paris from the invasion of the Saracen King *Y*soré; but he does not advertise his presence, and stays with a poor man in his hut in the moat, and gets him to help him as far as he can. After he has killed *Y*soré, he makes the poor man rich; he no longer wants fortune for himself.[29]

Nobles do not necessarily have the virtues of knighthood. Count *T*hibaut and his nephew *E*sturmi, at the beginning of the Great battle in the *Chanson de Guillaume*, are corrupt, cowardly, idle and boastful. It is not wrong to be boastful; the *Voyage de Charlemagne* is based on the theme, but every boast has to be made good (with the reluctant connivance of an angel). Roland's boasts before Roncesvaux are a part of the tragic irony, and they are made good by death. *T*hibaut and *E*sturmi are the opposite case. They run away, and their discomfiture is comic, and meant to be. Yet Vivien, whom they have deserted and who is going to die, reproves Gerard for speaking openly of their shame, because they are noble.[30] The poet has it both ways, he gets his laugh, and he reminds us to respect the counts. There are no cowards among the Saracens, however, or villains like Ganelon.

A man is often asked the question, 'who are you?' expecting the answer 'son of so-and-so', 'nephew of so-and-so', 'my mother's line was such-and-such', and, though we do not hear of long descents, such as they are they will take into account either the male or the female line or both.[31] This not only reflects a claim to nobility, but also demonstrates the poet's knowledge of poems about the same characters. Pride of achievement and pride of family are linked and are part of being *cortois*. The Aymerids or Narbonnais are an outstanding example, each the protagonist of his own poems or, in Guillaume's case, several. As Bueves de Commarcis tells the amir: 'our family is large and proud and confident, and backs up its kin'. In the episode at Nîmes, the young disguised Guillaume reminds himself that he is of the stock of Aymery; and when the old Guillaume gives battle to Ysoré incognito, the Saracen feels the weight of his blows and says 'you seem to be of the lineage of the Narbonnais ... I think you must be of the family of Guillaume'. His wife Guibourg reminds him that the custom of the lineage is to die on the battlefield; and better die than let the reputation of the family suffer or the heirs be ashamed. Guillaume finally, as he tells his cousin Gaydon, leaves his country for God (both are now hermits) because his wife and relatives are dead.[32] The same close alliance of brothers is the theme of the *Four Sons of Aymon* who rally to the family interest.

We hear a lot about the immediate family of the heroes, about whole families of heroes, but there are no long genealogies. Nobility might almost be spontaneously generated. Nobility is essential, but is as widespread among the characters of the poems as are gentry in Jane Austen. It extends fully to Saracens. King *A*rragon, for example, addresses his soldiers as *Franc chevalier membré* (illustrious) in exactly the same way as Christian leaders do: *franc chevalier nobile*.[33] To the world of noble privilege, which no villein could enter, Saracens had a natural right, if they could show *lignage* and *parenté*, in spite of being *felon* and *glouton* and *fil a putain* (see below, p. 107). When *O*tinel comes as ambassador of the Saracen King

*G*arsile to Charlemagne, the emperor asks him, 'Saracen, brother, by the religion you live by, what is your descent in your own country?' Naming his royal relatives, he passes the test ('*tu es assez gentis*'), and is judged worthy to fight Roland. Even when Saracens meet each other, they may be made out to ask each other's lineage: 'The King [*A*golant] asks: "What is your name, friend?" – "*E*liades. I am son of King *F*anis." Said *A*golant: "You are near to my line. I and your father were very close cousins."'

Nobility can be seen and recognised; 'the amir', says Roland, 'looks very much a baron', *ben resemblet barun*, where 'baron' means a soldier who is well born. *C*arahuel, best of Saracens, but in a much later poem with the same idea, 'looks a man of high nobility'. In another late poem, Roland takes service with the Saracen amir, who does not recognise him, but says that he looks like a knight with ancestry. *R*enoart and *G*uibourg, Guillaume's wife, are son and daughter of Saracen King *D*esramé; *R*enoart was enslaved as a boy, and bought by King Louis, who suspected his noble blood from his looks, and hearing that he was right, put him to work in the kitchens, where he would be kindly treated, for fear of his father and his other kin. When he wins the battle that Vivien and Guillaume have lost, he commands the obedience of the French because he is the son of a king and knows how to give orders (in spite of having been brought up in the kitchens), *Fiex de roi sui, si doi bien commander*.[34]

All these cases where Christians and Saracens recognise each other's nobility are remarkable enough. Perhaps the most surprising invention in this line is the main theme of the Provençal poem, *Daurel et Beton*. Beton, the high-born victim of Charlemagne's injustice, is taken by the jongleur Daurel to the court of the amir of Babylon, where he is brought up, ostensibly as Daurel's son. As a child he dominates his equally high-born Saracen playfellows, and, when the Saracen King *G*ormont attacks Babylon, Beton rides out alone to challenge him. At each stage of Beton's development, even as a young child, the amir realises from his behaviour that this can be no jongleur's child, and he is finally convinced by the challenge to *G*ormont. Finally he gives his daughter to him as wife (she becomes Christian) and sends an army to help him fight the French traitors who have misled Charlemagne.[35] Vivien, too, brought up by a merchant, is irrepressibly noble. The noble quality cannot be hidden, from Christian or Saracen.

There is a strange measure of Vivien's vulnerability. He is dying: 'in his body he had fifteen wounds, and from the least of them an amir would be dead, or a king, or a count, however powerful he was'. It seems that high position imparts a special capacity to resist physical weakness, but the measure is in any case equally Saracen and Christian. Another point is that family connections may also bridge the two societies. In *Maugis d'Aigremont* a Saracen nephew becomes Christian in order not to fight his own kin. In the same poem there is a burlesque combat with the monstrous Froberge who offers Maugis his ugly daughter as wife and adds the inducement that he will be well connected, *moult bien emparentez*.[36]

Nobility is perhaps most important when it comes to single combat. When *F*ierabras in the eponymous poem challenges all the Christian champions, Oliver accepts, but tries to hide his identity, making *F*ierabras highly suspicious. He is afraid he is being tricked into fighting an unworthy opponent: 'Who are you, what is your name and your kin?' Oliver pretends to be the son of an unknown vavasour, and *F*ierabras grumbles that he has never had to fight anyone of such low birth, since he was dubbed knight. If he kills him, what will people think of his being involved with a vavasour's son? The glory of victory is assessed by the status of the loser, rather as in schoolboy conkers; mortal combat is so intimate that, if one combatant is noble, so must the other be. The poet makes *F*ierabras as careful for his reputation as the professional he is. He knows the great barons of France by name and reputation, and he will not compound for less: fame is the spur. We are reminded that in a crucial stage in the action of *Roland*, Roland's decisions are formed by the thought of his reputation and of his family's honour. It does not seem to have entered the head of the poet

of *Fierabras* that it would be any different for a Saracen. When
Oliver at last admits who he is, *F*ierabras believes him – *bien sai
de boin parage est tous tes parentés* – because his fighting qualities
have enabled him to recognise the quality of his birth.[37] In the
combat which gives the name to *La Bataille Loquifer*, so like the
one in *Fierabras*, there is little talk of nobility, but Loquifer,
besides being personally formidable as a giant, is a knight and a
generous opponent and he and *R*enoart fight as equals and
almost as comrades. If *R*enoart is the son of a king, Loquifer is
accompanied by four 'crowned kings' and 'fears neither king
nor amir'.[38] There is no suggestion that we are not still among
the highest nobility.

   Nobility enters into strange fields. It is normal by our
standards that a Saracen *de grant nobilité* and *gentis hom et
de grant fierté* should resent an unjust lord, and even transfer
his allegiance to Bueves de Commarcis as 'rightful lord', but in
the same poem (*Le Siège de Barbastre*) the daughters of
Saracen kings who are looking for French lovers are introduced
as of *molt haut parenté* as well as *grant richeté*. In *Fierabras*,
*F*loripas the heroine assures Roland and the other French
prisoners that the five girls she is introducing to them are
de grant nobilité; presumably, if the worst comes to the worst,
the nobility of the genes will be assured. *O*rable, queen in
Orange and later baptised wife of Guillaume and called
Guibourg, in her unregenerate days was ambiguous. 'So much
the worse for her great beauty, when she does not believe in
God and his goodness. A noble could enjoy himself with
her.'[39] This at least is an ambiguous remark. What is clear,
however, is not just the great importance given to noble birth,
but the assumption that there was no difference in that between
Saracens and Christians. We are about to see that the chivalric
virtues were also fully shared by the Saracens.

THE SARACEN PREUX CHEVALIER

Not only the nobility, but also the feudal virtues of Saracens
seem more important in the poem than their false religion.
Though both are entirely fictitious, I do not think that Saracen

prowess or courtliness seemed so to the authors. When a Saracen character is sympathetic to his creator, he is often brought to become Christian, and in that sense also his chivalry takes priority over, or at least commands, his religion. When a *ber* and *cortois* Saracen appears, we suspect that he will be converted. We suspect the same of a woman when she is very attractive. But sometimes an enemy king or amir is allowed to die a Saracen, and die bravely, even in circumstances which would satisfy the requirements of martyrdom in a Christian (see Chapter 9). Whether he dies Saracen or lives baptised, it is shown again and again that he can be *cortois* and *gentil* and especially *preux*, before he becomes Christian, and sometimes without becoming Christian at all.

Et B*aufumes qui est pros et vaillanz* (*Prise de Cordres*), M*ala-quis, qui moult fu cortois et afaitiés* (*Bueves de Commarcis*) are both later converted; A*umons, li rois, li preus et li membrés, A grant merveille fu Aumes vertuos, mult fu corajos, Rois U*liens *fu molt preus et vaillant*, and G*orham, pros et hardis et molt cevalerous* – these, all from *Aspremont*, do not convert; in *Blancandin*, Sadoine is *cortois* and is converted, but so is the enemy D*aire*, who is not converted. One of four Saracen kings in *Narbonne* is specifically *preus et gentis*, and when Elie de Saint Gilles meets a Saracen he respects, he tells him so: 'By my head,' says Elie, 'You are a *vasal mout prous*. You would willingly have killed me if I had let you.' There may even be a passing, uninterested reference, like 'he's all right' – *1 aumaçour i avoit d'outremer, Preu et hardi por ses armes porter*.

In the class of foreshadowed conversions, G*anor of Maiogre* is outstanding; he is *le nobile baron* long before he gives his country to Christendom and becomes the second husband of Aye d'Avignon; and after it, Gui de Nanteuil, his stepson, recommends him to his mother as 'the best knight who ever bore arms or mounted a war-horse'. He takes up his stepson's family feud against the line of Ganelon and is more nearly integrated into the conflicts of European nobles than any other converted Saracen. Despite or because of his profound acculturation, descriptive phrases tend to stress his origins.

Ganor l'Arabis, *li rois des Arrabis*, and even (earlier in the story)
Ganor de Mahon. Yet the praise given to the Saracen *A*lderufe,
about to be killed in battle, is only less fulsome: *hardiȝ e prouȝ,*
Chevaler bon.[40]

If high birth is the condition of Roland's fight with *O*tinel
and Oliver's with *F*ierabras, what predisposes the two Saracens
to be baptised and honoured among the Christians ? Both begin
badly, *F*ierabras as the sacker of Rome, slaughterer of priests
and raper of nuns, *O*tinel, whose hand was sore for a week from
killing Christians in Rome, as a singularly aggressive and
provocative ambassador, out to pick a quarrel on his own
account as well as his master's. *O*tinel is the less interesting.
Although Charlemagne has sent his daughter to arm him, he
continues to jeer in a hostile way until he is suddenly stopped
by the appearance of the Holy Ghost. The battle of *F*ierabras
and Oliver is longer drawn-out. *F*ierabras offers Oliver the
balm with which Christ was anointed, which he has looted in
Rome; it cures wounds: '*Ber*, drink this balm . . . You will fight
better and you will be bolder.' Oliver, shown as pious in a
rather absurd way, will not take the balm till he has won the
fight, because sooner would not please Jesus Christ, but *F*ierabras is favourably struck by his prayer, which he overhears,
and again offers the balm in vain. Later, *F*ierabras gives Oliver
a blow that incidentally kills his horse. Oliver objects that this
is not in the rules, and *F*ierabras replies, 'You are right, but . . . I
did not mean to do it,' and offers his own terrible horse, which
has bitten and strangled more than a hundred people, to
Oliver; who again refuses, because he wants to take it by force.
So far Oliver has been indomitable, but consistently cur-
mudgeonly, and the courtesy in our sense has been all on the
side of *F*ierabras, who sums it up: 'Certainly, you are very
aggressive (*de grant fierté*) and it is folly to refuse my horse. I am
doing for you what I would do for no man born, now that I
know you are of such nobility.'[41]

Chivalry is more equally shared in the fight between *R*enoart
and *L*oquifer; *R*enoart is less grudging in his acceptance of
courtesies, and *L*oquifer is very angry when the supporting

Saracens look like intervening against the rules.[42] Yet *L*oquifer fights on to the death, the alternative to conversion; *F*ierabras is baptised (and inevitably sinks into mediocrity). The poet of *Fierabras* sees no need to explain the transition from the public image of the great ravager to that of the punctiliously courteous champion, and perhaps he is realistic: public villains are no doubt charming when you get to know them.

The poets may deliberately or without reflection have rendered the different points of view of two sides; *S*ynagon, who kidnaps and cruelly imprisons Guillaume, is *le boin roi honerable* to his kinsman who wants to avenge him. Usually the poets do not hesitate to impute virtues to Saracens, but recurring phrases such as: 'If he had believed in God, there would have been no better king'; 'He would have been a very good knight, if he had been a believer in God'; 'If he had agreed to believe in the son of St Mary, he would not have had an equal in barony'; and 'there would have been no Turk like him in the army, if he had believed in Jesus', reveal a special point of view: the Saracen has all the virtues but he is on the wrong side.[43] A unique position was reserved for *S*aladin; still the enemy of the Christians, he is also the model for knights, none is more courtly than he, *qui tant estoit courtois prince que nul plus*; he is *tres preu, tres courtois et tres exellent prince, Salhadin*. He decides to go to see the world, and particularly the French court, to judge its state and its nobility and the behaviour of the Christians. The Queen falls in love with him, 'thinking of his beauty and great nobility and high chivalry', she loves him 'more than she had loved any man before'. He attacks King Richard in England, and takes a part in tournaments. This is not meant to be grotesque; the ideal tournament might be conceived as an international match. *S*aladin is also in legend descended from the daughter of the Count of Ponthieu, who marries the Sultan before escaping back home with her first husband. He is deeply embedded in the legend of European chivalry.[44]

In a few cases the courtly virtues are attached to Saracens beyond any apparent requirement of the story. *G*orham in

Aspremont, the amir's seneschal and the queen's lover, is described as a pattern of chivalrous characteristics. He is wise and clever (*engignols*, ingenious), proud with the proud and compassionate with the humble; he is not covetous in his possessions and he knows how to give, both to the great, and to unimportant people.[45] The eulogy of *T*ibaut in *Foucon de Candie* is even more unexpected. From being a cuckold and rather ineffective villain for most of the Guillaume cycle, in the course of this poem he is suddenly transmogrified as *mout preudom*. He is skilled in the arts of war, particularly jousting, he knows how to harm his enemy and help his friend. He is debonaire, an accomplished lord who values a good man and does no injustice to any free man. No knight has ever better put up with the pains and efforts of war, or boasted about them less in the evening after dining. 'If he had believed in the Lord God, the true Justicer, there would have been no better prince in the world to govern it'.[46] These are the virtues of a lord rather than a king; but there is no compulsion of any kind to attribute them to a Saracen prince. The French will not invade France with him, and they save Christian Gandia by becoming his ally in a war against kingdoms further East. This admiration for and friendship with this Saracen is both sudden and gratuitous.

Roland is subtly ambiguous in its treatment of Saracen prowess. *A*bisme is the reverse of courtly and loves treason and murder more than gold, but *M*argariz of Seville is shown as gay and gallant, the beloved of the ladies. *C*hernubles of Munigre is monstrous. His hair reaches to the ground, he can carry four mule-loads if the fancy takes him; it is said that in his country the sun does not shine nor the corn grow, there is no rain or dew, but only black stones, and many say devils live there. When only *M*argariz and *C*hernubles survive of the twelve Saracen peers (a parallelism with the peers of France) *M*argariz charges through the French ranks, just missing Oliver, but Roland kills *C*hernubles, and abuses the body: Lout!' (*culvert*, 'serf'), 'You have put yourself in the way of bad luck. Mahon won't help you; a wretch (*truand*) like you will never win a battle.' Why this treatment for him? Because he is ugly, or savage, or a devil, or because he does not come from Seville? To the amir *B*aligant is given the phrase *ben resemblet barun*; he is fierce and aggressive in battle, but also white-haired and learned in his religion, which does not suggest a Christian idea of a baron. The use of the word *resemblet*: 'he looks a fighting man' (not 'looks like, and is not') is significant. His son, *M*alprimis, *mult est chevalerus*. They both recognise that Charlemagne is *preux*.[47]

In a number of poems of different date, Saracens reveal some pre-occupation with standards of chivalry. 'By my god Mahon', says King *E*rmine in *Bueves de Hamtoune*, 'if you became pagan, you would be *pruʒ hom*.' There is a good example of obeying the rules in *Elie de Saint Gilles*: 'It would be cowardice, King *T*riacle said so, If we five went to knock one man alone down'; and later, when *R*osamonde is defending Elie from her brother *C*aifas, she says, 'he is a good knight, spirited and bold, and you are mean, wicked and false.' *F*erragu, in *Entrée d'Espagne*, hoping for the honour of fighting Roland, says to his critics: 'You are not worthy to name such a man. By Mahon, I do not now see his equal, Roland is *preux*, and clever and proud.' *C*arahuel, in *Ogier*, is himself a paragon of chivalry, and also his opinions are courtly, almost judgements: 'Let the false man be dishonoured! And so he is, rightfully banished from honour on earth and from holy Paradise'. *B*audus, the Saracen king who changes sides in *Guibert d'Andrenas*, tells Aymery that there will never again be anyone so true and noble (*frans*, *jentils*), and that everyone says that there has been no prince more gifted with the right virtues (*plus vaillanʒ*). He may be being shown as a flatterer, but that would make no difference; there is no doubt that the ideas are shared. The *amustant* (ruler) in *Bueves de Commarcis* reproaches his daughter with having disgraced him, *con m'aveʒ vergondé*. By marrying Guillaume, *O*rable-Guibourg has disgraced *D*esramé her father and *T*ibaut her husband. In *Les Quatre Fils Aymon* the Saracen king *B*eges surrenders to Renaud on condition that he is not killed or subjected to *vilté*.[48] The assumption that ideas of chivalrous behaviour, as ideas of nobility, are the same among Saracens and Christians permeates this literature.

At first sight *traison* seems to be an exception. When *O*rable in *La Prise d'Orange* is helping the French prisoners to escape, one of them suspects that she is tricking them: 'God help me!' he says, '*O*rable has betrayed her husband, father, compatriots and fellow-religionist, so that it looks as though the treason is against Christians but not against Saracens. The fact is that treason is personal, a betrayal of individuals. The only difference for Saracens is that the special convention of this literature allows them to change their allegiance to new individuals, friends and kin, the Christians. But the rules are the same: 'You have deceived me (*m'avez vos traie*) says *L*icoride in *Simon* to her father, 'the word of an amir must not be broken', *parolle d'admiral ne doit estre faillie*. Sometimes *traison* is used in a more modern way. Subien, a Christian in *Blancandin*, is a traitor in every sense, to his lady and ruler, to his friends and his side; so is Abbot Henry in *Gadifer*, to his community and his God, and so of course is *G*anelon, *ki traison ad faite*. Yet all these cases involve treason to individuals, the lord, the friend or ally; it is hard to think of a case of treason to the kin. A Christian in Saracen country may offer his services, and when Gui de Warewic thinks he is being unfairly treated by the Christian emperor in Constantinople, he is ready to serve the amir of Babylon. What really is an offence is when the giant *A*morant, whom Gui is fighting on behalf of the King of Alexandria, is trusted by Gui, but does not keep his word. That, not serving an amir, is treason. Sometimes treason may mean little more than ill will, as in the case of the amir who plans to execute Aymery: *Li amirals fu plains de voisdie, De traison et de grant felonie* – trickery, ill will and great wickedness.[49] He does not owe Aymery loyalty.

A few special cases do nothing to change the pattern. In *La Prise de Pampelune*, *Y*soré has become Christian and changed sides, and is no longer a Saracen; his father *M*alceris has also changed sides, but he remembers his Saracen sovereign's kindnesses to him, compares Charlemagne's cool welcome, and changes back; he is then a traitor. In *Anseis de Cartage*, another Ysoré turns Saracen when Anseis dishonours his daughter. Both these 'traitors' are handled with some sympathy, because the personal ties, the ones that matter, go against the religious ones, which are officially overriding.[50]

In the story of Carahuel and Ogier, the Saracen and the Christian outdo each other in loyalty. *D*anemont, a Saracen king, is the only traitor, and it is precisely his treason which brings out *C*arahuel's loyalty. *D*anemont seizes Ogier treacherously, and *C*arahuel gives himself up to Charlemagne as a hostage for him. *C*arahuel's affianced lover *G*loriande, *D*anemont's sister, helps Ogier and he protects her. When the Saracens are defeated, the bodies of *D*anemont and *C*orsuble (*G*loriande's father, the amir) are found and given to *C*arahuel, together with all the Saracen prisoners, for once in a way excused the choice between the font and the axe. *C*arahuel will not change his faith, and leaves the Christian court amid sorrow and good will on all sides; he buries the bodies in Tripoli, marries *G*loriande and succeeds to the kingdom (or amirate). *C*arahuel, *mult cortois e sages*, best of Saracens, is unique in being allowed in spite of his prominence to stay loyal to his religion.[51] It is possible to suggest reasons why he is allowed, but none are necessarily convincing; what is clear once again is that the important loyalties are personal ties, and that Saracens and Christians have and apply the same standards.

There is almost nothing in all this that reflects actual conditions in the Arab world. The only pretence at verisimilitude is the use of special titles like *amiral*, *amustant* and *aumaçor*. They have no precise sense. *Amiral* in the case of the amir of Babylon sometimes seems to indicate an overlord or emperor, and may then reflect the title *amīr al-mu'minīn*.[52] Saracen potentates are sometimes supported by a number of *rois coronés*. Otherwise there is no attempt to portray Arab society.

Very sensibly from the practical point of view the poets preferred to create a world of their own, and the easiest world to create was a recreation of their own. There was little opportunity for actual experience of the Arab world, certainly not enough to inform all who composed songs or the parts of songs; even so, it is perhaps a little surprising that almost nothing that was certainly Arab or Muslim filtered into the songs. Having decided (in the sense of accepting a convention) to forget about authenticity, their choice of Saracen background was a wise one. They might have exploited a world of magic and enchantment, but those poems that have a magical element allow themselves a few physical impossibilities without seriously transforming the ordinary world where the action takes place (see pp. 58–9 below). The stories have nothing to gain from magic, and everything from a unitary and intelligible, familiar framework. Thus Saracen society as imagined is no different from European society as romanticised, and the ideals accepted for the one are accepted equally for the other.

COURTLY PASTIMES

We get the impression that the barons did not greatly care for leisure. When Guillaume has taken Nîmes, the fief he wants, he listens to the song of the blackbird and other thrushes and waits very impatiently for more war. Even the thousand girls from France for whom he sighs would only have passed the time until he could get back to business; and when his sexual desires are aroused, it is for *O*rable, the enemy Queen who can only be the prize of war.[1] War is the business of knights, and often of their ladies, who secure the lines of communication, recruit the tenants and at need stand siege themselves. Lords and ladies take an unmistakable pleasure in the fighting, which is not so obvious in their other pursuits. Sexuality never seems to conflict with it, and often leads to a useful marriage. Every other occupation lacks zest.

These other occupations are pastimes, to amuse the characters in the songs in the winter nights when there are no Saracens; they are literally ways to pass the time. Board games, chess and backgammon especially, are quite often mentioned, as a diversion for the barons, as a branch of learning for the women, and even as an accomplishment for an all-round knight. This applies indiscriminately to Frenchmen and Saracens. The texts are unconscious of any idea that things might be different among Saracens and Christians, or even that what games their heroes play are interesting. The games are a part of the background, which is taken for granted. *Avoir le goût du jeu . . . est, au moyen âge, un signe de noblesse.*[2]

In *Roland*, the elderly knights play backgammon and chess

47

while they wait in newly captured Cordova, and the young ones fence (although young men regularly enjoy board games too).[3] The benches at Orange where the barons are accustomed to play are empty in war, but, in *L'Escoufle*, waiting for the enemy does not interrupt play. At Orange, there is no change when Christians take over from Saracens; when Guillaume is there in disguise he finds that after dinner 'the pagans and Saracens play chess'. Desramé, in *Loquifer*, less intellectual, plays at backgammon and dice. In *Andrenas*, when Aymery is a prisoner, Gaiete (his future daughter-in-law) and the girls of her train have chess and backgammon brought to the count 'for his diversion', a rare case of both sides' assumed familiarity with these amusements simultaneously demonstrated. In *Loquifer*, chess and backgammon sets 'for his amusement' are offered to the purchaser by Saracen soldiers disguised as merchants, together with rich tissues and different kinds of hounds and hawks. The chivalrous Gorham of *Aspremont* is a good player of chess and backgammon, just as he knows about wild-fowl and sparrow-hawks and goshawks. When Tibaut suddenly becomes the model of an elegant prince, his accomplishments include the usual board games which he plays beautifully 'and without quarrelling'. When the daughter of the Count of Ponthieu begs the lives of her father and husband (unidentified as such) from her second husband, the sultan of Aumarie, she says that they will teach her chess and backgammon and fine stories; it is not that these are a peculiarly Frankish skill, but that the individuals involved are specially gifted. In the education of Blancandin, the board games go with hunting, and in *Aiol* they are an indication of a poor knight's gentle breeding. The Saracen heiress in *Gaufrey*, Flordespine, has had a full education, at fourteen and a half she speaks languages, knows astronomy, and 'how to play backgammon and chess also'.[4]

Chess twice plays a part in *Gui de Warewic*, in the plot and not just the setting. The (Christian) emperor's seneschal is jealous of Gui and entices him into the room of the emperor's daughter, Laurette, not in the hope of seducing her, but in order to play backgammon and chess. Then he denounces her to the emperor, who, however, knows that Gui is not that sort of hero, and would like him to have her anyway. Gui turns the offer down, because the Greek people would not want the son of a vavasour to become emperor. Even more crucial to the story is the game between *F*abur, son of King *T*riamor of Alexandria and *S*adoine, son of the soudan, who has bidden everyone to a feast. The players are already irritated by each other when Fabur puts *S*adoine in check. *S*adoine calls him *filz a putain* and hits him on the head with a rook, and then he in turn kills *S*adoine with the chess-board. From this drastic end-game spring the enmity of the sultan for Triamor, and important adventures for Gui, who becomes Triamor's ally. There is a similar episode in *Le Bâtard de Bouillon*, where the hero mates his cousin four times with the golden chess-men, and, after the cousin has four times called him a bastard and the son of a whore (more appropriately than is usually the case), kills him in anger, with the chess-board.[5] The prototype of these episodes has a purely Christian setting, as in *Chevalerie Ogier* and *Les Quatre Fils Aymon*. We should perhaps see these as war-games in a society organised for war, and Christians and Saracens receive the same training.

It is curious that we do not hear more about hunting, among either Saracens or Christians. From relatively sparse references wild-fowl and waterside hunts stand out slightly,[6] and this has no particularly Arab connotation. Hunting occurs in the background, as when Maugis cries off the court hunt in order to make love to the Queen.[7] It is one of the knightly accomplishments, and a part of education, like the board games. Different kinds of dog and of hawk are mentioned, but with no air of professionalism; the singers do not follow the hunt.[8] The newly moulted falcon is a favourite poetic image, but there is no national or cultural determinant in that.[9]

There is much more about feasting than about hunting. It is again apparent that the poets supposed there was no difference between Saracens and Christians, or deliberately presupposed it. They ignored important differences in this case.

In particular, their inclusion of wine in the most natural way in the world in any account of Saracens' eating, whether for sustenance or for feasting, is almost as remarkable as the system of pagan gods in its neglect of one of the best known facts of Islamic life and faith. Wine figures prominently, whether as served or as stored. In *La Prise d'Orange* King Arragon serves his guests, Christians, but disguised as Saracens, with bread and wine, crane, goose and peacock. Later, the heroes intercept two Saracens who are taking wine up to serve in the palace, and Guillaume finds the tower called Gloriette well stocked with arms and armour, with women for pleasure, with bread, wine, corn, salt meat, and two kinds of spiced wine (*claré* and *piment*). To please Simon de Pouille, the Saracens bring him 'to eat in plenty, rich roast peacock and wine in great plenty'; this might be meant as special treatment for a Christian, though it is probably not; Simon is expected to be converted, and it is most unlikely that Muslims would serve wine openly to anyone, though the scene may be meant to be private and privileged.[10]

When Saracens are stocking their fleet to sail to war they load wine, meat, biscuit and flour. Similarly, wine is stocked in the cellars of Reggio in *Aspremont*. The Saracen queen asks for food and wine when she falls into Christian hands, and not as though she were unused to drink. Indeed, this poem refers to the good wine of the East, *O beviés ses bons vins d'Oriant?* In both *Moniage Guillaume* and *Les Quatre Fils Aymon* an amir swears not to touch bread or wine until he has killed a Christian. And in *Fierabras* the Christians use for a font the marble vat in which the amir puts the wine when he is feasting. One Saracen who says that Mahon creates the good things of the world even includes 'wine and bread'.[11]

In *Bueves de Commarcis* the girls who entertain Christians in a tent serve wine and fruit and spices; if we can imagine free and respectable Arab girls entertaining men like this, there is no need to strain at the wine. One of the great scenes in *La Prise de Cordres* is the feast at which the wine is drugged, and the aumaçor kidnapped by his daughter Nubie and her

Christian lover, out of his own palace. Even without that, the behaviour of these Saracens is unseemly and more than improbable, with the father fondling his daughter upon his knee among all the men. When she brings the drugged wine, she serves her father first, and then all the Saracens around: *Et la pucelle les servit a bandon* (freely). Not only is this unthinkable among Arabs, it is hardly convincing for a Christian king's daughter: it is possible that the poet thought Muslims more, rather than less, free and easy than Christians. In the same poem the Saracens make merry, eating and drinking all they can take, and the wine goes to their heads, *Li vins est fors, o chief lor est monté*. Another example is Godin, son of Huon de Bordeaux, but brought up at the court of the aumaçor, where he drinks wine, even as an infant, because there is no milk there; habit does not exempt him and his friends from a hangover, *l'endemain lor dolu li chervauz*.[12]

There is no indication that these wine-swilling Saracens are doing anything untoward. Of course, there were and have been and are Muslims who drink, just as there are Christians who habitually do what their religion forbids; there are some factual assertions of Muslims drinking in the Middle Ages.[13] But in all the wine-drinking in these long songs there is no hint that wine-drinking is anything but the most natural thing in the world. We do not have to conclude that the poets knew nothing about Islamic society and religion; we do have to conclude that they described Saracen society as the same as Christian society, and I think it is more likely than not that this was a deliberate choice.

HORSES

Although there is less than might be expected about hunting, there is a good deal about war-horses; war is after all the best of outdoor sports, as well as serious business. A good horse is often, and often even by name, included in accounts of arming a warrior, and, although battles are not professionally described, poets rarely forget the horse in the course of a fight. The description of Turpin's horse might be an auctioneer's. *R*enoart's blows kill horse as well as rider; so do Roland's, and his horse Veillantif is killed under him.[14] There are more elaborate accounts that show simultaneously an affection for the animal and a callousness, both probably realistic as sentiments, although the descriptive detail seems habitually exaggerated.

In one part of *La Chanson de Guillaume*, the hero decides to change horses, and take the horse of the Saracen *A*lderufe who is disabled (by Guillaume) and dying. Guillaume kills his own horse, Balçan (Piebald): 'Ohi, Balçan, how wrong I am to kill you! As God may help me, you never did me any harm, in any way, by night or day. But I have done it so that no Saracen may ride you, and no noble knight be disgraced through you.' It is hardly surprising that *A*lderufe, though fatally wounded, doubts whether Guillaume is fit to own a horse. 'Ohi, Floricele, good honoured warhorse, I could never find better than you . . . Ahi, Guillaume, what a horse you are taking away! If only you were the man to take care of him!' Guillaume replies crossly that *A*lderufe would do better to see about getting himself an artificial leg; 'I will see to the horse, as a man who knows what has to be done; I have had many good ones, thank God!' *A*lderufe's dying words seem to be 'Ohi, Floricele, good-natured horse, there never lived such a warhorse! The wind did not blow as fast your pace, nor did the birds in flight keep up. You carried me here where I lost my leg. Guillaume is taking you and I have been ashamed.' Practically the same passage occurs earlier in the poem, when *D*esramé is wounded in the same way: 'Ha! Balçan, good warhorse, it was all for nothing, your noble body and your fine paces!' If this is the same Balçan as Guillaume killed a little later, he had not had him for so very long; but the parts of the poem are carelessly put together, and this passage is one of standard pathos, to be re-used like illustrations in an early printed book. There is another in *Aliscans*: 'E! Folatille!', says the dying *A*erofles, 'How many days I kept you! You carried me here where I was wounded, but all the same I am very upset about you . . .'[15] What is interesting is that the pathos is allotted to the dying Saracens.

There is some gruesome slapstick when *R*enoart and his monks are besieged in *T*ibaut's palace, and starving. *R*enoart suggests eating a monk, to give them a scare, and then decides to eat *T*ibaut's horse. He makes a sally, has to fight the horse, which kicks back, and then has a tug of war with the besieging giants over the body. The horse is torn in half and the besieged have enough to live on till rescue comes. Later in the poem of *Le Moniage Guillaume* comes what seems to be another set-piece of pathos. Guillaume has left his horse at the Abbey of Aniane when he goes to be a hermit; called back to the colours, as you might say, when King *Y*sorié invades and devastates France, he goes back to the Abbey to pick up his own war-horse. 'The Abbot had his horse brought, but it was worn out, and ill and thin and tired and feeble, and emaciated, because it had been put to carrying stones. The Abbot had it groomed and harnessed; the count saw it and began to weep. "Horse!", he said, "I am very sorry for you; you have had to endure great sufferings; but I do not know if you will be able to carry me. I shall never see such an excellent animal again." When the horse heard Guillaume speak, it knew him immediately, and recognised him well, pawed the ground and neighed and held itself proudly.' The horse then breaks away from its grooms and goes to its old master. This is touching, but at the end of the war Guillaume returns him to the Abbey, presumably to cart stones again. *A*lderufe's suspicions are after all not so wide of the mark; on the other hand, the monks had more need to cart stones than to go to war.[16]

This is an old man's old horse; a young man's old horse, Marchegai in *Aiol*, is allotted a big part at the beginning of the song, where the journey of Aiol and Marchegai from the Landes to the King in Orleans is a little like d'Artagnan's journey to Paris from Béarn. Aiol, with his old-fashioned armour and his 'very thin and worn out' horse ('he loved him very much') are laughed at in the towns through which they travel, though Aiol's prowess is fully exercised. Later in the poem we are told where Marchegai is, tied to a tree, or to a stone. He is fed, and he is groomed, but in this first journey he plays a bigger part. Whenever a drunk lays hands on him, he knocks him down and flattens him, revealing as much prowess as his master, if less *mésure*.[17] Marchegai is only remotely an ancestor of Rosinante; he reacts almost electrically to the spur, he takes part in a fight with Saracens, and prepares our minds to believe in the monstrous man-eating horse of a challenger to single combat.

When *F*ierabras kills Oliver's horse by accident in the fight, he offers him his own, a piebald sorrel, *bauçant sor*; there is no better horse alive. 'I can't understand how he did not kill you, because he has bitten and choked more than a hundred people, nor has he ever knocked a man down without devouring him; it is for that that I have taken him into many a fight.'[18] The poet certainly knew that horses do not choke people and that even biting is not their preferred method of fighting, above all that they are not carnivorous. The horse is just meant to be exaggeratedly monstrous, and exaggeration, here and often, is a joke.

The warhorse of King *C*orsolt in the *Couronnement* is wild, but credible. 'It was wonderful how wild the horse was, so uncontrollable, as I have heard witness, that only people it was used to could approach within a fathom of it.' It carried an immense weight of arms, but 'God! What a horse for anyone who could keep control of it! When it ran, neither the hare nor the greyhounds could keep up with it.' Naturally, Guillaume determines to have this horse, and in fighting *C*orsolt 'he spared the horse whenever he could, because he thought that, if he could get it, he could yet have the use of it.' When he kills *C*orsolt, he does take the horse, and rides back to Rome on it.[19]

Obviously the death of a horse is important in a battle[20] and to see your horse die is a bad moment. In the fight in *Loquifer*, when Guillaume kills *D*esramé's horse, *D*esramé is forced to threaten Guillaume's, if he will not come down and fight on foot. The horse is not only useful at the moment of truth; it carries the highest status. Gui de Warewic conducts his embassy to the sultan of Babylon with a high hand, and rides into the sultan's pavilion, and in his presence, on his warhorse.

The poets stress the splendour and beauty of the horse. Even in *Antioche*, with its proletarian elements, these qualities are noted. When *F*abur's is captured, it stands guarded by ten Arabs, 'quick and lively', *isnels et ademis*, 'the croup is large and square, the feet rounded or vaulted, nostrils wide and flaring, eyes brown and brilliant', it bucks and snorts, and *molt fu de grans fiertés*. Like master, like horse; the animal seems to share the chivalry to which it gave the name.[21]

It is not clear that Saracen horses are Arabian bred; *C*orsolt's proud steed, for example, comes from Aragon (under a Christian king since 1035); but they are presumably bred from Arab strains. They tend to be fast rather than heavy, 'faster than a hawk or a swallow',[22] or that is how they struck these poets. A good example is *M*alpriant's horse, which Elie de St Gilles manages to filch from him. The owner's first concern is for the safety of the horse, 'You are too rash! The rocks are high and the ford is dangerous. No one can turn round there, nor can a warhorse gallop', but Elie is content: 'He is riding the good warhorse that goes faster at the gallop than does the cross-bow or the arrow it sends. When he wants to be, he is behind, and when he wants to be, he is in front.'[23] The suggestions that Saracens will take better care of a horse may be meant seriously, and may have a foundation in fact. It is certain that a love of riding and admiration for the horse link the Saracens and the Christians of the songs.

LEARNING AND LANGUAGE

Sometimes the poets speak of what is happening as though it were doing so under their eyes and beyond their control; they appeal to God to bring their heroes safely through their perils; they almost enter the story themselves. Edmond Faral derived much of the material for his study of the jongleurs from such passages.[24] Here I want to note that they are sometimes self-conscious about their Saracen inventions, and are even capable of imagining that in some way their creations circulated in Saracen country.

The poets do not usually put jongleurs among the Saracens and they do not talk as though there were Saracen jongleurs. *G*anor's first act, when he becomes Christian, is to hire jongleurs to sing his praises, but this may only be part of his thorough adaptation to Christian ways. The jongleurs knew very well that they did not extend their own services to the Saracens, but they took it for granted that Saracens enjoyed some at least of the service a jongleur renders. *F*loripas, daughter of the amir in *Destruction*, has heard about *France le garnie* from songs, and the French had heard many good things about her, *ois et escoutés*.[25] Poems describe how a Saracen girl of high estate has fallen in love with a Christian hero on the strength of his repute[26] (when she does not do so at the sight of him riding by or battling) and this seems to presuppose some universal spread of reputation from one culture to the other. News may be conceived as passed through female slaves,[27] who might well be entertainers, certainly among Arabs, perhaps among Christians. *Daurel et Beton* is exceptional. Daurel himself is a jongleur, though '*considéré par son maître presqu'à l'égal d'un vassal*' (Rychner);[28] the amir of Babylon never forgets the difference between a noble and a jongleur, but Daurel's songs are liked and appreciated by the amir, whose kingdom is always treated as if it were Christian. If the poets knew anything about Arabs, they must have known that they had their own songs, but there is no evidence of what they knew. Daurel is not an exemplar, but there is an assumption that somehow the Saracens received the equivalent of jongleur services.

Daurel has no language problem, but generally poets were aware that a knowledge of language was useful to anyone who had dealings with real Arabs or imaginary Saracens. There was no inclination to hide this question, but it was usually treated casually. In a fight, all 'cry aloud in their own languages'. *B*audus, a Saracen who has turned to the Christian side, can pass a message to the Saracens 'because he knows their language well'. This seems obvious, but it might have been ignored, and very often it is. It is surprising how often the language difference is mentioned. The right man may well turn out to be the one who speaks the language: *qui sarrazinois sot*.[29]

'Sarrazinois' seems the logical language for Saracens to speak, and it is used by sober historians to mean Arabic; in the poems it means Arabic as much and as little as Saracen means Arab. Sometimes the Saracens speak Latin, or 'their Latin' or even Greek. *Latin* often means just 'language', although it often seems to mean a difficult or out-of-the-way language; and *Sarrazinois* can itself mean Greek or anything out of the way, just as Greek can mean Arabic. In one poem an amir calls someone and speaks to him in Greek, and later in another scene someone addresses him *en sor latin*; and in yet another the pagans pray to the god *en lor latin*, though there the poet may assume a liturgical language. Sometimes we get much wider claims to languages. Guillaume speaks Greek, and 'he had been well taught (latimés), he knew Sarrazinois very well, he had been trained in all languages'; later on, he uses Solomon-ese (Hebrew? the language of beasts?), German, Berber (?), Greek, Dutch, 'Aleis' and Armenian. This surely is a joke rather than pretentious ignorance. Blancandin 'knew how to talk all languages', and so he should, because he had been taught by one of his father's interpreters (or 'learned men'; *latinier* may be used in either sense).[30] Language is never a barrier; either whoever needs to, speaks the language, or it is conveniently forgotten.

Blancandin describes the whole of a simple education of a nobleman, the alphabet, then languages, games, dogs and hawks and horsemanship. Fighting on horseback and tourney-ing are omitted at his father's wish, on pacifist principles; this is to leave out, not just the final stage, but the whole purpose to which the education is directed. Beton, brought up by the amir in Babylon, can play chess and backgammon and dice and ride a horse at the age of five; at nine he is a royal squire, he hunts with dogs and greyhounds and with hawks and goshawks after wild geese and he can train a warhorse; and he still plays the noble board games. At eleven, he is taught swordsmanship by a skilled Saracen. Nothing is omitted in his case, and all is imagined to happen at a Saracen court. In the case of Godin, carried off in infancy by the aumaçor, he is educated for his high station, but we do not get so much detail; he has three *latiniers* whom he shares with the son of the aumaçor, and his father, kept informed by magical friends, is reasonably satisfied, though he sends Malabrun, with magical powers, to supplement the staple. The example of interchangeably Saracen and Christian education had been set in legend by Charlemagne himself, when he lived as a young man as 'Mainet' at the court of King *G*alafre.[31]

The education of a Saracen girl is congruous. 'The amir's daughter was very young but clear-complexioned and beautiful, noble in spirit, and well instructed in courtly teaching' – not very informative, but unambiguously establishing common ground. The amir's daughter in *Aiol* only learns languages, but she learns a lot. 'She knew how to speak fourteen languages well, she could speak both Greek and Armenian, Flemish and Burgundian *et tout le sarrasin*, Poitevin and Gascon, as the fancy took her.' The most learned of the amir's daughters is *F*lordespine; despite there being none so beautiful in all paiennie, 'big as that is', she 'was only fourteen and a half years old, she knew Latin well' (whatever 'Latin' means here). We saw earlier that she knew the board games, and we must now add that 'she knew about the courses of the stars and the phases of the moon, more than any woman in our time'.[32]

We hear a certain amount about Saracen skill in enchantment, but it is very vague, with a tendency to confuse mechanical and technical skill with magic. Simon de Pouille is not intimidated by the threats of *H*unaut, the 100-year-old sorcerer who is an experienced inventor, *l'enginneor prové*. Simon's friend's girl, *L*icoride, is frightened, but swears to outwit him; she is as good an engineer as he. His tricks are on the margin between magical and psychological, distinctly ineffective; Synados, Licoride's lover, finishes him off. When the heroine of *La Fille du Comte* is testing her father and husband without telling them who she is, she warns them that, being a Saracen woman, she will know if they tell the truth 'by art and astronomy'. Maugis d'Aigremont studies necromancy at Toledo, but it does not appear what he has learned; his prowess in battle and in adultery cannot be put down to his studies. In *La Chanson de Guillaume*, King Louis' Queen is libelling *G*uibourg when she says that she is pagan born and so skilled in 'many a dirty trick' and magic potion.[33]

It is difficult to know quite what to make of passages and references like this, or whether it is worth trying to make anything at all. They just may reflect the reputation of the schools of translation in Toledo, and others less important, and, if so, though the schools were under Christian direction, the fact of Arab science lies ultimately behind the rumours of enchantment. The old man aged a hundred in *Floovant* is described with rather more precision than usual; he is a sophisticated scholastic (*argumantez*) in the law of Mahon, and knows about the stars and the tides of the sea; the rest of the episode is valueless, but it is not foolish to associate learning in astronomy and religion.[34] In general, there are hints at great unknown forces: *omne ignotum*. But they are not taken too seriously, and the characters in the action seem able to circumvent or ignore such powers. The references do not seem to have any particular air of hostility.

Enchantment is a factor that counts for much less than in the Arthurian romances, and when a fairy world breaks in, it does not seriously disrupt the ordinary development of the plot. Arthur himself is not a character in our stories, and his brief appearance at the sound of the horn in *Le Bâtard de Bouillon* is a surprise in a Saracen world that has outlived the imagination of its inventors. Auberon, in the *roman* of his name, and even in *Huon de Bordeaux* and its sequels, and his brother Picolet in *Loquifer* and *Gadifer*, are hardly more than a kind of 'pagan', and Picolet, though independent of the Saracens, is their ally.[35] The fairy world, like Saracen necromancy, affects little more than the background to events; they are a third force, with no claim on reality, and have no special Saracen connotation.

There is an occasional straight assertion of Saracen skill in medicine. In *Li Nerbonois*, *F*orré, a doctor who claims he can restore a man cold in death to good health, is kidnapped from the amir's tent by the French; he is well born, the amir's chamberlain and the son of a king. As prisoner of the French he cures their wounds, and in the end he is baptised together with his cousin, another *preux* defector called *C*largis. This gives the doctor a much higher social class than he would have in Europe, and may suggest an idea that things were not the same among Saracens. In *Jérusalem*, the amir calls for the doctor *L*ucion to cure Peter the Hermit; he is the most learned doctor there has ever been. He is told to use medicine to cure the Frank and he takes a very holy herb from his medicine chest, which was discovered by Solomon.[36] That the herb should be holy is not a learned concept, and there is a hint at occult sources. None of this amounts to very much and it does not particularly interest the poets.

There is no apparent difference between the two sides in ordinary literacy. When Antequin, who has broken into Flandrine's prison, shoots a message out by arrow, it is Archbishop Turpin who sees that there is a letter fastened to the arrow, and who reads it, but this is not made out to be archbishop's work (either seriously or as a joke); Antequin, who wrote it down, is a sergeant, and he wrote at Flandrine's dictation.[37] Saracen lords are expected to read, *M*arsile in *Roland* for example. Both sides are alike and again there is very little interest in the subject.

THE CHANGE OF SCENE

There is no unmistakable sign that the poets thought the Saracen scene to be very different from the Christian, if different at all. There are a few indications that both appearance and manners might be unlike. When Guillaume plans to go into Orange in disguise, his nephew warns him that he will be recognised by his way of speaking and his laugh. This suggests that he personally might be recognised, not that any Christian would, though there no doubt was a difference in speaking and laughing between Europeans and Arabs. The disguise in *Le Charroi de Nîmes* is one of social rank, not of language and religion. The Frenchmen are pretending to be peasants and merchants, and this is the point of the action, though it has been made clear that the local peasants are followers of Mahon and Tervagant. The poet does not seem to have thought that there would be any difference in dress between European and Arab peasants, and in that area (which was raided, not colonised permanently) they would have been right. When Guillaume puts on the armour of a prominent Saracen, he is taken for the individual whose armour and arms are recognisable. When Bertrand is in Saracen armour, his cousin Vivien fails to recognise him, with nearly fatal consequences. 'What are you doing, you madman?' calls out Duke Naimes. 'Indeed I didn't know him', says Vivien, 'he was dressed in Turkish armour'.[38]

Cornafer is sent to spy on Aymery and to report on the state of Narbonne; his report is poetical, but there is no attempt to have him report information of military value. He has to report on Charlemagne too; if he were to be found out, he would be hanged, we hear, on Montmartre like a thief. Two more spies in the same story are Danebru and Matefer, who, when they are discovered, try in vain to buy impunity; they have each the right hand cut off, eye gouged out and nose cut off, and have to run through the army 'like greyhounds, calling on Mahon'. Clargis, Christian convert, friend to Aymery and favourite of the amir who does not know about the connection with Aymery, seems to travel successfully in both Christian and Saracen territory. Franks disguise themselves as pagans, or as 'pilgrims', who are assumed to be unrecognisable; the idea must have been that Saracen country had pilgrims wandering about and looking like pilgrims in Christendom. On one occasion, Simon de Pouille, having put on Saracen armour, is himself taken for a Saracen spy by the Christian counts: 'Let us go and speak to him and find out what his language is; he seems like a spy of the people of Apolin'. That he is dressed as a Saracen seems only a reason for suspicion, not for conviction; and that is right: he is not a Saracen. Blancandin, shipwrecked in Saracen country, sets about disguising himself thoroughly.

He says 'he will make himself a Saracen, and will speak their language, as he knows Sarrazinois well, and Latin well, and Greek well; he rubs his face with a herb, and then he is darker than a boiled pea.'[39] It is accepted that disguise is difficult, but the difficulties are dismissed very easily.

On the rare occasions when the poets show curiosity about cultural differences, the result is disappointing. 'What are they like, the people of France? Say on your honour; how do they live, there in your country?' asks *L*ucifer de Baudas of the French prisoners in *Fierabras*. Duke Naimes replies, 'When the King has given permission, they go and amuse themselves by physical sports, they fence and exercise in the fields; many go and play backgammon and chess. In the morning they hear Mass and worship God, and they give extensive alms willingly and freely, and they serve Jesus Christ with good will. They prove their bravery when they come to battle.' '"By Mahon!" says the King (*L*ucifer) "they all prove that they are idiots".' He tries to trick Naimes with a game with hot coals, and is himself, to everyone's satisfaction, burned to death.[40] The question *L*ucifer puts is a very good one indeed, and the poet who conceived it thought not only of cultural difference, but of what the difference might look like from the other side. This particular cultural imagination was not at all in vogue at that time, and it is difficult to suppose that the same man composed the pi-faced answer, like the caricature of a stuffy diplomatic style. Perhaps he had the audience guffawing with it. An interesting comparison is with the Paduan author of *L'Entrée d'Espagne* who has Roland teaching the Saracens table manners – a plate each and a dish between two[41] – and so demonstrates an awareness that customs may be different, and an arrogant assumption that the Saracens will be the less civilised. The vast majority of poems have no interest in cultural differences at all.

That applies to differences in customs. Sometimes poets remark on differences in war skills. All the fighting men on both sides are represented, or flattered, as tough, and anything else is comic; but it is gratifying to show the Frenchmen underrated. *G*ormont, a great Saracen King, when he sees his enemy eager to come to grips, says *ces crestiens sunt nunsavant*,[42] that is, they are making an error in judgement. Superiority in skill at arms is important for the Christians. They are good engineers, in the modern sense. When they build a scaffold to attack the city of Narbonne, the Saracens say, 'the French know a thing or two, *dist l'un a l'autre: "Molt sont François sachant!"*' In the thirteenth century certainly, there is a spontaneous pride in this engineering: 'So frightening are the machines to put down the Saracens', *tant erent hidus les engins*. So there is too in tactical skill, the placing of the better armed of the sergeants between the ranks of knights, by those who 'knew a lot about war', *Cil ki savoit de guerre tant*, and the knights themselves efficiently arrayed in their units. In the late romance of *Saladin*, King Richard sets 'men-at-arms with good experience and knowledgeable about war' to guard the shores of England from the skilled attack of the *courtois prince*.[43] The poets do not reckon these skills to be as important as morale and qualities of endurance, but they take them seriously and do not joke about them; we may assume that the audience did not want them to. The Christians are shown as better at war, but the Saracens are good too, good enough, as well as numerous enough, to keep the Christians up to the mark.

HISTORY AND GEOGRAPHY

The history and geography stated and implied in the poems are unintelligible in modern terms, and we should not start on the assumption that they were intended to be as accurate even as accuracy was then possible. There was an attempt to be 'accurate', that is, consistent, in the lives of the fictional characters in the songs, even throughout a long cycle; in the absence of easily accessible written texts, there were many variants in the plots, but a surprising consistency in the characters. There was no attempt at historical accuracy as we understand it now; fictional events seemed more important, and fictional Charlemagne, for example, as valuable as the 'real' one. Modern discussion of the historicity of the plots may be argued to accept this perspective up to a point. (I do not refer to the quite different discussion of contemporary historical influences on the texts.) For the poets, all their songs were 'history', as much as any chronicle, and they had no interest in the difference we perceive between fiction and history. For their purposes everything happened – or, it is the same thing, was conceived as happening – just as they described it, and they may barely have distinguished between complete inventions like *Le Voyage de Charlemagne* or *Gadifer* or *Simon de Pouille* and those which have a more or less hazy foundation in history, like *Roland* or *Aliscans* or *Aspremont* or *Couronnemont*. They must have known what they were doing when they added to or modified an existing story, included the name of some noble family to please a patron, or based the delineation of character on a living person, and still more when they made the whole story up, but I doubt if they thought it 'unhistorical' to do so. There was too much legend in history already, and also too much history in legend for that; and that is not, after all, an absurd point of view. History and fiction alike contributed to the total legend. The author of *l'Entrée d'Espagne* may have had his tongue in his cheek when he invented clerical authorities for the authenticity of his story of Roland, but, if so, he only honoured the convention. Jean Bodel insists that historical fact authenticates his song. The other way round, Philippe Mouské's *Chronique Rimée* slips constantly from one to the other, so that in his perspective Charlemagne enjoys an exaggerated and essentially fictional prominence.[44]

Very occasionally a genuine sense of history makes a brief appearance. Aspremont speaks of people dressing themselves in the way customary at an earlier time, *Si s'aparelle ensi con jadis fu*. A more elaborate example comes in the *Moniage Guillaume*, when the poet describes the invasion of France. 'At that time of which you hear me speak, the earth was not so full of people as it is now, nor so well cultivated; there were not such rich properties, or castles, or fortified towns. One could travel a good ten or fifteen leagues without finding a cottage or a castle or a town where one could find lodging. In those days Paris was very small.'[45] Such an exercise in historical imagination is more striking for being so rare, and there is no comparable attempt to imagine in what way the Saracen world might be different.

There is a taste for the exotic which has nothing to do with verisimilitude, and, though it is not greatly stressed, it persists throughout the literature. Thus we have Pharaoh (*Faraon*) used as a name or a title, and the names of other historical characters, chiefly from the Bible, but used with little apparent reason, other than rhyme (or assonance, or metre): *Salemon*, *Daire* (Darius), *Metusalé*. The ancient castle in *Cordres* is 'of the time of Abel'. Other poems of the Aymery cycle have a flavour of antiquarianism. There is an antique tower in *Barbastre*, and in *Aymery de Narbonne* Rome is referred to as *Rome qui est d'antiquité*. *Andrenas* refers to the *lignage Cayn* where a pejorative is intended, but Cain is not particularly appropriate.[46] *Huon de Bordeaux* and *Le Roman d'Auberon* embody a whole Roman history which is quite imaginary and just plays with famous names. Cesarius, emperor of Rome, marries the fairy daughter of Judas Maccabeus; his son, Julius Caesar, saves Hungary from the ravages of a giant and his father makes him its ruler; ultimately he also rules Austria, Constantinople, India, *Romaigne* and *Monmur*. In all this there is nothing more to the historical figures than the glamour of their name. Into *Auberon* come also the Holy Family, during the Flight into Egypt, and St George, who seduces the King of Persia's daughter (but she is helped by St Mary the Mother of Jesus in childbirth). He is Auberon's twin, and, in his turn, he, too, becomes emperor of Rome.

Parallel to this taste for a flavour of antiquity is a taste for exotic place-names and names of people, all wildly inaccurate. A name that recurs a few times is *Carfanaon*,[47] but apparently unrelated to the Gospel which must have made it familiar; its sound must have been its attraction. Eastern geography is a list of names and sounds. The lists in *Roland* are a good example: *cels de Butentrot*, of Micenes, of Nubles and of Blos, of Bruns and of Esclavoz, of Sorbres and of Sorz, of Ermines and of Mors, those of Jericho, of Nigres, of Gros, of Balide la Fort.

These are real names and imaginary ones mixed, high sounding and evil sounding syllables jumbled; and surely they have nothing but the sound to recommend them? So too in the *Chanson de Guillaume* the names seem almost to foreshadow Rabelais; we have *Encas de Egipte*, *Butifer li proz e li forz Garmais*, Turlen de Dostruges and many more.[48] Taking the poems as a whole, the main nations they cite are first of course *Sarazins* and *Esclers*; these two are interchangeable, and they are varied with *Turcs*, *Persans*, *Arabis*, *Mors* and even *Bedoins*. None of these is used in its proper meaning. The phrase *Sarrasin ne Escler* implies that there is a difference between the two, but there is none at all.[49]

The charm of the exotic is apparently confined to the sound of a name; imagination fails to conceive any new kind of country-side. The thought of *la douce France* which comes to heroes when they are in a tight corner is the only hint we have that where they are, in Provence or Spain, Calabria or Palestine, the countryside is different. This is true even of the second Crusade cycle, and in particular of *Le Bâtard de Bouillon* with its unalloyed geographical fantasy. Mecca is the principal city in a countryside no different from Picardy. It contains various imaginary cities, and politically, with its five kings, it is hardly more realistic. Desert always defeats these poets. This is Mecca, in *L'Entrée d'Espagne*: Roland perceives a city 'and in his opinion not Rome or Paris is as beautiful with its walls and towers and domed palaces'; there are 'meadows and copses and gardens', and within it 'many a trim tent, and many a silk standard fluttering in the wind'.[50]

The same indifference to authenticity obtains in historical geography. The Saracen King *G*ormont holds court at Cirencester, *a vos cuntrees*, as someone says to him, and he is evidently taken for a Viking; but the capital of the Arab empire in the same fragment is at *Leutiz*, home of the Slav Leutices, roughly Mecklenburg.[51] In the *Roman d'Aquin*, the Saracen invaders of Brittany are *Norois*. The Saxons cause particular confusion. Vikings are just understandably muddled with Arabs; both were invading at about the same time, and both devastated the monasteries, which had long memories; but the Saxons were as much the victims of Charlemagne as aggressors. They too appear as a variety of Saracen. In Bodel's *Chanson des Saisnes* they behave like Saracens, and have their pagan religion, exactly as in the other songs. In *Doon de Mayence* Saracens and Saxons seem more like allied tribes, two varieties of pagan; and in *Berte aus grans piés* a passing remark of circumstantially invented history tells us that at a certain time the Saxons had Saracen kings.[52]

If Saracens are misplaced in Europe they are only very vaguely placed in their own countries. Persia, India and Egypt, Nubia, Alexandria, Ethiopia, Armenia, are all names used indeterminately of places more or less to the East and inhabited by Saracens and Esclers and pagans generally. Babylon normally in the Middle Ages means the Babylon near Cairo, or, by metonymy, Cairo itself, in the time before the two places became one; in the poems it tends to mean a (or the) principal place of the Saracens without being precisely sited anywhere. In *Otinel*, the amir *G*arsile, who proposes, with the help of Charlemagne, and Roland and Oliver, to conquer France, England, Normandy and *Esclavonie*, already rules Spain, Alexandria, Russia, Tyre and Sidon, Persia and Barbary. It would be impossible to draw a map of Asia, or even of the Mediterranean, from the geographical data of any of the poems. There is some sense, not of direction, but of distance; Elie passes Baghdad and Hungary and 'Russia City' by sea, on his way to 'Sobrie'. The political trade of Gandia for Cairo lacks proportion, though the armies set off in the right direction.[53] But it would not be much easier to draw a map of Spain and what is now France. In the few days of a battle, Guillaume travels from Barcelona, to the Gironde, to Orange, to Paris, back to the Gironde, as well as doing a large part of the fighting. When we think about this, or consider that in another poem there is an underground passage from Narbonne to Orange,[54] we realise that the poets are not revealing their ignorance, or that of the geographers of the day. You could not draw even a simple linear map, such as charted itineraries in the thirteenth century, from the data in the poems. What the poets show is that they are simply not interested in verisimilitude at all. When they throw out the name of a place, they are indifferent to where it is. They like the sound.

This is nothing like an exhaustive survey of the Saracen cultural scene as the poets supposed it to be but enough has been said to illustrate the main points. There is no serious or sustained effort to present the Saracen world as different from the Christian. It is assumed that there is no important difference, apart from the Saracens' being wrong. Otherwise only superficial differences are conceded. Necromancy has no prominence or importance in the stories. Strange names have an undeniable glamour, but for their sound, not for the sense. If we generalise from very inadequate data we may conclude that the French have the edge in military skills, and the Saracens in medicine and in the care and breeding of horses. Saracens are dark, though their women are whiter than the hawthorn, and they have their own language, but there is no insuperable difficulty for a spy or a stranger on either side to pass undetected. In all the important things, in the preoccupation with war and in its ancillary sports, tournaments, hunting and board games, the two societies are conceived as alike. Contemporary scientific and academic knowledge has no reflection, and as far as we can tell, knowledge of Arab society has none either, or only an unidentifiably remote one. The poets simply omitted anything that might create a problem for them or complicate things unnecessarily, and they retained whatever favoured the telling of the story. With their relaxed approach to facts, they could allow their imagination to play freely. When it suited them, as it did when anything interested them in itself, as horses did, they made the Saracen world just like their own; and when they had no interest at all in a subject, such as geography, it suited them just as well to ignore verisimilitude entirely.

THE FAMILY,
WOMEN AND THE SEXES

Chastity was an invariable and essential part of the Christian programme, fully familiar to all Christians, and the more it might in practice be ignored, the more it was likely to be stressed in homiletic theory. Islam seemed to permit much that Christians were exhorted to avoid, which was according to the rules, strictly forbidden; and inevitably the clerical and learned in their polemic against Islam made a particular point of what they supposed to be a contrasting programme of unrestrained sexual licence. A few examples will reveal the tone and method, and allow a reader to judge whether they influenced the poems.

A twofold attack on Islam dates from early days: *luxuriosus* and *bellicosus*.[1] We are concerned with the first now. Christian criticism along this line goes back to at least the ninth century in both East and West; in Spain it was picked up again by Peter the Venerable's team for translating Arabic books about Islam, and it was renewed from oral sources in the Levant, in polemic material of the Crusading period.[2] It is a line that goes into casuistry and has its favourite themes, such as the law of triple divorce, a materialistic concept of Paradise and others.[3] Jacques de Vitry, a Frenchman who accompanied the Fifth Crusade and remained a few years in the East as Bishop of Acre before he returned home, explains with little accuracy the Islamic rules of marriage, divorce and concubinage. He reproves sexual pleasure even if it is legitimate: 'Those amongst them are considered most religious who can make most women pregnant' and 'they lie with their concubines and wives often in time of fast, because they suppose making love and desire are meritorious, either to satisfy lust or to generate many sons to strengthen the defence of their religion.' This is the 'wide and broad way' leading to death. Half a century later, the Dominican, Humbert of Lyons, says similarly, 'Nor did he teach anything of great austerity' (Humbert had presumably not attempted a Ramadan fast in high summer) 'indeed, he even allowed many pleasurable things, to do with a multitude of women, abuse of them, and suchlike', and thus, he adds, 'many Christians change and will change to the Saracen religion'.[4]

Scholastic methods only introduced a different technique to the same themes. A good example is the *quadruplex reprobatio*, also Dominican, in the thirteenth century. A religion must be holy and good, the author says, but this one is 'unclean, harmful and evil'. He then studies relevant passages from the Qur'ān, and the commentators and traditionists known to him. He states the law of marriage, but concludes that a man must have only one wife. Concubines are allowed; that, he answers, justifies adultery and fornication. He misstates the law of triple divorce, and he is shocked by any sort of divorce that may be given without cause stated. Then Islam encourages men to go into their wives ('their field') as they wish, and he takes the commentary to mean, *ante et retro*, and that in turn he does not take to relate only to posture. Against this he brings a string of arguments. Then he quotes a source permitting *coitus interruptus*, which he argues is against the command of God and the good of society; 'serious students', he says, need no further proof. So too with *effusio seminis extra vas debitum*, which is contrary to the divine law and the public good; no other proof is needed.[5]

This should suffice to suggest the tone and indicate the method. There is a good deal of authentic information carefully sought behind it, but the source materials collected with so much trouble are often misquoted and always misunderstood. It was common to assert what Islamic practice was, basing it on informants who could not know, as when Peter of Poitiers informs his Abbot that he has it from the best Christian sources, including an archdeacon, that the rule *insuper rem sodomiticam*, as he gives it, is a faithful guide to the actual practice of Muslims with their wives. St Thomas Aquinas adopted the dual condemnation of Islam, but pointed out the uselessness of arguing from authorities that the other side did not accept.[6]

This was the hub of the question. Christians could not think themselves outside the range of their own authorities, by whom their minds had been formed, and they had little to say without them; it was only one step further to use Christian witness to Muslim practice, where it was least reliable. The idea that there can be strict rules governing human behaviour, but which are different from those governing Christian behaviour, was too difficult for the theologians. To think again from the beginning, and recognise that a new set of rules was different, was arguably wrong, but still a set of rules to respect, was at that date beyond the scope of the training of the schools. Pastoral theologians knew, of course, that Christian practice fell a good deal short of the system they preached, but they seem to have assumed that, starting from what they considered a defective moral system, Muslim practice must fall exponentially short of that. The position to-day, when Islamic morals seem intolerably severe to most Europeans, would then have been wholly inconceivable.

Medieval theologians were not only the respected leaders of public opinion, but also the undisputed arbiters of behaviour. Theological opinion permeated most areas of thought, and through canon law, affected action too. Most of the polemists who wrote about Islam were scandalised, horrified and angered by the existence of an alternative system of morals, and especially sexual morals; their interest verged on the obsessive. The poets, however, did not feel committed to expressing the official line, and, although they observed the decencies, they showed little interest in the Christian virtue of chastity either.

SEXUALITY

I begin with two parallel passages. *La Prise d Orange* opens with Guillaume in a state of boredom because there are no Saracens to fight. 'If only we had a thousand girls', he wishes, 'French girls with their fine attractive figures, all these nobles would be amusing themselves with them, and I myself would be flirting; this would give me pleasure.' The poet remarks sardonically that the Saracens will give Guillaume more trouble, than he has had fun naked with the ladies, *que a deduit de dames nu a nu*.[7] It is fitting to compare this with the amir who is besieging Narbonne in *La Mort Aymery*. He sends his nephew to the land of Femenie, to fetch his beloved, to enjoy the amenities of Narbonne as soon as he has captured it; the meadows below it with the rose in flower in the month of May and the shade of the summer house where they can amuse themselves. She is also to bring 14,000 of her young girls. The fleet fetches them with song and drum and harp and viol, and so 14,000 beautiful girls get ready, 'some of the most courtly there were on earth'. They bring birds and wild beasts, tame monkeys and larks and blackbirds.[8] As so often, Saracens and Christians think alike. The numbers are exaggerated, but that is a joke characteristic of the convention, and we shall meet it often.

Other passages have only a remote plausibility. When the Saracen leader *A*umons is reproaching his discouraged fighting men in Reggio before the great battle, he reminds them of the ill-omened and braggart advice they gave him at home in Africa, in the great palace rooms painted with flowers, where girls with fresh complexions gave them loving kisses and they drank his best wines. In this nostalgic moment the wine is a warning to us, as it is also in the passage in *Orange* where Guillaume finds that the Saracen tower he has seized is stocked with provisions, drink, arms and women for enjoyment.[9] This is all wrong if it is supposed to refer to a practising Islamic country. Slave-girls and wine drinking might have come to the attention of Christians at the taifa courts and the memory have been distorted, exaggerated and transmuted in popular rumour; it is much more likely that these episodes spring exclusively out of European experience.

We should certainly not read anything specifically Saracen into references to quite ordinary philanderers. 'The ladies are his friends because of his beauty', says Roland of Margariz, 'any one of them who looks at him, her face lights up, and she cannot help smiling when she sees him'; and there is no other Saracen who is such a good soldier (*de tel chevalerie*).[10] Froiecuer, King of Aquilee in *Foucon de Candie*, has no equal as a knight, he is courtly, and 'he was so much loved by the ladies, if he wanted them to love him; that "Breaker of Hearts" is what the people of the country called him'. When King Tibaut suddenly becomes the type of the chivalrous ideal, he is 'loved by the ladies' and 'knew how to strike up an acquaintance with a beautiful lady when he saw one, and to persuade her to love him by fine words and fine gifts, not by overbearing her'.[11] Gorham (*Aspremont*), 'well-made and desirable', got many glances from the Queen, whose lover he was.[12] All these are gallant in every sense of the term, because love-making was one of the qualities of a good knight. The model of course is Christian.

Suggestions of the sexual freedom of Saracen women are also likely to be a simple transference of behaviour observed among Christian women and exaggerated. It corresponds neither to behaviour tolerated among respectable Arab women, nor even to the picture imagined by those Christian theologians who so stressed the lasciviousness of Muslim men exploiting or abusing their women. Aumarinde in *Barbastre* asks Corsout, 'What sort of people are the French? Do they love chivalry and the conversation of ladies for love-making? Who are the best of them? Don't hide anything from me.' He warns her: 'I tell you one thing for sure. If they catch you, you will soon be ravished.'[13] When Orable of Orange is baptised as Guibourg she makes Guillaume an ideal wife, but her reputation in her Saracen days was shaky, or her stepson Arragon slandered her: he despised his father for taking a young wife who has lovers in her tower and who prefers a young man with his first beard to her old and cuckolded husband.[14] In another poem, Guillaume asks King Louis for help desperately needed on the battlefield, and the Queen attacks the reputation of Guibourg as a former pagan enchanter; Guillaume replies by accusing the Queen of sleeping with two cowards who have run away from the battle, and with a hundred priests 'without wanting to call the chambermaid'.[15] This is another exaggeration joke, but one which indicates the single framework taken for granted for both Saracens and Christians.

In the *Chanson des Saisnes* (Saisnes are Saxons, but the author, Jean Bodel, makes them share the culture and religion of Saracens) Queen *S*ebile is a true wanton who pitches her tents on the river bank opposite the French army, and stills the jealousy of her husband, King *G*uiteclin, by claiming that she will get military information from her Christian admirers. '"Ladies", says the Queen, "Now we are well on the way to seeing the Frenchmen, as long as no one of us lets us down; when anyone has her friend, let her watch that she does not cheat him, but often enjoy herself and make love in her tent".' (they have pitched seven tents); 'what is the beauty of women worth, if they do not enjoy it in youth ?'[16] *S*inamonde, sister of the five kings of Hejjaz in *Le Bâtard de Bouillon* seduces King Baudouin in a determined and deliberate way – Vénus toute entière – and the Bastard is the fruit of this brief union. Later, she honourably marries Hugh of Tabarie, the hero's friend, saviour, and now stepfather. Her improbable behaviour is of a piece with the exceptionally implausible plot in its bizarre setting; but the poet sees nothing unlikely in her behaviour. He has her profess Christian belief for the occasion (one rare impact of canon law is the reluctance of heroes to sleep with non-Christians), and also makes her persuade the willing Baudouin with arguments that presuppose a long acquaintance with Christianity: the sin, she says, will only cost him a paternoster at vespers.[17] In these episodes there is a reflection, not on Saracen morals, but on the supposed morals of great Christian ladies.

Maugis d'Aigremont offers another pattern; Maugis is very free with the queens of Saracen kings, but the initiative is his as well as theirs. Here, as in the other cases, the total absence of restrictions, of the sense of respectability and seclusion normal at any period in a Muslim household, precludes an Arab model. The poet stresses what is going on. The court goes hawking, and Maugis has only to malinger; he finds the queen, and she straightaway embraces him, they find a room to themselves and get into bed where they are later seen intertwined: *Maugis et la roine vit dormir leȝ a leȝ, Bras a bras, boche a boche, se sont entracoleȝ.* It is much the same with Queen *Y*sane of Maiogres, who is even more wanton. She loves him so much 'that she cannot sleep by night or by day . . . the queen is in great torment for him'. She sends him a secret message; her husband is dead, but only just, and the proverb says that a young woman soon forgets an old husband. 'No one could count their loving kisses, They are lying in each other's arms' and making fast progress, when they discover that she is his mother's sister, and so escape incest at the eleventh hour.[18] The discovery that she is a Christian and a respected relation rules out any interpretation of this as Saracen behaviour; the fact is that it is regarded, for the purposes of a story anyway, as normal conduct for anyone.

This is a light-hearted story which provides the author with some amusement at the nature of the genre and its conventions. The giant who is fighting on the side of the amir of Persia offers him his daughter (the standard package, daughter, or sister, rich lands and conversion), she is bigger and uglier than her father and blacker than coal (or ink): in the passages parodied the Saracen heroine is always fair.[19] May the portraits of the wanton queens also be parodies? If they were, it would only further emphasise the implausibility of the theme, and be intended so to do.

Aye d'Avignon is in quite a different class from other loved ladies, and her *G*anor from other lovers. Kidnapped by Berenger (her husband's enemy and son of Ganelon), and taken to Saracen Aigremore, *G*anor's capital, she becomes *G*anor's prisoner. His intentions are honourable. The poet insists that he is unmarried. Whether from ignorance or deliberately, the poet gives no hint of the existence of legal polygamy, or any but Christian law. It would have brought a new genre of story into being if he had. Ganor asks: 'Who is this lady who is so beautiful? What is she to you, cousin or other relation? If it seems well and good to you to sell her to me for the best gold, I will take her as my woman and make her my wife.' He keeps her safe, defends her, and loves her long after (in his absence) she has been rescued; when Duke Garnier, her husband, dies, Ganor becomes the champion of the family, of her rights, and those of her son, Gui de Nanteuil. Devout Saracen, Ganor prays to his gods, 'Give me her to wife, by your divine pity; I seek no other paradise'; he goes on to pray to avenge Garnier and uphold Gui. All this is vouchsafed to him, and Paradise, of course, the Christian one, comes with Aye.[20] His having wanted to buy her in the first place is the more surprising. This might reflect concubinage, at that time not only legal, but of good repute, in Islam, but is, of course, limited to a slave and her owner. The story is too vague to echo the Islamic jurisprudence involved, but as far as it goes it does combine the ideas of respectability and legal purchase, of a kind alien to Christendom, which was familiar with slavery and with concubinage, but not with their legal control or their religious respectability. There is no sign of the horror that theologians felt at this last.

There is little doubt about the fate of 300 girls, 'daughters of knights', tied in couples and dragged in the train of the conqueror, given over to ruffians, for sale (*Aspremont*). There is some doubt, however: 'you do not damage goods you mean to sell.' Are these haphazardly emotive phrases only? In the same poem, Agolant delivers an ultimatum to the emperor which is several times repeated (envoy to emperor, emperor to barons, and so on). He must not only return the four gods taken in an earlier battle, but pay tribute, treasure, 1700 virgins (and as many beasts of burden), he must go in person barefoot and renounce his faith. His first reply inclines to vulgarity; he wouldn't like to go like that; he hasn't got a penny; the virgins would be a problem, no one could find so many; and as for the gods, they have already been broken up and given to the whores. In a more formal reply he says, 'In all my kingdom I do not know anyone so blackguardly that he holds his daughter or his mistress so low as to hand her over to an unbelieving pagan.' He makes it clear that he expects that the girls would be handed over to *putage*, crudely debauched, rather than experience the lighter and relatively respectable fate of enslavement.[21]

The married daughter of the Count of Ponthieu, falling into Saracen hands, is married by the sultan of *A*umarie: 'she saw well that it was better to act from love than under duress', being subsequently rescued and recovered by her original French husband. Two points show that there is no thought of Islamic law in the story: the sultan is free to marry her because he 'still had no wife'; and he makes her adherence to his religion a condition of marriage, which is not required by Islamic law and is implausible.[22] *Floire et Blancheflor* is outside the scope of our immediate enquiry, but let us note that the amir of Babylon who buys Blancheflor proves benevolent, but the poet does not suggest that his rights over her are legal, as distinct from pragmatic.[23] The proposed fate of Aelis in *Loquifer*[24] is not in doubt, and implies the same *droit de vainqueur* as *Aspremont*.

There are few other indications of the sexual social relationships of Saracens. In *Antioche* comes the idea that Saracens copulate with many women in order to procreate more soldiers to fight the Christians. This does not come in poems with more ordinary settings, and *Antioche* contains some authentic Crusading opinions and illusions, like this one.[25] The accusation that Islam favours homosexuality is characteristic of later periods and I do not find it in the poems. Prosper Tarbé, introducing an abbreviated version of *Foucon de Candie* in 1860,[26] understood the line, *il gisoit avec Marsemin son dru*, to imply homosexuality, although he identified the poem as in part a satire on Thiébaut, King of Navarre and Count of Champagne, admittedly promiscuously heterosexual. *Dru* can mean 'lover' but it means 'crony' as often.[27] This was not an age of private bedrooms, and even centuries later, when privacy was more common, we find Pepys driven to lie with his brother or a friend when beds are short,[28] of course with no sexual connotation. Most medieval writers and Pepys were happy to make their meaning quite clear and there were no sly hints. There is nothing in this point. Is there in the use of *mahommet* as a common noun to mean *favori*, *mignon*? This sense may as easily derive from the notion of 'doll' (as English *mammet*, from idol) and it is used to mean 'favourite' in the most innocuous sense, as of Joseph with Pharaoh.[29]

In accounts of the behaviour of Saracen women, and in accounts of Saracen sexuality generally, it is impossible to see the slightest attempt to portray Arab manners and customs, but equally there is no sign of the preoccupations of theologians, and hardly a hint of legal concubinage. On the other hand, the poetic fancy plays freely with known Christian ways. The great knights and ladies, both Saracen and Christian, behave according to the poet's fancy, but behave alike.

THE LOVER AND HEIRESS

We learn much about the poets' ideas of relations between the sexes and within the family from their treatment of their Saracen heroines. 'La paienne amoureuse', as Bédier called her,[30] is not just a stock figure, though it is a stock situation that the daughter of a great Saracen lord should fall in love with her father's enemy, help him to defeat her father, should be baptised and marry him. Thus she becomes the consort of her father's supplanter. (In the West it often happened that a man was succeeded by a brotherless daughter's husband.) With its variations, the Saracen story in this form was a recurring convention that must have been a great favourite with the audiences, and the plots have the same episodic complexity as *alf layla wa layla* or modern television soap opera, both satisfying popular demand. Occasionally the theme is handled romantically, but especially in the earlier poems, the heroine commonly and appropriately chooses the most efficient knight to fall in love with. He is successful in terms of a feudal economy and she is physically attractive, so that the plots flatter an audience committed to chivalry. It is curious that through a great part of many stories the initiative in action is female.

I shall take *Orable*, in *Orange*, first, because there are many archetypical passages in her story, although it is Guillaume who first falls in love, and she is the wife, not the daughter, of the ruler of the Saracen city of Orange. We saw Guillaume's thoughts already turned to girls while he waits for war; then *Orable* is described to him ('her figure is pleasing, slim and well-made, and her eyes brilliant like the moulted falcon'). It is then that Guillaume thinks that a nobleman could enjoy himself with her, and wishes she believed in God; he falls in love by hearsay and only gets deeper in when he sees her; he is distracted by his desire, but does not forget that his two desires go together: to get her he must fight for her. He will not eat bread or salt meat or drink wine till he knows how Orange and its marble tower are laid out, and has seen its courtly Queen *Orable* – the fortifications and the girl, the two essentials. 'Her love holds me and dominates me in a way I cannot think or say'. It is fortunate that he is not disappointed when he does see her; his blood races, on the contrary, when he finds 'the Lady of Africa' is 'whiter than the shining snow and more flushed than the flowering rose'. Many poets dwell lasciviously, like this, on flesh whiter than hawthorn, *blanche la char comme la flor en l'ente*. Perhaps this represents nothing more than the preferences of dark men, or possibly there may here be another element of nobility: noble ladies from ancient Egypt onwards have tried to keep their skins pale.[31] When Guillaume tells one nephew, Bertrand, that he cannot sleep, eat, drink, carry arms, ride or go to Mass, for love, another, Guielin, laughs at him, and so surely do the poet and the audience; Guielin continues to make digs at his uncle at different stages of the action. So does the poet, with a nicely calculated degree of parody. 'She was dressed in an ermine robe and under that a long tunic in worked silk, fastened tightly over her well-shaped body. When Guillaume saw her all his body shivered. "God!" said Guillaume, "it is Paradise here!"' Presumably this got a sympathetic laugh too; and certainly it did when Guillaume's nephew urges him to sit by her, put his arms round her and not be slow to kiss her; the kiss will cost only 20,000 marks, and much suffering for all the kin; Guillaume tells him not to jeer.

When Orable hears of Guillaume's prowess, we do not hear that her blood races, but she comments, 'Happy is the lady who has his heart'. She is that woman, and we understand that she knows it. She is soon calling her own side *felon paien*; these may be thoughtless phrases carelessly inserted too soon. They show that the poet already thinks of her as having switched her allegiance, and so, it turns out, she has. Guillaume begs her to arm him; she weeps for pity and gives him her husband's sword – never lent before. Her husband Tibaut starts back to Orange from Africa (in the Roman sense) and the poet in an aside warns him that he will have the greatest grief of his life, he will lose his city and his wife, *sa fort cité garnie Et sa moillier*, Orable *l'eschevie*. This is a key sentence. In a number of stories there comes this double conquest, the captured city and the wife who adds to the inheritance. In English history the classic case is Henry VII. Orable says, in a business-like way, that if she thought she would be safe, and Guillaume would take her, she would become Christian. She knows a secret passage for escape, which was constructed by her grandfather; this strengthens the presumption of her family title to Orange (Tibaut is an 'African'). She has now changed sides, and the Saracen eavesdropper who tells her stepson that she loves the Christians (in general) and Guillaume in bed, *au couchier*, in particular, says nò more than the truth. Guillaume's policy of head and heart has paid off.[32] In no poem is the harmony of political, economic, military and personal values better balanced.

The inheritance that can be expected to go with the heiress is still more emphasised in *Anseis de Cartage*. Anseis, left to rule Spain by Charlemagne after Roncesvaux, wants a queen, and his council propose Gaudisse, daughter of the Saracen king, Marsile (who, unlike the Marsile in *Roland*, has escaped the Christian victors), in order to secure the kingdom. When the

Christian counsellor *Y*soré defects, *M*arsile offers him the girl and the kingdom. Anseis manages to steal *G*audisse away, and in the end he gets both, though without Charlemagne's help he would have been destroyed by *M*arsile and *Y*soré. *G*audisse is a lively heroine, and well able to co-operate actively with Anseis, but we cannot say of her, as of *O*rable, that the most important initiatives in the struggle are hers.[33] I shall leave discussion of the motivation of the heroines till my chapter on conversions. Here I shall concentrate on their attractions, their cunning, and their relations with their fathers and brothers.

Perhaps the most cunning of all is *N*ubie, daughter of the *aumaçor* in *La Prise de Cordres*, and even the falling in love is her initiative. Most of the conventional descriptions of beauty are lavished on her, her body is *gent* and *bien fait* and *molé*, her flesh as white as hawthorn, her eyes like a moulted falcon: 'there is none so beautiful in thirteen cities'. *Blanche ot la char, brunete le sorcille*, the poet assures us again; he cannot restrain his accounts of her beauty, he says, none more beautiful in ten kingdoms. She has no sooner seen Bertrand (Guillaume's nephew), like most heroes at one time or another, the prisoner of his future father-in-law, than she loves him. There is description of his attractions too: 'pleasing and noble-looking and adorned with all the advantages, Broad in the shoulders...'; his eyes also are like the moulted falcon. She immediately and realistically assesses the price of love: conversion, the escape of the prisoners, the kidnapping of her father. Her unscrupulous ruses are ingenious, and, though they are not usually altogether successful, luck proves an effective substitute. She treats her father unfeelingly and deceitfully, much as if she were one of his Christian prisoners, and owed him nothing. Like the other heroines, she has changed her allegiance. She treats her father particularly shabbily when he is showing his affection in a boozy way. She says she will honour the Saracen people by serving the wine at the feast, and he seats her on his lap and kisses her. She means to drug his wine and all the wine, and so she does. When the *aumaçor* is in the hands of the French, who have escaped, Bertrand will not marry her without her father's permission. This recognition of the father's authority, even when he is the chief enemy, is unusual; is it bound up in the poet's mind with the legitimate succession to Cordoba ('Cordres')? The French apply pressure to the *aumaçor*, and he consents.[34]

This story of conquest, marriage and inheritance, this basic plot of French prisoners of the Saracens who are released by the daughter (or wife) of the king or amir (or *amustant* or *aumaçor*) has variations, but the general description fits pretty well the efforts of *M*alatrie in *Barbastre* and in *Bueves de Commarcis*, *A*gaiete in *Guibert d'Andrenas* and in the second part of *Cordres* (*Prise de Sebille*), *G*audisse in *Anseis*, *F*landrine in *Doon de Mayence* (slightly different, because she is the off-spring of a mixed marriage) and *E*sclarmonde in *Huon de Bordeaux*; it is only varied at the last minute for *R*osamonde in *Elie*. In *Simon de Pouille* and *Blancandin*, Saracen friends of the hero get the girl. *Enfances Ogier* is another variant which we will look at a little later, as at *Fierabras*, the most striking example of all. The loves of *Aye d'Avignon* reverse the roles of the lovers.[35] In all the stories family interest is the constant factor. We will come back later to the unfilial behaviour of these young ladies; there is no question of subtle psychological explanation. We have instead a total and irreversible redirection of loyalty and a lasting impression of the planning and executive abilities of these heroines, of their ingenuity, their quick reactions, their singlemindedness and their unscrupulous pursuit of their ends. The immediate purposes are obvious, the ultimate end is less so; we shall not be very wrong to suggest that it is the setting up of a feudal dynasty.

Sometimes a song will conform to only one part of the pattern or another. The fourteenth-century Provençal poem called *Roland à Saragosse* is short, only fragmentary, and delicate in sentiment, yet on the same model as earlier and often rougher poems. The story tells how Roland, with only Oliver in support (and their quarrel takes up a good deal of the surviving text) goes to Saragossa to see Queen *B*raslimonde. She has sent for him in a lost portion of the poem, she does not know him, they meet only momentarily, she gives him a cloak which he will wear for love; she warns him so that he can escape her husband's soldiers, and specifically she regrets that she cannot hand the country over to him, *Vos en rendria dels Sarrazins lo camp*.[36] Thus the notion of inheritance is present, although not at all as a practical proposition. There is no possibility that any Arab queen, or any respectable Arab lady, could behave like this; we are still with the Christian model.

The case of *R*osamonde in *Elie de St Gilles* is strange, and rather shocking, perhaps as much to contemporary as to modern susceptibilities. The plot has unrolled in the usual outline pattern, with its own variations; *R*osamonde is baptised, and the barons are standing round waiting for the wedding feast, when the archbishop forbids the banns: Elie has stood god-father at the baptism and set up a spiritual relationship; this would be good in canon law, but in the plot it is absurd, the question would never have arisen. The editor supposes that the adapter of the existing recension gave Elie another wife, because he wanted to integrate him into a known poetic cycle, and he knew that Aiol's father's name was Elie, and his mother's name not *R*osamonde. As it stands, it breaks the pattern; but feudal propriety and the need for endowment are satisfied when Guillaume d'Orange insists that *R*osamonde is entitled at least to as good a husband as may be available, and she gets her second choice. Who inherits her father's kingdom is not clear, but certainly earlier in the action her wicked brother *C*aifas seems to ill-treat her to prevent her marrying, and it is implied that he had an interest in this.[37]

Another variation in the pattern is the case of the unhappy *L*udie in *Le Bâtard de Bouillon*. She is the daughter of the *amulainne* of Orbrie, the enemy of the Bastard's friend Hugh of Tabarie; and she loves, is loved by, and engaged to, King *C*orsabrin of Mont Oscur. The Bastard falls in love with her, and Hugh promises that he shall have her. Indeed, the *amulainne* offers her to the Bastard, but he must change his religion. He kills the *amulainne* and tells *L*udie that he will compel her to marry him. She is angry, and says she would rather be killed

than make love to him: 'You have killed my father with your
sharp sword; how then should you be given love by me?'
Nevertheless, he baptises, marries and forces her. When he
goes off to war, she escapes to her lover. The Bastard kills a
charcoal-burner, dresses in his clothes, and smuggles himself
into the palace to his unwilling wife. She greets him and lets
him make love to her, because she has sent a message to
Corsabrin, who arrives in time to catch him naked in his bath,
and make him prisoner. But the Bastard is improbably rescued
by Hugh and Ludie is burned.[38] As the editor says, this reverses
the usual situation, and the poet's sympathies seem at variance
with his own story. Ludie is wily. and a deceiver, but she is
clearly much provoked. The Bastard, of course, is more than a
bit of a bastard. Yet in spite of all this, much of the usual
apparatus is there; the parental authority, the heiress, the
baptism and marriage, but the lady's loyalty to her Arab lover,
family and friends, her rape and forced baptism, make her
destruction inevitable.

I have described the deliberate wantonness of the Saxon
Queen Sebile. In Bodel's song we hear her wanton sentiments
but we only see her making love with an extrovert paladin as
promiscuous as herself. On her husband's defeat and death she
marries the lover who inherits the kingdom. But this is too
much for Bodel, and the dead man's sons try to avenge him;
ultimately, Charlemagne has to reconquer the Saxons and
settle the kingdom. The Saxons are 'Saracen' by religion and
law. The kingdom passes with the lady, the sons avenge their
father. This pattern of aggression and inheritance is largely displaced in the thirteenth century by the single-adventurer
model, and this is one explanation of why it is the hero's friend,
one who has a stake in the country, who gets the girls, for
example, Synados in *Simon de Pouille*, and Sadoine in *Blancandin*. Gui de Warewic avoids the heiresses his adventures
earn him, perhaps because in real life the prototypes were
mercenaries who never got near to the heiresses (or their
equivalent); Bueves de Hamtoune's story in this particular
respect is close to the older tradition.[39]

It is not invariable that Christians should benefit from the pattern of inheritance. *Carahuel*, the chivalrous Saracen beloved by Ogier in his *Enfances*, and by Charlemagne and all his court, marries the heiress to whom he was originally engaged and whom Ogier has protected. Until the defeat of his treacherous father-in-law-to-be, and more treacherous rival for his lover's hand he is beloved and treated with the patronage given to a faithful client (or 'friendly'); but when he is allowed to take the bodies of the fallen kings for burial, and the heiress presents him as her husband to the people of Sur (Tyre), he is acclaimed king, and fades entirely out of the Christian picture. Here inheritance has operated without Christian advantage. Marriages between Saracen and Christian societies may work either way. When in *Maugis B*randoine finds himself fighting Christians who are his kin, and he cannot beat them, he does just join them. When *F*landrine marries Doon de Mayence another mixed marriage has returned to Christendom in the next generation, but although *La Fille du Comte de Ponthieu* herself returns safely to Europe, she has left behind the child from whose line *S*aladin will spring.[40]

It is impossible to escape the repeated impression that a marriage is seen as conferring the right to the kingdom; as the poet of *Maugis* says, *La terre est a la dame de par son ancissor*.[41] This is impossible under Islamic law, by which a daughter inherits one share against every son's two, and daughters can never alone inherit the whole estate, even when they have no brothers. It is most unlikely that anyone was thinking of Islamic law at all, correctly or incorrectly. That the founder of a new dynasty should marry a daughter from the old is politics, not law, and might happen anywhere. The poet has created a new type, and *la paienne amoureuse* turns out to be *l'heritière rusée* as well.

Two Pairs of Siblings

Floripas, in *Destruction de Rome*, but more especially in *Fierabras*, is almost a caricature of the type, and her story is interesting in all its applications. The description of her beauty is more than usually fleshly: 'Dressed in damask, none was more attractive, her hair shone on her shoulders like pure gold, her flesh was beautiful and whiter than the snow in February, her eyes black like the moulted falcon, her complexion ruby as the rose on the rose-bush, her mouth just right and sweet to kiss . . .'[42] This comes from *Destruction*. *Fierabras* is even more anatomical – flesh (white as summer flowers), face (flushed like a meadow rose), mouth, teeth, lips, nose, forehead, eyes (moulted falcon), hips, flanks, breasts, hair, all appropriately catalogued, there is a great deal of it. In some poems, including this one, baptism ceremonies are the excuse for another light-hearted and lascivious description: 'They undress the girl, all the baronage watching. Her flesh was whiter than the summer flowers, And she had little breasts and a tall and slim figure, Her hair like fine gold much refined.' The assembled baronage were attentive: 'Desire was moved in the bodies of the barons'; and Charlemagne, 'the emperor himself has let slip a smile, For all that his hair was whitened and yellowed; So would his feelings very soon have been engaged.'[43]

*F*loripas' own behaviour also suggests sensuality. We remember her offer of five noble girls to Roland and his companions; we do not hear what happened in the end to them. She is a great temptation to a burglar to rape her. 'He comes to *F*loripas' bed, she is more beautiful than a fairy . . . He looks at *F*loripas. It would be good for him to lie with her, because she pleases him very much. The wretch has embraced her side-by-side, both naked'. At this she wakes up and gives a loud cry; we feel that anyone else would have woken sooner. All this must titillate and amuse the audience, a somewhat drawn-out bawdy joke, but this poem has no moments of delicacy on any subject. Fun does not stand in the way of *F*loripas' plan to marry Gui de Bourgogne. Nor does the life of her old governess, who is going to tell tales to the amir about her entertaining the Frenchmen; she is thrown into the sea, and when the Frenchmen are told about it, they get a good laugh. Similarly, when Duke Naimes manages to get *L*ucifer of Baldas burned to death by a trick it provokes various sarcastic jokes.[44] If what the poet sets out to convey is that *F*loripas is a sexy piece with all her eye on the main chance, he succeeds very well, and the distinguished Frenchmen she has chosen as her new companions seem the sort she will be happy with.

But however much she is treated as a 'sex-object', and though to the poet and his audience she is an object, she is conceived as a subject; she is dominant and dominating in performance. She chooses her husband, one is tempted to say, her consort; if there had been a cycle, like the Guillaume cycle, it would have been the *F*loripas cycle; *F*ierabras fades beside his sister, Gui de Bourgogne has no personality. In any sequel, *F*loripas would have become a noble Wife of Bath. Her ruthlessness shows most in her treatment of her father. *F*ierabras, long since converted to Christianity, and now unmistakably preux, tries everything he can to convert his father and save him from death. She presses Charlemagne impatiently to execute him.[45] Her motive may have been clearer to the audience of the day than it is now. Is she supposed to fear his enmity if he survives, or that, baptised, he might retain his kingdom and exclude her? What is sure is her inveterate hostility towards him, and there is also suspicion that there is some further motive not immediately apparent.

A somewhat different case, though at first sight it looks similar, is *G*uibourg's in *La Bataille Loquifer*. The poets of the sequels to *Orange* conceive the baptised *G*uibourg as having retained the powers of initiative she had as *O*rable. She has developed into an effective châtelaine who in times of disaster rallies the vassals, comforts and encourages Guillaume in defeat, plans for him, and sets him on the way to ultimate victory, which is gained with the help of her brother *R*enoart, the forgotten servant in King Louis' kitchens. The Saracens have not forgotten that Guillaume has robbed *T*ibaut of his wife and his lands, but *R*enoart is baptised and recovers his noble status. King *D*esramé, his and *G*uibourg's father, wants to wipe out the shame that she has brought on him and on *T*ibaut, and after *R*enoart has fought with and killed his ally Loquifer, he manages to kidnap *G*uibourg. She is roughly

treated, dragged by the hair, and is going to be burned.
Guillaume comes to her rescue, while *R*enoart stands neutral.
*G*uibourg helps Guillaume in his fight with *D*esramé, whom
in the end he kills (in another version, whom he seems to have
killed); *G*uibourg has taken a constructive part in bringing
about his death, or trying to, but she has not pressed eagerly for
it like *F*loripas for her father's. In *F*loripas' case, also, her
father was the prisoner of the Christians, whereas *D*esramé
is represented as raging against *G*uibourg: 'You are quite
crazed', he says to Guillaume, 'when you put that whore in
your bed'. *R*enoart, meanwhile, has problems of conscience.
Apart from being attacked by *D*esramé, *G*uibourg has given
her allegiance to Guillaume, she is his wife and companion,
sa feme et s'amie; for *R*enoart the case is less simple, and he is
torn between his sister, his friend Guillaume, and his religion,
on the one side, and his father on the other. *D*esramé puts his
trust in his son: *an son fil se fia*. *R*enoart mediates between his
father and his brother-in-law; 'I love you more than any man
alive', he says to Guillaume, 'for my sister, who is married to
you. See my father there, how he has humbled himself . . . I am
sorry for him, my heart is turned to him.' But *D*esramé cannot
lay aside his fury against *G*uisbourg: 'Son *R*enoart, Guillaume
has betrayed you, and so has that filthy whore *G*uibourg with
her perfidious heart, who has left Mahon, our god; and king
*T*ibaut, her rightful lord, she has shamed.' *G*uibourg defends
her joining in the fight: '"Brother!" she says, "Have a heart!
It is not surprising if I helped my husband".' *R*enoart cannot
bring himself easily to let his father die, 'My heart is much
troubled. People will say that I betrayed my father.' He presses
his father many times to accept Christianity, and if he will,
Guillaume will accept a peace; but *D*esramé is constant to his
gods: 'Your God, I defy him; I would no more believe in him
than in a stinking dog.' At last *R*enoart gives way: 'My thought
for you was kindly, but now you have violated my feelings so
that I can have no more sorrow or mercy for you.' *R*enoart,
like *F*ierabras, is anxious to save his father, but he shows much
more feeling and is much more anxious. *G*uibourg, like

*F*loripas, attacks her father, but it is in self-defence. The striking things are the frustrated sympathy between *D*esramé and *R*enoart, and the raging virulence of *D*esramé against Guisbourg.[46]

✕ AUTHORITY IN THE FAMILY

Women do not rule, although the government sometimes seems to pass through them. Their attachment shifts in a moment from their consanguinity to their affinity, from father, or father and husband together, to lover. When it is put like this, they sound unattractive, passive nonentities. But it is just here that we are surprised; we find, on the contrary, tough, realistic women of untiring initiative, politically and socially effective. The degree varies from case to case, but it is often true. 'Your heart is soft and feminine', says one Saracen king to another,[47] and what is meant in reproof between men would be equally unjust of many heroines. The sexual emphasis restores the balance; in most references to the heroine there is a word or phrase to remind us of her beauty;[48] sexuality is not always as strong as in *Orange* or *Fierabras*, let alone *Saisnes*, but it is a norm of behaviour shared by Saracens and Christians. Yet it is largely extraneous to the more important matter of young female initiative (or quick response to a male initiative); both these situations occur.

It would add to our understanding of the function of the women who dominate the stories to see it as to some extent a fantasy of revolt against parental authority, in an age when a father or guardian determined the children's marriages, and especially an heiress's. In the latter case, the lord was also a source of interference; and in the songs the father is also the superior lord. The origins of family pressures in adult life are beyond the present subject, but among its results are both the arrogance acquired by fathers (and other men of the family) in the exercise of their power, and the passive resentment of the young whose lives are disposed of in the interests of a family or a dynasty. Usually, the girl directly helps her lover to seize power in her father's territory, but sometimes the revolt against authority is more lightly or remotely triggered off;

*F*lordespine, in *Gaufrey*, for example, helps the Christian
prisoners just because she thinks they might help her to meet
Bertrand, whom she loves by reputation.[49]

The poems portray this revolt even in situations where no
Christian benefits from it. *C*arahuel, in *Ogier*, loves *G*loriande,
and, when her father changes his mind and gives her to another
and more powerful suitor, *B*runamont, her revolt against this is
not even 'justified' by subsequent baptism. When her father
and *D*anemont are killed, *G*loriande presents *C*arahuel to her
father's people as her husband and they make him king. That
is, their defiance of the father and king has succeeded, and they
rule in his place.[50] *L*icoride, in *Simon*, loves Simon's friend,
*S*ynados, not Simon himself, but they are both converted, and
they are recompensed for what they have lost, but do not
succeed the father whose power they have helped to destroy.[51]
The daughter of *A*limodés loves *S*adoine, the companion of
Blancandin. This case is remarkable for an explicit statement
of the revolt, couched in romantic terms, by the heroine. A
Saracen king called *R*ubion who is a suitor announces that he
fights for the honour of the lady he loves – 'To those on the city
walls he calls, "a battle for the love of my love"'. However, he
is not her love and she is not his *amie*; it is her father's idea that
she should be, and she prays to Mahon to let her marry instead
the man of her choice, *S*adoine: 'He and I are of an age; our
marriage would be good . . . I would be his lover, and he mine'.
She is protesting against an exogamous arranged marriage that
is politically motivated: 'My father wants me to marry an
aumaçor from overseas', whose hair and beard have turned
white. She conducts a military operation against her father,
who is very angry at her getting married without his permission:
'You have married without my consent, and you will repent of
it'. Not only that, she has tried to introduce a young man and a
foreigner into his land as king. The poem repeats his outburst
against her lack of submission, which seems the primary
provocation; and the young man he will hang.[52] A plea for
freedom of choice would never have been listened to in East or
West, still less would an act of insubordination have been

tolerated, least of all from a princess. Outraged husbands are rarer than enraged fathers. Marsile is angry, but less angry than might have been expected, when Maugis cuckolds him. In *Loquifer* it is Desramé, as disgraced father, not Tibaut the wronged husband, who tries to avenge the family honour.[53]

It would be misleading to suggest that family pressures and parental authority are generally or consistently resisted. The devotion and solidarity of the Aymerids exemplify the contrary, as do the four sons of Aymon. These family dynasties are fighting units whose members' reciprocal loyalty is deeply embedded in the moral system of the poems. Family sentiment is quite understood; the sorrows of bereaved parents,[54] the urge in Saracens to avenge their kin killed by paladins.[55] The fact is that new family groupings destroy old ones, and they may have been seen by their creators in an inchoate or vague way as forces of social change. That heiresses should marry new men and aliens against their fathers' wishes does not constitute a revolution, but it does suggest that a social order will inevitably be modified by the new management. It will affect the common people in only one way; whether Christian barons take over, or a Saracen king is converted, they must turn Christian.[56] This would mean changes in the family structure in the long run, but some of these the poets do not foresee, and others apparently do not interest them as they did the polemists. I discuss the process of conversion in another chapter, but here we should beware of seeing it as a prime motive. In the immediate discussion it has two functions. Poets use it to explain a predisposition on the part of a Saracen to love a Christian (though this is not the invariable pattern); and it sets a seal on the change of loyalty when it is confirmed by the act of baptism.

This conversion is only part of the story mechanism; the real revolution is the break-up of the Saracen ruling family. This may be a reportage of what actually did happen when Arab lands were conquered, but it cannot fail to reflect what was known to happen when lands changed hands in Christian Europe, and it is likely that it is also a way of talking about developments in Christian society and concomitant discontents in the Christian West, and especially in its overcrowded privileged class. There must be some explanation of the pattern of family break-up that these poems sometimes exhibit, and of the problem of why some Saracen fathers are subjected to great humiliations. The poet of *Cordres* felt that this was so, and, when he had extracted the maximum fun out of the tricks Nubie plays on her father, he allowed the Christians to respect the father's resistance both to the marriage and to conversion, at any rate for some time. That the sons in *Loquifer* and *Fierabras* tend in contrast to their sisters to be compassionate, rather supports the idea of the daughters' revolt. The anger of the fathers reads like something observed, and must have sounded more so. If these plots emphasise and often deride parental authority, the model may well be European rather than Arab, and it recurs often enough for us to be sure that it found a welcome in a European audience.

It becomes clear that there is no certain reflection of Arab life and customs or of Islamic law in the poems. There is no explicit reference to polygyny, in marriage or in slave concubinage. If *G*anor's attempt to buy Aye as wife does dimly reflect legal concubinage as defined by Islamic law, it is too obscure to carry conviction. Queen Ysané, captured by Saracens, is honoured and married by their king; nothing is said of her sharing him with other wives and slaves. The demand for girls as tribute from Charlemagne, in *Aspremont*, may reflect a folk memory of invasion and enslavement, but reveals no knowledge of slavery as a legal institution in Islam. The open and indecorous behaviour of Saracen girls, sometimes even promiscuity or wantonness at least in intention, is inconceivable among Arab girls of good family. The resentment of parental control might well have an Arab source, if it were not more likely to have its origins nearer home.

Badly as these girls behave from an Islamic point of view, there is no hint in the poems that their sexual morals diverge at all from Christian practice; on the contrary, if all behave rather too freely to be credible, at least all behave alike. The clerical and polemic line on sexual morals is totally lacking. Almost our only certainty is that the story always comes first, and the love interest favours an exciting plot. To have been able to follow their own road like this, the poets must have gone in total ignorance, not only of Arabs and Islam, but of everything Christian writers said about them; or else, they must have been completely indifferent to both. The second may be surprising, but the first is incredible.

5

VIOLENCE: HATRED,
SUFFERING AND WAR

THE OFFICIAL LINE

The second branch of the Christian polemic attack was that
Islam was in some special way a religion of violence and force.
In this case there was not the same minute casuist interest in a
series of specific though hypothetical acts that there had been
in the case of sexual morals, but it was not thought less important. The Cluniac Qur'ān, translated by Robert of Ketton, reads
for example (sura 88): 'For you are one who teaches, not one
who coerces', and a marginal annotator of the time who had a
more than usually extensive acquaintance with the subject
comments, 'So why do you teach that men are to be converted
to your religion by the sword? Why do you subject men by
force, like animals and beasts, and not by reasoning, like men?'[1]
Peter the Venerable himself thought this the most important
issue. 'After he says, "Do not argue with those that have the
law", he adds, "for killing is better than disputing". So what
shall I say? Words fail me to confute such an absurdity, such
animal cruelty, such disgraceful wickedness.' Vitry similarly
simplifies when he paraphrases the requirements of jihād;
'Whoever contradicts and blasphemes, let him be killed.'[2] Yet
an unrelenting religious coercion was for many centuries
characteristic of Christendom.

It continued to be imputed to Islam. To take two examples
from the thirteenth century, both very well informed Domini-

cans; William of Tripoli says, 'One article of belief of theirs runs like this: "the faith of the Saracens arose by the sword of Muhammad, and will perish by the sword which will be God's"'; and Ricoldo da Monte Croce says, 'The religion of the Saracens is violent and was brought in by violence, and so among them it is held to be quite certain that it will last only as long as the victory of the sword will remain with them'. Not only does Islam (he thinks) depend on the sword, but it does not enforce those points of morals that it lays down:

> Although the Qur'ān sometimes prohibits robbery and perjury and some other wrong things, yet that prohibition is a kind of permission, for it says, do not do such and such wrong things, which are not pleasing to God; but if you do them, he is compassionate and merciful and he will easily forgive you.[3]

Yet if Islam inculcates holy war and only half forbids robbery, Ricoldo has not quite the same conviction as in sexual morals that bad doctrine causes worse behaviour, and he even exaggerates, if only to shame Christians, when he says, 'they who have the religion of killing and death, choose not to kill each other, and the wretched Christians, who have a religion of life and commandments of peace and love, kill each other without mercy.'[4] This is a unique admission, but it is still based on the idea that Islam has an essential violence. Many authors recount, if only briefly, the rise of Islam as a sudden eruption and a quick conquest of Christian lands.[5]

In general, there is little knowledge of the law of jihād, of the Muslim doctrine of holy war, but canon law, as it relates to Crusade, is uncannily similar.[6] There is nothing that the law of jihād permits, that the law of Crusade does not also permit, but jihād enjoins on the conqueror duties towards the conquered Peoples of the Book for which there is no parallel in Christianity. To the conquered Muslim populations in Europe only a grudging and temporary toleration was offered, and with the authority of the church, said yet another Dominican, it is lawful and sometimes meritorious to attack Muslims, 'to despoil them and kill them and award their goods to the faithful'. In spite of this, all Muslim successes and conquests were seen as 'persecutions'.[7] We can sum up the general and inconsistent opinion of theologians: Islam is the religion of the sword; Muslims may be permitted to exist as such under Christian rule only for a limited time. This is not a statement of feudal rulers, who were ready to tolerate or massacre Muslims as might best suit their convenience at a particular time. How does all this relate to the songs, which have often been regarded as a kind of war propaganda? Do they suppose that Saracens are in some way more violent than Christians, and do they inculcate Crusade?

If in the stories the women often see to the brain-work, it is the men's part to perform almost superhuman feats of strength and endurance and indomitability, the function of efficient knighthood. Born in a lucky hour, the women who plan an escape route from trouble, and the men whose strength and daring get them into it and out again, seize every opportunity that the fantasy of their creators can devise, with courage, cunning and brutality. The poets constantly exploit an area of humour which fluctuates between burlesque and folk humour, but usually shows itself in one form or another of popular exaggeration. Probably they viewed with some irony the conventional phrases they used as appropriate to situations which frequently recurred, which were immediately recognisable and which the audiences expected and enjoyed. It is not likely that either poet or hearer took the sex and violence too seriously, the love, ambition and aggression which provide the staple plots in story-telling anywhere at any time. Absurdity and implausibility do not make adventure less exciting, and naturalism is not always more amusing. The brutality of these poems is not meant to be realistic.

We should be naive if we supposed that the poems were meant to be taken literally; naive, too, if we supposed them naive. The events of each story impress us gradually and cumulatively; this also is how the vein of humour of each particular author affects us. We can dismiss the callous presentation of acts of cruelty when they reach us singly, and the credulous repetition of impossible feats; they are not meant to be accepted seriously, callously or credulously. But we cannot ignore the cumulative effect of it all; violence, credible or not, creates an atmosphere. If we dismiss each separate inflated statement, we still retain an overwhelming impression of violence. This surely is a calculated effect: the grisly humour is even an evasion of authentic violence naturalistically re-counted. Exaggeration – size, numbers, strength, endurance – is the mode of humour, and it is in the case of violence that this is most important.

Solemn accusations of violence against Islam in learned treatises or even lowbrow histories are at the opposite pole from the fictional treatment of violence as a macabre joke.

THE POET'S LINE

Conventional, almost ritual phrases have a big part to play in this method of story-telling, and the most bloodthirsty expressions are just conventional. 'His blood and his brains poured out onto his feet' (the victim here is a disloyal Christian). 'He puts the two eyes out of the pagan's head and his brains fall at his feet'; 'with his great fist he gave him such a blow on the neck that he broke his spine and his back, and knocked him down dead at his feet'; 'he gave him such a great blow with the stick that his brains flew out in all directions'; 'he put his left hand on his head, and raised his right, and hit him on the neck, and broke his neckbone in pieces'; these are all cases of Saracens slaughtered by paladins. 'He hit his feet and wrists and head . . . and made blood and brains and wrists and feet fly away' (a fight between Saracens).[8]

Renoart is even bigger and more powerful than his brother-in-law, Guillaume; heroes have to be almost as big as the monstrous giants they sometimes fight, and this Superman strength (skill, too, is probably understood) is a quality of the greatest of the heroes. Renoart performs wonders with his *tinel*, the cudgel he prefers to the sharpest sword; this is a mark of his eccentricity, of his remaining, as he always does, somewhere outside the usual run of chivalry. He breaks a Saracen's

head in four places and scatters his brains in fifteen directions.
He knocks a man to pieces in a blow which also breaks his
horse in two. He kills poeple with his fists; if he hits them on the
back, he breaks the spine, if he hits them on the chest, the heart
bursts, if on the head, the eyes start out. When *R*enoart kills
one Saracen and his horse in a blow, Bertrand, who needs horse
and armour undamaged, complains that *R*enoart might kill
4000 in the same way. *R*enoart replies, 'You are talking nonsense', not at the idea that he may kill so many, but at the
suggestion that it would be feasible somehow to manage not to.
He points out that his cudgel is heavy and his arm strong, and
he just cannot give light blows, *Ne petit colp puis jo pas doner*.
Bertrand suggests that he might try giving a thrusting blow.
'You are right', says *R*enoart, 'I never thought of that', *Vus
dites verité. Mei fei, ne m'en ere pensé.*[9]

Modern taste shares this particular joke, if it appears in our
own idiom. 'The jovial way he would jump on the faces of his
opponents in the football field . . . won all hearts'; 'I shall kick
his spine up through that beastly bowler hat he wears. I shall
twist his head off at the roots.' This is P. G. Wodehouse, and,
as in the case of *R*enoart and the others, it is in the absurdity of
the violence that the joke lies.[10] On this particular point the
humour of two different periods happens to coincide, but they
do not overlap entirely. We also make a joke of what would be
acute mental suffering, if it were serious, as in W. S. Gilbert's
ditty, 'The criminal cried', or the line about beheading,
'Awaiting the sensation of a short sharp shock'; indeed, the
whole theme of 'The Mikado', we may forget because of its
familiarity, is exceedingly macabre. The chansons also extend
into subjects that do not have an equivalent to-day, just as
Gilbert takes up themes they lack.[11]

Guillaume in old age has lost his zest, but not his strength, his
skill, his spirit or his initiative. He makes his *moniage*, his
monastic profession, and tries to suffer indignity from robbers
as meekly as a monk should. But when the chief robber goes too
far (humiliating him by making him strip) he kills him with a
blow bare-handed, because he has promised his abbot not to

use weapons: he 'makes his two eyes fly out of his head'. Then to kill the rest of the robbers he tears the leg off his own horse, bowls them over, and finally prays God, with an unexpected tenderness, and unaffectedly, if disingenuously, to heal 'this wounded horse', a miracle which God indeed vouchsafes.[12] The poet has used the absurdity joke to laugh both at and with Guillaume's chivalry, and, in the grotesque episode of the horse's leg, perhaps at thaumaturgy, more probably at the joke of absurd violence itself. The violence which Guillaume, as well as *R*enoart, who also makes his monastic profession, employ against the monks is certainly beyond reason; the two *Moniage* poems, in most ways unlike each other, are alike in that Guillaume and *R*enoart severally disrupt monastic life; the monks resist, and soon plot against the heroes, who from time to time kill some of the monks with as much abandon as if they were Saracens.[13] This violence against the monks, as unrestrained by common sense as usual, was a joke that not only amused both poet and audience, but was the means of expressing the ambivalent attitude of both towards monks.

The violence joke is capable of considerable variation. Also in *Moniage Guillaume*, the protagonist breaks out of prison after seven years of insupportable privations which, if taken seriously, must be supposed totally debilitating, and runs through the city killing everyone in his way; the Saracens cry 'Guillaume has escaped; he is out of his senses and altogether enraged'. The escape is almost underplayed in contrast to the years of privation.[14]

The vein of exaggeration may be both serious and comic, and alternately, almost simultaneously, so. The defeat and death of Saracens is often comedy, but not entirely, and not frivolously. Although exaggeration may be used at any time and anywhere, a change of tone or a shift in the dominant sentiment may quite suddenly change the character of the poem. At the battle of the Archamp there is a much higher seriousness in poems or parts of a poem dealing with the death of Vivien and the defeat of the French than in those about the French recovery and the intervention of *R*enoart. There are comic episodes in the tragic parts and sad and serious episodes in the lighter ones. The *Chanson de Guillaume* is in two parts that the manuscript presents as a whole; but it is only with the arrival of *R*enoart on the scene, long after the passage from the one part to the other, that the story takes on the character of a rumbustious romp, with *R*enoart knocking Saracens down by the hundred, and the reversal of the defeat in a light-hearted triumph. This line of humour seems to lead on straight to Pantagruel's battle with the giants of Loup Garou.[15] Rychner treats the second part of the *Guillaume* as a distinct poem from the *Rainouart*, and they are separated by structure as well as by style and feeling; and even so he says: 'Les deux récits faisaient bien une sorte de tout'. The different uses made of violence (and other themes) in the *Chanson de Guillaume* in all their variety, only reflect the variation in attitudes of which the literature as a whole is capable. They run from Vivien at the extreme of chivalrous *démesure* to *R*enoart the amateur knight of the cudgel, who takes the huff because, when he has won the battle, he is not asked to dinner.[16] The joke is genuinely touching, and the tragedy is diluted by the extravagance.

Suffering

In the first part of the manuscript text, in the authentic *Chanson de Guillaume*, Guillaume is not pleased that *G*uibourg at home has not prevented the young brother of Vivien from riding out to the battle. His name is Gui. He says to Guillaume: 'Do you think God can forget, or that he can take care of great men and not do as much for little ones? There is no great man who was not born little.' The theme of an adolescent boy in danger or killed in battle touches off a moment of sympathy which is free of exaggeration.[17]

A number of stories of suffering, both his own and those he has inflicted, are attached to Vivien; most moving is his mother's lament when she has to give him up as a hostage (in his father's place. In this version his parents are living but his father is a prisoner of the Saracens). He has adventures as a hostage, but survives them successfully; his mother does not know this when she parts from him.

'Son Vivien! I do not send you, fine son, to take arms Nor helmet nor shield nor lance But to death, as I fear. The Saracens will take their revenge, Son Vivien, on your fine days of youth, Which were so sweet and seemly. I shall not see you again.'

She will keep a lock of his hair and his nail-cuttings next to her heart and look at them from time to time in her room.[18] This is not quite in the modern taste, but it is evidently sincere.

In another version Vivien's parents are dead and he is fostered by *G*uibourg; he leads a band of 10,000 young men like himself into Spain, where they soon make themselves felt: 'he lays waste the lands of the Turks and the Persians Kills the mothers and murders the children'. He 'was very noble and very chivalrous. From the time when he was dubbed knight, The young man had not a single day of rest From killing and maiming Saracens.' He wants to provoke *D*esramé, amir of Cordova, and he sends off a ship to him, manned by 700 pagans whose lips and noses have been cut off, 'there was not one who did not have his eyes gouged out, Or his hands and feet cut off' excepting four to take his message to the amir.[19] That this monstrous fancy should stimulate an audience is not a happy thought, but we must not let ourselves take it too seriously; we might find the poet laughing at us if he knew how we felt.

But Vivien himself is doomed to suffer and die in the defeat at the Archamp. As perpetrator or victim, he seems to attract horror stories. His death is a high-minded passage. When he is mortally wounded, his entrails hanging on the ground – 'there is no one who could have put up with it more' – fighting desperately but praying that he will never think of running away, but keep faith till he is dead; his last prayer is that he shall not give way a foot for fear. In the second part of the poem there is a new death scene in which Guillaume is with him and he makes an edifying death in the pattern that the church requires, a profession of faith, confession of all his sins, and communion, in spite of the absence of a priest (Guillaume

carries the Host).[20] This scene also stresses his wounds and
resistance to death. The earlier scene is the more absurd, but
it is also the more powerful. There is some comfort to the
listener in superhuman suffering and endurance.

A poet may put a lament similar to that of Vivien's mother
into the mouth of a Saracen woman by the side of her son's
body.

> His mother came running there when she saw her son
> lying bloody and dead, and weeping she cried aloud, 'fine
> son, Cadot, you are keeping too still! By Mahon, it is very
> wrong of you not to recognise me. Speak to me, why do
> you delay?' Then after she said, 'Misery! What am I say-
> ing? You are dead, I am sure of it.' Then she collapsed, her
> heart failed her and she let herself fall on the corpse to
> protect it.

This sort of occurrence was common enough, and no doubt a
singer had a passage or phrases ready to describe it, but that
does not make it insincere, nor detract from the way the poet
finds it normal to put it in the mouth of a Saracen mother.[21]

The devastation of war is generally described in a Christian
setting. One thinks of the trail of prisoners in *Aspremont*,
victims of horrible outrages, who call out 'Charlemagne, you
have so long forgotten us. What are you doing that you give us
no help?' There are accounts in *Destruction de Rome* and
Fierabras of the country round Rome laid waste; they have an
ecclesiastical slant, the incidents particularised being outrages
against priests, monks and nuns. But the devastation is general.
'When they had killed all that they could find, they set fire to
everything.' The French ride fast for Rome, but a good day
before they get there 'they see the country is everywhere
burning' and the city of Rome is too hot to enter.[22] There is a
description of war devastation in *Le Charroi de Nimes*, but the
emphasis again is on desecrated churches and torturing noble
women. When King Ysoré, in *Moniage Guillaume*, threatens
vengeance on France he says he will dishonour the Queen and
outrage the women and girls, and, when his men do invade
France, they do 'pull down the castles and towers, they burn

and capture and ravage . . . the poor people are much dismayed by it'.[23] The peasants are not wholly or always ignored. In *Aliscans*, Renoart listens to the grievance of a poor peasant whose cattle have been stolen (though, as he has cattle, is he not perhaps a rich peasant?); Renoart takes time off from the main course of battle to get his possessions back for him.[24]

The accounts of Christians ravaging Saracen country are less detailed, though we are left in no doubt that there is little to choose between the two sides as conceived by the songs. *Son pais gaste* is sometimes given as the reason for a Saracen King's invasion of France, and there are a number of references, more or less ashamed, to the raping of Saracen women.[25] Aquin's queen fears that she will be dishonoured bodily. It is natural that Christian troubles should get more attention; what is surprising is that there is as much as there is about what Saracens suffer. It was natural to particularise the sufferings of Christians sympathetically, and those of Saracens callously, but there is no pretence that the horrors of war were not evenly distributed between them, or that Christians and Saracens conducted war in any way differently. Gui de Bourgogne is exceptional when he proclaims, on pain of death, that no knight however highly placed, *tant soit de haute gent*, shall rob a Saracen of his gold or silver, his silks or hangings or clothing, or anything else, without authority.[26] The implication does not seem to be that the army and the leadership are inexperienced, although they are all young, but that discipline is good, and control of the booty in the hands of the leader; that these are better knights, and this a better way to behave. With many audiences this could hardly have been a welcome thought.

Scenes of individual suffering bravely endured have been perennially popular – in the Christian era, from the early lives of the martyrs to twentieth century thrillers. Our songs are not an exception. Threats of burning – considered a severe punishment, but not unheard of – were normal; Aymery is on the point of being burned when he is rescued. His son Guibert is in process of being crucified when Aymery rescues him.[27] These episodes are presented partly from the point of view of

Ermenjart, the wife and mother. There her courage is the theme, and so it is in the case of those who suffer physically. Fear in battle, on the other hand, evokes no interest or sympathy at all. Prowess includes the ability to suffer; it does not exclude the infliction of suffering, as in the case of the preux Saracen kings in *Aspremont*.[28]

The plight of prisoners is often mentioned and quite often described. They are often wounded – only wounds or enormous odds against them, or both, can explain how a paladin came to allow himself to be captured at all. Roland and his companions in *Fierabras* are wounded, but, as so often happens, their unshaken ability to endure, to fight, to play practical jokes, to make love, once again reminds us of the modern equivalent. One imaginary cruelty is when the Saracens make two Christian prisoners, weakened by starvation, fight each other as a spectator sport. It inevitably turns out that the precaution of weakening them lest they attack their captors is quite inadequate.[29] Prisoners are kept among toads and serpents so that they may be persuaded to change religion, or, if that fails, to be executed; they do not seem to be kept for ransom. Heroes kidnapped and sold to Saracens (it usually happens that way round) are treated as other prisoners, not as slaves.[30] *R*enoart, on the other hand, is enslaved as a child and bought by King Louis. A typical prisoner is Guillaume in old age, kidnapped from his hermitage by King *S*ynagon of Palermo and held for seven years: 'Little to drink and little to eat, a loaf of bread a day and plain water in a beaker . . . no one could recount his sufferings.'[31] In fact they seem to be recounted for their own sake; seven months would serve the purpose of the plot as well, except to show that after impossible privation Guillaume can come raging out and win his battle. In this, as so often, it is the love of the impossible that guides the poet.

BATTLES AND WARS

Battles, like whole poems, are often just a series of episodes. The scene tends to be particularised in the form of small skirmishes and, still more, individual combats, often one against one or one against many; there is no pretence at grand strategy or generalship. A battle may just go on till everyone on one side is dead; the retreat of the Saracens to the ships in *Chanson de Guillaume* is plausible in the midst of *R*enoart's implausibles. A commanding general is one who acts with outstanding valour and more than human strength. He is expensively armed and horsed. As hero, he sets the moral tone, and as count or marquis, he determines war and peace, but, as far as we can see or hear, he has companions, rather than feudatories, and many more knights than sergeants. In spite of references to feudal obligations, the spirit is the spirit of the old comitatus, on to which a good deal of individual eccentricity has been grafted.

The prowess of the Christian in battle is commonly measured by the numbers of the Saracens, though sometimes their own exaggeration is too much for the poets; when, at the battle of the Archamp, one man puts twenty thousand to flight, it is explained as a great miracle, *grand miracle que nostre sire fist*.[32] Sometimes the effect of large numbers is given by enumerating the enemy units; in *Roland*, the smallest enemy *eschele* is 50,000 men, and these groups are listed with exotic-sounding names which give a cumulative impression of great numbers.[33] The dangers seem greater and the battle harder.[34]

The actual battle is not described professionally. We must suppose that there were no technical howlers that would annoy professional soldiers in the audiences; jongleurs depended for much of their livelihood and all of their subject-matter on courts which were incidentally fighting units. The game of exaggeration will have favoured the poets here too; the audience will have expected to discount a great deal. At each blow the listener could visualise the technique for himself. The impossible feats of physical strength and endurance will have been the good-tempered envy of real soldiers, who no doubt could smile at exaggeration as well as anyone. This would apply even more to single combats than to general engagements.

War is the framework of all this literature and the normal

occupation of nearly all the characters, not excepting the clerics; it extends to monks and peasants. What in fact were all these wars about? The purely feudal wars do not concern us, but only those wars which are wholly or partly against the Saracens. We tend to think of these as 'Crusades', and even as some kind of 'holy war' from the 'pagan' side. There are, however, other aspects to take into account before considering this.

We have seen how frankly (in two senses) the motive of the young barons was to gain fiefs. They do so with the authority of their overlord, from whom they will hold what they conquer; Charlemagne grants Nîmes and Narbonne and Vauclerc in Saxony as if they were his to grant, when they are still in Saracen hands. Doon de Mayence refuses any alternative that is really in the emperor's gift. He wants to hold by a triple title, by conquest, by marriage, and as the emperor's man. At a lower level, Aymery in family conclave gives away the cities of Spain to his sons.[35] But it was also understood that the Saracens saw this process from the other side. At the Archamp, or Aliscans, *D*aneburs fights Guillaume because he is responsible for the death of a thousand pagans, and to avenge his brother; his friend *A*erofles fights to restore Orange to his brother *D*esramé and *O*rable-Guibourg to her husband *T*ibaut. In *Loquifer D*esramé fights to restore Orange and *O*rable to *T*ibaut, because Guillaume has 'by great wrong seized his land'. *C*orsout in *Barbastre* says that Guillaume 'has wickedly invaded our people'. In *Moniage Guillaume* the Saracen King *S*ynagon (the one who imprisoned Guillaume for seven years) has been 'killed on the field of battle and his land laid waste, his people killed and his city burned'; this arouses King *Y*soré 'who was of his kin' to avenge him. *O*tinel wants to avenge his uncle's death on Roland and *C*larel goes to war for revenge too; he hates Roland for killing his relative Samsoinie in battle, and is killed himself in the end by *O*tinel.[36] We can generalise so far as to say that many invasions are reprisals.

These songs do in their own fantastic way commemorate the Arab attacks on France and Italy in the eighth and ninth centuries of which the most spectacular was the sack of St

Peter's (but not of Rome-within-the-walls) in 846. The Arabs did not, as the Saracens of *Fierabras* do, loot the relics of the Passion; relics of the Passion were not at that time circulating in the West, and Muslims, unlike the Saracens, would not credit relics of an event they do not believe took place. The basic theme of *Couronnement*, of *Destruction*, of *Enfances Ogier* and the early part of *Fierabras* is an attack on Rome and its defence by the French. *Aspremont*, and in less degree *Couronnement*, recall the Arab settlements in southern Italy. But it is not the distant memory of old invasions that matters most. In most poems it is *France douce*, *France le delitable*, more than anywhere in the world, that excites the cupidity of a Saracen king looking for conquests. As concerns France as a northern kingdom, any memory must have been of Vikings, not Arabs, but Saracens here are deputising for Norsemen. When *G*arsile, rich king of Spain, and many countries East, offers Charlemagne a subordinate alliance, he proposes that Charles shall have Normandy and England, Roland shall have Russia, Oliver 'Esclavonie', but douce France is reserved for *F*lorient of Sulia: there is not a better man, *n'a plus preudome en tote paienie*.[37] The project of a conquest of France heightened the tension and gave the threat actuality as nothing else could. The idea of a take-over by *C*orsolt or *D*esramé communicated a shiver of pleasurable fear.

HATRED OF SARACENS

Are we just watching some kind of interminable football match? Or is there supposed to be real hatred on either side? The language of hatred and contempt which recurs constantly and often purposelessly, should be treated as simply conventional. Terms of this kind such as *pute gent*, *fils à putain*, *pautonnier*, *losengier*, *felon* (cas régime) and *fel*, *gloton* and *glot* are as vaguely pejorative as *baron* and *ber* are laudatory. They occur ritually, and even as forms of address. The pejorative terms cannot be taken to prove a deeply felt hostility unless that is the sense of the whole passage in which they occur, and in that case they will be associated with some other insult which is unambiguous. As a very rough rule, earlier poems treat Saracens in a more hostile way than later ones do, but even in *Roland* the Christian Ganelon is the only villain, and the Saracens do not behave badly; they are presented with respect and sometimes sympathy – their gods are not, but that is another problem. The famous line, *Paien unt tort e chrestiens unt dreit*, is commonly remembered as particularly aggressive, but in the context it is meant to reassure and comfort the Christians.[38] It does not mean more than 'our cause is just' in modern wars. Saracens rarely do anything disgraceful (anything, that is, that heroes do not do); if we remember that disloyalty is the only really disgraceful thing that ever happens in songs of action or in adventure stories, and that deserting other Saracens to become Christian is by special exemption not disloyal, we must recognise that it is all but impossible for them to appear in a thoroughly contemptible situation, and, though they are often callously derided in misfortune, they are rarely held up to execration, except in the mass, as *la pute gent*.

As an example of general vituperation, we may look at Vivien's exhortation to the barons at the battle of the Archamp; it verges on hatred. 'You've seen the *feluns Arabiz* who have killed your sons and brothers and nephews and intimate friends. They are not even asking for a peace or a truce. Let's avenge our dead.' But, on second thoughts, is this not, for a desperate battlefield, really rather mild ? It might do in a variety of war-time situations; it is another set-piece. In just this same language Gui de Warewic exhorts the Greeks to resist a Saracen advance. The passage is a little less impressive than in Vivien's case, but it serves.[39] In another case, Gui curses the *soudan* in his palace, where he is sitting with his kings; he ill-wishes him with the curse of the Creator and Saviour on unbelievers. This does sound like hate. Yet the poem as a whole is not consistently hostile to Saracens, and Gui takes service with the Saracen, King *T*riamor of Alexandria, against the sultan. The terms of Gui's curse may seem stronger to a modern taste than they did to the poet; they are a formal declaration, meant to spotlight the sultan as the bogeyman of this part of the story.

Most episodes that suggest hatred have either this formal quality or, at the other extreme, a personal motive. In the episode in the *Chanson de Guillaume* where King *D*esramé is badly wounded, and worrying about his horse (which Guillaume is taking), Guillaume's nephew Gui comes and abruptly kills the wounded Saracen. Guillaume reproves him. Gui replies that *D*esramé still had eyes to see with, and testicles to engender with. Guillaume concedes that it was right to kill the king; that Gui has a man's head on a boy's shoulders. This seems an act of blind hate if ever there was one; and yet the implications are not clear. Killing was not Guillaume's first thought; and the poet may be said to have two opinions. But there is also a personal side to this. Gui had his brother Vivien to avenge, the same motive as some of the Saracens have for fighting. Here is another example, from the *Moniage Guillaume*. After his seven years in prison, Guillaume says to his captor, '*S*ynagon, this is it. You made it very unpleasant in your prison: if I live long enough I will pay you back, and, as long as I live, you will not have a day's peace'. This is more anger than hate. 'The King will not take ransom for your person; he will have you roasted on coals, he will skin you like a dog.'[40] This is personal, and, taking the technique of exaggeration into account, no more than a mild joke.

The *Couronnement de Louis* contains a number of unusual dialogues, among them a strange tirade against God by King *C*orsolt, conqueror of Rome, who tells the pope that God has annoyed him more than anyone on earth; he killed his father with a thunderbolt, then ascended into heaven and will not come back. So *C*orsolt is avenging himself on Christians, and on clerics in particular.[41] This bears no relation to anything any Muslim could ever feasibly be thought to have said, nor is it likely that this poet believed a Muslim might think it. The comedian in him is here so much to the fore that it is not easy to be sure what he means, but this might be a joke about religion, or an actual bucolic blasphemy observed. It looks as though the poet thought that Saracens would be likely to feel a special animosity against clerics, but most of the passage relates to Christians and is put into *C*orsolt's mouth for convenience.

All the hatred seems to be conventionalised, formalised, almost ritualised, except where there is an urgent and natural reason for personal anger.

CRUSADE – THE HOLY WAR

The use of the word *martirie* and the idea of martyrdom are important. Theologically, martyrdom requires a free choice between death and apostasy. This requirement has come to define a martyr in English and other European languages as one who suffers for a cause, though it is also used loosely ('a martyr to lumbago'). In the strict sense, Crusading was not martyrdom; indulgences were given to Crusaders, and confession was a condition. True martyrdom, which wipes out all sin, would make these things otiose. So, too, in the poems; Turpin is an aggressive, fighting archbishop, but he does not think that death in battle against Saracens is martyrdom in the theological sense. The barons have to confess their sins, even if the penance he gives them in *Roland* is to lay their blows on hard in the battle (this of course is a joke). Vivien, when dying, confesses his sins, and so does Roland, who does not know that angels wait to carry his soul to Paradise.[42] However, Vivien does say, when he is encouraging the barons in their desperate straits to go on fighting, that St Stephen and the other martyrs were no better than those who have died here at the battle now raging.[43] This is surely bravado, a defiant claim that is meant to be understood in the certain knowledge that death in battle, even against 'the enemies of God' is not martyrdom in fact. The word *martyrdom* is more often used in the loose sense, without the meaning that Vivien has to define so precisely, by mentioning the protomartyr. It is used in Roland and elsewhere for the Saracens themselves: *cist paien vont grant martirie querant*.[44] *Martirie* came to mean the massacre of anyone anywhere, or just a beating up.

'Martyrdom' may have been used in a wide sense, but laymen were not insensitive to the new doctrine of indulgences, so closely linked to Crusade. It seems to be satirised in another of the remarkable dialogues in the *Couronnement*, in Guillaume's interview with the Pope, who offers him, for fighting, meat every day, as many women as he wants, and to be absolved (*quites*) of his sins all his life (treason excepted) as well as a resting place in Paradise. 'God help me!' says Guillaume, 'no cleric has ever been so big-hearted.'[45] If jokes are sometimes hard to assess across the centuries, this one is clear enough. The doctrine of indulgences might never have developed, if death in Crusade had been equivalent to martyrdom. The poems recognise this. How much Crusading is there in them, and how shall we understand any Crusading that we can identify there?

Considered in relation to Crusade, the poems fall into four classes. There are those which are set in Spain (including what we now call southern France) in the time of Charlemagne, or his son, or in another remote time. There are those that consist of adventures in the East, set in a remote period or otherwise. There is the second Crusade cycle, which is too fantastic to be considered close to actual events. There is the first Crusade cycle, which has many of the characteristics of the chansons de geste, but is recognisably close even in detail to the events. We have to look with special interest at this last class when we discuss the idea of Crusade in the entire genre.

The *Chanson d'Antioche* and the *Conquête de Jérusalem* are unlike the other poems, not only in their historical framework, but also in having less aristocratic emphasis. '*Quant à "la gent menue"'*, says Suzanne Duparc-Quioc, latest editor of *Antioche*, '*peu de poèmes épiques s'en occupent autant*'. Relatively to the whole Crusade, these poems give a much larger part than do most sources to Peter the Hermit, and the role played by soldiers who are not knights is considerable. They recognise a proletarian side to the Crusade in the vagabond *tafurs*, with their 'king', who has his own *barné*. This baronage rape the Saracen women and ward off starvation by cannibalism; victory will bring them regeneration, that is, they will have gold and silver, and never in their lives will they be poor again.[46]

The poems do not approve, but seem to understand them. Should we read their behaviour as a satire on the lords whose behaviour is only more discreet and more proper? The *tafurs* recognise Peter the Hermit as their special friend, and he himself plays an ambiguous part. He assents to Saracen worship of gods, out of prudence, and encourages cannibalism, out of realism; his religion is visionary, charismatic and uncontrolled, almost chiliastic. We are far here from the high clerical statesmanship of Pope Urban or the Legate, but would the audiences have failed to see that the *gent menue*, who are also *gent orible* in their hunger for life, women and wealth, are not so far from the ambitions of the great lords of the Crusade, or of the other *chansons de geste*?

The later adapter of *Antioche*, Graindor of Douai, is no *tafur*, but he puts a speech of barbaric Christian nationalism into the mouth of Jesus on the cross. It derives from a literary tradition of 'Jesus' revenge' and is a good deal less than evangelical. There is no 'Father forgive them' when Jesus tells the good thief and the bad that a new people will come from overseas to take such vengeance for his death that there will be no more pagans in the East and that the Franks will have taken over the whole country. They will be coming to avenge him, and kill the faithless pagans who have always rejected his commandments. The first instalment of vengeance will come with Titus, Vespasian and their company, who will well believe in 'God the son of St Mary'. The point here is not the terrible confusion of Roman emperors, Jews, pagans and Christians, but the notion of conquest and vengeance. 'Then will holy Christendom be exalted, my land conquered, my country freed.'[47] Obviously there is no lack of Crusading motivation here, and yet there are special points. The apocryphal scene on the cross and its folkloric forecast of the Crusade is not orthodox, but it would not be difficult to reconcile it with the usual grounds that justify Crusade as a recovery of Christian territory. It is not a bad *reductio ad absurdum* of what Crusade was supposed to be about. It is nationalist and popular and, it is no anachronism to add, it is an anticipation of colonialism.

Yet it is difficult to say how the first Crusade cycle songs differ from the rest of the corpus, except in being so much more closely tied to the events of the First Crusade and the places in Syria and Palestine where they occurred, than any other songs are to either time or place. This is a very important difference, which affects more than the mere setting. In other ways, however, we are struck by the similarities. The Crusade poems constantly remind us of the other songs in their themes and their forms of expression, often even in their phrases. The main theme of the recovery of Christian territory, in a popular sense that parallels the canonical theory of *terra sancta*, is shared by many of the poems about Spain. Jerusalem is the venue for some part of stories that belong to neither Crusade cycle – *Voyage de Charlemagne*, *Quatre Fils d'Aymon*, *l'Escoufle*, for example – but it has no historical actuality in them, and is as misty as any of the stories set in countries unknown to the poets or deliberately confused by them. In all the songs in which Christians conquer territory, whether in the East or in the West, they impose Christian rule by force, and this is the essential feature of Crusade proper, and is common to poems set in the framework of either Crusade or Spanish Reconquest. In the poems set in Spain, immediately Christian rule is imposed, so is Christianity, and Saracens must choose whether to be baptised or killed. This is part of the nebulous unreality of all the poems; Christianity was imposed everywhere in the West, but not so abruptly. Even the first Crusade cycle manages to suggest that Saracens will not survive, although that was not true, of course, even under Christian rule, in the East; the fictional convention is preserved within the broad outline of actual events, even in detailed episodes.

So far as the fiction of forced conversion goes, the poems are poems of Crusade. A Crusading sentiment is rare, and when it occurs it may even surprise us. There is a case in *Aliscans*, where a Saracen king asks Guillaume, gently and politely:

Why have you wrongly disinherited me and taken my land against my will? And in your walled palace you have beaten up my two brothers whom I loved so much, so that

> their blood ran in the gutters. On your head I will avenge
> myself.

This looks like another case of aggression in answer to
aggression, and Guillaume changes ground in his reply: 'You
are talking childishly. Once a man does not love Christianity
and hates God and despises charity, he has no right to live.'
This is a hard saying and a cold reason, with its touch of
theology ('despises charity') and canon law. It looks very
much as though it is brought in as the last refuge of an honest
knight. There is a curiously similar passage in *Chanson de
Guillaume* at the appropriate point, but it is in reverse. Guillaume asks the Saracen *A*lderufe why he wants to fight him
and he replies that Mahon rules the earth and decides who shall
be allowed to live on it; that there should be no Christian and
no baptism.[48] It is imaginative on the part of the poet to put
into the Saracen's mouth what (*mutatis mutandis*) he would
expect in the Christian's. The presupposition is that neither side
can allow the religion of the other to exist, and this is the
assumption throughout the whole body of songs and stories.

This, we must say, is holy war, and conceived by the authors
as being much the same on either side. There are few signs of
the canons that affected Crusading, and naturally there are
none of the rules of *jihād*. Since the religion of Mahon is not
Islam, we should not expect to see anything authentic of *jihād*.
As for the church canons, many of them were promulgated
after most of the poems had taken shape, but we should not
expect them to interest the poets in any case. The essential of
Crusade is there, all the same; but the question for us must be,
how important is it ? What is the use made of the holy war in
the body of the poems ?

For the most part, they reflect much more the attitudes of
the Carolingian age in which so many of them are set than the
new aggressive spirit of Crusade.[49] *Roland*, *Guillaume*, *Aliscans*, *Aspremont*, are all defensive: the war is to protect the
land and the people. The aggressive poems about the capture
of new fiefs do not seek profit where they Crusade; they
Crusade where they seek profit. The main motive of those who

travel East is a career of adventure which may take in a bit of Crusading on the side.[50] Even Charlemagne makes '*un voyage amusant et non religieux*' there.[51] Crusade is hardly at all a primary or original motive for fighting. The few simple rules (the font or the block for the vanquished, no marriage or copulation before baptism) form a background, constants in any plot but never its inspiration.[52]

The idea of Crusade relates also to the idea of the national epic. In English, as in French, 'national epic' is a special sense of 'epic' (OED), and the intention of the whole body of these poems is sometimes measured by *Roland*, both because it is a fine poem and because it has a simple theme. '*La France*', said Léon Gautier, '*a possédé, au moyen âge, une épopée nationale et chrétienne, et la chanson de Roland est notre Iliade.*' S.J.Borg, latest editor of *Aye d'Avignon*, says of that poem: '*notre chanson a vraiment peu d'épique, puisqu'il lui manque le concept capital d'un monarque luttant à la tête d'une France chrétienne contre l'Islam.*' This puts a point of view very clearly, but it is perhaps better not to involve French or Christian loyalties in the assessment of a long series of poems which range over every degree of solemnity and frivolity. Certainly, Frenchmen and Christians have more to be proud of in such a literature than resistance to Islam. It is possible to think of *Roland* as epic because it shows a hopeless and foredoomed battle against uneven odds, and not because Charlemagne defends Christendom. Rychner does not believe that the third section of the poem, the war with *B*aligant, belongs to the original concept of the poem, which it disrupts; I would add that it lessens the epic character. '*Il fallait, a-t-on dit, que Charlemagne, chef de la chrétienté, se mesurât avec Baligant, chef de la payennie, et le vainquit.*' This is a political idea, not an epic one. Yet, even so, it has little to do with Islam, and Rychner advisedly uses the word 'payennie', which avoids any semblance of endorsing a modern concept of the war against Islam. The poem would not be any poorer, or any different, if *M*arsile and *B*aligant ruled over Saxons, or Vikings, or Hungarians, or any other enemy. An enemy is required, to provide the occasion for heroic disaster, but the Saracen king and the amir of Babylon are just bogeys, as it might be Bonaparte or Pitt, a story-teller's convenience. In fact, they are entirely imaginary, and their character as Saracens is a work of imagination too, not an interpretation of Islam.[53]

The religion of the poems is certainly sincere, but it is not the primary motive for fighting; it is important, but in a supporting role. It reassures the combatants. The line, *paien unt tort*, is for comfort; it fortifies morale when it justifies the fighting that is already happening, a letter of guarantee from a spiritual bank under the terms of a victory contract with God. Guillaume says that his God has looked after him well; 'he who believes in him well will never be beaten'. Whatever their motives for fighting, Christians were fighting against non-Christians and therefore God was fighting for them. Does this amount to Crusading? No, in so far as the religious difference between the two sides only gives a moral justification to an existing quarrel. Yes, as reflecting the profit motivation of most Crusading in practice; and yes, in so far as it satisfies the legal forms, and technically it might easily constitute a Crusade. If a Crusade is for the recovery of the Holy Land, very few of the songs qualify, and only the first Crusade cycle does so seriously; but Crusade that was extended to Spain, and to the Albigensian war, and to war against the Emperor, could certainly extend to fictional wars against fictional Saracens. But by then the idea of Crusade was almost meaningless.

In the tenth and eleventh centuries the bishops attempted to limit the petty wars of the courts by means of a Truce of God which would restrict the days and seasons of war, and the people whom it was legitimate to attack (exempting peasants, clergy and even merchants) and some churchmen certainly thought of Crusade as more likely to absorb the energies of soldiers for a laudable purpose. Many of the chansons, especially those that portray land-hungry and adventurous young men, are set in just the small court atmosphere so attached to war as a pastime. The official exhortation to Crusade not only justified the barons in making war, but justified the poets in praising war as a way of life. We can say that in this way Crusade legitimised the moral system of war which had been not only a very rough but, in a certain class, very popular kind of sport. The church was also reluctant to approve the tournament, but it welcomed war against Muslims, and the reconquest of al-Andalus became a dangerous but enjoyable tournament, a sport in which the professionals might expect to be very highly rewarded. This more than anything shaped the attitudes of the chansons de geste, and later romances on related themes, to the questions of holy war.

THE USE OF VIOLENCE

What poetic purpose did so much violence serve? It is one answer that violence justifies itself from the story-teller's point of view; people enjoy hearing about it. Another answer is that it allows great scope for humour of the kind characteristic of these poems, even *Roland*, and for humour and tragedy to be almost simultaneous. The case of *F*ierabras typifies the problems imposed by scenes of violence, and the ease with which they may be disposed of. *F*ierabras, who boasts of the outrages and atrocities he has perpetrated, becomes almost instantly the noble and honourable opponent in single combat; his baptism is not sudden, but as soon as it has happened he becomes quite an ordinary preux chevalier. A theologian might explain this by saying: 'a man, however wicked, when you know him better, you may convert; once baptised, he should become a changed man; whatever he has done in his unregenerate days has been washed away in the waters of baptism, and what God has forgiven, we must not remember.' A humanist's explanation might be: 'the bogey figure, when you know him better, turns out to have many good qualities, and when you treat him properly and know him very well, you realise how good a man he always was.' The poet may have had something of both these interpretations in mind, but it is likely that he chose each next step in the story because he thought it would hold the attention of the audience. *F*ierabras fades out of the story when there is nothing left for him to do, when, in short, he is no longer violent. Violence against Christian clerics and people is not remembered against him, but, without it, he loses interest. He is no longer execrated for wickedness, because any hatred of how he carried on was unreal and mutable; that is not what the story is about.

The stories just need an enemy, but this produces excitement, not heart-felt hatred of a villain. No good story needs explaining or justifying. There is often a comic element close to high tragedy and a serious aspect to the most rumbustious joke. The compulsion on the story-teller is the story itself, and many stories are light-hearted; those that are not rely on tone and atmosphere, not realistic description. Hatred and anger are either highly personal or purely formal; Crusading is rarely the key-note. There is no trace of the polemic theory that there is something inherently violent about Saracen religion. Ferocity and toughness are admired, and most Christians would be very sorry to think that Saracens were more violent than they. In these poems, violence is fun.

II

THE GODS

WHY THE GODS? INTRODUCTORY

The requirements of a good story gave the poets the very same themes that the theologians chose for their polemic, and treated so differently. In our poems the Christians, far from condemning the morals of the Saracens, boast of outdoing them in violence, and of seducing their wives and daughters. This may more or less realistically reflect the ways of Christian knights, but was it not also a dangerous intellectual betrayal of the Christian argument against Islam? Was this a tendency which might almost have come to be seen as an antinomian heresy, or at least a culpable indifferentism? What saved the poems from anything of the sort was their absurd, and notoriously absurd, picture of Saracen religion. The evidence which we shall now consider is not quite like that in the first half of this book.

To attribute polytheism of the crudest kind to a religion which cannot tolerate any association of a creature with God (*shirk*)[1] has usually been thought of as one of the greatest howlers of history. Yet we have no right to take this for granted, or at least, to take for granted that it was done out of simple ignorance; and, if we do, we may make the more subtle howler of underestimating our ancestors: once more, 'the past is a foreign country'. We must consider the possibility that the multiplicity of Saracen gods is a deliberate fiction, and intended, not to deceive, but to amuse. We are alerted, not only by a degree of ignorance hard to credit, but by the total shift in attitude to the Saracens as soon as we come to the matter of religion. A poetic vision that makes Saracen society as like as possible to that of the Christians (apart from a little exotic

121

colouring) nevertheless differentiates Saracen religion as
sharply from the Christian as the authors think it can be. This
is the only way in which the two societies are seriously
differentiated in the poems; and it looks as though the poets
are not thinking of a suppositious Islamic model of religion at
all, but only of getting as far away as they can from the Christian one. The problem of how to avoid treating seriously a
matter considered very serious by the spokesmen of the
Church was solved by this 'ignorance' which, if it was deliberate, we should better call indifference to facts.

The notion of a multiplicity of gods is an idea almost as much
outside Christian experience as it is absurd in relation to Islam.
Attempts have been made, some very ingenious, to explain the
names of the supposed gods of the Saracens (such as Tervagant,
Apollin, Cahu),[2] while ignoring the need to explain the polytheist allegation at all. If the polytheist system was deliberately
invented by the poets, the etymologies might provide clues as
to how it was first done, or even when, but hardly to why it was,
or how it became fixed in its final form. Any explanation of the
absurdity is in the nature of a guess, but provisional assent to a
plausible explanation is better than continued acceptance of an
improbable one, and the presumption of the poets' ignorance
is arguably more improbable than any. This second part of the
book tries to consider again which explanation is the least
improbable. It is best perhaps to start with an idea of the value
of the polytheist convention to the story-teller.

What did the poets need in the way of a religion for their
Saracens? Everything suggests that their first priority was to
arouse and hold the interest of their listeners. The excitement
of the plots does not come only from danger to individuals in
battles with Saracens. Sometimes there is a threat of an invasion
which would raise Mahon to the altar in the great church of
St Denis in *douce France*.[3] The heroes' special dangers are
increased when they have to choose between death and a
change of sides which would be ratified by accepting the false
gods. Apart from the family of Ganelon, the gods are the
principal villains. They are not very horrible villains, and what

in themselves they add to the tension is almost negligible. Their triumph would, however, mean the destruction of Christianity, and this threat seems to be taken seriously, although the gods themselves remain almost figures of fun. If the Saracens won, their gods would win, and this spice of danger was important to most of the stories.

The false gods added this agreeable excitement to the poems, but they also took an undesirable kind of tension out of them. Any story of feudal war disturbed the conscience with questions of right and wrong – problems of loyalty and even of Christians killing each other – from which war against Saracens gave some relief, although it did not solve them. Behind these problems lay the one theological question that interested both poets and theologians, the problem of Providence. In a way, the poets had a fool-proof solution to it, because they themselves could play Providence and decide who should win; but a hero had to be in the right as well as lucky, or in the right in order to be lucky. It was essential to their idea of any religion that God or god should be vindicated by the ultimate victory of his people, and no poetic text about a defeat was left as it was, without a victory to follow that put disaster right.[4]

Unfailing victory over a wrong religion was an escape from a troubled conscience, but the religion had to be obviously and immediately seen to be wrong. If Christians and Saracens could not share God as they shared chivalry and sex and violence and games of backgammon, neither should they be divided by some abstruse theological concept. The Saracen opposition to the true God must not impede the story, and preferably should add to the amusement. To such a purpose the 'Tervagant convention' was very favourable, and all the more for having nothing whatever to do with Islam as it was and is. Why would not some simplified version of what the academics then thought to be the truth have done as well? One reason may be that there was nothing exotic about Islamic belief or practice to catch the imagination; its ceremonies and its doctrine (jurisprudence apart) were very much simpler and less splendid than those already familiar to Christians. But

more than this: not only would the truth about Islam have been
disappointing, but the polytheist convention saved the even
more tedious discussion of what might or might not be the truth.

We have only to consider the scholastic approach to the
existence of Islam to see how boring it would be in a song of
action, and how inappropriate. It can be stated in a summary of
the opening chapter of the *quadruplex reprobatio*, which puts
concisely what other scholastics put more diffusely but within
the same framework as the *reprobatio*. The *quadruplex reprobatio* is a thirteenth-century Spanish scholastic treatise conceived as a 'fourfold disproof' of the Prophet's Mission, almost
certainly Dominican in origin and commonly attributed to
Ramòn Martì. The writer begins by saying that he will refute
Muslim claims by applying to their revelation the test in
Matthew 7.20, 'by their fruits you shall know them'. There are,
he says, four fruits or signs which are absent; their contraries
are present. The prophecy must be veracious; God is pure
truth, it is sent by God and can include only what God wants
said; if anything in it is untrue, it is no prophecy. This seems to
labour the point, but it is normal scholastic method. So far
reason; the same thing can be shown from authority, adducing
Deuteronomy 18.21-2. The prophecy must be revealed in good
and moral, not evil and vicious circumstances, because God
is infinitely remote from uncleanness; the authority cited is
Psalm 100, *ambulans in via immaculata*.[5] Thirdly, prophecy
must be supported by miracles, and here it is ibn Rushd (as
'Abenrostus', not 'Averroes') who is cited. Finally, the prophet
must come with such a 'law' (or moral code) as is holy and
good, leading the peoples to the worship of the one God, and
men to holiness of life, harmony and peace, in accordance with
Psalm 18.8, 'the law of the Lord is unspotted'.[6] Here is a parade
of arguments and authorities to prove what no one (and
certainly no Muslim) would dispute, that a revelation must be
true, good and moral, and lead to worship of the one God, but
only on Christian assumptions would this be relevant to the
'disproof'. We recall Aquinas: 'It is clear that it is useless to
quote authorities against people who do not accept them'.[7] Yet

the *reprobatio* does tidily sum up the whole scholastic approach in point of method and the whole Christian polemic approach in point of matter. It is not an atmosphere suited to poetic fiction.

Although in the last resort their arguments rested on purely Christian assumptions, the serious theologians wanted authentic facts about Islam, because they always dreamed of controversy with actual Muslims who would accept their data, but their material was rarely irreproachable and shared some of the careless mixture of sensationalism and distortion that marks most chroniclers, and even encyclopaedists like Vincent of Beauvais and bellelettrists like Gerald of Wales.[8] The source of 'authentic facts distorted', which had the widest influence, was the pseudonymous al-Kindi.[9] The author of the *reprobatio* had access to good sources such as al-Bukhārī and Muslim ibn al-Hajjāj and the *sīra Rasūl Allāh* of ibn Ishāq which he used to show the incompatibility of Islam with true religion as he conceived it.[10] St Peter Pascual, in his use of the *sīra*, tended to invert fiction and fact, the corrupt information and the sound, by taking the facts that the Christians traditionally distorted for the distortions, and the distortions for the facts.[11] Ricoldo da Monte Croce subsumed his critique under the headings, 'loose', 'disordered', 'obscure', 'quite untrue', 'contrary to reason', and 'violent' – headings which aptly describe much of what he himself had to say.[12] Theological apologetics refuted Islam by standards acceptable as absolute only within the Christian system, and so all that it demonstrated effectively was an incompatibility, or at least a difference, between the two religions.

The methods and aims of such writers have very little in common with the methods and aims of our poets, who could hardly proceed by scholastic analysis without radically changing the character of their fictions and losing the attention of any audience but one of theological students. The price of their freedom from such restrictions was their indifference to facts. They were much less hostile to the Saracens, except in a purely physical sense, than the theologians, who, however, were in no doubt that Muslims are monotheist. Some of them want to prove that the Islamic apprehension of one God is at fault,[13] but they do not fall into the gross error of imputing polytheism. Occasionally they stress that Muslims believe in one God, and possibly this is a way of taking notice of the poets' convention.[14]

From the serious-minded writer we have to distinguish the run of chroniclers and gossip-writers who made use of whatever material, good and bad, that came their way; and with these we should include three poems, ambitious in concept but not influential on the opinion of the day, the malicious *de Machomete* of Embrico of Mainz and the more genial *Otia de Machomete* of Walter of Compiègne with its extended paraphrase in French by Alexandre du Pont.[15] This second class overlaps with the first, not only when an occasional serious or even accurate passage is included, but in the pattern imposed on the legendary matter they contain, a pattern that follows the same themes as the polemic: a contrived revelation, sexual indulgence and a religion of the sword. Our epic genre is a third and quite separate class from the other two. The three classes were first effectively distinguished by Y. and Ch. Pellat as *une tendance apologétique et polémique, que nous qualifierons cependant de 'scientifique'*; then *une deuxième tendance, encore polémique, mais de caractère essentiellement littéraire*, and finally *une troisième tendance toujours apologétique, polémique et littéraire, se réalise dans le genre épique*. They speak here of *une ignorance générale et totale de l'Islam en tant que religion et même, à quelques exceptions près, des fables qui concourent à la formation de l'image littéraire . . .*[16] What they call the *panthéon, de dimensions variables* is of course characteristic; I only want to leave open the question whether ignorance is involuntary or deliberate.

The overlap between the third class and the other two is minimal, except that a lack of scientific intention is common to the second and third. It is as though the poets, in adopting their pantheon, gave up the claim to insult Islam on any other grounds. They do not accuse the Saracen religion of inculcating any moral turpitude. The adoption of the false gods, just because they are totally unrelated to Islam, is not easily compatible with any serious attack on Islamic theology as it is, or even as it may be represented in a distorted form. The first two classes do distort facts, but the third by its polytheist fancy has precluded the possibility of doing so. There is an exception to which the Pellats refer.

A few of the songs contain a theme which stands out as belonging to the class 2 convention and is difficult to reconcile with the pantheon. In several poems, of which the earliest is *Le Couronnement de Louis*, some Christian says that 'Mahon' is not a god but a false prophet. In *Couronnement*, but not in all cases, there is a brief passage of abusive controversy; in some cases a passing reference to the well-known story is all. In *Couronnement, Il fu prophete Jhesu omnipotent* (in other versions, *Dieu omnipotent*); in *Aiol*, 'the Lord God first sent Mahon on earth to preach, to exalt his law' but 'he perverted the command of God'. *L'Entrée d'Espagne*, a late and long poem, fertile with surprises, clerical, intellectual, takes this further; the Prophet is shown as a former Christian leader (a form of the myth of 'Muhammad cardinal') whose ambition to become pope is frustrated and who then turns against 'holy baptism and God's law'.[17]

It is obvious that these interpolations – logical interpolations, they need not actually be the results of someone's touching up – belong to quite a different convention and attitude towards Islam. False gods might have false prophets, and pagan systems do include prophets, but the libel here is a false claim to speak for the true God. Yet in the poems where this anomaly occurs, the poet ignores the incompatibility. He does not allow it to detract from the polytheist convention, which he employs in the usual way. It is interesting to note that the same Saracen in the same chapter of *Turpin* carelessly refers to the Prophet both as *nuncius Dei* and as *Deus omnipetens* and that *l'Entrée d'Espagne* also refers several times to *Alakibir*, which can only be a form of *Allāhu akbar*,[18] but this too is not allowed to modify the convention in the poem.

This theme culminates in a crude and tasteless story about the body of the prophet which appealed to the poets and has attracted some attention from critics. It is an unpleasant idea that circulated widely in one form or another outside the chansons de geste and in the 'gossip' convention. It is renewed in some accounts that spread from the Levant during the period of Latin rule there, but it seems always to have been part of the Western tradition, together with other legends. In the ninth century in a closely connected form it was already considered old, and such stories have circulated among minorities under Islamic rule in both East and West.[19]

There are two reasons why this particular story may have attracted the poets who made use of it. One is that perhaps anything that shows the god to be false will do, however incongruously it does so. It is curious to find the poet who has imputed a gratuitous polytheism to the Saracens putting into the mouth of a Christian character a 'correction' to the effect that the false god is 'really' a false prophet. But not much is made of it. The songs would be sadly depleted for hearers who were given to understand that the Saracens no longer believed in their gods. A more important reason may be that it was the very unpleasantness of the story that they wanted. The point of the story is all they need to cite (*Doon de Mayence*, *Gaufrey* and *Floovant* are instances where everything else is left out).[20] That this is its chief attraction is indicated by its congruity with the fate of idols thrown in a ditch or broken up,[21] and by the fact that other common libels which are equally absurd (false revelation by a dove or animal)[22] but much less '*put*', less stinking, are never included. Many of the songs have their subtleties, but none forgo crude effects that any audience can enjoy.

These passages are the only significant intrusion of 'reality' in the usual distorted form into the total fantasy of polytheism. It strengthens the case for a presumption that poets knew of the polemic pattern and chose not to use it. In these few cases poets have simply not resisted the temptation to make use of a little ready-made scurrility. But there is very little intrusion from

outside, because the poets and singers lived in a different world
from the churchmen. As they had a system of morals which was
certainly not that which the Church Councils hoped to impose,
though it was closer to life as it was lived, so their attitude to
Saracen religion was not at all the official one. It is easy to
imagine how a theologically minded cleric might have written
a chanson de geste. The heroes would have had the virtues of
the ideal Crusader, of the *militia Christi* of St Bernard,[23] like
another and more blood-thirsty Galahad; and the Saracens
would have lived the sordid and disreputable life supposedly
inculcated by their religious jurisprudence. We need not regret
that no poem has survived that would parallel, for the Matter
of France, the Cistercian *Queste del Saint Graal* for the Matter
of Britain.[24]

Comparable to this slight infection of class 3 from class 2,
there is a little overspill of the idolatrous convention into
chronicles, but not specifically of the pantheon. There are
occasional references to idols as though they had actually been
seen, and the phrase *imago Mahumeti* occurs from time to time.
In an account which derives from the Latin states in the East, we
hear that Baghdad, 'where Mahumetus is, and (the) Caliphus',
is for Muslims what Rome is for Christians, and there is the
mahumeria there 'where Mahumetus the god of the Agarenes
is'.[25] To say that Muhammad is the god of the Agarenes does
not necessarily imply more than that the writer mistakenly
supposed him to be for Muslims what Christ was for Christians;
and to say 'ubi est . . .' does not necessarily mean more than that
the writer thought that the body or relics are there. What is
crucial is that a bench of gods, and particularly the characteristic Tervagant, do not come into the picture. The system of the
chansons de geste as a whole does not appear anywhere else,
but that some people acquired the impression that Saracens and
other non-Christians were idolatrous is likely.

We have to accept the nearly complete isolation of our poems
from all other medieval literature concerning Saracens, both in
its polytheist convention and in the total absence from it of any
serious polemic. As it was necessary to impute a false religion

to Saracens, and it could not be done in terms of the best scholarship of the day, what alternative remained? It might have been feasible to portray a religion with an anti-God or super-Satan. It would have been simpler, and would have fitted rather well the 'mirror image' Saracen world. It would have made the enemy more detestable. But there is a good deal of evidence that no one wanted them to be particularly detestable. This would have introduced all the venom of a genuine *odium theologicum*; and with it a degree and depth of hostility that apparently nobody wanted, and that could not have been varied at will, as the gods could, from a dreadful menace to an exploded hoax. The rather jolly approach to the gods as a set of bungling clowns would have been quite spoiled and the range of possible attitudes severely limited. The same objections would apply to making it a heresy, as some theologians did.[26] It would have made the authors serious, while restricting their freedom of treatment. Heresy does appear as a vague pejorative, so does the word *popeliquant*, but these are not specific accusations.[27]

As it is, although hardly a poem but ends in baptisms, converts need no instruction and there is no serious discussion of religion. With exceptions, the motives of conversion are a long-held but unexplained sentiment or sudden emotion, sexual love, hatred, disappointed ambition, revenge, fear of death, hope of reward, disillusion about the gods, even a miracle, but rarely reasoning. This may be realistic, but it does not go with speculative theology. There is a characteristic Christian piety which suits the narrative style of the poems but is never polemic in form.

The 'Tervagant convention' itself tells us most about the intentions of the general body of authors. The character of the gods, as they are made to act and be, and their cult as the 'pagans' practised it, tell us how far the whole conception is serious. How much was meant to be taken at face value was immediately understood by the audiences of the times, but is not so easily accessible to us. We can see that the system is flexible and that there were great advantages in being untrammelled by matters of fact and problems of plausibility. If the criterion is good entertainment, it is difficult to think of a theological system that would give better value than an absurd one.

The consistent use of the word 'pagan' for Saracens is possibly the only serious aspect of the convention. Its attraction may have been a sort of historical congruity in the minds of the poets, and many people, not only our poets, thought that Muslims in some special way enjoyed a direct continuity with the pagans of the ancient world.[28] If there was no other point of resemblance, they did inherit the position of chief non-Christian community known to Christians, who remembered the early centuries of persecution, not only in the Roman martyrology, but also in the cult of local saints, of which France had many. This will have lent one small touch of plausibility, in the eyes of Western Christians, without inhibiting in any way the inventive freedom of the poets, who show almost as little knowledge of antiquity as of Islam.

An escape from a tedious pedantry which would have alienated the attention and sympathy of audiences amounted to some defiance of the exhortation of churchmen to take the doctrinal as well as the military danger of Islam seriously; but attention was diverted from the natural link between professional story-telling and indifference to theology by ostentatious support of the Christian cause. This is not to say that the fiction of gods and idols was thought up in order to distract the hierarchy, and later the inquisitors, from the track of an indifferentism to which, once suspicion is aroused, it is always possible to attach a label of heresy or disobedience. Singers, as *joculatores*, were vulnerable;[29] and they were indeed guilty of indifferentism, but, as they imputed to the enemy a religion worse than any theologian imagined, they could not easily be faulted for lack of faith.

It is a delicate matter to probe the religious sentiments of people who should be presumed to be sincere believers but who are not particularly religious. It does not make it easier for us across the centuries that we have been contaminated by later religious and anti-religious controversy from which we have to prescind or fall into anachronism. There is a relevant example in an article of Gilson's entitled *Rabelais Franciscain. Chacun se souvient du chapitre XVI :* Des moeurs et conditions de Panurge, *et de l'anecdote du Cordelier qui, voulant se dévêtir des ornements sacerdotaux après* l'Ite missa est, *enleva, en même temps que son aube, sa robe et sa chemise que Panurge y avait cousues. Ce qu'il montra en pleine église, tout le monde le devine* . . . This was instanced by a critic, M.A. Lefranc, as an indication that Rabelais was an atheist. Gilson instances the lack of prudishness of the thirteenth century Franciscan historian, Salimbene, and we might add any number of Bacchic masses and such liturgical parodies as the *evangelia secundum marcum argenti*,[30] which would lose much of their point if we anachronistically supposed them to be gestures of unbelief. The critic's opinion was coloured by the post-medieval development of free-thinking and right-thinking schools, and perhaps by his awareness of the symbolic obscenities of the goddess of reason in churches; but in the Middle Ages, light-hearted blasphemy and indecency came easily to believers, and the transition from solemn to frivolous was barely noticed. We must expect to find religious questions treated at different levels.

It is impossible to be quite sure when and how far we are dealing with jokes, spoofs, ironies, sarcasm, reservations and implications which at the time were taken for granted, but went unrecorded as such; moreover, everything that was sung or read by a professional may well have been given meanings by voice or sometimes mime which our texts do not record either. Much that is left unsaid, to be understood, inevitably gets forgotten in time. Remembering that we cannot entirely recreate the preconceptions and sous-entendus of earlier times, and cannot wholly free ourselves of more recent preconceptions of our own, we come to analyse the system of the gods, their character and cult, their conflict with the Christians, and the service of the true God as it sheds light on the idea of the false.

WHO ARE THE GODS?

The first impression we get of the gods comes from the frequency with which the Saracens swear by them. This may be meant to draw attention to them, or it may just be that the singers like the sound of the strange names; it is at least clear that they do not want to slip them in unnoticed. Sometimes the oaths are just expletives, at other times they are threats of war and vengeance or prayers for help. In Roland, for example, 'If Mahon will be my surety', or, in battle, the ejaculation, *Aie nos, Mahum*, are as near prayers as make no difference.

After the earliest poems, references to the gods are usually a little more elaborate, and, although they are only passing references, they often have the look of a theological description: Mahon 'who has power to judge us all', or 'Apollin, sire Dieus, who caused me to be born'; or of an act of faith: 'by my god, Apollin', 'by my god, Tervagant', 'by the faith I owe Tervagant and Mahon'. These may be inverted: by Mahon 'your god' in the mouth of a Christian, 'by that God in whom you believe' in a Saracen's. Sometimes the attraction seems to be the sonority: 'and he swore by Mahon and Tervagant', 'he swore it by Mahon and Jupitel'. This effect is naturally not confined to oaths; the author of *Aspremont* liked to list four gods in a phrase repeated with variations several times: 'they gave him Mahon and Apollin, Tervagant and their companion Jupin' or 'Jupiter le grant'.[1]

Of the invocations of the gods, those that have theological implications are the ones that interest us here. In these, the gods are interchangeable, any or several of them as best suits the needs of the prosody. Each of the prayers or ejaculations, especially those that mention some activity of the god's, might be expected to indicate something about his character, or at any rate to specify a function peculiarly his own. On the contrary, they are haphazard. The choice of a qualifying phrase, like the choice of the god to name, may be determined by the assonance. The half-line or single line phrases that describe the gods may not necessarily have more point to them than this; but even if they are chosen for their sound, or perhaps from some vague sentiment, they must at least have been thought in nothing inappropriate, and it is likely enough that they seemed positively suitable in a general way, though lacking specific relevance.

There are phrases that express the relation of the believer to the god: 'whom I worship and believe in', 'in whom I put my faith', 'whom I must worship', and, with special significance, 'to whom I have done homage' and 'my natural lord', *seignor naturel*. There are those that describe the relation of the god to his creation: 'who has formed us all', 'to whom the world belongs', 'who has everything in charge'; and there are intermediate phrases that verge on one or the other of the general types: 'to whom I am given', 'the great justicer', 'who governs and guides us', 'who governs the age' (*siècle*). When Apollin is qualified as the one 'who caused me to be born', he has not been singled out as the god or patron saint of creation, of fertility, or childbirth; we can be sure of this, because it is nowhere else suggested; nor is there any indication that he is addressed as the individual patron of the speaker. Creation and fertility are attributed to Mahon, and we shall speak of this later. Moreover, the Lord God (Damedeu) is given similar attributes; 'who created all the world', 'whom I must worship', 'who has everything in charge', 'who caused me to be born'. Only references to God as *lou fil sainte Marie* are inapplicable to Mahon in principle. The phrase 'Who made the sea and the fishes', where there is no obvious relevance to the context, and must either be arbitrary, or meant only in the sense of the *Benedicite*, can be paralleled with Mahon.[2] Roughly, we may say that the Lord

God and Mahon are given the same attributes (each by his supporters), but, where it suits the poet, and for no reason apparent from the sense, Apollin or Tervagant may take the place of Mahon. All the attributes of God or gods (the Incarnation apart) relate to the government of the world, or of the individual speaker.

It is only their names that distinguish the gods from each other. We often get just that impression, that it is indeed only one single god who is being invoked under different names, and by names chosen indifferently from a rota at that. *Le Charroi de Nîmes* speaks of the hour of the day 'when they pray to Mahon and his idols (sic), and to Tervagant, that he should help them';[3] but it is not the general tenor of this poem that Tervagant is specially qualified to help, and certainly not of the poems as a whole. One god seems as well qualified as another, but some names occur more than others, and Mahon has a distinct advantage, often overwhelming, but rarely exclusive. Some names make only an occasional appearance, and in many poems do not occur at all, for example Cahu and Baratron, and even Plato – sometimes thought to be a mistake for Pluto – is invoked: *Mahon reclaiment, Apollin et Platon*.[4] Although the three most often recurring, Mahon, Tervagant and Apollin, are not always invoked together, they often are (or with Jupin, Jupiter as fourth) and, just as it is never quite clear that there is any particular theological reason for one rather than another, it is no clearer why it should be any particular pair, or group of three or more. Tervagant may precede Mahon, and Mahon may be omitted, even from some solemn invocation.[5] Few cases, however, are quite as striking as an occasion in *Enfances Renier*, when King *B*runamont solemnly pronounces his daughter's apostasy from 'Tervagant and Apollin and Jupiter le grant', and he repeats his formula, neither of them mentioning Mahon, whose name occurs often enough in the rest of the poem.[6] It is difficult to see any other cause for these irregularities than caprice.

There are other anomalies, including the extraordinary reference in *Raoul de Cambrai*: 'This Mahon does, and

Mahomés our god'.[7] Can this really be meant to assert two
separate entities ? In the sentence in *Elie de St Gilles*, 'We shall
be able to see which god is most authentic (*verables*), Mahon,
or Apollin, or Jesus', are these three equally alternative, one to
another, as this seems to say, or is Jesus alternative to the
remaining pair (it is a Christian speaking) ?[8] Nor are the gods
differentiated by regions; none of the parts of paienie seems
appropriated to a patron. There is a reference in *Orson de
Beauvais* to *Tervagant de Suzile* and Gaston Paris suggested
that this might indicate a Sicilian origin for the name,[9] but this
is a lead that takes us nowhere, because it has no confirmation.
Nor again are the gods appropriated by nations. We find
indifferently *la gent Mahon, la gent Apollin, la gent Tervagant*, as
well as *la gent paienne* or *Sarrazine*, and, I am afraid, *la pute
gent.*[10]

SARACENS AND PAGANS

It is beyond doubt that the creators or practitioners of the
poetic convention intended to portray a pagan religion; but
it seems that they did not know how to do so, having retained
from the past no idea at all of what paganism is like. It might
just be argued that they tried to construct a shamanistic
religion – a dimly apprehended godhead approachable only
through intermediate spirits – Tervagant and the rest – who
need to be propitiated; occasionally there is a priest or manipulator who might be cast as shaman. Such an interpretation is
compatible with some texts or some passages, but there is no
compelling reason to accept it, and on general grounds it seems
most unlikely that the poets would have had the knowledge,
collectively or severally, to concoct such a religion. If they had
constructed a pagan religion as scientifically as was possible to
them, we might expect them to have done so along the lines of
Clement of Alexandria's acute and unsympathetic analysis of
the kinds of idolatry,[11] but they had no access to it. In fact there
is no trace of the long passage in *Wisdom* to which access was
possible, had they been interested.[11] Interest in pagan religions
did not revive in the West in clerical and academic circles until

the accounts of travels to the Mongols began to circulate,[12] and the poets show as little sign of contact with authentic travellers as with academics.

It is not surprising that they did not have the little knowledge of comparative religion that the Christian tradition included, but we might have expected them to be aware of their own ancestral gods, Celtic or Germanic.[13] It is possible to detect fragmented Celtic folk-lore in the occasional appearance of a fairy world in the poems, but none at all in their treatment of the gods, not so much as the names. There is a great contrast with German and Arthurian epic and romance, permeated with folk-lore. Our poets were slightly more open to written tradition, in that the names at least of some of the gods of classical antiquity do survive, but it is little more than the names. Sometimes gods are conceived in the classical manner, but as nameless personifications (*Par le commandement d'Amours,* | *Pitiés et Francise et Paours*) and Love was inevitably more the poets' favourite than Pity, Nobility or Fear.[14] These figures are in just the opposite case to that of the Saracen gods, who are named and yet functionless. The classical gods are scarcely in better case; we should often be unable to tell them apart if we depended for our information on many of the poets who mention them.

Twelfth century writers in different fields, both theologians and on the science side, with a fair knowledge of antiquity, associated Muslims with Venus, both because of the supposed venereal laxity and because of the Friday prayer. Not so our songs. Venus does appear, though not in the form Aphrodite, not of course as Hathor or Isis, and as Astarte only in the form Ashtoreth, taken from the Old Testament, and used meaninglessly. When in *Pampelune* the city is taken from the Saracens, the 'temple of Venus' is consecrated as a church; in *Godin* Saracens bury a dead warrior in the temple of Tervagant.[15] Who can say what kind of temple and of temple worship the poets had in mind, if they had anything definite in mind? The classical apparatus of divine interference in the affairs of men – gods who promote their protégés' adventures or themselves make love to human beings – is foreign to our poems, and even the 'god of love' is no more than a literary manner of speaking. Where the gods of the Tervagant convention are, or resemble, classical names, the traditional attributes of the gods have been lost. Apollin has no recognisable characteristic of Apollo, and Jupiter those of his homonym only so far as his name may occasionally be used instead of Mahon's (or Tervagant's) to designate the creator and ruler; some poets like the phrase *Jupiter le grant*, but he is one of the least of Saracen gods, and poets just like various forms of his name, besides *Jupiter: Jupitiel, Jupitel, Jupinel, Jupé, Jupi, Jupis, Jupin*.[16]

In *Blancandin et l'Orgeilleuse d'Amour* we find two pagan systems overlaid. There are Mahon and Apollin, with occasional mention of Baratron, Tervagant, Jupiter, Cahu and Margot; and there are also the romantic *diex d'amors* and *Amors*, who get rather more mentions, but all very literary. For example, 'the god of love is very heartless' (*trop est . . . villeins*), because he makes the branches of the trees bud when the lovers are separated. We are supposed to recognise the sensibility, but no one is expected to believe in the god, not the reader or listener, the poet or the lovers or the Saracens. He is not a fertility or vegetation god, because he is not a god at all. On the other hand, the idol-gods are supposed to control the elements, and when they are ship-board and fail to calm the tempest, the heroic *S*adoine is converted.[17]

This touches on the only truly godlike function that Mahon is given, or that his Saracen devotees claim for him, that he is a god of vegetation. In *Li Nerbonois* Saracens say that Mahon must be held dear above all things; 'he made the calm and the wind and the tempest, and so he gives us our drink and our food'. In *Raoul de Cambrai* (thirteenth century) we read that Mahon 'makes it snow and rain and blow' and in *Gaufrey* (late thirteenth) that he 'makes the rain and the weather and the wind, and gives us wine (sic) and corn from heaven'. In *Simon de Pouille* (also thirteenth century), 'he makes the herbs, the vines and the wheat grow' and in *Huon de Bordeaux* it is he 'who has everything in care and gives us bread and wheat'. In the fourteenth century *Chevalier du Cygne*, Mahon is he 'who makes the wheat grow'. The *Roman d'Aquin* links Mahon with Quahu (usually Cahu), the two 'by whom all good things spring from the earth, and by whom the bread and wine are grown and all things by which we are sustained'. Early in the thirteenth century Jean Bodel said 'who gives heat and cold'. These examples come from all periods but the very earliest. One of the early examples occurs in *Le Charroi de Nîmes*, where the French accost a Saracen peasant who tells them that if Mahon has taken good care of his crop he should have got a good harvest of wheat; the French jeer at him for thinking that Mahon brings riches and plenty, winter cold and summer heat.[18]

Do these passages bestow a genuine pagan character as god of fertility on Mahon? The phrases occur haphazard, with no obvious relevance to their context, except to assert Mahon's dominance. Moreover, the same qualities are given to the Lord God, and in much the same way: 'who made the wine and wheat', 'by whom it blows and thunders'. There is a more complex type, which places God in heaven, while the earth, including the charge of the fertility of plants, belongs to Mahon. 'And when God rains, Mahon makes the plants grow' (*Chanson de Guillaume*) and Mahon says in the *Chanson d'Antioche*, 'Let the Lord God look after his heaven, earth is in my department' (*en ma baillie*). In the short phrases of which we have already seen a number of examples it is the same idea that is expressed or implied – Mahon 'to whom the world belongs', 'who governs all the world, heaven and earth and the sea with its waves', 'who has everything in charge', and, summing up all these, 'lord god of all authority' (*sire dex de grant signorie*).[19]

Assertion and counter-assertion may be presented as a kind of dispute: the fighting King *T*riaire asks, 'Do you believe in Mahon who governs the world?' and Elie de Saint Gilles replies, 'No, but in God the great master'. Saracens and Christians agree that the proof is in the encounter, 'we will see which to believe'.[20] The idea appears at its most elaborate in its earliest form, in the *Couronnement de Louis*, which Frappier believes to be the source of all the later passages. The Saracen King Corsolt says that 'God is above, over the firmament; down here on earth he does not have an acre'. He warns the pope that he and God must now put their case to the test; God has got the heavens, but the pope has got the land, and Corsolt must take possession by force (and kill the clergy).[21] Frappier diagnoses possible Catharism, because of the dualism, although there is nothing specifically Catharist in the passage.[22] In all these passages the underlying idea may be, not fertility, animal, human or vegetative, and not dualism of good and evil as the Cathars understood it, but rivalry for the lordship, for power and possession. Creation is important because it implies lordship (God rains, Mahon makes the grass grow), but possession is crucial (God does not own an acre). Lordship is what the Saracens and Christians are fighting for, and, equally, that is the point of the conflict between their gods. 'May this Mahon who is worshipped by us save you and give you victory as you desire.'[23]

Another weakness in the paganism imputed to Saracens is that they know no histories of their gods, no sacred stories; there is no myth in the sense that students of comparative religion understand it. Fertility and lordship are at the roots of myth; the most that we can claim for our poets is that they reinvented the religion without myth of creation or other sacred story, or hierogamy. It is only the rivalry for dominion that matters to them. Even in the Matter of Britain, pagan myths have survived only as tattered fragments that modern critics have to cobble together; in the Matter of France, there are only occasional and disjointed fairy fantasies. Of Mahon, Tervagant, Apollin and the rest, the poems contain no myth; the gods have no past, and so no character.

Although the pantheon is a failure, it was seriously meant. The constant use of the term 'pagan' is itself evidence of a persistent effort. The gods were certainly seen as at least the heirs of pagan antiquity. Roman remains, of which there are so many in southern France, and still more in Spain and Italy, are conceived as somehow related to the Saracens. As Bédier said of the pilgrims, 'Dans toutes les villes du Midi qu'ils traversent, on leur montre des ruines, faites, leur dit-on, par les Sarrasins'.[24] In the great eponymous poem, Gerard of Rousillon, with his countess, discovers a great treasure in the arena of Autun, through the intercession of St Mary Magdalen (this dates to the period of high popularity of the Bethany saints), but 'the Saracen people collected this treasure', *Ist tresaur amasserent genz sarrazine*.[25] The assumption that the 'Saracens' were a survival from and continuation of the ancient pagan world extended far beyond the Tervagant convention, and was seriously believed of the Arabs. It was not only the literary association with the goddess Venus. A distinguished canonist speaks of the pagans as having begun to judaise after the earlier canons about pagans were promulgated, that is, the people who used to make sacrifices that St Paul talks about eating are those who now treat pork as unclean. It is true that the former pagans of the Greco-Roman world had become either Christian or Muslim, and it was correct to say that some non-Christians of the old Roman empire were now Muslims, some Jews. This fact gives Islam a kind of continuity from antiquity. In histories of philosophy, even in the case of so wide and judicious a reader as Roger Bacon, Muhammad the Prophet appears somewhere chronologically indeterminate between Aristotle and Ibn Sina.[26] The word *Saracen* was used outside our convention for Romans and even for Clovis[27] before his conversion. In Malory's Book V, and in the *Morte Arthure* on which it is based, the Saracens form a large part of the Roman army (and not as auxiliaries). In *Lancelot du Lac*, Joseph of Arimathea converts a Saracen people (see below, p.253). When the *Roman de Troie* says that 'Neither Saracens nor Christians' ever saw such a funeral as that which Helen gave her brother Memnon in Palestine, it does not mean that Troy was divided between those two religions.[28] It is a way of saying 'everybody' (or here, negatived, nobody); Saracens here do service for all non-Christians, past as well as present.

Other authors took the logical step of placing the Saracen

gods themselves in ancient times. This is clearly explained by the *Roman de Thèbes* (the story of Oedipus). In those times 'there were no Christians yet, but throughout the world all were pagans. Some worshipped Tervagant, others Mahon and Apollin, and some of them idols, some images of gold that they hung in their treasuries, and others of copper or tin or silver, these were the poor people.' Here is a whole theory of comparative religion. In Jehan le Prieur's play, *Mystère du Roi Advenir*, a fifteenth century presentation of the Buddhist story, Barlaam and Josaphat, the Indian pagans in the early Christian centuries call on Mahon, and on Apollin with Saturn, and on Tervagant with Vulcan, and Jupiter le grant. But these are exceptions, and *Eneas*, contemporary with *Thèbes*, cites classical gods only.[28]

There are claims to pagan antiquity within the Tervagant convention itself. King Galafre, in *Couronnement*, having taken Rome and expelled the pope, claims the right of inheritance from his ancestors, Romulus and Julius Caesar. We are not to suppose that the author cared at all that he was confusing Arab and Roman history severally and together, but he let his fancy play over the unity of all non-Christians, and was content to allow the Saracens some sort of moral right. Here too we may recall the story of *Auberon*, with Julius Caesar, son of Caesarius, Judas Maccabeus, St George and the Holy Family. The author has exploited a number of legends; he wraps it all up in a fairy story. He omits Mahon and the gods, even Jupiter is only mentioned once, but the poem is closely connected to *Huon de Bordeaux*. This is a literary poem, and its editor, Jean Subrenat, says it is *le point de rencontre des Matières de France, de Bretagne et de Rome*. He also points out that its internal chronology is precise, and one may add that within the terms of historical fantasy it has a sharp awareness of the great non-Christian world.[29]

THE ORIGINS OF THE GODS

We do not need to go deeply into the interesting controversy about the origins of the names of the gods, but just enough to see how far it may clarify the character with which the authors meant to endow the gods. Basset pointed to the existence of a striking statue at Cadiz, probably of Hercules, which lost its head at the beginning of the eleventh century and was destroyed by the Arabs, who were looking for treasure, in the middle of the twelfth. This he proposes as the *Ymago Mahometi* of Turpin,[30] a memorable phrase to which a real statue may well have given substance. It is the nearest thing to an idol that the Christians were ever likely to identify in Arab Spain, and a classical statue might even perversely seem to confirm the continuity of pagans and Saracens. But it is difficult to see how one idol could give birth to a pantheon, and, if it could, we should want to know how. The big questions are not answered here.

Grégoire and the Pellats have brought forward ingenious explanations of the improbable names of the gods. Grégoire presses the argument that the chansons had some intellectual foundation for imputing idolatry to Islam, a point we shall refer to later. He stresses the correctness of the form *Trivigant* for *Tervagant*, and identifies it with Diana Trivia, long worshipped among the Scythians. He finds possible sources for the other gods (such as Chaos for Cahu).[31] Much of his argument is necessarily etymological, but he has no doubt that there was a deliberate attempt to put forward a plausible pagan religion, and that this was inspired and informed by erudite clerics who knew and supplied the classical background. No doubt the necessary knowledge was available, but why should the poets have taken over the names of the gods in this garbled form, but no other facts about them? Why do we not find learned works by these erudite clerks in which they themselves attribute the worship of Diana Trivia and other cults to Islam? And if the poets were open to the influence of learned clerics at all, why do they show no sign of the influence of what clerics were really saying about Islam?

Ch. Pellat sees 'Mahon e(t) Tervagan(t)' as a joint phrase: the *et* belongs with Mahom and *ervagan* is a poor transcription of *ar-rajīm*; Apollin would be *ibn-laᶜīn*, and the whole phrase would be an ill-wishing of 'Mahon' in Arabic. The phrase would have been broken up by non-Arabic speakers into three gods, and this triad would ultimately have been extended to an entire pantheon.[32] The argument is brilliant, and impossible to render in a few sentences. In the nature of things, it cannot be conclusive. If it were true, it would help to explain the lack of any precise character in the gods, whose Arabic genesis would not have been generally understood. It would mean that the poets found a polytheist system ready made for them, but it would still be true that they embraced it happily, and, however the names began, what is important for us would still be the way they and their audiences understood it.

Apollin, irrespective of the occasional late spelling *Apollon*, must surely have been understood as Apollo. There is also a widely accepted explanation that the name originated as Apollyon. We have seen many variations of *Jupiter*, but they can only be explained as more or less recognisable forms of the one word. Apollin is often associated with Jupiter, and both must be the gods of Olympus, however dimly apprehended. Apollin also occurs in company with Baraton/Baratron, which is at any rate another Greek association. The name of Apollo may well have been better known than that of Apollyon, which occurs only once in the relatively little known Apocalypse (he is known to Englishmen through Bunyan). Other Hebrew names occur as gods, Beelzebub and Ashtareth, but they are less common, and less common as partners for Apollin, than Jupiter. There is no general tendency to keep Greek and Biblical names apart. The *Couronnement* rightly speaks of the 'pit of Baratron', but Beelzebub and Nero are there.[33] These three names in association sounded right to the poet.

Vagueness about gods and evil spirits was theologically acceptable as well as consistent with a poor classical education. Apollin may have been thought of as Apollyon and as Apollo at the same time. It was traditional patristic teaching that the pagan gods were evil spirits, so that there was no necessary conflict between classical and Biblical sources for the names of gods. It is interesting, but not illogical, that the pagans of the

Old Testament and Jewish tradition should be assimilated to those of classical literature (if that is indeed what happened). From this welter of imprecise associations and memories in the minds of the poets, we may safely draw the conclusion most important to us, that the poets were as indifferent to the origins, as to the specific characters, of the gods of their invention.

SARACENS AND MUSLIMS

We have also to consider whether there may be any vague apprehension or distortion of some aspect of Islam in the religion imputed to Saracens. Muslims, with their deep-rooted horror of anything that may be seen as *shirk*, the association of anything that is not God with God, have suspected Christians of being guilty of it. Was there a colourable medieval counter-accusation against Muslims ? Three possibilities come to mind.

Ramon Lull (1235–1315) was in the invariable habit of arguing that monotheism was inconsistent with rejection of the Trinity but he was eccentric about 'proving' the Trinity by 'compelling reasons' (rationes necessariae).[34] A moderate form of Trinitarian rationalism was familiar in twelfth century theologians,[35] and later, but, as we should expect, there is little trace of an argument from Trinitarian monotheism in the poems, and there can be no attack on Saracen monotheism which by hypothesis does not exist. (The false Saracen Trinity I consider later.) A second argument used against Islam is that any belief in a false god[36] is idolatry, and any false belief in God is a belief in a false god.[37] There are hints of this idea in some medieval theologians, but it does not even begin to explain the creation of an elaborate system of idols, and is too abstract for a popular adventure story. Humbert of Romans in an ambiguous passage seems to speak of the call to prayer as the 'idol of Muhammad'; the public proclamation of the Prophet scandalised many Christian observers of the Middle Ages, but this is not reflected in the poems.[38]

A third suggestion appeared quite early in the twelfth century in the work of the converted Spanish Jew, Peter de Alfonso; it was on this that Grégorie largely depended to make the assumption of idolatry sound reasonable. Peter's imputation of the paganism of the ancients to Islam bears no resemblance whatever to the epic convention of gods; he did also describe the rites of the pilgrimage (the hajj), and referred to the circumambulation of the Ka°ba, as pagan.[39] Circumambulation is indeed a common pagan rite.[40] The Islamic belief is that it dates back to Abraham, but had been corrupted in pagan times, and reformed by the revelation to the Prophet. No Muslim questions pagan influences in the 'time of ignorance' (*jāhilīya*). Since sauce for the goose is not always sauce for the gander, the fact that Christians took over pagan worship, pagan feasts and holy places, might not prevent their accusing Islam over the pilgrimage rites; but there is no sign of it in the poems, or of anything approaching even Alfonsi's garbled knowledge of the hajj. Many poets are aware of the pilgrimage to *Mesques de Mahon*,[41] but Saracen pilgrimage was conceived as no different from its supposed Christian equivalent. The two conceptions are in fact very different, and this the poets did not know at all. They thought Muslim and Christian pilgrims looked alike; Charlemagne, dressed as a palmer, and spying on his own account, is not recognised by a dress that would stand out among Saracens, but by an interpreter who by chance knew him by sight in his own court.[42]

Meredith Jones asked himself whether the greetings between Saracens in the poems represent the fulfilment of an Islamic obligation, but inevitably concludes that they are Christian. He is thinking, not only of greetings proper, but of oaths, including the part-line descriptions of Mahon which we have considered when defining the character of the gods. Jones attributed these to liturgical and homiletic sources, but he treats this aspect of his subject with less than his usual thoroughness.[43] It is worth considering greetings and pious exclamations a little further.

We can safely dismiss ordinary oaths with the constantly repeated formula, 'by Mahon', 'by Tervagant', and so on, sometimes with two or more gods; these might just as easily be by God, or by a saint, or by a string of saints. It is true that the addition of qualifying phrases ('who made . . .', 'by whom . . .') does not affect their character as oaths. Greetings varied: 'Mahon save you, and the god Tervagant', the pious wish 'Maons will aid you' and, in a late poem, 'Mahon save you and give you victory', these and others like them do seem to be Christian greetings with gods substituted. 'May it please Mahon' and 'if Mahon gives the grace' are pious ejaculations which might as well be Islamic – for 'if God wills' – as Christian; so is 'may God be adored' – for 'the praise is God's' – in response to an important bit of information. In the last case *R*enoart, converted Saracen, is speaking. We occasionally find phrases in the mouths of Christians which sound more Muslim than many of those that are given to Saracens, particularly the acceptance of what God has predestined. An oath by Mahon's beard is in a class by itself.[44]

Can we reasonably suppose that there is some reflection of Islamic practice here? In this we should include the practice of Mozarabs, who may be assumed to have used the same pious phrases as Muslims in Arabic, and who might more probably have been known to and have affected Frenchmen in Spain.[45] The extent to which the name of God is in the mouths of every Arabic speaker, Muslim and Christian, and of Turks and Persians, has been remarked by European travellers over centuries, and the exchange of courtesies which to-day appreciably lengthens telephone conversations is traditional in a Muslim culture. It is the typical Muslim greeting or wish accompanied by response that is wholly missing from the poems. Also it is curious that the formula, 'in the name of . . .' is usually lacking, whether the Muslim (God, the Compassion-ate, the Merciful) or the Christian (Father, Son and Holy Ghost), but the absence of both obscures any explanation. Some of the expressions used by Saracens, or even by Chris-tians, are consistent with an Arabic influence on the authors, but there is nothing that can only be Arabic in origin, and any influence would have to be remote. We must confirm what we expected: this aspect of the question is negligible.

The argument in *Turpin*, that in the case of a Christian

victory, the Saracens will be baptised, and in case of a Saracen victory, Christians will be oppressed forever, suggests knowledge of Islamic toleration of the existence of Christianity, in contrast with Christian insistence on the conversion of Muslims; but not decisively.[46]

TRIAL BY COMBAT

A search for the sources of the gods does little to help our understanding of their function in the songs, and we return to the provisional conclusions we had reached: 'paganism' is important as bringing together everything and everybody of the non-Christian world; and the function of the gods is to claim the lordship and government of the world: 'we shall be able to see which God is most authentic'.[47] It is for failure to give the victory that the god is blamed and often punished. We can almost say that there is a contract, as, for example, when in *Roland* the great amir of Babylon calls on his gods in battle, and not only offers them fine gold, but also reminds them of his past services to them.[48] Again and again and at different levels of seriousness, it comes out that the gods are expected by their people to give them victory, just as the God of the Christians is expected to do for them. The poets may choose arbitrarily which short description to attach to some god they mention, but they take it from a group of such phrases, all of which express either the authority of the god or the speaker's allegiance to him.[49] The relation between any god and his followers must be that they expect help from him, but these poems are about war, and it is chiefly at each stage or aspect of the wars that his people, *la gent Mahon*, or *Tervagant* or *Apollin*, call on him for help. He is blamed for everything that goes wrong, as everything in the end does for the Saracens.[50] They are not only *felon* but also *preux*; their gods are never *preux*, every story disproves their prowess. *En tel Dieu doit on croire, que sa gent volt aidier.*

King *A*goland will not believe that his son *A*umon has not won his war; that 'he has been beaten or defeated by any man who has received baptism'.[51] Battles, whole wars, Saracen invasions turned back, Saracen cities captured, are all a test of strength between two sides; each side jeers at the gods of the other, and the victory identifies the true God. The struggle is best expressed in the great set-piece single combats; *F*ierabras, *O*tinel (once as Saracen and once as Christian), *F*erragu, *L*oquifer, *D*esramé, Maillefer, *G*adifer, may fight in what they see as a just war, as in the last four cases, or for the pleasure of fighting, as *F*ierabras and *O*tinel, and *F*erragu in *Entrée d'Espagne*, but the end of the fight tells us who the true God is in every case. When *O*tinel (as Christian) fights *C*larel, the latter says that he is glad to fight, because the religion *O*tinel has taken 'is not worth a berry against ours'; and *O*tinel replies that there must be devils in him that he should want to defend Mahon against him but 'I shall defend the Lord God and his religion'.[52] All these duels are constantly interrupted by speeches in which the champions, courteously or defiantly, recommend their opponents to change religions.[53] If the gods, severally or collectively, claim sovereignty, in a chronic state of war they are war gods.

GODS AND THEIR IDOLS

Saracen armies are sometimes said to carry a standard of Mahon; if this means a picture, it designates an icon little more plausible than a statue; the name written would be another matter. Sometimes the idols themselves seem to be standards.[54] Were the gods imagined as being simply their idols, the two terms being interchangeable, or as appearing in idols, the epiphany of some transcendent numen? Poems usually speak of the idol, Mahon, Tervagant, Apollin, Jupiter, as if it were the only Mahon, Tervagant, and so on. 'They are carrying Mahon their god with them'; or, 'Here is the mahommerie of the unbelievers: within it they have put Mahon and Tervagant, Apollin and Cahu and Jupiter the great'.[55] But sometimes it seems that the god is conceived as having a separate existence from his idol. In *Roland* the idols are destroyed in the war against *M*arsile himself, in the disillusion of defeat, but the great amir *B*aligant still prays to them, and in the end the 'images

and idols' in the synagogues and mahommeries of Saragossa
are destroyed again, presumably a different set, or set of sets.
In *Aspremont* the idols are destroyed, but the Saracens demand
their return and require an indemnity, and continue meanwhile
to pray to the gods.[56] In *Fierabras*, the amir *B*alan weeps with
shame to see Mahon and the gods thrown down and broken up,
but he blames Mahon for sleeping, he does not think Mahon is
no more; and he retains his faith to the end, and dies for it.
When *R*enoart, in *Gadifer*, captures the statue of Mahon, and
ultimately returns him to the Saracens, they seem to speak as
though the god himself had been kidnapped, but they do not
behave like ants who have lost their queen. In a number of
poems the gods are destroyed, but they are always there again
in the next poem. Indeed, if every 'mahommerie' had its idols,
no idol could be the god in any exclusive sense. It is not at all
clear in what sense Mahon and the rest 'were' their idols in this
convention which is sometimes more complex than it looks at
first. *Turpin* speaks of the gods as *simalacra* of the devil.[57]

It is conceivable that only one Mahon, and one of each of the
rest, was supposed to exist, and that poet and audience forgot
this at the end of a poem in which they were broken up, and
sometimes mid-poem; in this case there would be a magic
carpet also, because sometimes Mahon is in, say, Cordova, and
sometimes in Cairo. It is not at all likely that this is how it was
imagined. There is no sign whatever that such problems of time
and space occurred to any of the poets. Possibly the idea was
of a number of individual entities, each an idol-cum-god, many
of the same name, so that one particular Mahon is brought out,
one of the Tervagants speaks to his people, and so on. It is much
more likely that the poets did not think about this question at
all, certainly not carefully or clearly; but the convention, as
they operate it, implies some idea at the back of their minds,
which we can hope to set down in rational terms. We have to
explain a god who can be humiliated and insulted, propitiated
and worshipped, in his idols, of which there are a number in
several or many different places, but who survives the destruction of one of the idols, or of many. It might be that they

imagined an indefinite number of idols, belonging to a god who was some kind of potentially ubiquitous evil spirit, each idol only a local or temporary manifestation. The impression we get of the poets' own opinion is that they more often thought it was fraud than the devil; but they may have conceived the Saracens as believing in a god with local manifestations in idols here and there.

Psalms 113 and 134, 'works of the hands of men, they have mouths and speak not' might be familiar to the poets from the office in the monasteries. These are Vespers psalms, and, if not understood in the Latin, could have been known from the conversation of the monks, or of the poets' own goliardic colleagues perhaps. These passages, however, only assert that an idol is not God, and is lifeless. If the poets were thinking of Romans 1.23, 'the image of a corruptible man' or animal exchanged for the glory of the incorruptible God, that too leaves the relation of the god to the idol undetermined; the sense is certainly that the pagans, having known God, have turned away to the images, and that does not quite fit the Tervagant convention. Another influence may be 3 Kings 18.27 (in the Vulgate), where Baal is ridiculed as a false god who does not respond to the sacrifice ('perhaps he is asleep and must be awaked'); this is very much the tone of some passages in certain poems. But Baal is not here an idol; both Elijah and Baal's prophets offer a bullock as sacrifice on Mount Carmel.[58] We can only say that the Saracens honour the god when they honour the idol, and the god is punished when the Saracens are frustrated and disillusioned in failure and the idol is thrown into a ditch as not worth a dead and stinking dog.[59]

The Pellats' suggestion that there were three stages in the development of the convention, first Mahon alone, vice Christ, then a false Trinity of Mahon, Tervagant and Apollin, and finally the extension of these into a fuller but variable pantheon, is a sensitive response to the feel of the poems. As the gods have no distinct characters and are interchangeable, they might well seem to be in some sense all one, and an anti-Trinity would have suited the needs of the story as well as the pantheon does. Yet this is not the generally accepted version of the gods, and, though the three mentioned are the most prominent, groups of four and more occur often enough. Moreover, the very lack of differentiation which makes a common godhead credible makes an anti-Trinity on the Christian model unconvincing. No medieval writer could conceive a Trinity, true or false, except on the Christian model. Theologians of the twelfth and thirteenth centuries expected to explain the Trinity by Augustinian analogy ('memory, intelligence, will') and, if that was remote from the poets, the terms of the Creeds were not.[60] There is no parallel way to distinguish Mahon, Tervagant and Apollin functionally.

What I think happened is that the creators of the convention conceived and meant to portray a traditional pagan poly-theism, but had no more than the haziest idea of what that would mean in practice, and so constantly slipped into the monotheistic way of speaking most natural to them, even when manipulating their Saracen characters. It always makes perfect sense, if we substitute the word 'God' for any of the names in a polytheist phrase, or even the names of the Persons of the Trinity if there are up to three names. When the Saracens of fiction use the names of various gods indifferently or in groups, it is as if they spoke of one God, known by different names, or by several at one time, who is similar to the Christian God, to whom however he is opposed. In this way the authors came nearer to the truth about Islam than they would have wished, and without the least desire for authenticity. If we construct a summary of the creed implied by the texts, it will be contrary to their ostensible polytheism: 'one godhead, known by any or all of a number of names not carrying individual significance, and represented by idols which are in some way an emanation of his being'. It is not what the poets intended, but it is the logical reconciliation of the inconsistencies in what they said. Their monotheism was irrepressible, as was their Christian cast of thought.

There were Western clerics to disapprove of three dimen-sional statues of the saints which overstimulated the credulity of the simple-minded (*idiotae*). Bernard of Angers conceded that the image of the Crucified was received by the universal church and considered that the final test of an idol was whether a sacrifice was offered.[61] This test would leave the Saracen idols harmless, and that was not the poets' intention, but one poet at least saw a parallel between the crucifix and the 'Mahon',[62] and poets generally made so much of the idols that they presented them virtually as a false equivalent to the Incarnation of God in Jesus. It is as an incorporation or materialisation of the gods that the Saracens treat the idols in the poems, whatever it is they are supposed to be doing, and so too do the Christians treat them, even when they want to show that the god is an illusion. This would account for the difficulty in either distinguishing god from idol or identifying them as one, and would explain how the god can be punished in his idol. This is not more than a recognition of the implications of some aspects of the convention, but it helps to explain why the 'pagans' are, as pagans, so unconvincing and implausible.

A SUMMING UP

It is not easy to see just how the complex Tervagant convention came into being. Grégoire's theory presupposes a deliberate process founded on a theory of religious polemic which nowhere else exists. The Pellat theory, which depends on accident and misunderstanding, is more realistic. If we were sure, in a matter about which there can in fact be no certainty, we should still not know how so complex a system with its many variants came to be adopted by all the authors of epic songs and adventure stories. They can hardly have had a conference to discuss it. If it did arise in ignorance, it must have become deliberate, as all the poets stuck to their own peculiar convention and ignored the way other authors were thinking. It might have begun as a catch-phrase does, or the fashionable use of a technical word in a general sense, and effectively this is what the Pellats suggest. It is curious but quite probable that something which takes so big a part in the whole literature should have a slight and accidental beginning; and the question must remain open. It is the success of the form that the Tervagant system finally took that is important. We can only say that it was entirely fictional, and that people liked it very much. Perhaps the first was the reason for the second.

The trial by combat between the Christian and non-Christian worlds is a competition between God and god to be lord of this world. Who governs the fate of the men who fight for the earth they inhabit? That is what the stories are about, and even a reference to natural creation is a reference to the war for control of the land. Who rules? The end of each poem tells us, but the poem as a whole shows that the Lord God, *Damedeu* rules, not by special intervention, but by the victory of his Christians and their prowess. It is an encouragement that 'God has not yet forgotten us', but an encouragement to act. Christians win by their own exertions, God helping in no way that is different from that of real life. It is a realistic element in the convention, and sophisticated theology, both perhaps unexpected.

In fact, the story would suffer if two parties of equal prowess were not pitted against each other. It is some sort of justification for the fact that Christians always win that the two sides are not equal in their gods. Heroes invoke their God when they are in trouble; so indeed does the poet himself – *or ait Jhesu de Renoart pités* – as though the story were unfolding with the uncertainty of real life and not under the author's control. This means little more than 'will he escape? Don't miss next week's instalment'. When the Saracen invokes his gods, the tension is further increased: 'Mahon give you victory'.[63] The Lord God gives the victory through the prowess of his Christians, and they vindicate his truth. Mahon fails, in spite of Saracen prowess, and they fail to vindicate him. The gods, whether we see them as a pantheon or as different faces of one anti-God, are not particularly evil; they do not demand human sacrifice, like Moloch or Aztec Cinteotl. Their positive function is to fight and their negative function is to fail. In the last resort they fail because they are wrong and they are wrong because they do not exist.

THE CULT OF THE GODS

There are surprisingly few descriptions of what the idols looked like, and by and large they give a less horrific impression than some of the human and even animal characters whom the poets could conceive more clearly. Several of these come to mind immediately: *L*oquifer and *G*adifer (*ongles agues comme serpens crestés*), Ascopard in *Bueves de Hamtoune*, who deserts to the enemy, *A*morant in *Gui de Warewic* (cist n'est pas home, ainz est diable), and even *F*ierabras' horse. When in *Barbastre Clarion*, the converted Saracen, takes the Frenchmen into the mahommerie, there is an image so big that it is beyond the powers of an entertainer who sings to describe: *ne le saurait à dire nul jugleor qui chante*, but there seems nothing very terrible about it. It is done in a 'forceful style' (or perhaps primitive style – *ruiste façon*) but not a repelling one, *bien resanble baron*; it is like a man of great physical presence.[1]

In *Floovant* Mahon is brought in on four uprights, 'the old horror (*li vilains*) was very big and deep and square, forged and cast of the finest gold of Arabia, and amply skirted like a pregnant woman'. He is much the same in *Elie de Saint Gilles* clothed in a brown pall and supported by a tree from Syria (a cedar perhaps?). Tervagant in *Andrenas* has big arms and well carved fists. There is an occasional touch of horror, 'their mouths gaping, each seems a devil' in *Aspremont*, and in *Cordres* the idol howls through a serpent's mouth. When the gods are captured and handed over to Charlemagne in *Aspremont*, Tervagant and Apollin and Mahon and 'their comrade Jupin' the victors say, 'don't be afraid, Charles, son of Pepin', and perhaps we should suppose that they did indeed alarm him. The general impression is that they were strange and big, *estranjement estoit gros figurez*, but there is usually little more to it than that, and often there is less.[2]

What does strike us about the accounts of the idols is the splendour of the cult, derived from the great wealth with which the gods were supposed to be endowed. There is an unquestionable admiration for Saracen workmanship, and this extends sometimes to the setting of the gods, but not to the way they are made; perhaps their being made of gold, which the paladins would hope to loot, meant that their value as metal outweighed any other interest. The shining splendour was both valuable and good to look at. 'I am that Mahon who is so much feared . . . have I not greater riches than your god Jesus?' Although the *Chanson d'Antioche* is close to the events it narrates, it is as remote from the semblance of truth as any song of Charlemagne, and this phrase is representative of many such songs: 'everything was of gold and silver, shining and alight'. *Enfances Guillaume* describes recognisably the same scene more fully, 'the best gold in Arabia, green hangings, thirty lamps burning and twenty lanterns reflected from the precious stones, amethyst and topaz, like the light of the sun'. *Barbastre* describes the room in the palace where Mahon is, a fine room and very rich, with its brilliance and rich colour in the pagan taste, the birds that fly by day, the big ones preying on the smaller, painted on one side, the wild beasts on the other, and below the fishes and the traps in which fishermen take them, a room of such great value, gold and blue with so many painted flowers. When *F*loripas in *Fierabras* leads the French into the 'signagogue' in Aigremore, they see the idols, 'each one was made of the finest gold in Arabia'. One of the Frenchmen calculates:

> God! Where does all the gold gathered here come from? There is not so much in all Christendom. God willing, the king of majesty, Richard (of Normandy) could take Jupin to his city, Rouen, and build the monastery of the Holy Trinity; King Charles could take the others into his

treasury, and make his men happy and comfortable with the gold; and the minster of St Peter at Rome, which has been laid waste, would be richly restored with the gold of two of them.[3]

The idols were usually kept in a *mahommerie*, of which the architecture is not described, although it is sometimes just a room in the palace and, whether a room or something more, it may be a vault, *voute*.[4] In the case of the palace room, we must suppose a large oratory – large, because the idols are large. The idols seem more often to be kept put away in the ruler's palace than in an open building in the town, though when we hear of a conquered *mahommerie* turned into a church, we must understand a town *mahommerie*.[5] The words 'synagogue' and 'temple' and even 'temple of Venus' are sometimes used. In *Roland*, Apollin is kept in a crypt. The poet of *Godin*, a late poem of the Huon cycle, makes a genuine effort to paganise, and has the bodies of the dead brought to the temple of Tervagant, where they are buried, while their souls are devoutly commended to Mahon.[6]

In this matter we can be quite sure that there was nothing in any mosque ever captured by the Christians to lend the slightest plausibility to the notion of the idols, despite a few statements in chronicles that they had been found. Chroniclers, like journalists to-day, used the best information available to them usually, but they did not always have very sound information. Refugees or squatters might bring in household objects, but even these are most unlikely to have borne representations that could colourably be described as idols.[7] In any case, it hardly needed a precedent to assume that any religion would need a place for collective worship, and there was already the Christian precedent.

There is some relation between the *mahommerie* and the royal treasure. The idols themselves consist of precious stones and metals, but also treasures are sometimes kept in a *mahommerie*,[8] or Mahon is made to guard the treasure;[9] the treasure may also be separate.[10] Perhaps more significant is the offering of wealth to the god for his favours in war, rather like the ex-votos offered at the shrine of a saint.[11] Might this be a distant reflection of *ẓakāt*, the religious tax in Islam which was collected in principle for charitable purposes, but also when necessary in aid of *jihād*, holy war? We cannot say absolutely, no, because the possibility is not susceptible of disproof; but there is no sufficient reason to think it is. The obvious model for war tax was the Christian, but, though the church paid taxes for wars reluctantly, liturgical treasures and the treasures of shrines were not normally used for this. It is curious that Mahon and his fellow gods were not described as receiving feudal dues and accepting feudal obligations of knight service.[12] The idea of a clergy representing the gods is rudimentary in the poems, and as far as taxation goes, we can only say that a depository of wealth in the *mahommeries* strengthens the concept of gods dedicated primarily to war against Christians, and certainly the Christians considered the idols a prize of war.

These recurring pictures of wealthy idols must have been influenced by the impact of rich church treasures. The poet's imagination can only work on the facts of his experience. The precious stones and rich hangings are detailed and clearly conceived; they give the impression of experience. Everything else about the *mahommeries*, often even the idols themselves, is left vague. The idea that there is a connection between the gods of the Saracens and the European cult of saints has not always found favour, but, without suggesting that there was any obvious theological confusion between god and saint, I think it possible that they should be related as cult objects and liturgical furniture. Where else could the author feed his imagination? Paganism was a void in the mind of the poet, and, when he wanted a clear picture of a scene where idols were present, he could only fall back on the richest and finest cult he knew. For the descriptions of lights gleaming on gold and silver and precious stones there was no other original than the great reliquaries held in many European churches. A scientific review of these, or even a cross-section, would not be appropriate here, but as examples there come to my mind the reliquaries of St Maurice, in the eponymous town in le Valais, and the casket of St Denis in the Louvre; there are many more, and many have been destroyed in the course of time. These glittering structures of finely carved gold are studded with precious stones, as well as images carved or inlaid in coloured enamels. It would not take much imagination to suppose the same thing on an even grander scale. An even closer model may be the reliquaries in human form of which a number dating from the twelfth century survive. The severe looking bust of St Théau at Solignac in Limousin, in gilt and silver on wood, is as intimidating as any idol; and the bust of St Baudime at St Nectaire,[13] in wood covered by copper plates with reliefs in gold, was studded with precious stones. Bernard of Angers was much struck by the statue of St Gerald, count of Aurillac, on the altar of the abbey church he had founded. It was made of 'the purest gold and the most precious stones' and seemed to belong to some ancient cult of 'gods, or rather demons'; rustics would feel that the eyes were watching them, a kindly expression signifying a benevolent reception of their prayers. Bernard smiled and burst out to his companion, 'what do you think of the idol, brother? Would Jupiter or Mars have thought such statues unworthy of them?'[14] He did not say, 'would Mahon have thought such a statue unworthy?'. It was a matter of upbringing. He had had a classical education, and he was not a singer within the convention of our songs of action.

In the poems which make it a Saracen war aim to set up the image of Mahon in the church of St Denis, was the idol to replace the reliquary?[15] There may have been no association of the ideas of 'saint' and 'god', and still have been one of image with image. The Arab world was known to be richer than Europe, and thought to be richer than it was in fact; it was natural for the story-teller just to imagine a greater mass of precious stone and metal than he himself had seen. He had only to multiply his experience. And the poets who describe Mahon as grotesque also had a liberal supply of models carved in stone on the church walls; and scenes of the Last Judgement provided many more examples of hideous, distorted faces. They had only to transfer an image from one setting to another. The humour of grotesque carving went very well with the grotesque humour with which some poets conceived the gods.

THE LITURGY OF THE IDOLS

We come to the liturgical worship of idolatry. Once again, the loss of any tradition of pagan or idolatrous worship left the poets with great poverty of ideas. It is relevant to remember how little convincing detail of idolatrous worship the inquisitors of a later age were able to bring against the Templars, although both torturers and tortured had every incentive to think up something striking. The poets were equally uninventive. Except when the comic side of the gods is developed, their worship is treated with a pedestrian quality of imagination. The cult of saints, largely influenced by folklore, including perhaps genuine survivals of paganism, was much richer and more varied than the tame rendering of the cult of nondescript deities in the *mahommeries*.

The idols kept in town or palace *mahommeries* were brought out in procession on occasions of intercession. The gods were allowed rather more liturgy than theology, but here again the processions in honour of saints and carrying images and reliquaries, and processions for litanies, are a likely source of imagination. One of the most ambitious descriptions comes in the *Chanson d'Antioche*, with its occasional illusory sense of immediacy: Mahon is dressed up and brought forth by more than a hundred acolytes with a great sound of many different musical instruments and loud singing; the pope, apostle (the sultan) waits to adore Mahon profoundly.[16] There is a similar passage in *La Bataille Loquifer*:

> Then he had Mahon carried into an orchard, and he has gone on his knees to thank him, the pagans go there to thank him very much; they insist on making an offering for love of Loquifer, it is worth fully a sixth of a besant'.[17]

'Adoring' no doubt means bowing, kneeling or prostrating, what in Arabic is called the *sujūd*, though the descriptions, even allowing for the nonsense of the images, bears not the slightest resemblance to Muslim prayer. Might there nevertheless be some influence of the authentic Muslim *salāt*? The acts of adoration in the communal Muslim prayer are impressive, and, because all take part, simultaneously and in continuous action, are more striking than any Christian liturgy. But Christian liturgy is quite enough to illustrate what is meant by 'adoration', and *aorer* might mean little more than 'invoke'. There is no clear description of the act in any poem, and we are not likely to get much closer to it than vague references allow. In the *Jérusalem* story, Peter the Hermit 'bowed', *s'inclina*, 'while he thought quite otherwise', a disingenuous act of conformity which is specifically referred to as 'adoration' or 'worship'.[18] In *Aiol*, *M*irabel is told to go to worship Mahon and 'say her psalms to him',[19] a phrase which necessarily excludes any knowledge of the *salāt* but not necessarily observation of it without understanding of what was taking place. In *Enfances Guillaume* the Saracens 'all lie on the ground before him, beat their bodies to pay their respects to him';[20] only part of this is consistent with *salāt*, even cursorily viewed by a stranger. It is most unlikely that it was inspired by the flagellation of Shī‘a worship at Ashūra. As in so many other cases, there is nothing here to convince us of authentic Islamic sources, even distorted.

The descriptions of processions, and perhaps the one in *Antioche* especially, may well owe a good deal to the memory of processions with the relics of great saints. Notions familiar from the psalms may also have reached the poets: 'Princes went before, joined with singers, in the midst of young damsels playing on timbrels'.[21] This relates to the worship of the true God, but it might easily be combined with the thought of 'The idols of the Gentiles are silver and gold';[21] and we have already seen how the concept of a god seems influenced, or even determined, by the existing ideas of God. The bringing forth of Mahon also recalls a modern description of the Indian feast of Juggernaut,[22] but, although it is impossible that a Hindu cult should be the origin of the description, it warns us that all processions of holy statues must be somewhat alike.

Appropriately for gods whose principal function seems to be

to practise ordeal by combat, they are sometimes described as taking part in a military display or march. In *Aspremont* the 'four gods' (the usual three, with *Jupiter le grant*) are carried by the army: 'They carry their four gods before them; each one of them is raised upon a platform'; and to the sound of the drum, 'the Saracens salute them by bowing deeply, and dance and prance'.[23] In *Roland*, they sound the drums, place the idol in the highest tower, pray and worship, and then set out for battle. Later, the amir *B*aligant advances with a standard of two gods and an image of Apollin. He offers the gods new images of fine gold, clearly implying that the god is not the image.[24] *F*ierabras rides into single combat with the image of Apollin on his shield.[25] The 'standard of Mahon' recurs from time to time, and is certainly military.[26] In *Blancandin* the idols are embarked on shipboard for a naval expedition.[27] The dancing before the gods sounds truly pagan, despite the Old Testament precedent; standards and devices on shields are based on Christian practice; there were of course no images on Arab shields.[28]

In *Floovant*, the sons of King Flore, the hero's patron, betray him to the amir, who sends for Mahon. They address the image as *si ber*, and pray, 'Without you we could not talk or boast; we cannot prosper without your favour. We come to speak to you of our father Flore, we come to speak to you about the baronage of France'. The amir makes a rich offering, and a thousand Saracens rise up, and all cry, 'Mahon, lord! receive your due, we are at your will . . .' Then they consult an old, white-bearded Saracen, aged a hundred, and skilled in the law of Mahon; but they are critical of his interpretation of the god's will. This is not the only use of the gods as an oracle. In a few poems the idols are actually manipulated to speak or act fraudulently. The 'sathana' in *Antioche* speaks through Mahon to advocate war. In Simon de Pouille there is a Saracen pontiff, *G*oras, who makes Mahon say: 'I am that Mahon who is so much feared, served and honoured by Turks and pagans; how does it look to you, have I not greater riches than your god Jesus whom you, prisoner, worship ?' The consultation of the god as an oracle is clearer in *Enfances Guillaume*, where the Saracen King *T*ibaut consults Mahon, who advises him to set off with confidence, his adventure will succeed. *T*ibaut makes an offering, which the idol seems to accept. 'A Saracen entered there by such a way that the others did not see him at all'; it is evident that he manipulated the god secretly in the course of a deception, not a shamanistic ritual.[29]

In a general way, the poets make little use of enchantment in the plots, and in their descriptions of the idolatrous cult, the line between enchantment and fraud, or even simple mechanical skill, is a fine one. At a feast of Mahon, the amir of Babylon exhibits a cunning machine – wind blown along a pipe makes the birds sing, on an artificial tree – it is worked by 'nigromancy'; but does the poet mean that? Or, as the word was often used, just vaguely 'magic'; or is this after all only hyperbole for 'highly ingenious workmanship'? This is a toy (*jeus*), not part of the worship proper, but in other cases Mahon is suspended by a magnet, which is also 'enchantment'. Roland associates sorcery with fraud (*ne sorz ne falserie*) as sources of wholly imaginary mosque rites.[30] Magic and great technical skill are not sufficiently distinguished for some poets to wish to commit themselves to which is being used. There does not seem to be a universal poetic convention for the technique of worshipping idols or consulting oracles which are 'engineered', yes, but mechanically, magically or by diabolical possession? There are Hellenistic precedents for the notion of temple frauds, including the idea of a magnet, which could be entertained only by someone with no experience of magnets to tell him that they exert an increasing, not a static, attraction.[31] It is part of the plot to expose the fraudulence of the gods; imaginatively, the poets are trying to represent an alien worship, but not with a certain touch, or with any obvious success. What is the model? A classical oracle? A prophet of Baal? An actual shaman? These are all pagan possibilities, but, if the poet has not made his intentions clear, it is probably because they were not clear in his own mind. The public worship of the gods turns out to be hardly better described than their functions.

There are a few references to aspects of the public cult which do not have to do directly with worship, and which might be thought to reflect an influence of Islam itself. In *Roland* Marsile 'has a book brought before him. It was the Law of Mahon and Tervagant.' It is there to solemnise the swearing of an oath. There is a reference in *Aye* to the *loi escrite* of Tervagant, kept in the *mahommerie*. In *Barbastre* we hear that the Saracens pray *en lor latin*, that is, in Arabic. References to Saracen clergy are not happy; the 'clerks and canons' in *Roland*, the use of *apostle* for a high cleric, but there is the old man in *Floovant* who is learned both in science and in religion, and another old man learned in religion in *Orange*. These two examples of the casual reference that is compatible with the facts are untypical. European travellers contemporary with the songs often identified the qadi as the 'bishop', and this the poets never do, but they are not quite wrong to attribute Saracen leadership to the army. In *Le Charroi de Nîmes* there is a reference to the place of assembly and the law court, but these are not the *mahommerie*, and there is no sign of knowledge of the many uses of a mosque complex. There is nothing that might not more probably be based on purely Christian experience.[32]

THE PRIVATE CULT OF THE GODS

The public cult of saints may have been the model for the public cult of the gods as it is imagined in the songs, but it does not follow that it was the model for private invocation and devotions. The very occasional use of the term 'saint' for Muhammad[33] is probably not significant, though even a slip of the tongue or the pen may reveal a state of mind. So far as the practice and method of individual invocation goes, any influence of the cult of saints can only have been a general one at most. It was customary to pray for the suffrages of a number of saints, so that there would have been no problem about how in practice to imagine reverencing a quantity of numina, whether saints or gods. The war offerings to the gods would have borne some resemblance to ex-votos offered to saints. But this is as far as we can go. People, individuals, families, monarchies and even regions were put under the patronage of individual saints, just as churches and monasteries were. Their legends were known, though these were not always more than distantly relevant to their functions as patrons, even as patrons of sufferers from particular diseases, such as St Blaise for sore throats (he had been beheaded) or Lazarus for leprosy. The saints were highly differentiated and as individuals familiar to their clients in the cult. Nothing like this can be suggested in the case of the Saracen gods; if they had no characteristic functions like authentic pagan gods, they had none like Christian saints either. The language of worship in the poems does not help us to distinguish between the cults of saints and of gods. The poets speak naturally of 'worshipping' both God and saints, and 'worship' and 'adore' equally translate *aorer*; the language did not conveniently allow for the theological distinction between *latreia* and *duleia*. The private cult of the gods on the whole bears out what we suspected when we tried to analyse their theology; it does not resemble the cult of either pagan gods or Christian saints, but rather so many incorporations of a godhead. Although the same terms are used by Saracens to invoke their gods and by Christians to invoke either God or the saints, and by all to swear by any of these, we get the impression that Mahon and his companions are being approached as persons of a godhead. *B*ramidoine's prayer, 'Help us, Mahon, noble king' – *Aiez nos, Mahum, E! gentilz reis* – now our men are beaten and our amir disgracefully killed' has the very tone of a prayer to Jesus.[34]

Religious Feasts

There are a number of references to the feasts of the Saracens, sometimes called feasts of Mahon, but not always: *Une feste fesoit de son dieu Tervagant.*[35] As usual, that god is named who sounds best in the verse. One ingenious author devised a feast of the translation of Mahon, who has been brought to Mecca to lie in a reliquary;[36] this brings us back to the cult of saints as the model. Mahon is conceived here as one of the rich pilgrim-

age saints; but if this really means 'translated to Mecca', could
it be trying to reconcile Islamic fact with Christian fancy, the
flicker of fact that the Prophet was buried in Medina, and that
most persistent error of Christians, that his tomb in Mecca was
the object of pilgrimage? He is 'Mahon de Mecque'.[37] When
Roland, in the late *Entrée d'Espagne* approaches a city and asks
its name, he is told, 'this is Mecca where we go to worship God,
holy Mahon who came to preach to us' and Roland pretends
that he too has come to celebrate (*cellebrer*) Mahon.[38] When
the feast comes, he goes to the 'great temple' (of Mecca!) with
the Saracens, and is able to go apart to pray privately to the
King of Majesty. In the poet's mind the setting is a French
church. Probably something like this is what every poet is
thinking of who mentions a 'feast of Mahon'.[39]

The *hajj* was never understood; its importance in Islam was
not realised, nor was it recognised for what it was. The *ʿumra*,
had anyone known enough to distinguish it, would have been
more sympathetic, and more familiar as a type of pilgrimage,
because, unlike the *hajj*, which has no Christian parallel, it was
(and is) a private devotion made at a time chosen by the
pilgrim. The almost universal assumption that the Prophet was
the sole object of Muslim pilgrimage (and that his tomb was at
Mecca) meant a total failure to appreciate the Muslim
liturgical year. A reference to 'the great feast'[40] would be
perfectly compatible with actual knowledge of Islamic
practices: *ʿīd al-kabīr*, which 'great feast' translates correctly,
is current Arabic usage to-day. But it is not good enough to
establish positive knowledge of the Arabic term; anyone
might happen on so general a phrase. 'Feast of Mahon'[39] might
well refer to *maulid al-nabī*, the Prophet's birthday, rather
than to either of the major feasts; which (if any) were meant,
might depend on whether Mahon was conceived as god or as
saint. The use of these French terms does not prove knowledge
of Islam.

More frequent than feasts attributed specifically to Mahon
are Saracen feasts for occasions as indeterminate as the gods
they celebrated. In most such cases there is no reason for the

listener to think that these feasts are not the same as Christian ones. Occasionally they are positively assimilated to Christian feasts. A reference to Easter 'at the beginning of summer, after which Mahon will be celebrated'[40] clearly links Saracen and Christian calendars, but it is less clear just how it is meant to do so. There can be no permanent correlation between the solar and Hijra years; any Muslim feast may fall about Easter time, but it cannot do so for more than a very few times, the full cycle being almost exactly 33 years. Possibly the poet just thought that paganism must have its own Easter, with some vague memory of pagan feasts of Spring. He is most unlikely to have known the English word, Easter, or, if he did, to have known that it was a pagan word.

Equally ambiguous are references to the feast of St John (the Baptist). Saint John is a Christian feast, but set deliberately at the pagan midsummer, and celebrated both in the Mediterranean and in Germanic Europe. Among explicit references to the Saracen St John's day are in *Barbastre*: 'At the feast of St John we shall adore our gods', and in *Aye*: 'This was the feast of St John the noble (*le baron*), which pagans keep much better than we do'.[41] This pagan commitment to St John is hardly an integral part of the Tervagant convention, but we get the impression that in a minor way it seemed so to a few poets; even so, this whiff of paganism was mediated through the Christian feast. Our suspicions are reinforced when King Ermine in *Bueves de Hamtoune* celebrates Apollin at Yule, but a few more or less isolated cases prove little.[42] We cannot be sure that these references are among the many attempts to show Saracens as pagan; we can, however, note that there are no feasts of those holy men whom Christians, Muslims and Jews all revere, Abraham, for example, Moses, Joseph or David.[43]

SARACEN DISILLUSION

The negative side of confiding in a god of war and offering him treasure for victory is the bitter disappointment of the war-leader when the god lets him down. His disillusion is one of the great comic conceptions of the songs, and one that seems never to have palled. The failure of the gods to deliver the goods is integral to the Tervagant convention; though Saracen disillusion is only one of the ways in which it is emphasised, it is the most interesting.

There is a very good example in *Fierabras*; whenever the amir *B*alan is told of some set-back in the course of his war with the Christians, he promptly blames Mahon. When he fears that the French will get away with his treasure, he threatens Mahon as an ineffective guard: 'when I get hold of him, I'll make him weep; cursed be the god that cannot make himself feared'. *S*ortibrant, his counsellor, tries to correct him: 'he is not to blame if he has gone to sleep; he has stayed a long time awake to guard the treasure. The French are great thieves, that is how they robbed him; this once, good lord, you must forgive him.' The jokes come quickly, comedians' patter disciplined by verse: the gods get tired, the French are thieves, Mahon is treated like a naughty boy. *B*alan becomes increasingly exasperated by Mahon's incompetence. When he hears that Charlemagne has forced the passage of Mautrible and that *A*golafre is dead, he exclaims: 'wretched tired-out god, you are not worth a nut; *F*ierabras did well, when he defected from your religion; anyone who puts his trust in you will be dead and defeated.' But *B*alan's case is not a simple one; he is destined to choose death, rather than desert his feeble ancestral gods. *S*ortibrant again reproves him for insulting Mahon, and the sequence is repeated in similar terms after the Christians break up the idols:

> 'Mahon!', said the amir, 'you are too forgetful; you are fast asleep when you put up with such a disgrace. I have seen the days when your power was great, but now you are too old, it would have been better if you had not been born: you are no help, you are senile.'

*S*ortibrant again objects:

> My lord, you have a bad habit of speaking so contemptuously about Mahon; from the hour he was born there has been no god like him; he gives us abundance of wine and

corn. When he has reflected, he will think of something to do; he is angry with you for knocking him about yesterday, when you broke his nose [*B*alan did this in a rage of frustration]; when his bad temper has worn off, he will deliver the Frenchmen up to you, just you see.

Mahon is brought in to preside over their counsels, and the war proceeds. Much more fun is extracted from the picture of an incompetent old god who can be roundly abused, than from any reminder to the audience that the god exists only in the imagination of the Saracens. The counsellor's protests serve to rub the joke well in. The amir and his crony discuss Mahon is if he were an old guard-dog due soon to be put down.[44]

In this poem passages of frustration and disillusion are exceptionally fully developed, but something of the sort is quite common, and there are regular disillusion scenes: 'he cursed his gods', 'he cursed his god Mahon', 'he fell dying to earth and was stretched out, cursing Mahon his lord'. Often phrases reproach the gods specifically for inefficiency: 'very harshly he blamed Mahon and his powers', 'these gods of ours have given up, they did rotten work at Roncesvaux, they let our knights be killed, and failed my lord in the battle'; 'he! you rotten god, your power is finished' and 'Mahon really is shamed and disgraced'. The charge that the god is sleeping also recurs. 'Mahon, lord, now you are asleep', and '"Mahon!" said *N*asier, "I think you are sleeping"'.[45]

An angry and disillusioned Saracen will go to greater lengths of physical violence against his idols than breaking a nose. There is a maritime variation in *Blancandin*, where Mahon, Apollin and Baratron, embarked on a war vessel, are thrown overboard for failing to quieten a storm. Violence short of total destruction takes on a ritual look when it is offered to the god at the moment of reproach. In *Orson de Beauvais*, the Saracen King *Y*soré 'runs to the synagogue, catches hold of Mahon, he hits him four times on the neck with a stick, "Rotten good-for-nothing god, you are not worth a button!"'. This symbolic little comedy is taken a step further in *Enfances Guillaume*. When the French throw missiles at the god with impunity and

give him 'over a hundred wounds', the Saracen King *Ti*baut
is so shocked that he himself joins in the physical attack on a
god so contemptible that he cannot defend himself. This makes
the Saracen people angry: 'Wicked king, what are you doing,
when you insult and damage our god?' Mahon, he says, is
'dead and overturned'; it is like a liturgical response. So is the
'dialogue' – one of the interlocutors speaks by his silences – in
Elie de St Gille, where the Saracen *M*acabré calls three times
on Mahon. 'Noble and gallant god (*gentieus dieus de boin aire*),
can you do nothing about the impertinent Frenchman who is
provoking you?' Then again, soon after, 'Noble and gallant
god, pay attention to what I want to say about the impertinent
Frenchman who is so greatly provoking you, stop him for me
there!' He threatens the idol's eyes and ears. Finally he says,
'Noble and gallant god, you have betrayed my faith, for the
Frenchman has got away and I shall never catch him'. He
knocks him about and finally knocks him over, and the people
get angry, 'Wretched arrogant king, why do you provoke us,
lay our god so low and punish him?'[46] They make *M*acabré go
and ask the god's mercy a hundred times. In this worship,
turned to abuse and then again reversed, by a disillusioned king
and a believing people, each in turn either honours or dishonours the god in his idol; the reiterated *gentieus dieus de boin
aire* is comic, ironic, yet formal, the key note of a mock ritual
which descends to crude assault.

A comparable passage in *Gui de Warewic* is equally ritual but
is otherwise different; it reads like a case of summary justice.
The sultan pronounces judgment: 'I have given you much
service and done you honour, but to-day you have deserved ill
of me; I will reward you and I will serve you with a stick'. He
will not ask for the gods' help again.[47] Still insulting them, he
breaks them up and throws them out in the mud. Although we
infer that judgement and execution have taken place before the
court, this time we hear no popular protest. But he has not given
up the fight in giving up the gods; he sends as far as the Red Sea
for the aid of every Saracen of wealth or strength. This is an
unusual variant in the theme of disillusion; more often the god

is blamed each time he fails to produce victory, lordship and dominion. As the best illustration of the theme in its more serious vein we may quote the encounter of King *C*alidé with King *U*lien, fresh from the Saracen defeat in the first Aspremont war ('dead is *A*umons, his prowess is gone for nothing') – 'the blessing of Mahon be on you; are the Christians converted to our gods ?': *C*alidé asks eagerly – or is it hopefully ? Or complacently ? Or anxiously ? It is difficult to tell. *U*lien can only reply, 'Our gods have betrayed us; and all their skill and their luck have failed them', and he describes how ten thousand Frenchmen, 'strong and tough (*preux*) and bold' have defeated a hundred thousand picked Saracens, and have then turned their attention to the four gods, which they have passed on to filthy whores to break up. He seems to be piling on the agony; the whores are a new note, the idols were too valuable to be thrown away like that. But '*A*umon is dead, we have all retreated';[48] the failure of the gods is here more serious because the defeat of the Saracen armies, and their own capture and destruction, follow a more than usually serious Saracen threat to Europe.

The worship of idols, liturgically propitiated with offerings before battle, and blamed, rejected and deliberately destroyed after defeat, endorses the conclusions we have already reached about the character of gods who are more than their idols, who are hurt, but survive, when their statues, in all or any of which they are 'incarnate', are broken, or broken up. The implied reference to the prophets of Baal is compatible with the humour which is present, not only in the more light-hearted songs, but also in more serious 'epic' treatment of the war, where it has the rather sour flavour of the Old Testament story itself. Like the original audiences in their time, we may find ourselves sometimes in danger of suspending our disbelief in the existence of these unlucky clownish gods whom ridicule has called into being rather than laughed out of existence. Certainly, the disillusioned believer seems in these poems to think that a real god is really asleep, and that a god who has let his side down can really be punished.

Poets and theologians have this one thing in common, that both set up an antagonist that they can knock down; and the breaking up of statues is hardly more naive than breaking down the arguments that one has oneself imputed to one's opponent. In fact the gods are a sophisticated conception, which we can recognise as soon as we accept the purpose for which they were conceived; they are quite implausible as objects of a serious cult, but not as a part of a story. Each song is the story of a Saracen defeat, commonly symbolised as the failure of the gods, where defeat and failure are each the measure of the other. It is understood that every Christian knows that the gods do not exist, but in practice they enjoy a spurious life, hardly more spurious than that of the Saracens themselves. It is not explained how the Saracens expect a god to help them; no doubt he was to be Providence, and manipulate events, but we need not suppose that the poets had their ideas about this very clearly worked out in their own minds. All that we are told is that he has not influenced events favourably to his followers, and this makes his relations to them clear enough: he embodies their luck. They reject their palladium when their luck fails. Their disillusion is about an inefficient motor in the war machine, and, if the poet leaves them still thinking that the god is just feeble and negligent, rather than that he does not exist at all, this may be because poet and audience have no great interest in this last purely theological point. Even converts seem to imply that the gods they desert exist.

Disillusion has its own ritual, a primitive sacred drama, in which Christians themselves may take part. Before *B*alan's disillusion with Mahon in *Fierabras*, Gui de Bourgogne finds himself in the role of Elijah; when *F*loripas shows the Christian knights the idols, he says sarcastically that their inflamed eyes (which are red jewels) show that they have been sleeping.[48] This is the curtain-raiser to the series of *B*alan's bouts of anger with the god. The whole play of the disillusioned Saracen acquires the character of a counter-ritual. It may be no more than a prayer, like *B*alan's or *M*acabré's complaints, like *D*esramé's at *R*enoart's victory over *L*oquifer, 'O! you diabolical god, your power is finished, when one man alone can put my people to shame';[49] or, when the joke is cruder, and the ritual is extended to actions, the amir who smashes up his own gods makes the same point with greater finality. In either case, the worship is reversed, to mark the humiliation of *la gent Sarrasine*, who earlier bowed in hope and expectation before the splendour of their gods, but now solemnly curse Mahon and Tervagant.

Christian Triumph

Pagan worship of the gods is even more decisively reversed when the Christians seal their triumph by acts of destruction, or sometimes, while the war is still in progress, extend hostilities to the persons of the gods. This is often straight knockabout humour, often less subtle than the passages of Saracen disillusion. It is natural, especially when the gods have been given an important role, that the tension should be released by a scene of destruction. This is something distinct from the Elijah theme. Sometimes it is the Saracens themselves who knock the gods about, in the angry mood that follows disillusion, from which it is distinct, although it is a logical consequence. When Christians do it, of course, it has nothing to do with disillusion; for them, it is an act of triumph, for Saracens, an act of despair.

The most matter-of-fact example of breaking up the gods is in *Roland*, which says simply that the victorious Christians search the town and break all the images and idols in the mosques with iron hammers and axes; it is circumstantial and unembroidered and gives an impression that the authors really did think that there were idols in mosques. *Roland* has always carried conviction by describing its fantasies in matter-of-fact terms, but it has been a false model to which other songs do not quite correspond. Later accounts of breaking up gods are more frankly fanciful; and there is a destruction of the idols, done by the Saracens themselves, earlier in *Roland*, less matter-of-fact but a more influential model. Apollin is grossly abused, robbed, hanged, rolled about and broken up; Tervagant is robbed of a jewel, and Mahon is thrown into the ditch and fouled.[50] Here is the prototype of the confusion of the god with the idol.

We find the sack of a town and of the *mahommeries* in *Barbastre* and also in *Orson*, where the Tervagant and the Mahon are broken up for the sake of the gold and silver.[51] The riches of the idols are closely connected with the notion of loot, which, unlike the discovery of idols, was a fact of military experience. The secular booty which would be expected from a Saracen war is transferred in the songs to this occasion of fantasy, the triumph over the gods. In *Aspremont* the gods are left on the field when King *A*umons' army retreat, and are handed over to Charles; the booty is shared out with a curious attention to detail in the division of the spoils that reveals the triumph it prolongs in the telling – at any rate in one version: an arm to this vassal, a left side to that one, a thigh, a right shoulder, the head, each to named Christian barons. In all versions, Charles says that the profit should go to the knights who do the fighting.[52] A similar account in *Andrenas* is only a little less specific. There is a sharing out, 'to one the leg, to another the sides', but the lucky vassals are not named. In *Fierabras* there is less a division than a self-service. 'They came to a room where Mahon was, with Apollin and Margos, where the gold glittered and each one took his share' (Roland took Apollin, Ogier Margos and Oliver Tervagant).[53] The humiliation of the gods is brought very close to the enjoyment of the loot in this kind of story.

In *Barbastre* it is part of the adventure of war when the Frenchmen break up the gods as soon as they are introduced to them by their Saracen ally *C*larion. Later in the same poem, the experienced *C*orsout, describing the French to King *F*abur's daughter, says, 'Foully was our people invaded and the image of Mahon completely broken up'. In *Enfances Guillaume* the destruction of the gods is even more directly part of the war. Another Christian onslaught on the gods which falls mid-adventure is rather different: *M*irabel, Saracen turned Christian and recaptured by her father, is told to worship the gods, but she knocks them about; and, when the Saracens say 'this lady is mad', she tells them that they can see the god is not alive or kicking: gods lose their power over anyone who is not afraid of them.[54] This is an episode of Christian triumph with aspects of Saracen disillusion, as is the great scene in *Simon de Pouille*, where Goras, the Saracen *apostoile*, enters the idol of Mahon and speaks in a terrifying way. Simon is unshaken and breaks the statue, driving Goras into Tervagant, and, after a similar, briefer sequence, into Apollin; the last blow on Apollin kills Goras. When Goras has seen that Mahon will not 'keep him safe' he has moved to the 'body' or 'person' of Tervagant, in a phrase in which some notion of false incarnation seems to appear at the very point where the fraud is revealed. In another version of *Simon*, the Saracens think that the statue suffered when it was battered.[55]

Another special case occurs in *Moniage Rainouart* and *Gadifer*, two linked poems in which the folk-hero side of Renoart is developed rather than the baron, who is courteous to his opponent and as filial as his father will allow, in *La Bataille Loquifer*. That is not quite right either: it is more that he is an innocent, ignorant of Christian culture. When he and his monks are besieged by hostile Saracens in their King Tibaut's palace, he stumbles across a Mahon, who is guarding Tibaut's treasury, is nearly fifteen 'measured feet' tall, made of the best Arabian gold, and holding a stick in a threatening position. Renoart challenges him, but there is no sort of light there and he 'thinks that this must be a man in the flesh', so that when he gets no reaction, he says angrily, 'You are too sure of yourself (*trop estes fier*) when you will not speak'; he hits him in the face and knocks him down. The fall makes such a clatter that 'certainly it seemed that the palace had been over-turned'; after a bit, he goes on and feels the hard sides of the statue, and 'he knows Mahon by the face and the nose'; to the monks who have come up he says, 'honourable lords, look at the god of the wretched pagans; whoever believes in him must be quite out of his senses: in this god all my family believes'. It is surely not wholly accidental that this poet imagines Mahon as looking, even in the dark, like a man in the flesh, *hom carnés*. This is Renoart's private triumph over Mahon, combined with his public avowal of his family's religious allegiance.

He takes the ritual of triumph a good deal further. He hangs the Mahon from the walls of the palace in which he and the monks are besieged, above the ditches, so that they can urinate on the statue's face, *pour li compisse et la bouce et le nes*; when daylight comes it will upset the Saracens. 'Thrown out in the ditch' is quite a common epic cliché for Mahon and the other gods, though none is quite like this one. That the gods should be subjected to indignities and insults is essential to the Christian triumph, and their humiliation. In the case of *Gadifer*, Renoart is realistic about his hostage, and trades Mahon back as a peaceful gesture; then the Saracens want Mahon to wake up and revenge himself.[56] The poet of *Gadifer* exaggerates the notions of other poets; he supposes that Mahon can be recognised by his features (and apparently still in the dark), and he allows his Saracens to believe that when his idol is grossly insulted, he is asleep, but can be expected to wake up and take his revenge. The fight with Gadifer at the end of the poem is, says Runeberg, *l'une des imitations les plus pitoyables qu'on puisse se figure-, d'un original dont la valeur n'est déjà pas trop grande.*[57] Gadifer *crie, hurle, roule ses yeux*. Yet the line between a poor calque and a good parody is a fine one; and similarly in the treatment of Mahon. That the god is a delusion has never been made clearer, but the Saracen belief in him is delicately balanced between that in an idol who is a god and that in a god who is incorporate in a statue, but exists independently of it.

The episode outside the treasury has a curious parallel earlier in the story, when Renoart is first trying to become a monk. He finds himself alone in the monastery chapel, where he sees a large gilded crucifix. He thinks it is alive, he speaks to it, tries to encourage it to come down and talk to him; then, after speaking to it irritably but politely (*Dist Renoart, vassal, a moi parlez*), he finally consigns it to the devil (*au vif deables soies tu commandé*).[58] This clowning is not simplified, in one version of the text, by the explanation that he takes the crucifix for *home charnel*, never having before seen a crucifix or an altar. The poet is familiar with the story in *Aliscans*, he knows that *R*enoart was supposed to have lived since early youth in King Louis' kitchens; and there is certainly no intention to cast doubts on his Christian allegiance. Ignorance of church interiors is inconceivable in the circumstances, as the audiences will have understood; and no doubt they enjoyed the spoof; but the parallelism between the Mahon and crucifix stories, if it was deliberate, is striking, and is revealing, if it was not. *R*enoart is shown as acting consistently. The joke is that he does not recognise a simulacrum, but this extends in a way to all the Saracens in relation to their gods. One wonders how close the parallel with the crucifix was meant to be.

Summing Up

In his book, *The Overcrowded Barracoon*, V. S. Naipaul describes a visit to the 'chapel' of Martinique Hindus – he puts their 'Hinduism' in inverted commas – and he speaks of 'a degraded form of the degrading *kali puja* which, though Catholic converts, they still practise' in a temple with large figures 'crudely sculptured and painted' – 'the features pathetic in this setting – aristocratic and serene'.[59] That situation cannot compare in essentials with that of Christian authors making up a religion for someone else; but the two have in common the invention-cum-survival of a pagan ritual by people with no very clear idea of what they are doing. The Saracens' images of their gods were not described as crudely made, or poor, or serene: just the contrary; and yet the sense of futility which Naipaul so effectively conveys accords also with the ultimate impression of the gods that we get from the chansons. It is the futility of amateurism; and our highly professional poets are amateur whenever they try to create something that does not interest them, such as Saracen practice of a religion unfamiliar to them. That is why the gods at their grandest seem so futile, and why the descriptions of their public cult seem to be recollections of the public (not the private) cult of saints. The gods are best conceived and portrayed in their humiliation.

The search for Islamic originals of the religious practices

ascribed to Saracens, for reflections of *salāt*, *zakāt*, *jihād*, though not conclusive, is unrewarding. The models are from nearer home. In the European experience reflected in the 'song of action', society was usually at war, and, as a standard was known to rally soldiers in battle, the idols were supposed to rally Saracen sentiment in the stories. When Louis IX off Damietta in 1249 knew that the *enseigne de St Denis* was landed, he straightaway landed himself;[60] and what a right-minded king took seriously made an appropriate model for the imaginary worship of the imaginary god of an imaginary enemy, whose gods of battle are a fragmentation of one way of looking at the Christian God. As for the clerical theory that Islam gave the endorsement of religion to the pursuit of violence, nothing like it in any way occurs to the pagans of the poems, where both sides think alike about the unvarying state of war, and, more to the point, no-one ever pretends otherwise. Rooted in the same violence and the same moral system as Franks are, the gods inculcate nothing that is not normal and acceptable to Christians. The imaginative weakness in their conception inevitably pervades their worship, they are just symbols of conflict. Their wealth, their gold, and jewels and rich hangings only contribute to the Christian store of loot. Ostensibly their function is to ensure Saracen victory, but their true function in the songs is to symbolise Saracen defeat, and this is their true liturgy, upbraided by their own followers and thrown in a ditch by their enemies. The gods excite and amuse, but that is all; after that, the poets' interest in religion goes dead, as if the current had been switched off.

CONVERSION

The reasons that poets give for a Saracen to become Christian look pretty thin, morally and intellectually. They are much more interested in conversion as an event in the course of the story, than in any religious justification. Many of the conversions follow the same pattern, and are without the rational argument that would be considered appropriate nowadays. I do not mean conversion in the sense of a change of heart, such as people experience at a revivalist or charismatic meeting, but in the sense of a change from one religion or sect to another. We think of this as a matter of long and careful thought, painful, often contrary to sentiment; perhaps the prototype is Newman, as Augustine might be of the change of heart. The chansons are concerned with conversion as a change of political allegiance. Although the converts of the chansons de geste and romans rarely explain their new religious conviction, they reverse all their sentiments, their loyalties in particular, from the moment of changing allegiance; so that conversion, however unreasoning, is always total, much as in the case of the worm eaten by a robin in *archy and mehitabel*.[1] It is often the matter of a moment, between two lines of verse, with loyalties reversed in the blink of an eyelid, as if it had never been otherwise.

Conversions rarely have reasons, but they always have a motive; whether there is an argument or not, some explanation is forthcoming. These motives can conveniently be grouped under the headings of threats and bribes; the bribes may be gold, or lordship, or both, often with a woman too, or occasionally revenge for a real or fancied dishonour. A captured

Christian expects to be bribed first, and then threatened; but, though he may be tempted by great wealth to apostasise, Saracen converts to Christianity are also rewarded and do very well for themselves.

The best-known Christianity renegade is Ganelon, who betrays Charles from motives of jealousy, and only afterwards is given a financial reward. 'I want to give you a great quantity of my possessions', says *M*arsile the Saracen King, 'ten mules loaded with the finest gold of Arabia'. The defector's employer wants to make it clear that the motives of defection are sordid, then as now; Ganelon's motives are, however, shown as progressively degraded, with a subtlety lacking in the later accounts of other traitors.[2] Runeberg makes this point in connection with the case of Abbot Henry, in the sequel to *R*enoart's fight with his son Maillefer. The Abbot is a good deal provoked before he slides into treason, and he turns out to be a relation of Ganelon's and, as it were, predestined to corruption. He tells King *T*ibaut, 'I have given up God, I am given over to the Devil; it seems to me that your god Mahon is to be highly valued'; and he tells the monks that there is to be no more singing or matins, he wants no more of that sort of monastery:

> So I believe very heartily in Mahon and Tervagant. I will not deceive you about my plans: beautiful women, fast and frequent. Anyone who refuses is an idiot, so come to an agreement to do the same, otherwise life is finished.[3]

All this is a joke or tease, but it curiously does recall the clerical polemic against Islam as *via lata*, the life of self-indulgence religiously endorsed.[4] The difference is that the clerics contrasted the Islamic rule for all men with the Christian one; the poets here are contrasting what the pagans can offer a convert with the *via angusta*, the life of austerity of the monks, *via angustissima*. In the form of the usual bribe for conversion, the joke is on the monks.

To consider whatever payment a convert receives as a reward for defection is only one way of looking at it. A convert in real life gave up every connection with the society to which he belonged, family, friends, country, and no doubt his new friends must have had an obligation to set him up in a viable position in life.[5] This would be humdrum reasoning for a poem in which there is often an exaggerated offer of women and wealth to a Christian prisoner who seems to expect it, even if he means to refuse it. The classic offer receives a near-perfect expression in *Simon de Pouille*. 'If you will serve and honour Mahon, he will give you possessions and riches, and many well-born young ladies as wives and companions'. Simon is too careful to hurry into martyrdom. He temporises cautiously and receives an earnest of future reward in a fine meal of sumptuous roast peacock with rich wine.[6] A typical passage comes in the fight between *A*goulant and Raimon in *Anseis*; *A*goulant wants Raimon to believe in Mahon, if *A*goulant can take him under his wing; he offers *Esclavonie* in fee, and his sister *G*aiete. Raimon in return offers half Spain on behalf of Anseis. Gui de Bourgogne offers all Spain.[7] These offers are usual in single combats, and such combats occur often. *L*oquifer offers *R*enoart his sister, wide lands and a share in the conquest of the sweet kingdom of France. Such offers are not motivated by fear so much as by an access of good-will and a sense of fellowship between combatants. *R*enoart does not make a counter-offer but spurns the proposal; he values *L*oquifer's words at a straw, and the gods at a hanged dog.[8]

The bribe and the threat may be linked. When Guillaume is offered a choice between joining profitably in the conquest of France and being hanged like a thief, he replies, 'Glous! May the Body of God harm you! You shall not kill me for all the gold in Besançon'.[9] It is typical of him, as so many poets conceived his character, that he should refuse the first horn of the dilemma by denying the feasibility of the second. We also find a threat standing alone as an inducement to apostasy, as when a Saracen says, 'Give me the Frenchmen into my charge' (they are prisoners) 'I will take them to Ireland, my town (sic), and make them worship Mahon and his idols'.[10] This menace adds excitement, our flesh ought to creep. A poem, not one of the earliest, about Aymery, progenitor of so many sons, gives an example of a classic response to the threat. He is captured, he is badly wounded and very weak (as well as very old); all he wants is to get his strength back, to be able to go on fighting. 'If you will adore Mahon, you will be healed and recover', they tell him, an offer nicely adjusted to the character and the situation. He refuses, of course, and they prepare to torture and burn him before the walls of his own city (by capture), Narbonne. Inflexible, he calls up to Ermenjart, his wife, on the walls above, 'Don't give up the city, whatever the Saracens say to you; let them burn me.'[11] In *Jourdains de Blaivies* and other poems, the captured Christians are threatened with prison or death if they will not adore the gods.[12]

The story-teller is simply interested in the adventures of his heroes, including their temporary misfortunes at Saracen hands, and at the end of each campaign likes to demonstrate how complete the victory is. He gives the impression therefore that the Saracens concentrate on bullying or buying the Christian elite, when they get hold of them, and that the Christians baptise or behead entire populations as they conquer them; but there is not much in it. Christians make short work of captured amirs who will not accept baptism, and a conquered Christian population expects ill-treatment or death. Each side offers the other in turn the carrot and the stick. Charlemagne sends the same sort of ultimata as he receives. His messenger repeats: 'he commands you by me that you agree to give up Tervagant and Mahon'. He can also be persuasive in person: 'deny Tervagant and Baraton and believe in the Lord God', he pleads; and, in a friendly way, 'Let me hear your voice. Do you want to go on fighting? . . . Friend, give up Mahon . . . I will straightaway give you this kingdom' (the kingdom of the Saxons).[13] Others make similar offers on his behalf; we see Anseis, who expects to stay there, offer half Spain; Gui de Bourgogne, who did not, offered all of it for a conversion.[14] In *Aspremont*, *A*umons, in his duel with Charlemagne, offers to make it worth his opponent's while if he will deny Lord God; this is before he knows who he is; afterwards, as Charlemagne says, he who wins the fight will get the vast lands in dispute, effectively all of continental Europe.[15] The bribe at best resolves itself into an offer of feudal subordination; it is an invitation to a disguised and honourable defeat, whichever side it come from.

Dishonourable defeat is conversion under the threat of death. There is not a great deal of difference between Christians and Saracens in their treatment of prominent individuals, but there is some in their treatment of whole populations. Christians overrun by Saracens suffer enslavement and devastation, a fair enough summary of what the Saracen invasions of France and Italy looked like to their victims, and perhaps a genuine historical memory. Saracen populations are treated rather more drastically in poems than they actually were, at any rate immediately after conquest. The poet of *Aymery de Narbonne* describes with appropriate relish the massacre of Saracens as the city is captured, as well as the looting of gold and silver from the mosques.[16] At the capture of Conibres, in *Orson de Beauvais*, all the Saracens are killed, except the 'beautiful and distressed' girls who are willing to accept baptism.[17] At the *Prise de Pampelune*, the defeated populace are quick to demand baptism on terms reassuring if not flattering to Charlemagne, who is in fact pleased that they do so before he exacts it.[18] In quite a different story about a capture of Pamplona, all the Saracens who 'do not want to believe in God' are killed, but those who accept baptism 'do not lose 4 pennyworth' of their property.[19] When *G*anor becomes Christian, his people must do so too, or he has their heads off.[20] Normally followers of Tervagant and Mahon get this choice between the font and the axe: conversion is a Christian war aim, completing subjection, and it is taken for granted rather than proclaimed, but apparently exacted (unless the poet forgets to tell us about it). The Saracen supporters of Maillefer, after their defeat, 'pagans in abundance' (*paien aplenté*), 'who would be baptised and blessed; they had escaped from the battle, and so they wanted to accept holy Christianity, and with one accord because of that to worship God'. Their fear was not without cause, considering the order that had been given: 'go and cut all their heads off, if they do not want to be baptised'.[21]

Both fear of death and desire of gain are closely connected with the great theme of the poems, the victory of Christian armies or the success of a Christian adventurer. The fate of the people generally, Saracen and even Christian, is in the background. Heroes occupy the foreground, and cannot be afraid. They sometimes bide their time with prudence, like Simon de Pouille who waits for the convenient occasion to break up the gods; and, in their different ways and for different reasons, both Peter the Hermit in *Antioche* and Roland in *l'Entrée d'Espagne* bow down like Naaman in the House of Rimmon. These episodes are, however, concerned with outward forms that have nothing to do with true conversion; as is the case also when a pagan ruler offers to be converted, as a diplomatic ruse.[22] Heroes are also not seriously tempted by offers of gain, which their prowess is going to obtain for them anyway. In answer to the challenge: 'Have you ever seen a god so fine and so rich (as Mahon)? – He gives me whatever I ask for', Elie says that he would take the idol if he could and break it up to pay the soldiers.[23] This is a variant on the usual smashing of the idols theme, and reminds us that paladins have nothing to gain from Mahon, from whom they propose to take everything. The only adequate reason as the poets see it for a Christian to turn pagan is in order to avenge himself. The rest of this chapter looks at examples that justify our hoping to extract interesting motives for conversion from the words or the actions of the convert, in almost every case, Saracen converts to Christianity.

POLITICAL CONVERSIONS

Some of the more plausible conversions are, at least in their setting, political. Otinel, the aggressive Spanish ambassador to Charles who fights Roland, and jeers at Roland for wanting to convert him, is anti-Christian; but after Charles has prayed, the Holy Ghost descends 'and moves his heart by Jesus' command'. Otinel and Roland embrace, and Otinel gets Charlemagne's daughter, the bribe he had already refused when Roland offered her (Belisant is Roland's cousin as well as the King's daughter) and it is still Roland who presses the marriage on the King. The miracle, in poor taste, and even poorer as theology, is unrelated to any action of Otinel's. The poet ensures that he does not actually marry his affianced until he has proved himself a *preux franc chevalier* in the later course of the poem. However much we analyse the different aspects of the story, the sole stated reason for the original conversion remains the miracle. The rest of the poem is the story of Otinel's acculturation, and in that sense of his true conversion. He has not lost face over the manner of his conversion in the first place, and he boasts to his Saracen enemies, as they have now become, 'Charles the King has given me Lombardy, and Belisant, beautiful and shapely; I'll never love a pagan in my life'.[24]

Something like a miracle works another face-saving conversion in *Blancandin et l'Orgeilleuse d'Amour*. Blancandin forms a close friendship with a Saracen king's son, Sadoine, and they go off together on an adventure of war and conquest. Their ship rides into a bad storm, and the gods that they have embarked with them prove unable to save them. Prayer to the Christian God stills the storm, though realistically not until they are off course, and they jettison the gods. The episode is not much stressed. It is a convenient way of getting an obstacle out of the way of the friendship of the two heroes, a popular theme in itself, and part of the political setting of the story. The poet has found a dignified, and in his opinion plausible, way of converting the hero's friend; in so far as this propounds a reason at all, it is that the gods fail to protect, the theme of Saracen disillusion as we have seen it. Sadoine has a lover, and she too becomes Christian, but only by way of her attachment to him.[25] Conversion here is to make a group of active characters cohere. Sadoine in some ways resembles Synados, in *Simon de Pouille*. Defeated in a skirmish, Synados is depressed about the massacre of his men, and decides that Mahon is not worth a penny. He becomes Simon's invaluable and even irrepressible ally, to all intents and purposes another Frankish knight, with the special advantage of knowing the enemy and his language. His lover, Licoride, in the rôle usually the hero's lover's, is converted for love, but with a show of reason, by a thumbnail creed.[26] Most change of religion springs from the now familiar disillusion with Mahon because he has failed to give victory.

An even more improbable political convert is *B*randoine in *Maugis d'Aigrement*; he is the son of the Christian Queen Ysane, Maugis' mother's sister, and the *preux* and valiant King *A*quillant, now dead. He and Maugis exchange insults, and, as usual in these cases, offer, or threaten, the conversion of the other. 'Give up Mahon, who is not worth a penny, and all those bad gods who cannot help you' – 'I would let my limbs be cut off my body before I would give up or deny Mahon or Tervagant or Jupin, so worthy of esteem, for your clumsy God, who is not worth a penny'. But in this case we do not need to reach the point of disillusion; when honour is satisfied by a few bouts, Maugis tells *B*randoine that they are cousins, and *B*randoine replies, 'Cousin, say no more, I will do it straight-away for your friendship's sake. For love of the family relation-ship, Mahon shall be given up and denied by me, and so I will believe in God who was crucified'. For those audiences family ties and the solidarity of the kin were motives more credible than they have become to-day. *B*randoine's people are of course baptised too, and 'those who did not want to do it had their heads chopped off', as usual.[27]

*G*anor's conversion does not follow the usual pattern. Its frankly romantic motive is very striking ('Ahy! Mahon, rich god of strength, Margot and Apollin and Jupiter also, give her to me for wife by your abundant grace, and I will seek no other paradise'); he could not make it plainer that he is happy to reject his religion at the same moment as he confidently prays to his gods. Whether we are meant to take his motives seriously, the results are more remarkable still; after he is baptised, his conversion turns out to be as political as anyone's, as he takes part in Aye's family feuds as the friend and ally of his stepson, Gui de Nanteuil.[28] In one version of the sequel to *Aye*, 40,000 of *G*anor's subjects who have somehow escaped alive and pagan from their master's font turn Christian for love of Gui,[29] a more dignified reason than fear, but also one that further emphasises the commitment of *G*anor's Saracen world to European feudal politics. Ellen Rose Woods has related *Aye* to the current development of feudal society,[30] but we are concerned here with the simple basic point that an apparently arbitrary and very personal conversion immerses *G*anor and his people in a particular political situation. But I do not think the poet supposed that there was any difficulty in acculturation; and in this little group of poems *G*anor is after all not in fact unique: *G*randoine, amir of Iconium in *Gui de Nanteuil*, holds Charlemagne's niece, Flandrine, in his prison, but is happy to turn Christian to gain her consent to marry him.[31] This gentlemanly behaviour, like *G*anor's when Aye is in his power, but not free to marry him, was doubtless meant from the first to seem improbable, but perhaps only as much as it would in the case of a Christian lord. The feudal nexus is more important than the religious allegiance.

The theme of the Saracen client king, intelligible in the context of *Reconquista*, makes an appearance in some stories set in Spain. *B*audus of Balaguer in *Guibert d'Andrenas* is convinced by his own defeat that Christianity is true, and a practical allegiance to adopt, and it is interesting that he insists on rescuing his wife and having her baptised too.[32] In this case the sequence of defeat, disillusion and conversion is less a personal problem than an effective political manoeuvre. He would have been more useful to the Christians as their client king if he had remained Muslim, that is, he would have, if the Saracens of the poems had really been Arabs and Muslims. In *Prise de Cordres* the parallel character *B*aldus acts as Christian ambassador to King *J*udas of Seville, his uncle, who naturally challenges the renegade in an uncomfortable encounter. He explains his story and his motives very simply. 'My wife and I could not escape; I could not hold out against the French, and so I had myself taken to the font and baptised'[33] – an explanation which would commend itself (if it were not fiction) to no theologian, whatever his faith; but in our convention it is acceptable to both sides.

Although Saracen society resembles Christian society so closely, it is not suggested that there are normally social links between the two. There is an exchange of opinions, also in *Cordres*, between a pagan king, *G*alerian, who is trying to recover the captured aumaçor, and *N*ubie, the aumaçor's daughter. 'Why have you rejected our religion?' he asks, rather politely ('demoiselle Nubie'), and names Saracen women who have stayed Saracen; 'you are cutting yourself off from the company of your father and from all our pleasures'. She answers sharply, 'Damn your company! Because of you certainly I have left Cordova, and I shan't go back there all my life; but I pray God, the son of St Mary, that I might have you again in my power; you would not last long if I had'.[34] He is surely appealing to her memories of a circle of family friends, and she is asserting her new allegiance, not subtly, but at least plainly.

Another straightforward case of political conversion is Clarion in *Barbastre*. He considers that he has been unjustly robbed of his lands and rights by his Saracen feudal superior, and he is looking for a chance of restitution. He turns to the Christians because they will give him a better feudal superior – Bueves – and he changes his religion almost as a matter of course.[35] In *Anseis de Cartage*, Charlemagne has left Anseis to rule Spain, and Ysoré to advise him, but Anseis allows himself to be seduced by Lutisse, Ysoré's daughter. Ysoré is driven distracted: 'I am disgraced, and will no longer seek God or love Anseis my lord', he says; 'I will go to King *M*arsile' (the Saracen) 'I will leave God and follow Mahon'.[36] Together they nearly destroy Anseis, and their story is shown as tragic rather than reprehensible, so well is the motif of the disloyal lord understood. A feudal dispute in which the poet seems to have some sympathy for both sides occurs also in *La Prise de Pampelune*. *M*alceris, the defeated ruler of the city, becomes Christian and wants to be admitted to the fellowship of the *douze pairs*, which is refused. He has a son *Y*sorié, who becomes Christian at the same time. *M*alceris reverts to his old allegiance to King *M*arsile, and to the gods he had deserted, Mahon and

Tervagant, while *Y*sorié remains 'loyal' and, as well as fighting on the Christian side, gives Roland useful military information about the Saracen fortifications. At the moment of decision, *M*alceris and his son are in bed in the same room, within hearing but not sight of each other, and *Y*sorié hears his father soliloquising aloud as he reflects that he has deserted the gods and the king (*M*arsile) who has done so much for him, given him his sister as wife, by whom he has had his son, *vailant et preus*, *loiaus e avenant*. He has left the king who honoured him, for a king who gives him neither honour or reward. His history seems to give the lie to all the offers of reward for conversion. His crisis of conscience, with its mixed bundle of motives, evokes the poet's sympathy for what is undeniably a great offence: 'Neither young man nor greybeard can trust you, because you abjured both Mahon and Jesus Christ'.[37]

There are varying degrees of sympathy and understanding for Saracens who refuse conversion (we shall see some cases in greater detail later) or even who revert to paganism. *M*arsile himself, in *Anseis*, is offered safety by Charlemagne at the price of conversion. He asks what the various courtiers do; seeing their wealth, he refuses to desert his own gods for a God whose 'messengers', the poor, are neglected. 'I prefer to have my head cut off'.[38] The same story is told in other contexts,[39] and is, of course, in principle a common theme of medieval satire; but in this homiletic satire on Christians, the part of the Saracen in it is to sharpen its point. Quite a different case is that of *G*uischard, a converted Saracen and *G*uibourg's nephew, who is wounded at the great battle of the Archamp, where Guillaume has promised to keep an eye on him. *G*uischard does not want to be treated for his wounds, but just helped on to his horse and given something to drink. 'Then I will go off to Cordova where I was born. I will no longer believe in your Lord God, for I cannot worship what I cannot see. If I had prayed to Mahon I would not have had these wounds in my sides.' Of course Guillaume will not help him to do a thing like that; he is embarrassed for *G*uibourg's sake. He pulls *G*uischard up in the saddle and a Saracen immediately cuts him down.[40] The argument, 'I cannot worship what I cannot see' perhaps sheds a little more light on the way the poets envisaged the worship of idols. The nostalgia for one's native land is treated sympathetically. As always, the competition of two gods who fail or succeed is taken for granted.

There is another and rather different class of Saracenised Christian. In *Raoul de Cambrai*, Bernier claims the supposedly Saracen *C*orsabré from King *C*orsuble, who is under an obligation to him. *C*orsabré is really Bernier's own son Julian, kidnapped as a boy and brought up as a Saracen. Both sides accept it as reasonable that a born Christian, brought up as a Saracen, would deny the pagan gods; *C*orsuble is happy to discharge his obligations so easily.[41] Had Saracens really been Muslims, such a thing would have been out of the question. Although the poets are unforgiving to Christian traitors, such as Ganelon or Macaire (*Aiol*) 'who denied God and turned to Mahon', they do not seem worried when Christian-born children are brought up as Saracens; there is at any rate nothing that a straight war cannot put right for a *G*odin or a *M*aillefer, both of whom, of course, by blood were half Saracen; and both cases are modified by magic. Finally, the poets who know that in the end these people will return to the Christian faith have no need to concern themselves too much. Yet their conversion is much the same as that of any Saracen amir, and it is surely a little strange that their early Saracenisation is taken so coolly. When Godin is lost to his kidnappers, the child's father, Huon, comforts the wretched mother by telling her that 'the Father Redeemer wills it so', while fortifying her resignation by the thought of Godin's future greatness as a king of Babylon, that is, as a prominent Saracen ruler.[42] The case of Isembart, a traitor like Ganelon, is quite different, but he too is allowed to repent, and in the surviving fragment we leave him lying on the grass, *sor la fresche herbe*, praying, 'have pity on me, Father, God . . .'[43]

'Political' conversions are distinct from the usual pattern of reward and threat and disillusion only in being given a more convincing social context, but they may vary greatly from case

to case. *O*tinel's conversion is arbitrary, but its material rewards
are substantial. The converted Saracen ally is the most plausible, in that he reflects however imprecisely the pattern of
Mediterranean politics; unconverted, such allies would be
wholly credible. It is into this same pattern that we must fit
those who change sides and even change again, whether they
do so for bad reasons or good ones, for motives sympathetic or
otherwise; they come as near as possible to recognising the
unitary nature of Mediterranean culture, not only in games and
sports, in sexual and war-like activities, but even up to a point
in religious allegiance. The whole business is shown to be most
business-like, however, in the Scottish burlesque of the
fortuitously knighted collier, *Rauf Coilyear*. As he rides back
from Charlemagne's court to the moor where he lives, he meets
an enemy: 'Ane Knicht on ane Cameill come cantly to hand'.
They fight because they are knights and without pretext, and
Rauf is the more delighted to discover a pretext after all, when
the enemy knight turns out to be a Saracen, as he might have
suspected from the presence of a camel on a North moor.
Roland comes up, and he does not interfere in the battle, but he
does try to persuade the Saracen ('Sir *M*agog') to give up his
faith in Mahoun ('Fy on that foull Feind, for fals is thy fay') and
marry a rich Christian duchess:

> Wed any worthie to wyfe, and weild her to win,
> Ane of the riche of our Realme be that ressoun.

Sir Magog does not think that the financial offer, the 'Grassum',
is enough:

> Thy God nor Grassum set I bot licht;
> but gif thy God be sa gude as I heir the say,
> I will forsaik Mahoun, and tak me to his micht.[44]

The author of the burlesque misses nothing in the convention,
neither the girl, nor the profit nor the choice of a winning god.
The change of allegiance is advantageous, without other
motivation; this is common to many different sets of fictional
circumstances, and the arbitrary decision, or choice of moment

to decide, in the Scottish joke brings this point home to us again.

THE HEIRESSES

The pattern of conversion of the heiresses is a special one. We might have expected that those daughters of amirs who fall in love with Christian barons, for whose sake they deceive and desert their fathers so unscrupulously and with such enterprise, would have had or at least claimed substantial grounds for changing their religion, something persuasive that carried conviction. Far from it; here again religion was the side you belonged to, not a state of mind or an opinion, and their reasons for changing religion are just their reasons for betraying their fathers to their lovers. In their case, more clearly than in any, religion is allegiance. They change allegiance because they fall in love, but their falling in love is arbitrary and explained only by their seeing the hero in battle or riding by, or even just by hearing his reputation.[45] This may be enough for falling in love, but it is too little to persuade us that a total change of allegiance is reasonable. Once more, we are dealing with a convention, not with realistic fiction. The heroes' ability to attract the girls physically seems to spring from a predisposition in the girls in which the change of religion is certainly not a primary motive.

Guillaume and the other sons of Aymery illustrate this in the songs devoted to one or another of them. In his conquest of Andrena, Guibert gets the usual help from the king's daughter, Gaiete, who has the singular honour of saving Aymery himself. She slips almost imperceptibly into Guibert's arms, and even more so into the Christian faith, although she is not named among those who receive baptism after the Saracen defeat. Malatrie in *Bueves de Commarcis* is a little more intelligibly motivated; she has been captured by Girard, which makes her falling in love with him plausible. She is recaptured, but in her allegiance she has defected for love: 'for Girard her heart is very sad and disturbed' and she wishes she had become Christian 'for her heart was entirely given to God'. The poet emphasises her sincerity; when later she is able to send Girard a message, she begins by saying that she believes in God, who created the world and with his body redeemed sinners, and only then goes on to the immediately practical part of her message. Yet, for all the poet's display of her sincerity, her conversion is strictly a matter of her marriage to Girard. She illustrates another interesting point when she slips straight-away and apparently without any instruction into Christian theology (*pecheours racheta*).[46] It occurs to few poets to wonder how a Saracen would acquire such knowledge. The author might credibly have made her confidante, *F*landrine, a Chris-tian, say a Mozarab, but he takes familiar knowledge for granted and does not think what links there might actually be between Saracens and Christians – another indication among so many that the Saracens of the songs are not meant to be real Saracens.

The *M*alatrie of *Le Siège de Barbastre* shows little interest in Christian religion and a great deal in Christian knights. The poem ends with the baptism of most of the Saracen cast, and it is as a reward for Christian gains, including much rich booty, which she has prompted, and for the conversion of the Saracen prisoners, among whom is her father the *amustant*, that King Louis awards her in marriage to Girard, whom she has desired, night and day, for the last month. Once again, plenty of bapt-ism, no fuss, no objection, and we get the impression that every-thing will go on much as before. An outstanding contrast and exception is the short passage near the end of *Roland* in which *B*ramidoine, Queen of Spain and *M*arsile's widow, is taken prisoner by Charles to France, where he wants her to be con-verted by love; and when finally she has heard 'so many sermons and edifying stories that she wants to believe in God and be christened' she takes the name of Juliana 'and is a Christian by true knowledge'.[47] This insistence on willing conversion and proper instruction is just what is usually most obviously lacking, although pressure exerted along those lines became the normal and preferred clerical pattern for subject Muslim peoples.[48]

In another poem of the Aymery group, *Prise de Cordres*,

*N*ubie, the wily, is also given this mixture of motives, love and religion; she will receive baptism for love of 'God the son of Saint Mary', but expects to get Bertrand, the hero, in return. Her story is complicated by her relations with *B*aufumé, who might have come under the heading of 'political', and who is her liegeman, totally devoted and bound to her. From the age of seven he has wanted to adore the Lord God, but not dared to show this in public. It is once more thought unnecessary to explain how such a Saracen might come to have this wish or acquired the knowledge from which it could derive. Whatever his reason, he is put forward as a spontaneous and disinterested convert; but in the course of the story he develops an interest, as *N*ubie, without whom he will not act, opens up to him the possibility of a career as a Christian baron. Although his baptism is deferred to the end of the poem, he acts, and the Christians treat him, as a Christian knight. When he is captured by the Saracens, his danger as a renegade is no less than he has feared: 'God, do not let me go back to my religion!'; but not only is he rescued, but *N*ubie's father is captured in his turn, and pressure is put on him to agree to *N*ubie's union with Bertrand. He gives way, and all are baptised. *B*aufumé does not have to change his name, but he does have to be dubbed knight again in the French way, *à la françoise guise*, and so completes his acculturation. The one poem offers three cases each with its own motive, *B*aufumé's long-standing conviction, *N*ubie's falling in love, her father's surrender to pressure. He is not shown as afraid; but he accepts the decision of Aymery, to whom he appeals as his feudal superior, since he is now in his *baillie*. Both as aumaçor and as prisoner, his principles are authoritarian, So, too, in *Barbastre*, 'The amustant was baptised, and without resentment, and he took the name of Aymery, for love of that open-hearted man', as others in the story take the names of Guillaume and (for the King) Louis. Religion could hardly be more feudal, and yet all these conversions proceed from the sexual enterprise of the girls, and political motivation follows in its wake.[49]

Another case of a converted royal daughter is that of

*M*augalie in *Floovant*, 'son of Clovis' the Merovingian. Yet again the heroine helps the hero out of captivity and asks to become Christian, but the plot is more complex than that. There are two heroines, of which one, Florete, is a Christian anyway; and there is more *traison* than usual, because her brothers betray Floovant and his squire Richier to *M*augalie's father. Still more unusual, the two heroines are competing for Floovant's love. He considers himself bound to *M*augalie (not with any apparent regret), but she is prompt to promise conversion, responding perhaps to the competitive stimulus, and Richier gets Florete.[50] As well as giving some sort of hereditary claim to her family lands, for which it is only a necessary but incidental preliminary, baptism is the means of entry into Christian society at least as much as a religious exercise. Anseis too has two lovers, and, though his case and Floovant's are different, there is something common to them; he sleeps with Lutisse, and so dishonours her father, Ysoré, who defects; he steals *G*audisse, King *M*arsile's daughter, no doubt to strengthen his hold on Spain; and their marriage is given a romantic respectability by their mutual physical attraction, the description of the charms of her body, her admiration for his style in fighting: 'I will take holy baptism for you'. The story illustrates clearly how baptism is the initiation of a socially and politically acceptable heroine into a new world, but not primarily in a religious sense. The daughter of a noble adviser, though Christian already, is ineligible on more important grounds than religion. Baptism is a ceremony of acculturation likely to be its primary function also in the many other cases that blend sex and inheritance, though it is not always equally obviously so. *M*arsile's widow in the same poem enters Christendom in the same way; no sooner is his head off than she is baptised and allotted a suitable husband; so too with the queens in *Aspremont*. *R*osamonde, who is not allowed to marry Elie for whose sake she has been baptised, might feel her baptism to be a cheat, especially since it is the spiritual relationship now obtaining from his sponsoring her in the ceremony that has prevented the marriage; but Guillaume and the other barons feel that she has a right to marriage and quickly find her a suitable husband. It is marriage, not love, to which she has an admitted right, and her baptism as well as her social position entitle her to it.[51]

That baptism was an entry into Christian society does not of course mean that it was not taken seriously as the first of all sacraments, but the devout life did not dominate European ways in the poems. Moreover, if baptism as an admission ticket to Europe was only a form of conversion by offer of reward, there remained also baptism by threat. *Roland* is exceptionally tender of Bramidoine's convictions, because happily she was easily convinced of Christian truth; there is no suggestion that any other conviction would have been tolerated. The threat to the men who refused conversion on either side was death, or, in some cases of Christians, privation and imprisonment; for women, it seems to be implied that it was most often enslavement. The Arab raids on Europe in the early Middle Ages did take great booty in the form of prisoners,[52] and if the chansons reflect this, then their hints would be consonant with a European supposition that the men were wanted to be put into prison and the women as concubines for the harem, in the romantic nineteenth century sense. Doubtless both were wanted in fact for any segment of the labour market, but there is no suggestion of realism, only this vague reflection of a folk memory of prisoners taken, and figured in Ysané, Maugis' kinswoman, in Aye, or in Aelis in *Bataille Loquifer*.[53] But there is no firm indication in the fiction of any pressure exerted on Christian girls that was not exerted on *Sarrasines*; certainly Sebille in *Saisnes* expected to be carried off and baptised. In *Daurel et Beton*, least realistic of songs, Erimena is happily disposed of in marriage by her father, the friendly amir of Babylon, even at the price of baptism, her conversion forced, in fact, by a Saracen gesture of friendship.[54] The Christian women captives mostly escape their dilemma, but the compliant Saracens are really in no different case from the enterprising heroines who seek what the others just accept: by their baptism they enter Western feudal society.

When the traditional themes are modified by a more personal approach, it is the credibility of the political setting that is most affected, as by the magical influences in the *Huon de Bordeaux* group. As to baptism, Huon turns the screw by piously refusing to have sexual relations with a pagan; in so doing he is conforming to canon law,[55] but some might say, degrading baptism even further. When *E*sclarmonde gives him her allegiance and rescues him from her father's prison, he is willing to anticipate her baptism; it is Oberon who forbids them to do so, and imposes various misfortunes on them for copulating impatiently.[56] If we were to take Huon's motives seriously, we might suppose that he thought her consent to baptism good enough, or we might think that he refused only so long as he needed to stimulate her into helping him escape. In any case, this is only a variant on the theme of conversion for love.

Occasionally heroines take part in arguments about religion of a kind which is, we shall see, more often met between men who are fighting each other. *M*irabel in *Aiol* has in common with *E*sclarmonde that the hero of the poem, pious, honourable churchgoing Aiol, wants to make love to her, and would if she were christened, but he does not want to shame the law of Jesus by doing so sooner. She is little short of crazy when she hears this – *por poi que n'est dereves* – but first just replies, 'I have not thought about it'. She does think quickly and says: 'The religion of Mahon will never be disgraced by me, I would rather be killed'; she even has good religious reasons: 'For Mahon is my god, and he administers great justice; and he who trusts in him is afraid of nothing'. Aiol tellingly ripostes, 'Mahon be damned and anyone who trusts in him! For his powers are not worth a rotten apple'.

*M*irabel picks this controversial style up from him. She is baptised, she does marry him, but her father recovers her, and wants her to return to the worship of Mahon. Staunch to her new faith, she cries, 'Let me go! When you force me to worship him, it fills my heart with fury about it', and she herself starts to break up the idol. When her father says that she will suffer for this, she answers, 'How can such a useless thing help you?

Anyone who has no fear of it makes it lose its powers', an argument curiously psychological that evokes the whole disillusion theme. *Y*doine in *Enfances Renier* finds herself in a similar predicament, and her father has already stoked the fire for her; he is particularly upset that she should believe in anything so silly as a god whom the Jews put shamefully to death. Perhaps *G*aiete puts the logic of heroine conversion when she is afraid for the safety of Guibert. He assures her confidently that the event will show which religion is the richer, but she, when she prays, warns 'God who made sea and wind' that he must strengthen Guibert's powers, or she will no longer believe in him.[57] When there is discussion at all, it is about which God is the strong one; but often heroines see no need to discuss what is only the ticket to a good feudal marriage. Whatever motives, ostensible or hidden, there may be for wanting marriage, marriage is the motive for conversion, and the only problem is, as usual, between God and gods to choose the winner.

Two Family Groups

We have looked at the families of *F*ierabras and *R*enoart before, and in their conversions they are interesting also. These two are certainly among the most striking of the defectors. In the one case there is only the pair, *F*ierabras himself and *F*loripas his sister, to discuss. The single-minded *F*loripas naturally makes no bones about adopting the religion of the knight she means to marry (and why she means to marry him we must infer from a variety of possible motives). 'I have loved a knight of France called Guy of Burgundy, from a distance ... for him I will believe in the king of holy majesty'. She consistently subordinates everything to her marriage plans; she has her governess thrown into the sea, and she cannot wait for Charlemagne to execute her father. Like so many, but more unambiguously than most, she has no religious reason for her conversion, and is quite certain about her priorities. *F*ierabras is in rather a different case. At the beginning of the song he is a terrorist, destroyer of Rome, pillager and violator of the innocent, thief of the Crown of thorns. Once he is satisfied that his opponent

is of noble status, he and Oliver fight in an increasingly comradely way that is characteristic of such scenes. Each makes
his position clear: 'You will lose your head, if you don't believe
in God', Oliver warns his enemy, who in turn presses Oliver to
give up his native faith, marry *F*ierabras' beautiful sister (presumably this means *F*loripas) and share with him his invasion
of France. Oliver replies, 'You are talking nonsense. I shall not
give up God, nor his honoured saints . . .' and throws in also
that he could not believe in gods you can chuck into a ditch like
a dead dog. *F*ierabras calls this démesuré, which the language
certainly is, though usual enough, and the argument, that the
god is powerless, is the invariable one.

There is a kind of divine intervention, but it is not part of the
essential development of the plot, as in the case of *O*tinel, but
rather the story-teller's device for prolonging the action without boring his public. An angel appears privately to Charles to
reassure him about the outcome, but the combatants do not
know this. When finally *F*ierabras is beaten, he asks for
baptism, and he insists that Oliver is bound to see him through:
'if I die Saracen, you will be responsible'; and Oliver pities him
and does want to have him baptised. If he is baptised, he will
not be killed, and the problem is referred to Charles, who has
not forgotten the havoc done. The suppliant promises to return
the looted relics. If he is accepted, other pagans will turn to his
new faith, and if he dies Saracen, it is now Charles himself who
will be responsible. When *F*ierabras says, 'From now on I do
not care a farthing for all my gods', he is giving the reason for
his conversion; 'Oliver has beaten me, I don't want to hide it'.
Charles consents and orders the baptism; inevitably, *F*ierabras
becomes the model of a preux chevalier, though rather a minor
character now.[58] *F*ierabras does not act out of fear; he has
shown himself strong to attack and enduring in defeat. He is
a valuable recruit. He and his sister have in common that both
want to join the winning side, but we miss the point if we forget
that this is a religious reason. Success has identified the true God.

*R*enoart, his son *M*aillefer, his sister *O*rable/Guibourg and
her husband Guillaume form a more complicated family group;

with those who remain Saracen, *D*esramé, the siblings' father, and *T*ibaut, *O*rable's Saracen husband, they permeate a major cycle of songs. Do their motives reflect the usual themes? In fact *O*rable slips into Christian faith imperceptibly. In *Orange* we are not even told clearly when she falls in love with Guillaume, who with his nephew, both in disguise, asks to see her in her absent husband's palace; her husband's son *A*rragon inveighs against her supposed infidelities, and she receives them decorously, if a little flirtatiously. Insensibly she slips into helping them. When they are imprisoned in the tower, *O*rable, still at this stage swearing by Mahon 'whom I pray to and worship' asks for their custody, which her stepson refuses, blaming her for agreeing to see them in the first place. In the prison, nephew Guielin is still jeering at his love-sick uncle: 'send to *O*rable, the lady of Africa, who out of love will help her lover'; but in the *laisses* following this is just what she does. She would quickly get them out, she says, if she thought she would be safe from trouble, and Guillaume would take her. And so it happens, but without mention of her falling in love or reasons for her change of heart.[59] Guillaume's sexual excitement about her is both described and laughed at; there is no hint even that she finds Guillaume a fine knight, until she is fully committed to him. The song does not hint at her adventures in other poems. It is clear only that she is uneasy and unpopular in her husband's household; Orange seems to be inherited from her own family, and she does not seem to be related to her husband; finally she becomes the devoted and courageous wife celebrated in other poems. Her actions are quite unexplained.

*R*enoart's story is outwardly different. His years of lowly service in King Louis' kitchens have scorched his skin, and he has slept and got drunk without his bothering about his religion, or anyone else's bothering either. When his fantastic qualities as a fighting soldier mark him out as chivalrous, however eccentric in preferring his very effective club to a sword to which he is not accustomed, his high lineage is discovered or remembered, and inevitably he moves towards baptism. He is like his sister in taking sides and making war on the Saracens before he becomes a Christian in any formal sense. Unlike her, he has not made the same simple and final transfer of allegiance, and certainly he does not owe the Christians more than he has already repaid by winning for them the great battle of the Archamp which Vivien and Guillaume have lost. Because the lost battle has the same proportion as the *Battle of Maldon*, and the battle that the giant from the kitchen wins is a comedy, though I think a fine one, we forget *R*enoart's sensitivities, and that is also just what we are meant to do. At any rate, Guillaume forgets, or someone in the clerical bureaucracy of Orange fails to invite him to the celebration dinner. *R*enoart grumbles that he was never baptised, or even at church, although he has won the battle; now he will worship and serve Mahon, and come back to do to the Christians what he has already done to the Saracens. As he goes, he sends his sister a loving message, and to Guillaume a challenge. They send men after him with a pledge of amendment, which he rejects, but Guillaume then goes himself, taking *G*uibourg with him, and she reconciles the two.[60] The forgotten invitation is no more ridiculous than the dinner invitations refused in the parable. *R*enoart, who now is baptised, becomes Christian, not under threat, not for reward, not through disillusion or because he has been defeated, but because he has been and remains part of the Christian host. *R*enoart, always a bit of a clown, has the most dignified reason for conversion, but in his case, too, of course, it is the gate of entry to European society. The same may perhaps be true of *G*uibourg.

The single combats that *R*enoart fought against *L*oquifer and against his own son *M*aillefer are worth a quick look, though they are very like the other debates between enemies in mortal combat of which we have already seen examples and shall have to see more. The description of *L*oquifer as horrific outdoes the similar one of *F*ierabras, as in a still later poem *G*adifer's will outdo *L*oquifer's, but *L*oquifer has more moral character and better morale, so 'that he fears no man, neither king nor amir'. The opponents jeer good-humouredly at each other. *R*enoart speaks of the boat that has brought him to the island where they have chosen to fight: 'It is very sound and solid, if you will believe in Jesus Christ, it will easily carry us both back', and *L*oquifer says, 'By Mahon, you have let yourself in for a fit of madness, unluckily for your brave and noble person'. When some of his treacherous colleagues try to take advantage of a truce to attack *R*enoart, *L*oquifer is furious with them for breaking the word he has given. Each appeals to the other: 'I see that you are very brave and tough. Give up God and I will spare you, let us be comrades'. 'Brother Saracen, we have eaten together; you are very loyal, full of loyalty. *Ber*, believe in God, we shall be agreed, and the pagans will be christened through you.' *L*oquifer refuses because 'God has no power here'. When the Saracen leaders at a meeting press *R*enoart to desert 'Guillaume and his barons' he replies, 'I could never think of deserting Jesus of Majesty'.[61] I suppose that this might just mean that if it were only Guillaume and his barons, he would desert them; but it seems more likely that he does not distinguish between Jesus and the feudal world that acknowledges him. In any case, conversion for either side is a question of loyalty.

In his *Moniage R*enoart fights his own son Maillefer, and, each in the name of the appropriate god, they give each other a hard time. 'Vassal, your god has surely forgotten you, you can tell he has little power, Mahon on whom I have called has more.' *R*enoart laughs at the idea of believing in a god who can be thrown in a ditch, and prays that Maillefer will give up Mahon 'willingly and by his own choice'. And so in fact he does. When they discover their relationship, Maillefer is horrified at what he has done, and bitterly reproaches himself for the blows he has given his father.[62] The filial relation is far more powerful than the religious connection, and the audience, who did know who the two combatants were, has long foreseen a conversion without loss of face for Maillefer.

DISPUTES AND REASONS

We have seen some exchanges between Saracens and Christians, but they are a regular feature of the songs and were clearly thought to be important by singers and public, so that we should look at some of them more closely. In many cases, the Saracen participant refuses conversion to the point of death, less lucky than *F*ierabras, who knew when he was beaten.

*R*enoart is again involved in the fight between his father, *D*esramé, and his brother-in-law, Guillaume. Linked to both sides by kinship and affection, he acts as a kind of umpire; religion is the factor finally decisive. 'Believe in God, who set the world up', says *R*enoart, trying by all means to save his father's life, but *D*esramé replies, 'Shut up! Your God? I defy him. I will no more believe in him than in a stinking dog.' Just before Guillaume's final blow, he recapitulates his and *T*ibaut's grievances (wife and daughter abducted, country laid waste) and ends, 'I believe in Mahon, who has lordship over so much; I will never have help from your God, for his power is not worth a rowan'. *D*esramé has already expressed disillusion in Mahon: this is unexplained loyalty to a failed god. It is much the same in *Fierabras*, though the tone is more violent and strident. The amir *B*alan has made the series of virulent attacks on Mahon that we have seen, and, defeated and captured, he makes his final vicious attack on a god he holds 'lower than a stinking dead dog'. He seems ready for the font, and so thinks Charles, who has had it brought out in readiness. But the amir refuses to abjure. 'As long as I have life, I will stick to Mahon.' *F*ierabras begs him to change his mind, and begs Charles to be merciful, while *F*loripas only begs him to get on with executing their father. Then the amir makes his last attack on the Christian religion; five centuries have passed, he says, since Jesus was stoned (sic); anyone who thinks that he has risen again must be a sick man. Charles accedes to the single-minded importunity of *F*loripas.[63]

The motives of *D*esramé and *B*alan are not clear. If we talk in terms of character, we can say that *D*esramé has the courage and loyalty of his children, *R*enoart and *G*uibourg; and *B*alan, as well as these qualities, is cross-grained, sceptical and obstinate, suitably enough for the progenitor of *F*loripas and

*F*ierabras. But these poems are not primarily psychological
studies and character drawing to so fine a degree does not seem
to have been the aim of the authors. It may well have seemed
fitting to them that root-and-branch enemies of Christendom
should die in their misbelief; Guillaume's victory after a long
struggle, still more Charlemagne's headsman, symbolise
Christian triumph. From this point of view the lesson of
*D*esramé's case is that he is struck down while he persists in
trusting Mahon and despising God; and in *B*alan's that,
although he is totally disillusioned about Mahon, he sticks to
him and attacks Jesus, and so is rightly destroyed by the
machinery of Christian justice. As ever, God is vindicated and
Mahon humiliated.

The whole theme of disillusioned belief must be related to
this question of conversion. Why does the aumaçor, *N*ubie's
father, give way, when others die obstinate in their paganism?
The poet's decision seems arbitrary. He might be humiliating
the aumaçor, as Saracen ruler; or he might be sentimentally
reuniting him to *N*ubie, as father to daughter. His consent to
baptism must be related to the poet's wish to show him freely
consenting to the marriage of his daughter. In a related poem,
*J*udas, King of Seville, refuses conversion, and puts Mahon's
power to save him to the test, by jumping off the battlements –
a test predestined to fail and one few Christians would be prepared to put their own beliefs to. 'Are you hurt?' the Christians
jeer at his shattered body. The reason why *M*arsile rejects the
religion of rich courtiers is obvious up to a point, but the
episode is better told in a clearer setting in the Turpinus
chronicle, and it is not particularly appropriate to *Anseis*. These
cases are to some degree anomalous.[64] *A*quin is typical in
emphasising the trial of strength when the amirant complains
that he is expected 'to desert Mahon the powerful to worship
your rotten failed god – of course I shan't do it'. It is the theme
we have met so often: 'we shall be able to see which is the
authentic god'.[65]

In the *Couronnement de Louis*, King *C*orsolt, nephew of King
*C*alafre, says that he is going to kill Guillaume in the time it

takes to lay the table for dinner. Guillaume begins a long
prayer, and Corsolt jeers at him for being so crazy as to believe
in a god who in fact will not help him – masses, sacraments and
weddings are only a puff of wind.[66] It is in reply to this that
Guillaume tells the story of Mahon as 'prophet of Jesus' who
went wrong.[67] 'Christianity is all madness' says Corsolt, and
prays to Mahon, but more briefly than Guillaume to God.[68]
Corsolt manages to cut off a bit of Guillaume's nose (hence his
nickname, 'Shortnose'), but Guillaume gets, and takes, his
chance to finish him off when he tries too rashly to get back to
dinner in time. Corsolt has remained consistently hostile and
impenitent throughout. It is interesting that the Christian
Romans threaten St Peter that if his champion dies no one will
say any more masses in his church.[69] Does this mean that a
Saracen victory will put an end to all pilgrimage to St Peter,
or is it a threat – in the light of the pilgrimage trade, an
improbable one – like the threats the Saracens utter against
Mahon when he does not quickly produce the right result?

Gaufrey is another poem that introduces the idea that Mahon
was 'really' a false prophet, not a god, like Tervagant, out of
nowhere. Nasier's duel with Robastre, the old friend of
Gaufrey's father, Doon, begins with mutual insults. Nasier,
one of those hideous monstrous Saracens whom Christian
prowess so often reduces in single combat, addresses Robastre
as 'old man', but is told that 'Turks' will stop troubling Christians when they are all baptised. 'You have preached enough'
says Nasier, 'You know well how to sermonise; I think you are
a monk, to know how to talk so well, the Devil has had you
taken from your place'. The point that Jesus is a failure as a
god is made again: Nasier laughs at Robastre for imagining he
might give up Mahon, 'so valiant', for Jesus, who let himself
suffer, and his body moulder on a cross. 'On guard! I don't
want to talk any more – Mahon is worth more than Jesus
Christ, and this is how I prove it'. When Nasier manages to
scalp Robastre he says that, how that he is tonsured, he can
be a monk or a canon, a prior or abbot, even, if he likes, a
Roman cardinal, as he has a red cap. When Robastre claims

that he will pay back what he has been lent, *N*asier says that he is afraid neither of him nor his God, whom Robastre will have denied by evening; he is assuming that defeat in battle will convert his rival, and when Robastre knocks his eye out, he immediately attacks Mahon for allowing it. Because both story and argument are about who gives the victory, they are closely interwoven.[70]

The late *Entrée d'Espagne*, often intellectually a little different, elaborates variations from *Turpinus* on the single combat debate. It begins, not with the idea that victory will test the power of the gods, but that it will decide which god shall dominate Spain, a sensible and prosaic thought. 'He does it for Mahon', says Roland of *F*erragu, 'and I for Jesus Christ'. The argument drifts in and out of the usual channels. *F*erragu boasts that he will show by 'living force' that the Lord God sent Mahon on earth, as the protection of all he has created shows. This is the clue for the version of Mahon as 'false prophet'. This exchange suggests that the author is imagining the Saracen claim as equating Mahon and Christ. In any case, *F*erragu ripostes that the Jews convicted Christ as a thief and nailed him to a cross between two thieves. (As always, the debate is un-Islamic; for Islam there was no crucifixion at all, although the Jews attempted it.) So far, the argument seems to be about rival ideas for an incarnation. Roland can hardly contain himself when he hears the thief sneer, but does contain his rage enough to cut *F*erragu's cudgel in two. *F*erragu is upset 'just like a child when he loses his pet bird', and reproaches Mahon, which brings us back to the more usual theme. The Christians are shown as expressing greater solidarity; at the end of this day's fighting Roland goes home to encouragement, *F*erragu has to rebuke his friends' jeers, and insists that he will humble Roland's pride or die.

On the next day Roland prays to the Holy Virgin to help him, because he is in real need, and *F*erragu derides him, 'Listen to that great confidence trick! (*briconie*) Your God is dead and his people are ill-used . . . It is folly to pray to a dead man . . . Believe in Mahon and your soul will be saved'. Roland then

tries to explain the death of Jesus, leaving *F*erragu uncon-
vinced and indignant at a fraudulent god who went about
teaching such beastliness (*tel glotonie*), and only to die. This
theme of the failed god reads like a Christian heresy, and that
surely is how this author conceived it, although we come on
to more imaginative conceptions of how an ignorant pagan
might think, not, of course, a Muslim with a well-developed
theology of God and prophecy. Roland is angry but he later
lets *F*erragu sleep in safety and comfort, the comradely feeling
brought into many single combats, and *F*erragu is touched.
Now he is willing to negotiate, and he plays the usual court
card – he offers Roland his sister, royal on both sides, and half
all the lands he will conquer and rule.

Roland then undertakes a degree of serious persuasion which
is rare in the convention, although many of its familiar features
recur. The poet takes very seriously the idea that the crucifixion
is a weakness, and he has Roland explain that it is one thing
for a man to go to his death because he cannot help himself,
quite another to go willingly and able to avoid it: men should
honour and serve the one who does that. *F*erragu's gods are
there only to betray him and laugh at him and insult him; they
are going to take the souls of the Saracens to the Devil. He
begs him to believe in God who will save his soul. *F*erragu says
that he already believes in God the great (*Alababir*) and he is
willing to be converted and escape hell if Roland will explain
everything to him. Roland begins with God the Creator, and
*F*erragu accepts this as truth, adding 'we find it quite different
in our teaching'. However, he goes on to describe God as
creator of earth and sea and air and fire, and man and earthly
paradise, and asks why this is not enough in common to them
for there to be no further quarrel between them, between *Amis*
and him. *Saracins frere*, says Roland, you want to believe in God
and not believe; but you have to believe in the right way, in
Father, Son and Holy Ghost. *F*erragu asks, 'What thing is the
Father, what the Son and Spirit?' When Roland speaks about
the Incarnation and the Virgin birth, *F*erragu opines that no
one is or has been born unless a man engendered him, and no

virgin woman has given birth; do you believe it? he asks, and when Roland says, yes, he promises to be baptised if Roland will show him how this may be.

Roland begins to show signs of irritation: 'you have not been following!' When *F*erragu asks 'was he a true man?', Roland assents, and *F*erragu says that he cannot believe in God's eating and drinking, still less dying; a stay for a few months followed by a return on high might just be credible. How was the first man born? asks Roland; *F*erragu answers, from mud, he did not have a mother. Roland stresses the prophecies of the virgin birth and *F*erragu falls back on the argument that if he could accept a virgin conception, he could not believe in virginity maintained through parturition. Like the natural growth of the fruit from the flower, without rupture, replies Roland. In the end *F*erragu confides his real reason for not being baptised: 'Most of your people will not say that I am being baptised of my own free will, but that I have done it for fear'; he would not disgrace his family for all the gold in the Orient. Roland tells him that he is quite wrong, he would be honoured for it, and, when *F*erragu suggests that they get on with the battle, Roland cries with exasperation, 'Son of the Devil, born of a devil, you do not want to believe anything I tell you!' He provokes *F*erragu into explaining that he is invulnerable, except in the navel, and this enables Roland to finish the battle by killing him.[71]

In all this there is a considerable display of clerical virtuosity by Roland, but it is not this that makes the argument – of which I have only given fragments – exceptional; the reasonable and credible points put by *F*erragu are one anomaly, and the intellectual level of the whole dispute is another. Some of the discussion verges on a genuinely Islamic controversy, but no sooner does it do so than it seems to spring from total ignorance of Islam. This is at a fairly elementary level. It is true that Muslims object very much to the idea that God can engender, but the Qur'ān firmly teaches the virginity of the mother of Jesus. Of course it rejects the whole concept of the Incarnation, and it denies the historical occurrence of the crucifixion. The Islamic thought is rather that God would not allow the Jews so to treat a prophet, not at all that that prophet was disgraced or even that he failed. Yet in the objections that *F*erragu makes to the doctrine of the Trinity there is much that a Muslim would accept; but of course there is no question that Muslims do not think God the eternal creator.

This discussion has been given lengthy treatment since it draws attention to what most such arguments are not. If *F*erragu is only occasionally plausibly Muslim in his objections and frequently the contrary, he is often a Christian heretic, and almost consistently a free-thinking rationalist. But it is at least a reasoned discussion, and Roland's replies, to which I have not given much attention, are a sensible presentation of orthodoxy, if they do fall short of the highest standards of the Schools. Out of the context of the good comrade battle debate there is little dispute, even of the kind, 'I hit harder, so my god is true'. The conversion of *B*alan in *Aspremont* is predetermined in reasoned talk, although it actually occurs in battle. *B*alan goes as *A*golant's ambassador to Charlemagne's court, where he is Duke Naime's houseguest. They talk about religion and Naime gives a strictly uncontroversial and historical account of Christian Biblical belief – I mean by 'uncontroversial' 'not intended as matter for dispute'; for a Muslim there would be disagreement about the facts, for a true pagan it would be a new story altogether. Here is one of few conversions in a more modern sense, just as *F*erragu in *Entrée* was one of few intellectual disputes. *B*alan is convinced (perhaps predestined, being fair in colouring?) but he is linked to King *A*golant by personal obligations, he is his benefactor, and his son is his seneschal and the Queen's lover. When Naime in turn comes to *A*golant's court, *B*alan returns his kindness, but there is no further talk of religion. It is only when all is lost in the great battle, and he is about to be killed, that he gives up his old life and faith: he had gone into battle believing in God and praying 'that my body and soul be not severed before I have been regenerated at the font'. He gets more than this minimum, baptism under the name of Guitekin and a place as a Christian knight;[72] but, though he has had the usual reward, he has been persuaded, not forced, and neither expected nor covenanted for the reward. A very unusual case.

A last case outside the usual run is that of Ogier's friend Carahuel, in the late thirteenth century poem *Enfances Ogier*, the unconverted Saracen who is sympathetically treated. It is entirely realistic and entirely untraditional, that a Saracen should be a good ally without baptism. His personal loyalties to Ogier and generally to Charlemagne's court supersede religious, social and cultural loyalties. That he should stay Saracen (except for a half-hearted rumour inserted perhaps at popular demand that later he and his bride became Christian) and be much loved by the paladins is contrary to the whole tendency of the convention and the usual feelings of poets and hearers. When Charlemagne hints that he need not worry for estates if he becomes Christian, he replies, like any Christian hero refusing his bribe, 'Lord, I do not value at a penny that which you offer at a whole gold mark'; he would rather be impaled, or burned or drowned than desert his religion. Charles hangs his head with disappointment and others, the Pope, Duke Naime and many others, Ogier himself, all try to persuade him but

> King Carahuel looked at the barons, and saw the love which each one showed him; in his heart he thought of them very highly, and he thanked them for it very well and truly; but in no way did his heart change, and he said that Saracen he would remain all his life, and Saracen he would die.[73]

We have seen that loyalty is the key to *Ogier* and equally the key to all religious allegiance, but it is very abnormal for loyalty to be allowed to extend to Saracen faith and not end on the block. Carahuel leaves in an atmosphere of sorrow and love. The arguments that he decides to ignore are not given us in much detail, but are clearly of the same kind as Naime's to Balan in *Aspremont*. It is these that are used when an ironic spirit is required by the story, but it very rarely is.

SUMMING UP

Conversion after defeat is never seen as cowardice: it simply recognises the end of religious dispute. The result of the fight has proved the true God. It is here that the football club analogue seems relevant; the defeated Saracen transfers to the other side with even less fuss than one player to another club. The conversion of many of the Saracen heroes falls into another category; no one does more than they, often no one does as much, to ensure the Christian victory which is the failure of the pagan gods. They, like the converts that I have called 'political', have transferred their allegiance, and their conversion has nothing direct to do with the virtues of Christianity. But why do they want to transfer allegiance? In one form or another, the answer is almost always that the pagan gods are false, losers who hold a good soldier back – or a good heiress back. The basic motive of nearly all conversions is, in one form or another, a desire to enter European society, and there seems no explanation of why they want to do that other than that quite simply it is the best. It is natural that poets singing to please an audience, whether aristocratic or popular, should found themselves on that very simple conviction.

All the common themes reflect this attitude. Offers of reward for conversion to either side, threats of torture, prison or death, are only forms of rivalry between two societies, each of which claims to be the one that works best; and the stories in one form or another are all about which does work best. The converted Saracen is not disloyal, because his god has freed him of all obligation in failing him. The Saracen gods have a kind of contractual obligation to their people which their failure dissolves. This does not mean that Christian faith in the poems is reduced to faith in the God whom an author of a fiction can cause always to win. There is an element of that in the stories; as they are stories, there could hardly fail to be. Yet the Christian faith of the chansons is not only sincere; it has characteristics of its own. But in the conversion of Saracens, and for that matter the conversion of Christians to paganism, abstract discussion and theory of any sort have little part to play. Had Saracens really been meant to be Muslims, we should not have escaped the actual statements of the Qur'ān, at least in some attenuated form. The Qur'ān does say, in different places, that the Messiah was not crucified, that the Messiah was not and did not claim to be God, and that there is one God, not three.[74] It does not say, however, that Jesus was a failed god or that he was disgracefully executed, as occasionally a Saracen is made to say, most explicitly in the *Entrée d'Espagne*; but fourteenth century Northern Italy, from which this work comes, is not a probable provenance for authentic Qur'ānic material. The attraction of calling Jesus a failed or feeble god was just that it recalled and restated the main theme of all conversions, the relative strength of God and the gods, of Christians and Saracens.

CHRISTIANITY

The remaining area of enquiry is the religion which the heroes opposed to the Saracen gods. It is no surprise to find that the poets had their own characteristic way of presenting Christianity, and it is an integral part of the convention. It is sometimes a good deal closer to Islam than anything they thought up for their Saracens; there is no reason to suspect Islamic influence in that, but it parallels the crypto-Christianity in the concept of the gods. Yet singers who so often neglected official church ways of thought shared with the theologians their concern about God's vindication of the right cause by victory in battle. Here we have one point of underlying agreement in all Christians (Muslims of course had the same problem). The independence of most theological ways of thinking implies a neglect of the clergy which is reflected in the way the poems treat them. When it comes to the monks, there is a further implication of moral uncertainty. The knight's life, which the chansons celebrate, and the monk's, which they respect, are incompatible. One way of dealing with violence is to treat it as a joke, as the poems often do; and one way of dealing with monastic repugnance to war is also a joke, first to make the monks act like Saracens (either by themselves or in actual alliance with Saracens) and then to treat them accordingly, as in the two *Moniage* poems discussed below. The poets do not seriously doubt that the monastic vocation is best, or that killing requires repentance, and this strange equivalence of monks and Saracens is the last ambiguity in their attitude to Saracens that we shall have occasion to notice.

There is even little reflection of half-Christianised pagan and magical survivals at a popular or illiterate level, although this was an oral art. The supposed relics of the Passion, whose recovery after their theft at the sack of Rome forms a principal theme of *Fierabras*, verge on the magical. When they are recovered (there were in fact no such relics in Rome) the authenticity of the crown of thorns and of the nails of the crucifixion is proved by their being able to knock the enemy out at a distance. Also among the holy relics is a balm (in kegs) with which *F*ierabras can cure his wounds, and wishes Oliver, whom he is fighting, to do the same. The similar balm in *Bataille Loquifer* and that in *Gadifer* are both just magical, but in *R*enoart's fight with Maillefer in the *Moniage* the sight of a stone from the Jordan (though Maillefer forgets to use it) is similarly healing. The magic introduced into the *R*enoart and Huon groups of stories by Picolet, Auberon and their associates is fantasy rather than superstition, but even superstition and a corrupt cult of relics are unimportant in the religion of the songs.[1]

Part-line phrases, an extended epithet or a relative clause, are often very alike and sometimes the same, when they are used for God and Jesus or for Mahon and Tervagant or one of the others. A phrase that has a specially Christian sense is 'king of majesty' or 'Jesus of majesty'; less characteristically Christian and closely similar to phrases used for Mahon, are 'who made the sea and the wind' and 'who made the salt sea'.[2] This similarity only tells us that Mahon and his colleagues were conceived as claiming rivalry with God as Creator and Ruler of the world, as we have already seen in other contexts. Much more informative are the long prayers uttered in the course of the action, 'prayers of crisis', often amounting to a full sacred history. The Biblical story is the expression of faith most characteristic of these poems.

A good example of the sacred history is the long passage recalled by Aymery, in a thirteenth century poem of disputed date, when he watches the fire that has been prepared for him burning fiercely. 'Glorious Father who made the world', took

incarnation in the Virgin, 'chose to be born for the ransom of
the world', who put St Peter in Nero's field (the traditional site
of the martyrdom, a favourite reference), who threw Jonas up
from the belly of the fish, who protected Daniel from the lions
and forgave the Magdalen, 'when you were a guest in Simon's
house, and she went on her knees before you, at your feet, there
she wept from a good disposition . . . she has a fine reward for
her service, that she is there above in your great house'; who
passed Moses across the sea and drowned the people of
Pharaoh; 'you who made the river Jordan issue from its source,
and sat on a stone in the middle, with the water running round
you; the angel from heaven put the chrism on your forehead
and St John said that your name was Christ . . . you went deep
into the desert . . .' and so on until Maundy Thursday 'when you
gave yourself up to the Passion'; and to the peroration, 'save
me from the anguishing fire'.[3] This passage, greatly abbreviated
here, is representative of these prayers which recapitulated the
chief events of salvation. They tell God what he did; Labande
finds an exception in a late poem, but it just tells the Virgin
Mary what God did, and the prayer is different only in shifting
from the second person to the third.[4] In early poems there is
some emphasis on St Mary Magdalen, which roughly conforms
to the period of the Bethany cults in the South and West of
France.[5] The episodes recounted are normally examples of
divine protection, the events from the life of Christ seem chosen
as distinctively redemptive, but the same is true of Old Testament references. They are clearly addressed to an audience
that, we already know, likes to hear about adventures. If so
much piety seems unrealistic, or at least uncharacteristic,
Aymery in the case cited is back on form in a line or two,
shouting, 'son of a whore, what are you waiting for?'[6]

There is a similar prayer in *Orange*, and another rather
neater and simpler, but the most famous prayer allotted to
Guillaume is in *Le Couronnement de Louis*, where it provokes his
dispute with Corsolt. It is not exactly a prayer of crisis, because
Guillaume is far from being reduced to the straits in which in
the other example Aymery found himself: it is a prayer before

battle. 'Glorious God, who made me, who made all the world at
your will and set it within the sea; and formed Adam, and then
Eve, his companion' and, it goes on, they ate the apple from a
fruit-tree in paradise, 'a great disgrace which they could not
hide', they are sent to earth, to 'dig and labour and suffer and
endure mortal life'; the story takes in Cain and Abel and then
Noah ('all beasts, male and female to restore the world') and
so promptly to the incarnation ('flesh and bone ... and the holy
blood') in 'Bethlehem, the wonderful city'; by now the second
person is used again, though for several lines at a time, as in the
episode of Herod, the third person takes over naturally. The
life of Christ is somewhat summary, passing from the nativity
events to those that precede the Passion, his going round the
land teaching the people, the desert fast and the temptation, and
then direct to Palm Sunday. The washing of the Lord's feet in
Luke, always attributed in the West to St Mary Magdalen, is
prominent and detailed (and placed after Palm Sunday) as are
the curious two lines, 'in his simple goodness, he has sent away
the rich and turned his heart to the poor' – a reminiscence perhaps of the Magnificat? The story passes normally through the
Passion, and up to the Resurrection; like St Mark, it barely
goes beyond the latter fact, with the addition that it is the Risen
Christ who harrows hell.[7] The chronology is odd in most of the
prayers and there is a little legendary additional matter. The
angel who anointed Christ at his baptism in the Aymery prayer
is an example. In *Couronnement* there is an obscure reference to
the raising of St Anastasia[8] by the child Jesus, and Longinus the
centurion of the crucifixion[9] gets a good mention. These are
much less important than the overwhelmingly Scriptural,
simple and straightforward telling of the sacred story in which
there seems no joking for once.

These prayers have been well studied, and I will mention the
details of only one more. The account of religion which Duke
Naime gives *B*alan in *Aspremont* and which effectively converts
him, is not a 'prayer of crisis' in its context, though very like
one in content. Naime takes his guest through the sin of Adam
and Eve, and the people who remained in sin till the Flood,

when Noah was saved. He describes how after that the people were punished in hell 'just as the beasts are led to the market', until God took pity on his people, in the incarnation, his baptism, crucifixion and harrowing of hell, where he released Jacob and Joseph, Abraham and Noah.[10] The story does not read any the worse for not being set as a prayer, and so not recurrently in the second person singular. Sometimes the prayers show an almost fictional recreation of a scene. The short creed put to the amir in *Fierabras* asks him to accept Jesus 'who restored this world, and hid himself in the holy girl, the Virgin', was crucified, buried, rose again, ascended into heaven: this summary sounds no different from the creed, but there is also an imaginative immediacy which enlivens it: 'right in front of the apostles he rose there above to the sky'.[11] For all these virtues, the prayers are indeed very similar, and there are many of them, so that of course there are variations in the sameness of both content and style.[12] The ambitious *Entrée d'Espagne* elaborates to an extent that we may call it a catalogue raisonné of salvation, rather than a simple list of the main events.[13] Repetition is inevitable, since there are only so many episodes in the Bible that are relevant to the theme. It is more surprising that there is as much variety as there is; Edmond-René Labande's analytical tables make it clear at a glance that there are great differences of detail between them all, and between them and any homiletic or liturgical source.[14] It is not always obvious that the choice of episodes has been chosen to suit the immediate context, but there seem to be no obvious incongruities.

The poets may have a minor interest in their choice of particular episodes or in the way in which they describe events from Scripture or, occasionally, legend; but such points may distract us from the main effect that is intended and is achieved. All of them make us think of the general sense of the liturgy, particularly perhaps the series of prophecies (in the sense of God's mercies to his people) of the Easter Saturday liturgy in the old Roman missal, but also of the series of Roman prefaces and parts of the old Roman canon of the Mass and of the new

eucharistic prayer.[15] We do not have to suppose direct
liturgical sources but rather an ultimately liturgical inspiration.
There are shorter passages that have something in common
with the style of the collects. The prayer which in a short space
sums up all the prayer of the heroes is Roland's dying prayer,
with its great human dignity. He has prayed to be forgiven 'all
his sins, great and small, that he has done since the hour when
he was born'; now he ends: 'our true Father, who never lied,
who raised Lazarus from the dead and saved Daniel from the
lions, save my soul from all danger from the sins I have committed in my life'.[16]

These prayers have attracted the attention of many good
scholars; the key work is Labande's *le credo épique*; he
follows more systematically the example set by Léon Gautier
in constructing an analytical catalogue of themes, based on 41
chansons, some of them containing several examples (*Aiol*
seven). There has been criticism of the prayers as illogical and
unchronological in their presentation of God's mercies.
Labande pointed out that they seem most stereotyped in their
earliest appearances and contrasts the occasional fresh and
charming presentations of some themes in the late decadence
of the main tradition,[17] doubtless because religious verse was
then in fashion. It is sensible to consider the prayers as part of
the story, rather than as religious interludes. Some scholars
have thought the inversion of the Resurrection and the descent
into hell in *Couronnement* a prototype,[18] but even in the same
prayer the Gospel stories are unchronological, and inversions
are so common in the genre as a whole that, as Labande says,
citing the crossing of the Red Sea after the penitence of Mary
Magdalen, '*on est parvenu là à un comble d'indifférence*'.[19] Such
indifference is perfectly sensible, if we consider that the
purpose of the prayers is simply to establish God's merciful
interventions in the economy of salvation, and not to teach
theology or conduct a Bible class. These passages are not, and
we must not be seduced into thinking them, catechetical. The
order in which they were related did not matter to the teller or
the listener, and the order in which they happened to come to

mind, or best suited the prosody, was as good as any.

Similar but abbreviated prayers reinforce this point. Roland's dying prayer is an example, and if Lazarus precedes Daniel, it in no way affects the effect desired. Another example is: 'God, who let himself be pierced by a lance on the cross for the great sin done by the first woman when she gave her husband the apple (as it is written in Rome)'; here the logical sequence explains the chronological, but the choice of the lance to expiate original sin is arbitrary, and a little earlier the same poet, writing much later than *Roland*, picks out a favourite reference: 'God who was put on the cross and forgave Longinus'.[20] Traditionally, Longinus prefigures the conversion of the pagans and represents the piety of soldiers, both good relevant reasons why he should be brought in, the latter particularly sympathetic to a feudal context. It is difficult to think of any ulterior purpose that might have dictated the choice of references. It is quite possible to be historical without being annalistic, and by contemporary standards the prayers are free of major legendary additions, as Labande says.[21] Prayer is not silent and it can often be overheard by Saracens, who may jeer;[22] the prayers do not read like polemic, despite their resemblance to the statement of faith by Naime in *Aspremont*. They are certainly not written by or for theologians although their theology is orthodox and consistent; but there is no obvious homiletic model, and no interest at all in subtle definitions, least of all of Trinitarian beliefs, and they do not clearly distinguish Father and Son by function; to appropriate functions to the Persons of the Trinity was a theologian's interest. The 'credo' neither asserts articles of faith like the Nicene creed, nor condemns errors like the Athanasian. It shows a practical interest in the economy of redemption, and redemption was a familiar idea in a feudal world where ransom was commonplace.

USE AND PURPOSE OF THE PRAYERS

Why are these passages of Christian faith introduced at all? It is possible to suggest several explanations, all of which may be true. The most obvious purpose is to heighten the tension in the story. If the hero's situation is desperate, the prayer will increase the tension by postponing the dénouement. If it is exciting, but less than desperate, the prayer itself must impart some sense of urgency. In the case of ejaculations, when the poet himself intervenes in the story, exactly as if the events he recounts were really taking place, we are made to feel that the issue is uncertain, that the poet himself does not know what is going to happen. 'God and the noble St Marcel help Maugis! – 'May God who was hung on the cross take care of them!' – 'Now may Jesus have pity on *R*encart!'[23] In a more subtle way, the prayers remind us that every Saracen war is a threat to Christianity, that the beliefs of every listener are at stake. There is reassurance too, but even that helps to recall the dangers which only God can avert. Elie says to his adversary: 'by my head, you are a very tough vassal. You would willingly have killed me if you had been allowed to, but God loves me from the heart, and will always keep me safe'.[24]

There is no sign that the prayers are meant to illustrate the psychology of the characters who pray. The poets do not have a modern novelist's interests, and although there is character-isation, the prayers are not individual or in character. They are universal, prayers such as every man would pray, and their universality is itself a function. The poet wants to make his audience recognise its own faith in that of the heroes, and it will in fact recognise in the poems a common background of universally accepted facts. It would be seen as folly for a hero to neglect prayer, as much as to neglect any other engine of war. If the functions *orare* and *pugnare* were commonly differ-entiated, the fighting men could pray, as well as the bishops could fight. Certainly they did not pray because they were particularly devout, but because they were preux and cortois, and because they quite understood that they were sinners. A spontaneous moment of devotion now and then was normal. Indeed, in this artificial and so often fantastic literature, these passages are among the most practical and ordinary. They link the airy fiction with the every-day and familiar.

It was not claimed that the soldier's life was easily compatible, in society as it was, with the Christian moral system. The dying hero prayed for forgiveness (even Vivien, even Roland) because a soldier's life was well known to need it. The protagonists of these poems are sinners as well as heroes. The listener is told that the angels are only waiting to carry Roland's soul to Paradise, but he does not know it or expect it. It is a bonus thrown in in lieu of living happily ever after. I do not think that the poet means more than that a fiction, because everything in it is an invention by hypothesis, may anticipate also the judgement and the mercy of God. Oliver gets no angels, though he has Roland still living to mourn him; Vivien's dying consolation is the Host. Gui de Warewic is warned of his approaching death by the archangel Michael, but he has lived a life of suffering as well as battle and is preparing for death by a hermit's life. Guillaume, too, becomes first monk and later hermit, but, though his soul is taken to heaven (and his story finally confused with that of St William of Gellone) this is because of his ascetic and eremitical life of penance, and the sins of which he has repented are forgiven. His sins are not in doubt, and his first abbot took it for granted that a knight would have many killings to repent.[25]

May there have been a kind of contract, implied and understood, between the Lord God of the songs and his paladins? The Christian established his loyalty to God by his prayer, in a way that just fighting, with its many material rewards, could not; on the other side, the theme of the prayers established God's loyalty to his people, whom so often in so many different circumstances he had protected. The heroes did not claim martyrdom in the theological sense, but they knew that their fight was good and officially approved, and its profit on earth might reasonably be expected to be carried on in heaven. For those who died before they could collect their share of the booty, there was a substitute: 'who dies here will have a very good share of paradise'.[26] This is not intended as a precise official statement, though its implications would go well with indulgenced Crusading, which makes fighting (for those who fight the right people) a kind of penance. It is inconsistent with the sense of sin of which we have been speaking. Perhaps we could say that in return for fighting God's cause, they expected either to win or to get compensation in the spirit. If there was some thought of implied contract, then the prayers that express it are highly suitable; the events in the story of God's mercies are told with a narrative technique that is obviously congruous with songs of action and romances of adventure. If a soldier lives, he has time to repent, and if he dies, his dying is his penance. The story-teller keeps this delicate balance with his Biblical prayers.

There is a more important function of the prayers, one at any rate that is of universal interest. The long prayers normally end by an assertion that they are true, and Labande rightly dismisses Scheludko's contention that this is a near-magical incantation.[27] It is explanation enough, as Labande says, that the authors believed that faith merits grace; although it is not spiritual grace, but material intervention for which the heroes pray, it is puritanical to call this magic. There is no positive indication of a magical intention, or of any notion that God can be compelled by a verbal formula. On the other hand, the poets are here at grips with one of the few problems that troubled theologians and laymen equally, the problem of Providential support for the right side. Muslim victories troubled theologians, although they always maintained that Islam was peculiarly the religion of the sword, which it could hardly have been for long without victories; and they troubled soldiers whose morale often requires some assurance that the enemy is wrong. The standard explanation is that God punishes Christendom for its sins, but the polemists have been busily explaining that Islam endorses and encourages sin, and yet Muslims are allowed victories. It was indeed difficult for anyone nourished on Old Testament texts to suppose that true belief might not earn at least the material reward that it would itself prosper in the world.

One theologian and polemist, Ricoldo da Monte Croce, took the problem personally and very seriously, in letters, apparently written in Baghdad, where he saw evidence of the fall of Acre and of the death of his friends and colleagues. God seemed to be endorsing the Qur'ān, he complained, even implementing it, and doing so by miraculous intervention. Ricoldo sought a private revelation to explain this, and in a sense he got it, that there is no new explanation. He thought that God told him to read Gregory on Job (certainly one would think the one book in the Old Testament which could answer his questions). On 'God will speak once, and will not repeat the same thing twice', Gregory comments that there can be no private revelation: 'He has provided for our instruction, by what he stated to our fathers in holy Scripture', and, as Ricoldo very well knew, when pushed to it, that meant that God castigates some, as his friends, that they should fear him, and others as his enemies, that they should be punished. That, as he said, left him more worried than ever for the fate of Christians remaining in Muslim territory.[28]

This is realism in theology; but if there is no worldly solution, so that priests and soldiers alike must learn to live with their fears, this would not do in an epic poem or in any adventure story. The poet, of course, can determine the course of events, and can play the part of Providence, as long as he is plausible, and stays within the limits of his convention. So, in the end, the Christians always win, whatever the difficulties that castigate them meantime, and entertain the audience, which, however, was accustomed to a final victory, and would not have tolerated anything else. Of course, the poets do not solve the theological problem. They do not quote Job when they describe a setback, but perhaps they do feel that the invariable final victory of the Christians needs a bit of explaining. Are they not saying in these prayers – and intending no blasphemy – that in the light of so many true victories and escapes, from Exodus to the Resurrection, there is nothing implausible in one more, or several more – either in fact or in fiction?

This is another reason why they should insist that each pattern of events taken from Scripture is authentic, and therefore, of course, that God is authentic, which reminds us that the gods are there to be proven failures. The poet can afford to replace realism by a fantasy in which God finally chastises only his enemies; but he does so usually without miracles, and the poets were better theologians for letting Providence work through chance. But in the last resort no statement of faith needs explaining. The poets liked to nail their flag to the mast, and remind the audience of its Christian identity; in fiction there was nothing else to differentiate heroes from Saracens. This brings us to the last and perhaps most important step. The authenticity of the Bible sequences rubs off in fact on to the songs. A cycle of poems, with its repetitions and its rediscovery of familiar characters and references to familiar events in other songs begins insensibly to take on the appearance of history, and the succession of fictional generations evokes the passage of real time and events.[29] A kind of modern sacred history of the exploits of heroes almost parodies the sacred histories of the Bible and the liturgy.[30] The acts of a Roland or a Vivien, the progeny of an Aymery or a Doon, joined the tail of the Scriptural procession of sacred figures, several of whom were themselves secular heroes, a Magdalen or a Longinus, and some of whom were not even notable for the holiness of their lives or the depth of their repentance, an Adam, a David, a Solomon. The *gesta militum*, the acts of a Guillaume, a Renoart or an Ogier, were linked to the *acta sanctorum*. The poets conferred on Charlemagne a place of fame in the history of European relations with the Arabs greater than he deserved or sought. As the Charlemagne literature penetrated the scholarly world and was taken for history,[31] so the events of fiction were easily attached to the divine mercies recorded in Scripture and in tradition. In our modern world, liberals, Marxists and believers in various political doctrines fit events as they occur into their own particular legend. The poets were doing the same thing with imaginary events, and making their heroes' prayers less a theological than an historical justification.

THE PRAYERS AND ISLAM

Is there any possible connection in the authors' minds between the narrative prayers and Islam as it is? We have found no positive sign of interest in Islamic realities up to now, and this is no exception. Just as the gods seem to be fragmented notions of the Christian idea of God, not of the Islamic, so there seems no reflection of the Qur'ānic presentation of the prophets who are common to the Qur'ān and the Bible; there are no Saracen counterparts to the prayers, and no Saracen references to the prophets. The stories of Abraham, Jacob, Joseph, Noah and so on are not the same in the two holy books, and Muslim and Christian concepts of these figures are a little different as a result. There is no sign in the chansons that the poet is aware of this; the Christian sacred history, New Testament and Old alike, is assumed to be the sole source of knowledge about the events and the people concerned. If it is absurd that the believers in one God should be set up as idolators, it is equally absurd that the figures known to Christians from the Old Testament should not be given a part in a religion which consists of a revelation that continues from prophet to prophet.[32] Here we have one more indication that Saracen religion is not meant to be Islam in this convention.

Yet the authors of the songs were much closer in this to the Muslims than they knew. In stressing the story of God's mercies and his intervention through the prophets in men's affairs, they shared an attitude with every devout Muslim, whose religion daily makes him conscious of the rule of God, and who hears stories that illustrate it every time the Qur'ān is read aloud. This shared affection for the sacred history of the ancients and repeated awareness of God's interest in ordinary events created a natural affinity with Islam of which the Christians were themselves unconscious. Although their fictions are conscious of God's immediate action just as are Islamic histories, there is no evidence of mutual influence which cannot be better explained as part of the shared cultural inheritance. As on every point where there could have been

communication between the cultures, there is none. No
Saracen is shown as knowing anything of the Qur'ānic Jesus,
and there is no indication that the prophetic occasions singled
out and included in these prayers are chosen because they are
areas of either agreement or disagreement with the Saracens.[32]

Does the Christians' use in the songs of phrases possibly of
Islamic origin (*si Dex l'a destiné* or *so Deu plaist, se fera* to
represent the Arabic *insha'llah*) affect this argument?[33] We
can neither prove nor disprove it. Although the phrase is
characteristic of Arabic (and used as much by Eastern Christians as by Muslims) there is nothing about it inappropriate to
Western Christianity and it may have developed spontaneously. If there is an Islamic influence here, it would be likely
to be unconscious and it would be certain to be unacknow-
ledged.

The stories make certain assumptions about the Saracens'
ideas of Christianity,[34] but no Saracen seems ever seriously to
suggest that the Christian God does not exist. The attacks on
'Lord God' that we have looked at deny only his power and
efficacity, at least in this world. Perhaps no concept of atheism
was possible. Each side says that the other's gods are not worth
a shelled egg or a rotten apple, or whatever it may be, and to our
mind denying the power of the god is tantamount to denying
his existence. The poets do not seem to think so. We have seen
disillusioned Saracens talk as though their god, now admitted
to be useless, still existed, and it is in the same way that they
deny the power of God, as long as they hope to defeat the
Christians, but they never say that he does not exist. The
perpetual rivalry of God and gods is essential for the entire
literature; as Mahon often seems a dim reflection of the Christian God, God seems conceived by the fictional Saracens as a
kind of Mahon. As Mahon has so little character except as a
war god, the Saracen criticism of Christianity is in terms of just
that, hence the sneers at a failed crucified Jesus, and hence too
perhaps the long prayers which tell us what Christian belief
really is. The real Muslim objections to Christian belief do not
come into this at all. Sometimes a poet carelessly makes a

Saracen use Christian phrases which even within the convention would be impossible, such as *Jesu de magesté*. It does
not change anything to say that it is indeed the poet, and not the
Saracen, who is careless, because his carelessness springs from
his inability to conceive a world which does not accept 'Jesus
of Majesty'.[35] It is an effort for him to recall that his Saracen
ought to be jeering. In *Destruction de Rome* and *Fierabras*, the
Saracens do not doubt the authenticity or the efficacity of the
relics of the Passion that they have looted,[36] although Muslims
do not believe that the Passion occurred in the way that
Christians understand it, and such relics must necessarily seem
false to a Muslim, not, of course, to the Saracen of our convention. When we hear of 'the holy shroud in which God was
wrapped'[37] from the mouth of a Saracen, we do begin to wonder
whether this can be just poetic carelessness. The Islamic belief
that Christians have distorted the sole revelation of the one
God has no echo in the Saracens of fiction.

THE CLERGY AND THE MONKS

The relationship of the whole literature to monasticism in
particular and to the clerical orders in general is a larger
question than concerns us, but it is of some importance to our
subject. Just the fact that the poets ignored the vast clerical
polemic against Islam is itself a measure of their dissociation
from the clerical world. There was a wide gap between the
poets and most curial clergy, and between their conventions
and those of the monastic chroniclers. The greatest gap
separated them from the Schools, despite references to learned
clerks or documents.[38]

It is obvious that the poets reveal little idea of the working
of the church – or, it must be said, of the households of any
great lords. A great household was an administration, we may
almost say a bureaucracy. A magnate, layman or bishop,
would have had a number of clerks, not only to perform
devotional duties, but also as clerical, secretarial and administrative officers. Turpin and one or two other bishops appear
without supporters, or any household of their own; we see

Turpin himself reading a message ingeniously delivered by
arrow, as if he were a chaplain. Yet in *Roland* he is himself a
nobleman, and dies as a knight should, with his entrails spilling
out on the battle-field.[39] A bishop, like any magnate, was
surrounded by knights as well as by clerks, and neither lords
secular nor lords spiritual appear in the chansons realistically;
but in the case of the lay lords there is a dynastic reason.
Bishops had little to gain from the singers and the singers seem
rarely to have bothered to give much praise to the bishops.
Popes figure little in these stories, but most where the sack of
Rome is in question. Conceivably some confused memory of
the Roman church of the tenth century is reflected in the Pope
of the *Couronnement* who offers Guillaume the mercenary's
wage of as much food, and as many women and sins as he
wishes, for life.[40]

The few references to a Saracen religious establishment
betray little interest in the subject. *Roland's* picture of Saracen
'canons' is not taken up elsewhere, and the occasional references to men learned in the law (*fuqahā'*?), necromancers and
manipulators of idols,[41] amount to very little, certainly not to a
widespread interest; but, as there is so little reflection of the
powerful Christian church, is it surprising to find even less of an
imaginary Saracen pagan establishment, and less still of anything authentically Islamic?

However unclerical the interests of the poets, monastic
influences seem to have made a strong impression on them. The
ignorance of the poems, not, surely, of the poets, about the
great households, does not extend to the monasteries. References to divine services, whether office or Mass, are infrequent,
though not enough so as to need explaining. The pious Aiol is
introduced as a steady church-goer. The chief interest in
prayer was in individual prayers, and formal prayer was not
often required by the story. Two kinds of public prayer that
do make an appearance are absolution before battle (where it
is Turpin or someone like him in arms who usually officiates)
and vespers, matins, compline, the great offices of the church
and the *opus Dei* of the Rule of St Benedict, the primary function

for which monks exist. The prayer of the great monastic churches appears as the norm of peaceful prayer.[42]

The influence of the monasteries is unmistakable but not obtrusive. It is not that the monks have imposed their ideas on the poets, but just that they are often there in the story. The poets often laugh at them, sometimes acidly, and the dominant ideas of the poets, including their prayers, bear no clear sign of monastic influence. The monastic presence is often neutral. Great monastic houses are mentioned from time to time as sources of the author's information; Cluny and, most of all, St Denis; and there are slight references, such as 'it was the feast of St Denis'. Cluny, apart from its influence on monks everywhere, was a strong local influence in southern Burgundy, and St Denis was a royal monastery, a seat of political power, the *maîtresse maison* of *la douce France*.[43] When Saracens threaten to invade France and instal the worship of Mahon where it will make most impression, it is the church of St Denis that they specify.[44] I am not entering the controversy about monastic and pilgrimage sources of epic legend to which Joseph Bédier made so unforgettable a contribution. A connection certainly exists between poets and monks, between fighting heroes, and the local legends of saints. A particular story may have its special association, such as *Moniage Renouart* with Brioude and *Moniage Guillaume* with Aniane and Gellone.[45] One of the first adventures of Aiol is to rescue monks under attack from brigands, admittedly in a part of the poem which occasionally approaches the devout. The height of *démesure* in Raoul de Cambrai is to burn the nuns and their abbey. If a knight prays aloud the Saracen who jeers at him may use such expressions as 'little clerk' or 'monk', and though these are pejoratives that the poet can hardly endorse, there is always some hint that a hero's function is to protect monks, rather than pray himself.[46]

Moniage Guillaume and *Moniage Renouart* are typical poems in most ways, but exceptional in their treatment of monks; their theme after all, is the religious vocation of a penitent hero. *Moniage* means 'monastic profession', and the subject is an interesting one. The treatment of the theme, and of the monks as a community, is simultaneously serious and comic, in the true tradition of humour at once ribald, fantastic and devout. The idea of Guillaume, the hothead of *Nîmes*, lovesick in *Orange*, desperate in the *Chanson* and in *Aliscans*, as a monk, has enormously funny possibilities, and has, too, a persuasively authentic ring. The poet develops both sides, though there are many adventures in the second redaction which do not concern monks at all. Gulllaume's acceptance in the monastery is serious, but only just. He presents himself, as an angel has told him to do, and he is readily accepted by the abbot.

> 'Lord Guillaume', [says the abbot], 'fine noble lord, many a man have you killed and slaughtered; you can no longer put off your repentance. For your sins, of which you have committed twenty thousand, you will be a monk and submit to privation'.

But the tone of the poem changes almost immediately. When the abbot asks Guillaume if he can read, Guillaume replies, 'Yes, lord abbot, without looking at the book', and the abbot and the monks laugh, not, at his naivety, but simply at the joke he has made. The fun develops side by side with something more serious: 'the count was now a monk, he had taken the habit; he heard the service of God very willingly, and he did not evade Mass, or matins, or tierce or nones, or vespers or compline'. But the monks get nothing to eat, because Guillaume gets it all, and even needs twice as much cloth to wear as they do. They plot to get rid of him, by sending him through a robber-infested forest to buy stores. He is wearing his habit, and he tries to behave like a monk; when he is attacked he makes a great effort to submit humbly to being stripped. The abbot, as part of the plot, has forbidden him to use arms, but, when he is tried too far, he kills the robbers unarmed. Finally he gets home, but kills several of the monks when they try to shut him out. He is forgiven, and they make it up: 'we can replace them with plenty more', *Ja d'autres moines recoverrons plenté*; but the angel appears to him again and sends him off to be a hermit. The monks agree that this is best.[47]

The monks' plot occurs also, with variations, in the longer

second redaction of this poem. The original conflict is exacer-
bated by his quarrel with the cellarer for not treating a highly
placed visitor with honour;[48] he takes the food he thinks right
for the occasion by force when he is refused, and in this version
he finally kills the prior by throwing the abbot at him. None of
this slapstick should deceive us into supposing that the poet is
not serious about Guillaume's religious vocation. In this
version his life as a hermit is interrupted for some years by new
Saracen adventures, but these are intended to prolong the
story in an interesting way, not to obscure the *moniage* itself. He
achieves an ascetic life in both versions of the poem, praying
and cultivating a herb garden. It is clear that his inability in the
monastery to stick to the monks' diet is just a joke; he eats very
little when he is a hermit. When he comes across his cousin,
now a hermit too, each being at first unknown to the other, they
eat a little grain in boiled water, rye bread, apples and nuts, and
drink cider; better, says Guillaume nostalgically, as the two
ageing hermits happily recall their plentiful fare as lords and
knights, than peacock, swan, capon and venison. Guillaume's
life as a hermit is treated quite seriously: 'the count has made
himself a very fine building, the noble count made a chapel
there where he serves God'. He may still fight the Devil, even a
giant, but he has given up Saracens, 'he will no more carry arms
or start a scrimmage, he will serve God in the early morning
and the night watches'.[49]

At one level the monastic vocation is seriously treated, at
another monks are killed with the same happy abandon as if
they were Saracens. At a third the theme can be made a vehicle
for anti-clericalism. When the robbers attack Guillaume in his
monk's habit, he begins by threatening them with excom-
munication, but they defy 'clerk and priest and bishop and
abbot' to put them in prison; still thinking him a monk, the
leader says, 'you are too rich and have possessions in abundance; you ought to give it to poor people and amend your
life'. The poet of *Aliscans* is in the same mood as this when he
makes *R*enoart distribute the food of the monks of St Vincent –
as much as he has not eaten himself – to the poor, who then pray

God, the true justiciar, that the lord abbot will keep this new almoner to go on distributing food in the future. Yet these luxurious comforts of the monk's life were too sparse to satisfy a knight, either Guillaume or, as we shall see, Renoart; and the monks in their turn criticise the ways of chivalry, as when the abbot takes for granted Guillaume's sins, not only as a killer, but as a robber of convents and abbeys too.[50] Religion can accommodate ribaldry and mockery without much difficulty, but there are certain obvious oppositions, the church and the poor, the knights and the church, and between the different groups, lords, tenants, townsmen, outlaws, which are reflected in the chansons, both as conflicting interests, and as different callings that employ contrasting techniques.

Moniage Rainouart (with *Gadifer*) teaches the same lesson in a different way. J. Runeberg, in his study of the *Renoart* poems,[51] rejects the suggestion that they deliberately parody *Moniage Guillaume*, and certainly each poem exploits the same comic situation differently. The *Guillaume* has less burlesque than the *Renoart*. Whereas the penitent Guillaume begins by going to the abbot in the regular way to ask to become a monk, Renoart, though equally penitent, begins by assaulting a monk whom he happens to meet, in order to force him to change his habit for Renoart's lordly clothes. Guillaume really has a vocation, though he does not immediately find it. It is not coenobitic; he is plausibly shown as capable of humility, but not of obedience. He cannot fast in the monastery, but he fasts very well in the desert. Renoart's case is quite different, although his repentance is sincere, even touchingly so. Like Guillaume, he repents of killing, but he has more to repent; he killed Saracens, but they were many of them his own friends and family. 'I have done many bad things', he says, 'seen my brothers put to death and my father wounded', and he reflects that 'whatever they were, they were sent to me by God'. So, too, in *Aliscans*, he reminds Guillaume of all he has done for him: 'I am descended and was born of a high family . . . yet I have killed my noble relatives and even killed my brothers and my friends'. Gadifer refuses him the use of his balm, because he is the killer of his own kin. In *Loquifer* he feels his duty to his father, although he is his enemy, and he is conscious of the unbelief of his family; when he knocks the Mahon down in *Gadifer* he says to the monks, 'in this very god do all my relatives believe'.[52] The poets show him as recognising his love to his family and friends, his shame at their unbelief and his repentance for having killed them. It is *R*enoart's dilemma that, although he must repent of killing his own people, his true vocation is not to a life of communal prayer, or even, like Guillaume, to a life of solitary prayer, but to fighting the Saracens, just what he has to repent.

This is the underlying problem, but there is another unresolved conflict at a more practical level. His soldierly calling means that he must have plenty to eat, and no nonsense about not eating meat; yet the abbot tells him that he must come to matins at night, fast four times a week, wear a hair shirt and eat no meat at all. He replies rather solemnly, 'by that Lord who suffered on the cross', that he must eat well (though he specifies ham, and birds in pepper, the latter surely more for the sake of the verse than that of the sense). He will indeed sing, 'often and a great deal', and he will scour the country-side for Saracens, and if he finds them, he will not leave them worth two shelled eggs.[53] The poet (apart from having his little joke) is not condemning fasting. He is just insisting sensibly that monastic and chivalric purposes and processes are incompatible.

*R*enoart is a comic figure, but a respected one, and there is a good deal of the folk-hero in him. Although he insists on his royal birth, his deliberate use of the cudgel to overcome knights armed with the swords he despises must be meant to appeal to audiences below the knightly class. He distributes the monastery's food to the poor, he takes up the cause of a despoiled peasant.[54] He is not lecherous; his faults are hardly more than those of a young schoolboy, he eats too much, he sleeps too much; admittedly he also drinks too much. He is definite about preferring food to sexual pleasures: 'There is no joy like drinking and eating; plenty of it is worth more than making love, kissing and embracing and holding in your arms';[55] so he cannot be a real folk-hero. With drink or without it, he oversleeps, but, when he is aroused, he is invincible, and, however late he is, he is never too late. The comic proliferates around him. As an idea for a plot, it is démesuré to make the abbot, in despair at *R*enoart's intractability, turn defector, and betray both *R*enoart and his own monks to the Saracens; but the joke is as much against the monks as against *R*enoart. After his grotesque failure to recognise that the golden crucifix in the monastic church is an image, he goes to bed, and wakes up only to realise that 'the night was fine and morning was near, and the monks were singing loudly and clear'. He runs to the church but dares not go in for fear of 'the good fellow sitting on the pillar' (the crucifix), and determines that he must join in from outside. 'And then *R*enoart thought that he could sing well, and he began to cry out loud, just as he used to shout at the battle of Aliscans-sur-mer' – 'it makes the great minster shake and echo'.[56] Except when he makes war, *R*enoart does everything wrong. The poet succeeds in conveying the impression of a good man lost in an alien society, trying to play the part appropriate to him, but not always sticking to what he can do. If *R*enoart had really been an Arab, or any foreigner, much of this account of one who knows he is *en estrange pais* could have stood;[57] it nowhere depends on the pagan interpretation of Saracen religion either. Joking at the expense of foreigners would be out of place where Saracens are imagined as sharing one culture with Christians, but there is compassion in the joke, and the heart of it is the juxtaposition of the monks and the Saracens. The poet has managed to make *R*enoart's simplicity and single-mindedness somehow moving and sympathetic. A poem which has not been much admired, and which makes its first impact as a gross caricature, is sensitive and original in many of its details.

At the final count, *Moniage Rainouart*, as much as *Moniage Guillaume*, witnesses to the monastic influence on the chansons. It is, naturally, a secondary influence. The songs are largely about war, a little about love, only very occasionally about religion. Clerics support the war, and 'Christians are right',[58] but they do not take nearly so large a part as they did in the actual Crusades in the East. There is a tension between the life of a soldier and that of a monk in the songs which tends to reduce the importance of the whole Saracen question. In a list of monastic virtues there is not much that the poets would wish to claim on behalf of knights; there is an inherent incongruity, and if there were not, it would still do nothing to improve the story. Neither St Bernard's ideal for the Templars nor the ecclesiastical ritual of dubbing brought war and religion together successfully.[59] In the Vespers hymn *iste confessor*[60] the list of virtues – *pius, prudens, humilis, pudicus / sobrius, castus fuit et quietus* – includes only two (*pius* is too ambiguous) that our poets ever see as knightly virtues, and those two equivocally. Guillaume is prudent, Vivien the reverse, Guillaume is better loved, Vivien perhaps more admired, as all the world reveres a martyr, whatever his cause. Guillaume also becomes humble in his old age, but the qualities *fier* and *orgueilleus* are commoner and go more comfortably with prowess. There are no gurus in the songs and the knights direct their own spiritual lives according to their own standards.

All the same, many poems show awareness of the monks, and from the two Moniage poems we can infer a serious commentary on the monastic profession. The monks are familiar to the poets, but they are naturally viewed from the outside; most of what can be seen and heard in choir is reflected in the verse. The daily office, orderly, unhurried, and carefully sung, is seen against *R*enoart's absurd attempt to sing. Guillaume's joke about his literacy draws our attention to the liturgical texts. Both the Moniage poems give us a clear impression of the poverty of the monks' habit and of that of their table, although in other poems the bandits and the poor indicate poets who think otherwise. We can take at its face value the abbot's condemnation of knights' work at killing. In their plots against their two illustrious but disruptive *conversi*, there is a caricature of the monks' search for peace, itself in total opposition to the theme of the poems. In the tendency of both heroes to force the door of a monastery that has been closed to them, and to kill the porter, there may be a fantasy for some slight resented by an importunate poet, or perhaps monastic porters were a standing joke to the fraternity of jongleurs. The life of liturgical prayer, the *opus Dei*, the way of asceticism under the sign of pax and the Rule of St Benedict, have been clearly observed. What naturally is missing is the internal life of the community, the activities of the monks in study, discussion and writing – the composition of sermons and commentaries, even histories – but none of these would be seen from the outside. The monks are choir monks; for work in the field we turn to Guillaume's life as a hermit, self-supporting in prayer as well as herbs. Behind the fantasy and the ribaldry there is a perfectly sensible estimate of the monastic vocation.

This makes all the clearer the contrast between a monk and a knight, and that contrast underlies not only what the poems directly concerned with monks have to say, but the whole literature generally. The poet of *Roland* makes no less a cleric than Turpin say so explicitly: a knight 'must be strong and proud in battle, or he is not worth four pence, and ought to be a monk in one of the minsters, where he can pray all the time for our sins'.[61] Monks and knights make a poor appearance in each other's rôles.

CONCLUSION

It seems beyond question that the poets established their orthodoxy abundantly, with sincerity and simplicity. It also served their main purpose admirably. It suited the story, and the prayers which were narrative were themselves stories within the story; all the purposes served by the prayers were ways that helped the story along. But they were also ways of evading serious polemic; there is no trace in them of any knowledge of Islam, and as statements of faith they are equally good for explaining the Christian religion to anyone of any other belief. Their most remarkable achievement is not just that they evaded what theologians say about Islam; they also evaded what theologians say about Christianity. They made their own statements of orthodoxy and they ignored ecclesiastical formulae entirely. Their clergy have never met the Gregorian Reform, and I should not like to vouch for Turpin's knowledge of canon law. Monks occupy the background a little more realistically; the Moniage poems burlesque them, sometimes moving to satire, but have a fair conception of the monastic vocation. The poets have therefore achieved an astonishing degree of individual independence without damaging their perfect orthodoxy.

The signs of Christianity in the songs are not many, but are crucial. There are the long prayers, peculiar to the convention but amounting to a substitute liturgy; there are abbreviated prayers, which are not essentially different; there are ejaculations ('who made the world'). There is a consciousness of the Christian life lived in monasteries. These, not their morals, are all there is to show what Christians are, and to contrast with the imaginary religion of pagan gods: except of course that the stories are about fighting pagans, and this is where it was convenient to have as the perpetual enemy the 'Saracen' who could be identified with true Saracens, to the presumed approval of all the authorities.

In the course of a long history of Conciliar and episcopal condemnations, *joculatores* and even *joculatrices* had learned how to do without Church approval; there is always a black market, and Edmond Faral brings together a number of instances in which churchmen, like other feudal lords, made full use of them.[62] This is not the only subject on which church councils reiterated condemnations that showed how little they were observed. The distinction between the jongleur proper, needed to sing the lives of saints and for other respectable purposes, and the buffoon, who could carry the burden of condemnations, was conveniently notional, but a serviceable one. The claim to authenticity was another way to disarm criticism, as when the Paduan author of *l'Entrée d'Espagne* claimed in the course of the poem to have learned clerical authority for his 'facts'. It would certainly have been disastrous if any serious charge of heresy could have been added to the existing ones of frivolity and obscenity.

This is where the theme of war against Saracens, obscured by fantasy, but backed up by other proofs of orthodoxy, could earn ecclesiastical neutrality, or even approval, and we can presume it succeeded. The chansons de geste, presented as a form of sacred history, were making a claim that fell only a little short of being on a level with the lives of the saints. This would hardly have stood up to serious examination, but the convention of the poems is calculated to block the view of any over-enquiring official mind. What if the poets did show a sublime indifference to the facts ? Only a pedant would object. It was encouraging and diverting to hear how victory proved that pagan gods were false, and who had any reason to care whether or not this was falsely attributed to an Islamic setting ? Those who wrote seriously about Islam wrote for intellectuals, academics and clerics and missionary friars, and they ignored the poets as the poets ignored them. I am not claiming that the chansons de geste are crypto-heretical. There is no anti-Catholic bombshell hidden in their verses, but to tell a good story and to make theological propaganda are incompatible; and the whole is made safe at the point where the theologians and the story-tellers have a common interest: the true God gives victory. This knotty problem for the theologian is for the poet the purpose and the culmination of every story.

III

CORROBORATION

I began this enquiry in the hope of identifying an unofficial medieval view of Islam in the body of chansons de geste, and generally the poems of the Tervagant Convention. Other evidence of unofficial and lay attitudes is not concentrated in a single convention, or even a single genre, but the briefest survey will illustrate the many elements that are common to the Tervagant convention and to other lay witness, and will show how little except the pantheon itself is peculiar to our convention alone. We can recognise unofficial and lay sources, not only in lay poetry and fiction, but in memoirs, chronicles and even treatises by clerics who may reflect a point of view not their own. It would not be practicable, without writing another volume, to search all clerical sources for evidence of what laymen thought, but I shall cite one or two examples in this chapter, as well as examples from the other sources. This short survey is meant to illustrate, not to exhaust the subject, and to show that the pantheon is the salt that gives the chansons their savour.

The *Chronicon Salernitanum* is essentially a city record and reflects better than most of the chronicles of the period of the Arab invasions of Italy the conditions of warfare at that time and the low morale of the Christians. One point of especial interest in the Arab siege of Salerno in 871 is the occurrence of single combats between Salernitans and Saracens, a process that led, as in epic and romance, from a challenge to the death. Christians seem surprised when all goes well; a Christian answers a challenge with reluctance, though he fights bravely, and even a victory is described with little echo of the glory.[1] In all the chronicles of France and Italy of the ninth and tenth centuries, it is not so much the ineffectiveness of the defence as the extent to which Arab invaders found local collaborators that stands out. Liutprand, bishop and chronicler interested in high politics and courtly motivations, remarked that the Arab settlement at La Garde-Freinet in France flourished because the people of Provence called in the help of the Saracens,[2] and this seems often to have been the pattern, not only in France, but in Italy also. This was not quite the same pattern of treason as in the chansons, where it is always found among the great courtiers, rather than among lords attached to their own lands. 'Treason', indeed, is the word for what happens in the chansons, but it does not really fit the events of history. The ravaging of the country-side and the capture of considerable numbers of prisoners for the slave market in Ifrīqīya and Egypt are also reflected in the chansons. Liutprand and other writers clearly distinguished Arabs from Spain and those from North Africa (he himself calls the Tunisians 'Carthaginians', *Poeni*);[3] this is quite contrary to the custom of the chansons, where all Saracens are one, by however many names they are known.

Least like the chansons is the slowness of the Christians to defend themselves: the Arabs jeered, 'where is their God now ?', and so 'God moved the hearts of the Christians to make the desire to fight stronger than the desire they had before to run away'.[4] This tepid reference to a counter-attack organised by John XII nevertheless looks forward to the new spirit of *corage aduré*, to the recovery of Spain, to the Crusade in the East and to the inspiration of the chansons. Equally there is something in the atmosphere of the earlier and dispirited centuries that reminds us of the chansons; if from the songs we could take away their characteristic spirit of aggression, the residue might be uninteresting but in tone it would resemble the earlier age. Despite the enormous numbers always attributed to the enemy, the actual fights related are a series of small encounters. Some of the best known of the songs are about defensive wars, *Roland*, *Aspremont*, *Couronnement de Louis*, and many others. Saracens are wrong and Christians are right, but there is no great theological venom. Neither songs nor chronicles show any curiosity about the invaders. Historically, the Christians made the same discouraged resistance to Arabs and Magyars alike, and the word *Esclers*, Slavs, may refer to the Magyars who devastated Italy, just as Saracens is sometimes used for the Vikings who devastated France.

Although the songs are sometimes set in a Europe that suffers invasion, they have more obvious affinities with the aggressive, invading Europe of their own age. The *Gesta Francorum* is the work of a fighting soldier, who adopts some of the attitudes of the heroes of fiction. Phrases recurrent in the poetry are echoed by the *Gesta* in its comment on the Turks:

> Certainly, if they had been firm in the faith of Christ, and in Christianity, if they had chosen to confess one Lord in Trinity . . . and had believed with a sound judgement and faith, none could have been found more powerful, or stronger, or cleverer in the arts of war.

He adds: 'I will tell you the truth which nobody can deny';[5] this is surely not a magical formula, but surely just for emphasis; it is true that the omission marks above represent something very like the 'prayer of crisis' in embryo. In the same passage we recognise the same Frankish pride in toughness: the Turks 'thought that they could terrorise the Frankish people with the threat of their arrows, as they had terrorised the Arabs, Saracens and Armenians, Syrians and Greeks'.[6] Then, again, conquered peoples who will not change their religion are sometimes killed. 'They captured all the inhabitants of the place, and those who would not accept Christianity they killed.' This treatment extended to prisoners taken in battle, deliberately *ad terrorem*: 'so as to make those that remained in the town more wretched'.[7] The most notorious of the massacres was at the capture of Jerusalem, where the victorious army boasted of being up to the ankles in blood, and 'the whole Temple ran with their blood', and 'our men captured a good number of men and women in the Temple, and those they chose, they killed, and those they chose, they kept alive'.[8] Less

frank than *Antioche*, this compares with *Conquête de Jérusalem*
very closely. The army also believed that the conversion of the
enemy was a negotiable point.[9]

The polytheism of the enemy is taken for granted, but not
stressed; it comes in imaginary conversations that break up the
narrative. Karbuqa ('Curbaram') is made to say, 'I swear to
you by Muhammad and the names of all our gods'; and the
Fatimid amir defeated at Ascalon similarly says, 'I swear by
Muhammad and by the holy spirits of all our gods'. Bréhier
says, '*Le point de vue de l'Anonyme est le même à cet égard que celui
des chansons de geste*'.[10] It is nearly, but not quite, the same.
Oaths sworn by Muhammad and the gods are ambiguous about
the person of the Prophet but it is at least clear that the writer
thinks that Saracens and Turks are pagans; probably his idea is
vaguer than that of the chansons. There is no actual mention of
an idol, and there is no Tervagant, Apollin, or Jupin or their
companions. Karbuqa's mother tells him of an oracular prophecy that 'has been found in our scriptures and the books of
the nations', which Bréhier, surely rightly, refers to the
Methodius or similar prophecy.[11] If, as it seems to be, the
Gesta is representative of knowledge and opinion in the
'pilgrim' army of 1096–9, at an unintellectual level, the knights
had a great deal in common with the chansons, of which they
were a potential audience; but the *Gesta* seems to reflect more
diverse outside matter, and it is just where its supposition of
Saracen and Turkish paganism is vaguest that the Tervagant
pantheon takes over in the songs.

Most of the *Gesta* is a serious record, with passages of fiction
interpolated; the *Cantar del Cid* is a fiction with strong historical
roots. It is more realistic than the chansons de geste, and it
treats many of the same themes. Its Moors, in the place of
Saracens, tie us immediately to the peoples of Spain and the
Maghrib, in contrast to the infinitely extensible Arabs and
Persians, Norsemen and East Europeans inhabiting foreign
parts undefinable. Its world is Spain, divided between Moor
and Christians; Morocco, source of Moorish reinforcement,
and Barcelona, inhabited by Franks, are already foreign.[12] The

poem is set in places that existed and among events that happened, although the plot, like that of many chansons, is centred on the relations of the hero with his overlord and on the conflict between a new and an old nobility.

The *Cid* makes more out of the lure of booty as the purpose of fighting than the chansons do.[13] The Cid and his followers are in business, and they think of their profit with the single-mindedness of Union negotiators demanding an overdue pay-rise. When the Moors attack, it is the occasion for him to tell his wife and daughters in a famous phrase that they will see 'how we gain our bread'.[14] He is a pious sort of robber: 'I thank you, spiritual Father', he prays, 'we are in their country and are doing them all the harm we can'.[15] When he and his men hear of another Moorish invasion, they are happy, because 'this will increase their profit, God willing'.[16] The word *ganançia* is also used in this same poem to mean 'usurious interest',[17] and the Cid's attitude to his gains is very much that for which the newly rich are everywhere notorious.

His wars are more realistically told than those in the chansons; the violence is only occasionally exaggerated, and there are few battle horrors.[18] There is no pious pretence at Christianisation after conquest. Relations with the Moors are immediately credible. Terror is a weapon of war, the Cid's ravaging of the country-side is a matter of policy. The poet knows that the Moors really suffer.

> [They] do not know what to do. They cannot get bread anywhere. There is nothing a father can suggest to his son, or a son to his father, nor can a friend comfort a friend. It is bitter trouble, gentlemen, to be short of bread, and to see your children and your wives die of hunger.[19]

It is hard to parallel this degree of realism in the chansons. Yet the Cid cares about his relations with the Moors. He is just as happy to make kindly use of them as to ravage them. 'We cannot sell the men and women Moors, and we shall gain nothing by beheading them', he says after capturing the fortress of Alcoçer, 'let us live in their houses and make use of them'. If this is to enslave them, he does not hesitate to sell the

stronghold of Alcoçer back to the Moors when it suits him.[20]
His alliance with a Moorish client kinglet as much as anything
persuades us that the political situation is authentic. Aven-
galvon is his ally and friend, faithful, hospitable and brave; he
is the Cid's 'friend of peace', he is the ideal and idealised
Moor.[21] When the victorious Cid catches fleeing King Bucar,
the invader, he first offers him his friendship. He does not offer
him baptism. Christianisation has no part in his plans, but when
Bucar rejects his overture, he kills him.[22] In the *Cid*, no one
troubles to say that Christians are right and Moors are wrong;
religion is not discussed. There are neither baptisms nor idols.
The name of the Prophet occurs only as a battle cry: *Los moros
llaman Mafònat e los cristanos santi Yague*;[23] is he somehow
equivalent to St James ? The name of God, *el Criador*, is often in
the Cid's mouth, and so are St James and other saints, and
something like the long prayers of the chansons occurs. And to
piety is added luck; the Cid is the man 'who was born in a lucky
hour', 'who belted on his sword in a lucky hour',[24] phrases
constantly repeated.

The Cid does resemble some of the heroes of the chansons in
his interest in horses, especially his Babieca, won from the King
of Seville, and so fast that it was famous over all Spain:[25] this
quality was the most prized even in a war-horse. There is also
an equivalent to the Turpin of the chansons, Jerome, characteristically made Bishop by the Cid himself. The Cid takes to him
from the moment of his first arrival as a young priest looking
for a chance to kill a Moor. Jerome, like Turpin, is bishop-
cum-chaplain, and we see more of them both on the battlefield
than in the church. Jerome makes an explicit bargain: 'I sang
Mass for you this morning', he says, and in return he wants the
privilege of striking the first blows. His own job is to give
absolution before the battle, and he more than fulfils it. 'He
who dies here fighting face to face, I take his sins on me, and
God shall have his soul', he promises. He is a successful soldier.
'We'll see how he fights', says the Cid professionally; but, as
the poet realistically puts it, 'through good luck and God who
loves him, at his first blow he kills two Moors'. He has his

difficulties, but after the battle he cannot keep count of the Moors he has killed, and his share of the booty is enormous.[26]

Yet the Cid has no claim on choirs of angels. He died on Whitsunday, 'may Christ have mercy on him, and on us all, righteous and sinners'.[27] He is never idealised. Nearly all the themes of the chansons are present in the *Cantar del Cid*, but all are treated more earthily. The subject is the same; it is the treatment that is different. The French heroes and the Cid alike exist to champion Christendom, but they are all infinitely remote from the concern of a Peter the Venerable.[28] They do not care to know the truth about Islam, and the Cid actively desires his Muslims to remain so as his subjects. The Spanish poem has no trace of the Tervagant conventional pantheon.

There are also useful comparisons with other fictions about the Saracens that do not have the Tervagant convention. One of the earliest and most relevant is *Partonopeus de Blois*. King Sornegur, invader of France, is at once a 'Saracen' and a Dane, and ultimately honourably defeated and repatriated by agreement. The particular honour of his defeat is that he is so shocked by the treachery of a supporter that he comes in person into the French king's court to apologise. It is an aristocratic story, and the traitor is a churl by birth. 'It is the character of a villein to be very high-handed towards someone he fears, when he has a chance to do him harm', or, as the English version paraphrases it, 'For thus ys ever chorles kinde . . . Curteyse, esy and debonowre, Tylle that he may have tyme and leysowr Hys master to do summe fowle dyspyte'.[29] This is a direct transplant of a feudal attitude to the mouths – and situations – of Saracens. Sornegur and Partonopeus are worthy opponents. Partonopeus is *'li plus beaus hom qu'aiue feist Deus'*, and Sornegur is pleased and proud when he hears that his challenge to the French is going to be taken up by him: 'he is the most distinguished of the French, and I render thanks to God for his great mercy'. Sornegur receives that characteristically Christian measure of praise: 'they would have had in him a valiant king, if he had believed in our religion'.[30]

In the three-day tournament which takes up all the last part of the story, and is the framework for the dénouement of a complicated love plot, the great challenger is the *soudan* of Persia, who is in love with Partonopeus' lady. When all the contestants arrive, they include both Christians and pagans, and among the latter seven kings from *ceste nostre Aufrique*, who will be judges; they have a high reputation, as good educated clerks and good knights, for their common sense and sound argument. One of the Christians is a new friend of Partonopeus', Gaudin of Blois, who comes from Spain (Blois?), 'where God is neither served nor invoked'; he is the son of a rich vavasour, who did not believe in the Creator, and when Gaudin, travelling in France, came to Tours, he rejected Mahon and Apollin. The soudan is the favourite, Partonopeus is anonymous, the other two pagans among the élite of the tournament are King Sades of Syria and King Anpatris of Nubia. Third among the Christians comes the King of France. There are several close fought encounters between Partonopeus and the *soudan*, who claims to be the better knight, 'I am worth more in *cortesie*, in sense and chivalry...'[31] and so on. In a final and fatal fight, the sultan is killed. In another version, of which the extant English poem is an example, the *soudan's* last fight is replaced by a disputed adjudication which he loses but is unwilling to accept. Yet the poem as a whole, and in both forms, witnesses to the huge part allotted to Saracen nobles in a story which is a hymn to chivalry. It could hardly do without them, although they might as well be Tibetans for all that there is characteristically Saracen about them. Religion hardly enters in. Sornegur speaks of God only,[32] but his monotheism is not repeated in the account of the Saracens taking part in the tournament, and, as they come from Arab countries, and Sornegur is a Danish 'Saracen', this could just be construed as a jibe at Islam. The gods of the pantheon are just mentioned, although they have no part of any importance to play in the story. In the alternative version, the sultan is willing to be converted to marry the lady, but he and the other Saracens at the tournament are only vaguely indicated as pagan, and by implication. It is as knights that they are important, and they provide the standard against which the hero's prowess is measured, and it is on them that his sword is sharpened. The story almost qualifies as belonging to the same convention as the chansons, but it differs from them, in degree at least, in the exaggerated fantasy of its chivalry, Christian and Saracen.

There are a number of poems that have some Saracens in them, and we should look at a few more examples. It is tempting to read too much into the troubadours' repertory listed by the author of *Flamenca* in the late twelfth century. In a deliberately wide field, matter of Rome – Alexander, Hero and Leander – Daedalus, Cadmus, Orpheus, Julius Caesar – the Old Testament – Goliath and David, Samson and Delilah, Maccabees – matter of Britain – Percival, Eric and Enid, Tristan, the Fair Unknown, the Fisher King – matter of France – Charlemagne, Clovis and Pepin and Gui de Nanteuil – and many more, none of it placed carefully in categories, is included 'how the Assassins act under the direction of the Old Man of the Mountain'[33] (*shaykh al-jabal*). The matter of France is the thinnest, no Roland or Oliver, no Guillaume or Aymery; this is strange enough, but the inclusion of a fragment of contemporary history is stranger still. The French subjects included have a bearing which is primarily feudal, not necessarily Saracen at all, and the only unquestionably Saracen subject is 'current affairs', a sensational theme, but a remote one. The lesson of this is to remember the limited impact of the convention which is my main subject, and this is at the same time a further reminder of how tight and sealed up that convention was.

Floire et Blancheflor is another variation on an increasingly familiar pattern. We are not concerned with it as a story of oriental origin, cousin by common descent of the *alf layla wa layla* complex which is so much more recent.[34] I find it difficult to accept the theory of Dorothee Metlitzky which makes it a reconciliation of East and West, because I do not think we should read too much into the happy ending of a romance.[35] Yet there are aspects of the story which relate closely to themes we have recognised elsewhere. The story is again aristocratic, but it does not make so much out of the social discrepancy

between the daughter of a Christian slave (whose father in any
case turns out to be a *preu* and *cortois* French knight) and the son
of a pagan king, as it does out of the theme of life fidelity: 'une
véritable idéologie de l'amour-vertu', says its most recent
editor, a fidelity that began in a shared cradle.[36] Elaborate
descriptions are a facet of this short poem, such as the account
of the journey to Baudas (Baghdad), an imaginary port set
high on a rock, on the way to Babylon (Cairo), where the amir
has a kind of harem of young girls, kept strictly secluded; he
takes one a year, and beheads her afterwards; but the author
does not seem to recognise the harem as specifically a Saracen
institution, and public opinion among the courtiers is represented as favourable to the lovers, 'they all said that it would be
a great misfortune that they should have to die like this'.[37] The
Trojan cup which plays a part in the story, made by Vulcan,
brought to Rome by Aeneas, inherited by Caesar, adds to the
pagan connections of the story,[38] but the pagans are never
identified as Saracens, though they sound a good deal like the
Saracens of the chansons de geste. They have some sort of
religion, since they have a bishop, and some other pagans
celebrate Palm Sunday; they drink wine freely; there is no
mention of their God or gods.[39] The only unambiguously Arab
notes are the place-names and the titles of *amirail* and, in
Spain, *amaçon*.[40] The notion of Saracen is almost totally
engulfed by the notion of pagan, and this reminds us that it is
largely so, though not to this extreme, in our chansons. The
pagans experience the usual propaganda of the faith: Blancheflor baptises *F*loire, and he baptises his knights – as with Aye,
religion is matrilinear when it is Christian; as for *la gent vilaine*,
their baptism takes a week; 'those who refused baptism and
would not believe in God' were either burned or chopped
down, but they are good people who can easily be persuaded
to do right.[41] The eponymous couple are the destined grand-
parents of Charlemagne,[42] and the poet's attitude to pagans
can figuratively be described as ancestral to the usual attitude
of the chansons.

The situation is much the same in *Aucassin et Nicolette*,

though here the non-Christians are called Saracens, without stressing it. Whether the name of Aucassin has its origin in al-Qāsim is, as Mario Roques says, unprovable and unimportant.[43] The geography is unusually plausible, although *Saisne* is once more confused with *Saracen*.[44] An essential of the plot is the King's objection to his son's marriage with a slave-girl, contrasting in that with the plot of *Floire*. The theme of mésalliance ends when Nicolette turns out after all to be the daughter of the King of Carthage: *cil estoit ses peres, et si avoit dose freres, tos princes u rois*.[45] Despite this mass-production of nobility, her high birth averts all danger of contamination between classes (the *dérogation* of the ancien régime?), but it is Saracen high birth and counted by Christians just as good as a Christian one. Nicolette behaves throughout with initiative (*'adroite et énergique'*, as Roques says), where Aucassin is rather clod-like, though brave.[46] Here is a variant on the *paienne amoureuse*. There are no gods in the story, and the pagan aspect is, as in *Floire*, inchoate.

Another and later kind of *roman* is that of the soldier adventurer, prose parallel to *Simon de Pouille* or *Bueves de Hamtoune*, and indeed *Fouke Fitz Warin* is the rewritten version of a lost poem. In one episode, Fouke falls asleep on his ship, there comes 'un hydous vent' which breaks the mooring and sends him to sea. Woken up by two sergeants in the harbour of '*la cité de Tunes*', he is welcomed by the King of Barbarie and befriended by the King's sister. The King is at war with the Duchess of Carthage, and a knight is needed to take up a challenge to single combat. Fouke offers, on condition the King will be baptised, and the challenger turns out to be Fouke's brother, also in an overseas service. They postpone the rest of their battle after this discovery and overnight persuade the parties to make peace, the King marries the Duchess, and he and his men are baptised.[47] This is part of an attempt to glamourise the actual history of the Fitz Warin brothers of the first half of the thirteenth century, and episodes from adventure romances are grafted on to the English background. The King's sister plays the part of the *paienne amoureuse* up to a point, although she cannot become Fouke's wife, who was known, or his mistress, which would not have been seemly within the convention that all this was imitating. Her rôle nevertheless hints at what was not asserted. Fouke tells her a story about how the girl he loved at home loved someone else more, and, making love to him, betrayed him to her real lover, who put him on the ship. The King's sister comments, *cele demoisele ne fust geres cortois*. The question of religion is taken very lightly; there is one mention of a god: *plust a dieu Mahoun*.[48] This near-parody is so light a confection that we can only note the familiar assumption of an international concept of cortoisie, and the tendency to confuse actual events and fictional conventions.

Fragments of Saracen conventions are scattered in late romances. The author of *Le Roman du Comte d'Artois* (fifteenth century), in order to flatter the Duke of Burgundy, chose for his subject 'un ancêtre peu connu du même nom et lui ait attribué les qualités réelles on désirées du duc'; but he handles an imaginary political situation and a war against the King of Granada adroitly enough. The King is made out to be an aggressor who threatens Castile, bringing in to help him the amirs of Tunis, Barbary and Fez, but he has his point of view: 'intending to be avenged for all the troublesome losses that the Christians had caused him'. There are three references to Mahon, none to Apollin, Tervagant or Jupin, Cahu or Baratron, but two of the Mahon references speak of him as a god, e.g., *le puissant dieu*.[49] In this age the Tervagant convention is beginning to tire; in *Saladin*, Mahon is still healthy, but Apollin and Jupiter are attenuated and Tervagant himself has disappeared.[50] Although there had always been some books of Saracens without the pantheon, they had been the exception, and now were increasingly the rule. The *Jehan de Saintré* by Antoine de la Sale presents a Crusade battle with the pomp of a tournament, and chivalry itself seems more pomp than war.[51] It only hints at a consciousness of the real Ottoman danger, a hazy reminiscence perhaps of the Nicopolis disaster.

In Book v of Malory, *Of King Arthur and the Emperor Julius* there are again plenty of Saracens but no gods at all. It is a fourteenth century poem, adapted, that puts us back into a remote and confused pagan Rome, contemporary with Arthur, when Rome was no longer pagan, and harking back in its genealogies to the Greeks and the Jews – to Alexander and Maccabees and even to Joshua.[52] We can compare *Auberon*, absurd Roman fantasy and the epitome of anachronism – yet both avoid any anachronism with Mahon; the other poems of the *Huon de Bordeaux* cycle are not Roman, and have the pantheon, and this surely conscious handling of the difference is the more unexpected.[53] Malory v takes the near-identification of Romans and Saracens further: 'And thus were the Romaynes and the Sarazens slayne adowne clene', he says, and he makes Lancelot kill the Emperor Lucius, 'and in his wey he smote thorow a kynge that stoode althirnexte hym, and his name was Jacounde, a Sarazen full noble'.[54] The *Morte Arthure* which Malory adapted is closer in style to the chansons de geste; for example, when the King 'with a prynce metes That was ayere [heir] to Egipt in thos este marches' he strikes him so as to cut through prince and saddle and horse, and dis-embowels the horse, all in a blow, Until the death of his knights is avenged, the King will accept no ransom, 'There myghte no siluer thaym saue their lyues, ne secoure, Sowdone, ne Sarazene, ne senatour of Rome'.[55] The assimilation of 'sultan and Saracen' to 'senator of Rome' is here most nearly complete, and once again it endorses the pagan identification of Saracens without mention, in Malory or the source, of the gods. I shall give one last example of this. In *Lancelot du Lac*, Joseph of Arimathea converts a thousand Saracens whose villainous king announces as soon as Joseph has gone that he wants 'to bring back all our people to our first faith, for the one I have just taken does not please me'; he recalls the high barons to the gods and turns the common people back to their 'mahommerie' by threats and a few judicious martyrdoms.[56] *Mahommerie* here means the religion, not the place of worship, and there is no indication whether it is an anachronism or bears the general sense of paganism. But all these examples tend to show the association of Saracens with the vaguest possible conception of paganism, and even omit Mahon and Tervagant.

We now turn back to realistic history, and do so by way of romantic feudal fiction encapsulated in a serious dynastic history, the famous story in Orderic Vitalis of Bohemund's imprisonment by the Danishmandid ghazi, and his rescue by the converted daughter of the ghazi, 'Melaz', whom he does not marry, but talks into marrying another Norman. It is just possible that this is the origin of the theme of the paienne amoureuse in the West, though it is not possible that such a thing really happened; it is much more likely that Bohemund's propaganda picked up and exploited a story already circulating. If, as has been suggested, 'Melaz' is the Greek *melas*, it diverges from the usual form of the story, in which the amir's daughter is the fairest of the fair.[57] Some other episodes in Orderic reflect romantic origins and suggest episodes from the chansons, for example, the imprisonment and sufferings of Odo Arpin, vicomte of Bourges,[58] which might be Aymery's or Orson's. Orderic also gives us a miniature disillusion scene, when some Muslims say to the ghazi: *En execrabilis Machomes deus noster nos prorsus deseruit.*[59] This confusion about Islam in Orderic may be of a kind we have met before, by false analogy with Christ, or it may be another of the chansons' loans to him.[60] King Baldwin's escape from Ramla is another story that Orderic tells in the style of a troubadour.[61] That is not to say that some of these episodes did not happen – Melaz is entirely imaginary of course – but that the writer interpreted and retold them under the influence of epic poetry and its romantic developments. Odo Arpin became a monk, and in Orderic's romantic tendencies we may recognise the authentic imaginative link between baron, monk and jongleur.

I turn to Joinville. It is not fanciful to suggest that Louis IX was conscious of playing the rôle of Charlemagne or his son Louis in the chansons. His attempt to charge the very first Saracens he saw might come straight from an adventure romance.[62] He approved the knight who knocked down a learned Jew invited to Cluny to dispute with the greatest theologian (le plus grant clerc). The abbot thought the knight crazy, but the knight thought the abbot crazier, and the King agreed – only a very good theologian should dispute, and the only way for anyone else to defend Christianity was to stick his sword into the unbeliever's stomach.[63] Turpin too would have agreed; but the King did in fact anticipate the disappointed hopes of theologians for successful disputation. His practice with Muslim prisoners was reminiscent of the last lines of almost any chanson, if distinctly less draconian. In the canonisation material utilised by Guillaume de Saint-Pathus, the first example of the King's *debonnereté* was his command not to kill Saracen women and children, but have them brought for baptism, and even 'as far as he could' not to kill the men, but have them put in prison. After his own release, and while he remained in the Levant, 'forty or more' Saracens came to him asking for baptism, including some 'amirs and high men among them'. He fed them, and had them instructed by Dominicans, took them back to France with him, made them rich and married them to Christian girls.[64] It is hard to avoid the impression that in practice as well as in fictions the title of 'amir' was imputed too easily by Christians to Arabs; it would have been easy to impose on Louis, if those with enough *sarazinois* chose to do so. These converts might even have been Eastern Christians. Christian loyalty also mattered to the King as much as to Charlemagne. He sent away a well-dressed and fine-looking Saracen who turned out to be a Frenchman converted to Islam since the Fifth Crusade attack on Damietta; he was married and prosperous, and must have seemed to have accepted the traditional offers of women and wealth for apostacy.[65] But Louis also insisted that renegades who turned back again must not be reproached or blamed;[66] it was fear of reproach, the French-born Saracen told Joinville, that deterred him from going back to France.

It is not only to the King that things happen that echo the songs of action; did these influence the actual events, or only Joinville's memory during more than fifty years since they took place? His own chaplain, like a little Turpin, laid out nine

Saracens in battle. Count Walter of Brienne quarrelled with the Patriarch; before battle he asked for and was refused absolution, but the Count had in his following a 'valiant cleric', bishop of Rames, who assured him: 'Don't worry your conscience when the Patriarch won't absolve you, for he is wrong and you are right. And I absolve you in the name of the Father, the Son and the Holy Spirit. And now let's get at them.' This bishop had campaigned before with the Count who this time, however, was captured. The Arab army besieging Jaffa brought out their prisoner and hung him up on a gibbet by his arms, and announced that they would not take him down until the town surrendered; he told the defenders not to give up, and threatened to kill them himself if they did. In the end, Cairo merchants who had suffered losses from his depradations were allowed to finish him off. Joinville calls this a true martyrdom.[67] There are several figures of fiction here; the absolution before the battle, a little more complex than usual, the scene in front of the city walls, like those with Aymery and Guibert before Narbonne,[68] and a tale of ill-treatment in prison; the claim to martyrdom is more than poets made for their heroes, but the battling bishop, old campaign comrade, is a familiar figure.

The chivalry of the songs and the chivalry of the battle-field are not total strangers to each other. At the technical level there is the shared interest in banners and coats of arms; and still more an interest in horses is common to history and poetry.[69] There is even a case of a challenge to single combat modified by practical tactics. A Genoese knight was covering the retreat of some poor people in the gardens outside Acre. 'While he was taking them back, a Saracen began to call out in *sarriẓinois* that he would joust with him if he liked. And he said that he would do it willingly.' As he made in the direction of the challenger, he saw a group of Turks to the left, who were waiting to see the joust and laid out three of them, and still brought his charges safe home.[70] Little things too recall the minor occupations of chivalry in poetry; the *shaykh al-jabal* sent the king presents that included chess and backgammon. The Count of Poitiers, one of the King's brothers, was a gambler, but *jouit cortoisement*, giving his winnings away.[71]

Joinville as much as any jongleur used expressions of chivalry for Saracens quite naturally. He speaks of the *chevalerie au soudanc* and of *serjans sarrazins*; these are technical rather than ideal identifications. Joinville also makes judgements based on chivalrous values: 'he was one of the best knights in all paganism (*paiennime*)'.[72] Jean Sarrasin is making both an ideal and a technical assessment when he says that outside Damietta the Crusaders killed 'the greatest lord of all the land of Egypt after the sultan, both a good and tough knight and an expert at war'.[73] Joinville certainly extends expressions of honour to Saracens, as much as any poet. Speaking of Fakhr al-Dīn, son of Shaykh Sadr al-Dīn, he comments: 'these are the people who most in the world honour old people, and so God has saved them from *vilain reproche* into their old age'. He also reports the distinction made by King Philip Augustus between *preuhome* and *preudome*: the preudome has prowess, which is the gift of God, but 'there are many preuhome knights in the land of the Christians and of the Saracens, who have never believed in God and his mother'.[74]

The resemblances between history and fiction spring largely from common techniques and technology of war; also the amusements of gentleman soldiers did not vary greatly. Joinville does not bring anything like a scholastic mind to his matter, and there is nothing to which he is indifferent or about which he is incurious. In spite of the inevitable confusions of old age as well as the passage of time, his mistakes are never stupid. These are ways in which he was unlike our poets, who so concentrated on their main purpose that they were always indifferent, usually incurious and quite often stupid about other things. Theory is outside Joinville's interests, and therefore theology is. He reports a curious little inverted 'disillusion' scene. One of the interpreters, who may have been having him on (he claims that the amirs would like Louis as sultan) says that if Muhammad had allowed him to suffer as the king had suffered, he would not believe in Muhammad as the King did in God. Perhaps he was a converted Christian; he made the sign of the cross.[75] But Joinville missed the significance of that and supposed he was getting a genuine insight into a Muslim's thoughts. He never mentions idols or gods; he gives no sign of even having heard of the Tervagant convention.

By the later part of the thirteenth century the spirit of aggression against the Muslims was largely exhausted, though not of course the spirit of individual adventure; the mercenary and the merchant replace the land-snatcher and the bandit. It made a difference to the spirit of aggression. As far as Crusading goes, the watershed came somewhere between the first (Egyptian) and the second (Tunis) Crusade of Louis IX; Joinville refused to go to Tunis because he thought that both he and the King should stay at home to protect their own people.[76] There was a good deal of self-analysis by the Christian clergy at the time of the Council of Lyons of 1274; they realised the apathy of the public while they hoped for renewal. Humbert of Romans analysed the opposition which he saw as arising in tepidity. People were objecting on pacifist grounds: Christians should not shed blood, as Christ and the Apostles did not; so much blood had been shed and would be shed yet, the blood of the harmless as well as those who did harm; it is unwise to tempt Providence to stir up an enemy who is satisfied and quiet; it is all very well to defend oneself, quite another thing to invade the Saracens. We do not persecute Jews, we should not persecute Saracens either; nor will anything spiritual be achieved, the Saracens will not be converted, but turn to blasphemy, and those who are killed will go to hell. There will not even be any temporal gain, because the Christians will be unable to hold any lands they may conquer. Humbert also analyses the motives, as he sees them, for this lukewarm attitude: the avarice of the clergy, who squeeze the tenth out of the poor, the death of Crusaders and the failure of Crusades; the hopeless task of overcoming such multitudes of the enemy; and the worldly wisdom that tells us that trade cannot flourish in Crusade.[77] He himself has aggressive answers to all the objections, but he represents at most the enthusiastic wing of church opinion. All the opposition may be summed up as 'stay at home'; as with Joinville and as with Humbert's objectors, so with the poet Rutebeuf, a great satirist of opinion: 'I want to stay among my neighbours'; the speaker wants the sultan told that if he invades, he will be sorry, but the speaker will not go and look for him. 'If God is anywhere in the world, he is in France, there is no doubt; don't think that he is hiding among people who do not love him'.[78]

When all that was left of Crusading was the looting and the murder, enterprising freebooters like Chaucer's Knight, noble and commoner alike, found profit at the sack of Alexandria in 1365, for example;[79] not only merchants, but ships' captains and doubtless pirates, made profit from trade with papal licence and again with multiple excommunications.[80] Yet the surge of aggression was over, and, though the songs of action were not songs of Crusade, the same change of spirit outmoded them also. The former Crusader, Philippe de Mézières, happy participant in the Alexandria massacre, had mellowed when he wrote his 'Dream of the Old Pilgrim'. No one in Lower Egypt is in rags or maimed, the hospitals are open and full of sick people under care or convalescent; there is no fear of thieves, 'what I have got, it is mine'; but the Mongols (in error for Mamlūks?) have usurped the lordship and their self-seeking is masked beneath a pretence of good government.[81] This is reasonably generous, and clearly based on sound information. On the other hand his Upper Egypt is pre-Chalcedonian and his Maghrib equally uninformed.[82] His geography is quite irresponsible but he cares for facts when he knows them.

The real shift away from the spirit of unending warfare is best seen in individual travellers. Already the great travellers of the thirteenth century, such as William of Rubruck,[83] took a vivid interest in all that they saw, for its own sake, and they recorded it with self-authenticating accuracy. With the fourteenth and still more the fifteenth century the number of accounts circulating in Europe increases, and pilgrims are soon outnumbered by diplomats, among whom Rubruck may himself be counted. Outstanding among travellers on mission of the fifteenth century is Bertrandon de la Brocquière. He watches everything, he likes people and he enjoys doing things with Muslim companions. His account of the *dhikr* is not an explanation from the inside, but it is an accurate outside observation. To illustrate his attitude: 'The Turks are happy and joyous and enjoy singing chansons de geste, and those who want to live with them must not be at all pensive or melancholy, but must be cheerful'. The cultural comparison ('chansons de geste') is new; this is not the old assumption that French songs will be known to amirs' daughters. Equally new is his inclination to accommodate himself to the ways of others. His good-bye to the *mamlūk* Mahomet, who had taken him under his wing – 'a man outside our religion who had done me so many kindnesses for the love of God' – shows his friend warning him not to be too trusting, because there are bad Saracens as well as bad Franks.[84] Here both men reveal a complex awareness of their differences. Like the earlier poets, Bertrandon sees no great difference between Franks and 'Turks', but now it is based on knowledge, and perceived beyond the superficial differences. This new approach resembles the poetic convention also in its relation to the clerical assessment of Islam, which cannot be said to have changed in any particular of importance. Experience of actual travel brought a new convention in literature into being, but it was still pragmatic and lay.

The use of this cursory look at examples of non-ecclesiastical writing over a very long period is only to note the many sides of the chansons de geste that appear in other forms of writing, from romances to personal memoirs. They illustrate many lay attitudes and opinions adopted in spite of official guidance in quite a different direction. The examples chosen are not atypical: until the late medieval travellers, it is difficult to find any record, other than the ecclesiastical polemic, that took accuracy about Saracens very seriously. Other writers than the theologians, though they were all orthodox Catholics, were interested in Saracens only so far as they suited their various purposes, though these might vary from historical description to total fantasy.

My antithesis between lay and clerical may be misleading.

Clerical status is not irrelevant, because the 'official' line was, of course, the Church line. The poets of the chansons de geste and the authors we have considered in this chapter were concerned with the profession of soldier in one form or another, or else with the status of nobility, and often with both. The distinction is less in the status in life of the authors than in the purpose for which they composed their works. A better antithesis than lay and clerical would be between polemic and entertainment. Some laymen entirely accept the purposes of the authorities of the church; some clerics do not. Monks are a special category. In the Middle Ages they fitted into the feudal power structure, but their basic purpose was to get out of the world, and let the world, if it wished, come to them. Any writer will draw on a variety of sources, and monastic chroniclers use unmonastic material, as Matthew Paris derived information from the court as it passed through St Albans. All the monasteries saw a greater or lesser stream of visitors. The Salerno stories quoted above are taken from a monastic chronicle but describe the behaviour of fighting laymen. Entertainment at one level or another was certainly a major purpose of all chronicles. The first concern of most books discussed in this chapter and throughout the book, is fighting, and that is why it contrasts so unmistakably with all theological polemic. When it is not fighting, it is love; these are the two subjects that best entertain.

Most of the material reviewed in this chapter, both history and fiction, is concerned with chivalry and battle, and certain themes stand out naturally; the chief are prowess, both skill in warfare and moral toughness, a concept of honour and loyalty, courage of course: all the fighting virtues. Also characteristic is the alternation of sensitivity and brutality, of cruelty and compassion. The Saracens always make the same sort of appearance as the Christians, and in the books about lovers too, including the passage from Orderic's monastic chronicle, Saracen and Christian behaviour is the same. The formal hostility to the *felon Sarazin* is gradually replaced by the happy or unhappy experience of travellers. Until then the attitudes of

Western chivalry to the Saracens was surprisingly static, and much the same in different kinds of literature. There are many different ways in which the subject is treated, but very little in the appreciation of Saracens.

The songs of the Tervagant convention share these character-istics, and it is difficult to define a way in which they are really distinct. It is not quite enough to say that they are songs of action and romances of adventure, although action and romance are essential to them, and a story devoid of swash-buckling can hardly belong. Yet the love episodes of many songs seem no different from stories devoted to love – *Floire* or *Aucassin* – except only that the plot reverts to greater violence sooner or later. It seems so slight a thing to judge by, yet it is the religion which is finally characteristic of the con-vention. The vague attribution of paganism seems to be general, and tends to take in both the dimly remembered or apprehended pre-Christian past and the whole non-Christian world of the authors' own day. This is true of nearly all stories and of many histories; only academic apologetics was differ-ent. *The Battle of Maldon* is a desperate defence by Christians against a wanton Danish attack, but there are no angels waiting in the wings for Brihtnoth. 'Thought shall be the harder, heart the keener, Courage the more, as our strength grows less.'[85] This is purely heroic, whereas our songs are cheered up by their Christian awareness at the moment of death; and they are cheerful overall. The contrast between Christians and pagans is a useful tool in the skill of story-telling, and, though we can see more and more clearly that 'pagan' means no more and no less than 'non-Christian', it is only in our songs that the special Tervagant convention – the pantheon, whether it includes Tervagant himself or not – gives paganism some sort of defini-tion. It is not a very good definition. As a religion it is implaus-ible, as a comic invention it is highly successful, but in any case it is the least variable of all those factors which must go to make up our definition of the genre. It is the one thing that makes the songs stand out.

CONCLUSIONS

The points established by the analysis in the main part of this book seem to be almost entirely negative, but not therefore unimportant. The poets show no interest at all in Saracens, that is, in Muslim Arabs and Moors, as they actually were; they chose to see them as an extension of Western Christian society as they understood it. When they say 'Saracen' they do not mean 'Saracen', because they are making no explicit assertion about Saracens at all. We cannot say positively that they never reflect an Islamic reality, but nothing that they say is unquestionably Muslim in origin, and little of it is likely to have an authentic source, even a very distant and distorted one. We can positively assert that they do not reflect at all the official Christian theological and polemic attitude to Arabs and Muslims. The sexual behaviour of Christians and Saracens is all one; we can assess it as somewhere between that of which the polemists accuse the Saracens, and that to which the moralists exhort the Christians. There is no serious difference either in the attitudes of the fictional Saracens and Christians to warfare; both of them enjoy it, both are professional soldiers. The entire literature is about war, with episodes of love and religion interspersed, but it never descends to the hypocrisy of supposing that the first two are particularly Saracen, or even that the third is exclusively Christian. Saracens are called 'pagan' and there is a persistent effort to link them with the pagans of the ancient world, as well as a confusion, perhaps inherited, between the Arabs and the pagans of the barbarian invasions of Europe.

At the same time there is no imaginative effort to understand paganism, and very little literary knowledge of it; reflections of ancestral pagan beliefs and practices are equally sparse. 'Saracen' relates to any nation that is not Christian, and the gods are a joke about non-Christians. Just as Saracen society is not at all Arab, so there is little authentic pagan belief described and no authentic Islamic religion. Sometimes by accident where Christian and Arab ways coincide, the Christian social model is serviceable enough for Saracens to look like Arabs; the gods are meant to be outrageously different from anything Christian, yet here too we can detect the influence of Christian dogma on the description of the gods, and it is difficult not to see the vaguely imagined cult of the gods as shaped by Christian liturgical worship. The only constant factor in the gods is that they were set up against the Christian God and in the test of battle proved to be worth a rotten apple.

So much in the songs is sui generis. On the negative side it was a remarkable achievement to cut themselves off from nearly all other writing at both elevated and debased levels, no academic abstractions, of course, but none of the notions of fraud that fill out the lighter chronicles either. The exception is the story of the false prophet which occurs occasionally; but that, while retaining much of the nastiness, does not include the absurd methods of religious fraud that occur very frequently outside the convention. Even this one story, occurring rarely enough, never shakes a poet from his main presentation of the false gods: it is a little libel used to 'correct' a big one. Nothing seems to affect the 'Tervagant' convention; it is entire, and nothing seems to fragment it. The devotional parts of the songs have a character entirely their own, and, although we can guess at possible sources, and even suspect that the type of prayer is very old, we do not know why they take the form they do, or why the singers decided to go their own theological way. They are most independent in their ambiguous attitude to holy war. Penance and sin are normal poles in a soldier's life; admittedly dying in the right cause is an acceptable penance, but a lifetime of fighting Saracens does not absolve a knight from his killings, as the two Moniage poems illustrate. The *Renoart*, in addition, shows specifically the sin of killing one's kin, even Saracen kin. Abbot Henri in *Gadifer* is only a monastic Ganelon, but the monks in the *Guillaume* plot as craftily and are killed as carelessly as if they were Saracens, and unlike Henri they have no Saracen connections. Killing is a sin that requires much expiation, and it is also a game undertaken lightly; as there were plenty more monks to take the place of those who were killed, so there are always plenty more Saracens. But is it really much more than a game? The serious epic moments which Gautier and other critics of the nineteenth century thought of as the French defence of Christendom against Saracen aggression are epic because they tell us about brave men fighting hopelessly against great odds, not for reasons of high politics or rarefied religion. All the songs about a great Saracen menace are about invasions of Italy or France: the last section of *Roland*, all the songs of the Archamp battle, all of *Aspremont*, and all the songs about attacks on Rome; they do not reflect anything of the aggression characteristic of Crusading, until they cease being epic, in the phase of counter-attack. When there is aggression, it is usually frankly land-grabbing. So just as the Saracens are not really Saracens at all, and the gods are a glorious hoax, so the Crusading is not Crusading as the Popes conceived it: the two kinds of war, like the two kinds of Saracen, are altogether different. We may be sure that the authors of songs in this convention preferred to do everything in their own way, and we must take this thought into account throughout.

They used ancient and modern material, and out of the amalgam they made good entertainment; to that single end they were prepared to adapt anything. There are modern parallels that help us to assess what they did. In one aspect the chansons resemble Westerns. Indians are a convenience in a Western, an enemy that provides excitement and that can be fought without appearing as individuals, and the heroes, intent on the struggle, are undistracted by complex human sentiments. The only enemies among the palefaces are bad men too bad to arouse sympathy, and they may be traitors in relation with the impersonal Indians. Only the occasional Indian is a person and is sympathetic; in the mass they are aliens whose ways are understood less than those of horses and dogs. This is much the same in the case of Saracens, the impersonal mass, the menacing danger, they can bite the dust without our tears; occasionally one of 'us' is a traitor, one of 'them' is a friend. They are worthy of respect, a good enemy, difficult to conquer, a chance of glory, always numerous and their leaders notable for prowess. The authors of the chansons and of the Westerns alike found the right enemy for the stories they wanted to tell.

This particular appeal to the audience is deeper than a religious prejudice, which is acquired and can be eradicated, and is itself only another symptom of the animal instinct of aggression. Lorenz has remarked that a man's 'most noble and admirable qualities are brought to the fore in situations involving the killing of other men, just as noble as he is'. He is not the first to say so, but he has related the fact extraordinarily clearly to its biological origins. It explains also the pleasure that an audience takes in hearing an account of these qualities in action: and this is precisely what the 'songs of action' are about. To add that 'men may enjoy the feeling of absolute righteousness even while they commit atrocities' is to refer primarily to the actual events of history, including much that was actually done on Crusade; our authors, though invulnerably righteous, do not dwell greatly on Christian atrocities, but take them in their callous stride, without turning a hair. The aggressive instinct in fact serves a range of objects 'from the sports club to the nation';[1] no discrimination is necessary for this instinct to find expression. Indeed, as soon as we begin to discriminate, our aggression begins to evaporate.

The deeds of superhuman strength which many of the heroes perform have another parallel, in the comics which portray protagonists of superhuman powers, Superman, Batman, Spiderman and others. The fantastic powers that these characters enjoy of appearing, disappearing, flying and generally ignoring the laws of physics, appeal to the same quality in the reader as the deeds of the heroes of the songs whose strength is superhuman; as when Guillaume strikes a man in half, through helmet, brain and body, to kill the horse, or Renoart kills hundreds with his cudgel. The chansons are indeed more realistic than the modern fantasies, which are inherently impossible, where the songs only exaggerate matters of ordinary experience. Playing with physical possibilities is a kind of humour which satisfies a wide popular need.

The songs are not Crusade propaganda, as I once believed, but they are good propaganda for a life of daring and adventure; they are often very individualistic. They are not at all ashamed of private advantage or profit, unless a slightly defiant note in references to booty reveals, not shame, but a hesitation to boast.[2] In warfare we are most concerned with the exploits of individual knights; the knight with the most marked individuality, in all those poems of his cycle where he is the true protagonist, is Guillaume, and he admits that there is a better life when he becomes a hermit – but it is the individualism of the hermit, not the community life of monks at which he becomes proficient. The Middle Ages are thought of as an age of anonymity, and that is largely true for the creators of works of art, but it is not true of imaginary characters; there, there was a cult of individualism which flourished on the depiction of physical marvels, miracles in the case of lives of the saints, fantasies of prowess in the case of the knights. Within the noble class, knights get ample scope.

There is a third modern parallel to the poems, in the creation of a closed and self-sufficient and wholly imaginary little world. This takes a number of forms in our own day, all of them popular at one level or another. There have been the literary sagas about some family who pass through several generations; a series of sequels allows the reader to relax in a cosy world where he can have all the pleasures of the familiar without the sorrows of real loss.[3] In a shorter space, but in the serial form that has something in common with the traditions of oral verse publicly recited, Dickens had the same ability to bring a sense of personal loss to readers who in fact had lost no one. P.G.Wodehouse did not admit his readers to a world of change and death, but the imaginary and self-contained scene he constructed diverted a large and highly discriminating public. The chansons create the same sort of imaginary world, one which in no way seems to reflect the ordinary lives of the feudal lords it is chiefly concerned with, but does often relate episodes coherent in themselves and faithful to life, as observed in the streets or the monasteries. In this way they resemble the soap operas of television, where an imaginary world takes over from reality, and week after week, sometimes even day after day, a group of imaginary people experience many rather ordinary adventures, but a huge audience enjoys living in their fictional world and seeing their troubles enacted. These parallels do not have the same degree of fantasy as the chansons, but all alike create a world sufficiently convincing for audiences and readers, when they enter it, to find release from their own problems. In all these cases, and including the chansons de geste in their cyclic character, the people of the imaginary world become very familiar to the hearers or readers. Perhaps the parallel is even closer with the worlds created by science fiction, of which a good example is provided by the Dune series, or worlds with no pretence at all to plausibility, like the *Lord of the Rings*; all these reach a large and intelligent public. They combine the separate world of the sagas and soap operas with the physical fantasies of the comics and, *mutatis mutandis*, this is just the combination we find in the chansons. The latter make up their imaginary world out of fragmentary realistic scenes alternating with exaggerated acts of prowess, all set in a greatly simplified world of feudal lords where the Saracen element might just as well be made up of invaders from outer space, for all the authors care about authenticity. We have to think of Mahon and Tervagant and the rest as anticipating the space invaders of twentieth century science fiction. The Mekon, of the Dan Dare serial in the *Eagle* of the 1950s in Britain, designed for boys whose fathers might find it relaxing too, made a similar appearance and had a similar function to

Mahon's in the chansons. This is the right level of absurdity for the gods.

I am not saying that the chansons were the 'same' as their modern parallels. We cannot say that they 'were' the soap operas, the science fiction, the comics, the cowboy stories of the Middle Ages, or even an exact equivalent, but we can say that they responded to much the same needs in an audience. The poets were not conscious of writing literature, but of patching up an evening's entertainment; they were amusing a public which would pay them, and be willing to listen again, and pay again, if they were amused. Their songs show every sign of being meant first and last to entertain, and inevitably it is we who obscure this, because we cannot hear them under the same conditions as their original audiences. We can only treat the results as literature, because our texts are the written ones that survived, and scholars necessarily subject them to the normal rigours of textual criticism to establish the form they were in when they were written down. This is the nearest we can come to the original entertainment, and so we tend to forget that oral entertainment was their purpose and the only criterion by which their authors would expect them to be judged. It is the amusement value of the gods that we need to judge.

It cannot be said too often that authenticity would have added nothing to the amusement value. The poets cannot have thought that it would have added to the pleasure of their audience if they had been concerned to present an Arab world as nearly as possible as it really was, or they would have shown more curiosity about other cultures than a meaningless taste for exotic names. They wanted to get on with a story of battle and high life that did interest them, and the long survival of the whole genre in its different manifestations is proof that their estimate of their audiences was correct; their taste was formed by their experience as singers in front of a diversity of listeners. The Saracens were well enough devised for purposes of story-telling to stand the test of the consumer. We cannot put poems to the same test, because the only possible audience for the songs now is no longer a mass of soldiers, officials, merchants, their hangers-on, the promiscuous assemblies at courts, at markets and at fairs. The audience now is confined to those ready to make the effort to read old French, and it is remarkable that these poems, in the form of a mere written record of the song that was actually sung, can still give pleasure, sometimes great pleasure.

Authenticity was itself no sufficient safeguard against fantasy. There is no question but that the theologians sincerely sought authenticity, although their motive was only to refute Islam the better for knowing more about it; against their will sometimes, they gradually eroded the legends that libelled Islam, although we still live in the afterglow of some of them.[4] In spite of this, they too in their own way were writing fiction. It was different in kind and used a different technique. They wanted to persuade where the poets wanted only to entertain, and they wanted to convince in order to persuade. They began from the hypothesis that belief governs behaviour, and many people would agree with them, though not perhaps so far as to suppose it the sole control. In any case, they lacked the means to find out enough about Islamic belief; and in addition they had a second and covert hypothesis, that people will always behave as badly as they are permitted to behave. This is implicit in the attacks on sexual freedom in Islam; if divorce and polygamy and concubinage are permitted the result will be promiscuity. This is a fiction, but it was believed because there was promiscuity in Christendom, where these three things were forbidden. They do not seem to have known about the Islamic moral category *makrūh* – of things discouraged but permitted, such as divorce; this is a deceptively subtle distinction, and easily but mistakenly assimilated to the concept of venial sin. But if they had it would have made very little difference. They were too attached to the fiction that everyone will get away with as much as he can.

When a theologian speaks well of particular Muslims he does not see that this is incongruous with his own thesis. William of Tripoli, a Dominican on the spot, saw much to admire in Baybars, especially his strictness in respect of public morals (his suppression of homosexual behaviour, of prostitutes and of drinking) and his well-organised army.[5] Ricoldo, one of the few major polemists with experience of an Islamic society not dominated by Christian rulers, himself realised the contrast between his experience as he recounted it and his theories as he expounded them. His experiences were themselves perhaps fictional to some extent; it is impossible that he never heard a profane song in Baghdad, though it is possible that he did not recognise it as such when he heard it. If he exaggerated a little the virtues of the learned Arabs it was to shame the Christians. Yet he continued to condemn Islam for its mild prohibitions which 'amounted to a kind of permitting', and attacked the laxity of Islamic law as he saw it, for its effect on moral behaviour.[6] This is a presumed effect, and contradicted by both Ricoldo and Tripoli in practice. When they reported facts, they were no longer playing with fictions, and did not see that their experience showed that the supposed ill effects of error had been greatly exaggerated. The seekers for authenticity had their own fictions and fantasies, not just in their materials, but in their methods of handling them.

If their sincere search for authenticity did not help them to escape fiction, the poets were better off with their own kind of fantasy. No accurate information that led to serious polemic would have improved the stories. There were interesting travellers contemporary with some of the later poems, William of Rubruck in the thirteenth century, Bertrandon de la Brocquière in the fifteenth, but their accounts of the people among whom they went are interesting partly because they are well observed and well told, but also because they are true. Theirs is the authenticity of observation and experience, and potentially more useful to composers of fiction than that other kind of academic authenticity of the theologians. Ricoldo's own *Itinerarius* might have been of great use, in spite of its being spoiled by its sometimes unbalanced and doctrinaire criteria. Most other travellers of the times were less observant and less original, but even so it would have been interesting, if later poets had made use of such information as travellers provided, in order to imagine the settings of their adventure stories.[7] In practice the fourteenth and fifteenth century second Crusade cycle is more fantastic than those earlier songs that have Charlemagne's times for their background; the convention was too firmly established to be able to adjust to any radical development of this kind.

Our poets were making up historical fiction, and we should perhaps judge them as we judge writers of historical fiction of modern times, in their choice of material as well as in the use they make of it. Most people would think that Walter Scott's best novels are those set in the eighteenth century, because of his vivid understanding of the history of his own country, and his stories set in the Middle Ages, often good stories and based on research to which the library at Abbotsford bears witness, contain much more personal fantasy; curiously, the *Talisman*, with a setting comparable to Eastern chansons, may be thought the best. Alexandre Dumas père, despite learned friends and solid collaborators, lacks in his Valois and Bourbon romances the immediacy of his contemporary stories. Thackeray achieves an astonishing sense of period in *Henry Esmond*; Dickens in *Barnaby Rudge* and *A Tale of Two Cities* hardly troubles, and, granted his choice of subject, may well have been right. Manzoni cared deeply for historical accuracy. In our own days the Duggans, the Renaults and Yourcenars have all had the benefit of nearly two centuries of historical research, yet they impose their own interpretations, in Duggan's case a realism imposed on periods that range from Romulus to the high Middle Ages, and extend geographically into the Near East in both Roman and medieval times. There are a vast number of writers of historical fiction nowadays, and most impose a very personal myth on history. I am not reviewing the genre and my personal judgements and preferences may be sound or silly; I wish to make the points that all historical fiction must create its own myth, that the sense of period varies, and may not correlate with research, and the importance given to research also varies. Above all, every one of these writers has naturally, inevitably and quite justifiably made something quite personal out of the people, including well-known historical figures.

These points are well to bear in mind when we think about the historical originals of characters that have become wholly fictional in the chansons. The poets had their means of research, both local legend preserved partly in documents in the monasteries, as Bédier insisted, and an unbroken oral tradition which alone can explain the surviving memories of Christian defeats and the sack of Rome. Their treatment of personalities to whom an historical origin can be traced, a Roland, Oliver, Guillaume, Ogier, may be historically muddled, but it may also be more or less deliberate. It is as reasonable for them as for modern authors to make what suits them, deliberately accurate or inaccurate as the case may be, out of the personalities of history. What they did marvellously succeed in doing, and this doubtless because theirs was a living oral tradition, was to solve the problem of 'sense of period' at least in *Roland*, in *Aspremont*, in *Couronnement* and the rest of the Guillaume cycle, especially the poems about the great battle of the Archamp. The concept of an imperial France surrounded by pagans who must be forced to become Christian is authentically of the time of Charlemagne: 'France' because the sentiment of the poems is often concentrated on the relatively small area that was originally France, 'imperial' because Charlemagne, in the songs as in fact, is constantly interfering in the affairs of peoples on the fringes of his empire. The Saragossa episode is relatively unimportant in the reign of the real Charlemagne, and there is no evidence that he did not treat Arab rulers with the respect due to equals, no evidence that he confounded them with unconverted pagans, such as his Saxon enemies and subjects. Into this picture the poets have blended two later impressions, first, the weary and often unsuccessful defence against the Vikings and the continuing invasions of Italy, rather more than France, of the later Carolingian period; secondly, they have interwoven the new spirit of aggression that expressed itself in Spain, in Norman Sicily and in the First Crusade. It is obvious that the early phases of the Reconquista have inspired much of

X for an opposite p of v, see Aebischer

the Aymery cycle, poems entirely about Spain, such as *Anseis de Carthage* and *Gui de Bourgogne*, or partly so, such as *l'Entrée d'Espagne*, *Fierabras*, *Aiol* and many others. There was of course a real siege of Barbastro, but it does not correspond to the story of *Le Siège de Barbastre*, though it may have inspired it.[8] So much more important than the historicity of episodes or characters is this blend of three moods from three different periods of a past that may have been only dimly remembered, or may have been better remembered than we think, and conveniently adapted. This blend has been so well done that it gives a unitary impression. As historical fiction it takes no more liberty with the past than much modern writing. But one important point for us to remember is that of the three moods representing three different periods the first two are concerned primarily or entirely with true pagans, and that Muslim or Saracens play a major rôle only when we come to the third. They have given the enemy their name to add to the name of pagan, but their part in the historical fiction is to provide a worthy adversary, not a plausible religion. That came from older strands in the weave. The only poems that present contemporary history, *La Chanson d'Antioche* and *Histoire de Jérusalem* by a tour de force assimilate it on the whole successfully to the old convention.[9] Finally, in the poems as a whole we are liable to find compliments to patrons in the form of characters actually modelled upon them, or of the names of their ancestors included on lists of honour.[10]

On the one hand the authors seem to have blended as many elements into their fictions as any writer of fiction to-day would think normal; on the other hand they seem to have had every motive to avoid authenticity in presenting the Saracen world to their hearers, and to allow memories of the alien pagan horde at the gates of Europe to swamp all thought of the Arab present. Pagans neatly balanced Christians moreover; writers who were aware of actual facts about Islam and travellers as they began to write accounts of their expeditions, were conscious of the existence of the Eastern Christians in Saracen country; in the poems there were no Christians except Latins, and the plots were a good deal simpler in consequence. Out of the mass of material they inherited from their colleagues and predecessors or acquired from monastic archivists they chose a sensibly simple and straightforward scheme.

'Saracen' was only the top and visible layer in a stratified complex, and much that goes on in the poems does not belong at that level at all, and is not an assertion about Arabs or Muslims as they were when the songs as we know them were sung. The memory of paganism was a bad dream from the past, a memory of encircling hordes that had had somehow to be contained, and nothing was remembered clearly about their religion except that they destroyed the Christian church and people. There had been Arabs among the invaders; they had not left a clearly distinct image behind. At the later date, the date of our songs, audiences were not afraid of any invader, some of them were themselves the descendants of Vikings, and the authors could invent what religion they liked for their composite creature, the 'Saracen'. Nothing in Islam as it was was suitable material. If the subject had been treated realistically, one concept of revelation against another, the story would have been lost in abstractions. If the invention of gods vaguely associated with pagans was certainly more amusing than the official grim polemic against Islam, it was also more suitable in the context of battle than the libels on the Prophet which the chroniclers and others found amusing, up to a point. That point would soon be reached with constant repetition, and the discussion would inevitably have been more acrimonious. There is more hostility in such an argument than can ever be attached to a patent absurdity. The Tervagant convention calls for no serious polemic, although it does not exclude serious discussion if it is wanted; there is always room for any unbeliever to question Christian dogma sceptically: Ferragu in *Espagne* is an example. The convention is less hostile and also less boring than any serious allegation: it is insulting, because it is irresponsibly frivolous, but it is not founded on theological hate.

The stories would have lost entertainment value without the gods, because of their profoundly comic possibilities, and the consequent flexibility with which they could be presented, now sinister, now absurd. The way to look at this is surely to consider how much it would have impoverished the stories to be without them. The theme of war between the armies of the true God and the armies who served a set of buffoons for gods was still exciting, because the enemy was powerful, but anyone could tell that these gods were foredoomed to fail. They gave the right balance between tension and reassurance. We might almost be watching Bottom the Weaver when we see the infatuation of the amirs with Mahon, until he lets them down by losing their battle for them. It would be less exciting with no religious threat, and it would be much less funny. Above all, the gods were the poets' own; the poets controlled their own invention, and no theologian, no chronicler, no literate writer at all even wanted to intervene.

It is difficult to say how far all this was conscious and deliberate. It is also difficult to say how much it mattered to the authorities that the *joculatores* should take their own line in everything. The articulate churchmen, the polemists in particular, almost certainly overestimated the appeal of Islam to the Christian public in Europe; but in Muslim countries the opposite almost would be the case. Islam was no attraction in a non-Muslim country, because it was not its ideas that were likely to appeal; the appeal of Islam would be in a country where the community as a whole was Muslim. The religions are sufficiently similar for a transition between them to be intellectually fairly easy, and adherence to one or the other is usually a question of very deeply felt loyalties. Two hypotheses would explain the ecclesiastical concern. One would be that the authorities' concern was simply with the small Latin communities – traders, soldiers – employed in Muslim countries, and not at all for the faith of ordinary people in Northern Europe, or even in Spain or Syria/Palestine, so long as Christian forces were advancing or in control. Another hypothesis would be that the Western Church inherited Mozarab experience and could not forget the days of Muslim dominance, when Islam may have offered practical attractions.

There is no evidence at all that either of these explanations of the theologians' concern is true, and no hard evidence explains the rage of the polemists; we must just presume *odium theologicum*. There is no sign that it was any less when more remote from Muslim areas, and it cannot have been indifference to Christian attitudes in Europe that left the songs uncorrected by ecclesiastical censure. We have seen, as we went through the evidence, that the poets' absurd religion of polytheism, negative, unattractive to anyone, unlikely, it might be thought, to sustain the loyalties of the most imaginary of Saracens, might disarm the suspicions of authority, who certainly could not fear that anyone would want to adopt a religion so unattractive as the poets allot the Saracens. If the authorities noticed it, they could not have been happy about the absence of hostility or moral condemnation, but they seem to have tolerated this indifferentism, in spite of their own excessive concern. That this concern was not echoed by singers may have seemed unimportant to them and unsurprising in mere entertainers. The greater the absurdity, the more likely it was to be ignored, and we cannot say whether this was a calculated effect, or a happy chance they were able to enjoy. The unending war within which all the songs take shape must be presumed either to have obscured some of the implications, or else to have compensated for deficiencies.

There is little sign of academic or other clerical criticism of the poets' ignorance, beyond a mild insistence by some theologians that Islam is monotheist. Guibert takes the *plebeia opinio* to be that the Muslims believe only in the Father; there is no question of idolatry here. *Plebeia* might mean the 'general' or 'common' or even 'lay' opinion. *Plebeius* would suit any of our poets very well; and certainly as a body they were neither clerics nor intellectuals. Alan of Lille regards the designation 'Saracen ŏr pagan' as a popular or common one. Neither refers to the Tervagant convention at all,[11] or even to the one apparent folk memory which associates all the non-Christian invaders of Europe as pagan – or 'Saracen' – and which by itself lacks all precision; it certainly does not imply the artificial system of the songs. The Saracen pantheon, so distinctive in itself, and unchanging over centuries, must have been maintained against all the evidence that reached, for instance, monasteries and their chroniclers, who were as remote as the poets, Jean Bodel for example, from the scenes of Arab conflict. Certainly the convention must have been deliberately maintained, however it began, and whatever the motive. We have, however, no reason to suppose that the poets who practised this convention took it seriously outside their own stories, although something of that sort may occasionally have happened. I would not like to claim that no one ever believed these fantasies. Something that is often repeated becomes respectable and acceptable simply by familiarity, and many people may have believed, not fully consciously perhaps, but half-believed in, accepted or half-accepted, Mahon and Tervagant and the rest. But it would be much rasher to argue that the poets, in upholding their convention, rigorously believed it to be true.

Beyond doubt, theirs was an autonomous world, created and maintained by them, and unlike anything else in the Middle Ages. It not only isolated them from Islam itself, and from what other Christians had to say on the subject, it was a tight little world which only the hearers of the songs would share with the singers. Yet it was rarely esoteric; because it was a world at war, it was business-like, and it was essentially one where courage mattered: in men who were seeking lands, profit and adventure that might lead to satisfied ambition, in those, some Christian, some Saracen, who knew how to die bravely; and in the enterprise of women who planned and executed, who so often took the initiative, and who, in a tight corner, were as daring as their lovers. It was a world of normal emotions. There is almost as much about the relations of fathers with their sons and daughters as about the love of two people sexually attracted. In the longer cycles, enough time passes for love to be seen to persist in marriage, as between Aymery and Ermenjart, and between Guillaume and *G*uibourg; it is when *G*uibourg dies that Guillaume turns to his monastic profession. The spotlight is on the Christians, but the Saracens also love each other and love their horses, fight and die bravely, share a conception of honour with the Christians. In this autonomous world the pantheon stands out as different, although there are other unrealistic elements, besides the gods. The great lords fight but do not seem to rule, they exist only as individuals, set apart by their calling as heroes, and by the apparatus of historical fiction; it is here that the comparison with the *Cantar del Cid* is most illuminating. The gods are isolated too, at least from any recognisable religion, but they are at once fantastic and down-to-earth, menacing and comic, and always ready to prove by their ineptitude that 'Christians are right and pagans are wrong'. We should not entertain the idea that they are meant to be anything but creatures of fiction.

NOTES

Where different editions or sources of the same work are used,
they are normally indicated in the notes in the same way as in the
bibliography; but where no contrary indication occurs, *Antioche*
is quoted from Duparc-Quioc, *Aliscans* from Guessard, *Loquifer*
from Barnett. *Simon* means *Simon* (1) and *Ogier* means *Ogier* (1).
Couronnement (2) is cited as A B or C, as printed.

CHAPTER ONE
Introductory

1. The most important articles on the pantheon are listed at
ch.6, n.3, and the whole bibliographical range in this field
is so vast that it is not appropriate for me to try to cover
it; there is no difficulty of access to good bibliographical
material. But it may be practical to mention some works that
I have found useful and relevant, and which have a general
bearing on all or some large part of my book, rather than
on particular issues. Works that relate chiefly to specific issues
are cited in the notes on the appropriate places in my text.
The first of the more general works are, of course, the classics,
Léon Gautier's *Les épopées françaises*, vols I-IV, Paris, 1878-92,
Joseph Bédier's *Les légendes épiques*, Paris, 3rd ed, Jean
Frappier, *Les chansons de geste du cycle de Guillaume d'Orange*,
Paris, 1955, and the editors' introductions to most of the
editions cited; there can be few articles with more concentrated references than C. Meredith Jones, 'The Conventional Saracen of the Songs of Geste' *Speculum* XVII, 1942;
it suggests or implies most of its interpretations, rather than
states them. W. W. Comfort, 'The Saracens in the French
epic', *PMLAA*, LV, 1940, approaching from a different angle,
has a different interpretation from mine; to this add his
'Chanson de geste and roman d'adventure', *PMLAA*, XXIX,
1914. Reto R. Bezzola, 'De Roland à Raoul de Cambrai, Les
origines et la formation de la littérature courtoise en
Occident' in *Mélanges de Philologie Romane et de la Littérature*

Mediévale offerts à Ernest Hoepffner, Paris 1949; Italo Siciliano, *Les chansons de geste et l'épopée (mythes – histoires – poèmes)*, Biblioteca di studi francesi, Turin, 1968; René Louis, 'L'épopée française est carolingienne', *Coloquios de Roncesvalles*, 1965; Ramon Menendez Pidal, *La Chanson de Roland* (French translation) Paris, 1960, André de Mandach, *La Naissance et Développement des chansons de geste*, Geneva, 1961-77, 4 vols to date); Paul Aebischer, *Rolandiana et Oliveriana, recueil d'études sur la chanson de geste*, Geneva,1967; R. F. Cook and L. S. Christ, *Le deuxième cycle de la Croisade, deux études*, Geneva 1972. There are also, of course, background works less closely related to the subject matter, such as I. G. Isola, *Le Storie Nerbonesi, romanzo cavalleresco del secolo XIV*, Bologna/Genova, 1877-91 (on a special subject which I have no space to include), or R. I. Burns, *Islam under the Crusaders, Colonial Survival in the 13th century*, Princeton, 1973 and Henri Pérès, *La poésie andalouse en arabe classique au XIe siècle*, Paris, 1953. E.-R. Labande, *Etude sur Baudouin de Sabourc*, Paris, 1940. A. de' Magnabotti, *I Reali di Francia*, 1947, and A. Ceruti, *Il Viaggio di Carlo Magno*, 1871; Gaston Paris, *Histoire poétique de Charlemagne*, Paris, 1865, and Anouar Hatem, *Les poèmes épiques des Croisades*, Paris, 1932; Gervase Mathew, 'Ideals of Knighthood in late Fourteenth Century England' in *Studies in Mediaeval History presented to Frederick Maurice Powicke*, Oxford, 1948, and *The Court of Richard II*, London, 1968; J. T. Reinaud, *Les Invasions des Sarrazins*, Paris, 1836; Marc Bloch, *La société féodale*, Paris, 1939-40 and, in addition to works by Georges Duby cited in the notes, much of the collection, *Homme et structures du moyen âge*, Paris and The Hague, 1973. This is not intended to be a general bibliography. The reader who is interested in a more detailed analysis of many of the themes of this book is recommended to read Paul Bancourt, *Les musulmans dans les chansons de geste du cycle du roi*, 2 vols, 1079 pp., Aix en Provence, 1982. The writer takes a more traditional view of the poets' intentions than I do, but the purposes of the two books are different. I had not seen this until my own was in the Press.

2. See the discussion and bibliography in Ellen Rose Woods, *Aye d'Avignon: a Study of a Genre*, Geneva, 1978.

3. Jean Rychner, *La Chanson de Geste: essai sur l'art épique des jongleurs*, Geneva and Lille, 1955. Edmond Faral, *Les Jongleurs en France*, Paris 1910 (cf. his *Les Arts Poétiques du XIIe et du XIIIe siècle*, Paris, 1924.

4. *op. cit.* 149-50.

5. Based on lectures given by Professor Mahdi in Cairo in 1974 and confirmed with him direct. See the introduction to his forthcoming edition of the Arabian Nights.

6. *op. cit.* 25.

7. *op. cit.* 155.

8. The two versions have been published; see my bibliography of texts quoted. They diverge at laisse 67 and rejoin at (1) 77, (2) 98. Summary in Barnett (2) 1.

9. 'D'un viel estoire li cante' 2e rédaction 1202; 'Volés öir de dant Tibaut . . .', Ière, 446-50.

10. Council of Elvira, Héfélé (Leclercq), vol.i, pt.i, 255 canon 60.

11. E. A. Peers, *Ramon Lull, a Biography*, London, 1949, and see Norman Daniel, *Islam and the West* (Edinburgh, reprinted 1980) 121-2. *Vita* in *Opera*, Mainz 1721, reprinted Frankfurt 1865.

12. Text in J. Kritzeck, *Peter the Venerable and Islam*, Princeton, 1964, *Liber contra sectam* 231 (lib.i).

13. See Norman Daniel *The Cultural Barrier*, Edinburgh, 1975, ch.9.

14. M. T. d'Alverny and G. Vajda, 'Marc de Tolède, traducteur d'ibn Tumart' in *Al-Andalus*, xvi (1951) 128/30ff. Cf. M. T. d'Alvenry, 'Deux Traductions Latines du Coran au Moyen Age' in *Archives d'histoire doctrinale et littéraire du Moyen Age*, Paris, 1948, 126.

15. *Itinerarius* in J. C. M. Laurent, *Peregrinatores medii aevi quatuor*, Leipzig, 1864, cap. XXII *de operibus perfectionis Sarracenorum*. Cf. infra 95 and 271.

16. Lepage inclines to accept this Saracen, but I find him impossible to swallow.

17. See below, ch.11, n.64.

18. For knowledge of ibn Tumart, see Marc de Tolède, xvi.1 and 2 and xvii.1 (1951-2).

19. This is the sense of both Roman and Arab usage.

20. E.g. J. Riley-Smith, *The Feudal Nobility and the Kingdom of Jerusalem*, London, 1973 and Burns, *op. cit.*

21. Matthew Paris, *Cronica Majora*, vol.2, 399 and *liber addita-mentorum* vi.348 (both RS 57); Oliver of Paderborn, *Historia Regum Terrae Sanctae*; Roger Bacon, *Opus Majus*, ed. Bridges, vol.1, 266. See also below, 129.

22. Lull, *Vita*, 6, in Peers, *op. cit.* Found from time to time in early missionary records: G. Golubovich, *Biblioteca Bio-biblio-graphica della Terra Santa e dell'oriente Franciscana* (Quaracchi) esp. vol.2

23. C. Haskins, *Studies in the History of Medieval Science*, New York, 1927, 70-9.

24. E.g. Matthew Paris, *op. cit.*, vol.3, 40 (Historia Damiatina).

25. E.g. Michael Scot's astrology in MS Bodley 266, fo.20v-25r and cf. the popularity of ʿAlī ibn Abī Rijāl in Latin (*de iudiciis astronomie*, Venice 1485, Basle, 1551, and many MSS).

26. *Roland*, 1015 and cf. below, ch.5, p.108.

27. L. P. Hartley, *The Go-Between*, London, 1953.

28. See n.1 above. For the poems referred to, see the bibliography of sources, and so in all cases where there is no specific quotation.

CHAPTER TWO
Chivalry

1. E.g. *Simon de Pouille* or *La Chanson de Saisnes*. (The Tennyson quotation above is *The Idylls of the King*, *The Passing of Arthur* 408.)

2. The first Crusade cycle is a biased history of actual events (see *Antioche*, *Jérusalem* in the plot summaries); the second, considerably later in date, is a fantastic series celebrating the Bouillon family but scarcely related to history (see plot summaries, *Bâtard*, *Baudouin*, *Chevalier du Cygne*, *Pontieu*, *Saladin*).

3. *Chronicon Salernitanum* in *Monumenta Germaniae Historica* (G. H. Pertz) Scriptorum tomus III, 530, ch.113ff. (This theme is more fully developed in ch.11.)

4. *Gaydon*, 4802ff.

5. *Maugis*, 4113-28.

6. *Roland*, 1162-8.

7. Notably in *Fierabras* and *La Bataille Loquifer*; cf. 40-1.

8. *Orange*, 1888.

9. To the works mentioned (see bibliography) add *Amadas*, 1368-1418. For *Doon* see 6339. Reference to Gui de Bourgogne and Anseis de Cartage is to the eponymous poems. The principal songs of the Aymery cycle (leaving out Garin and Guillaume poems) are *Aymery de Narbonne, Les Narbonnais, La Mort Aymery, Le Siège de Barbastre, Guibert d'Andrenas, La Prise de Cordres et de Sebille* and *Bueves de Commarchis* (a later version in a style of *Barbastre*). Mainet: see under *Mainet* in bibliography, also *Cronica de Espana* 597-9 and *Turpinus*, cap.xx.

10. *Charroi*, 81-2, 88-9.

11. First cycle: *La Chanson d'Antioche* and *La Conquête de Jérusalem* (with *Les chétifs*); for the second cycle see *Le Chevalier du Cygne, Baudouin de Sebourc, La Fille du Comte de Pontieu, Le Batard de Bouillon* and *Saladin*.

12. See 106-7.

13. Georges Duby, 'Les "jeunes" dans la société aristocratique' in *Annales, Economies, Civilisations*, Paris, 1964, reprinted in *Hommes et Structures* (ch.1, n.1).

14. *Chanson de Guillaume*, 1305-9, 1339-40. Phrases like *corage aduré, coraige vaillant, Aymery de Narbonne*, 923, *Charroi*, 1348, *Roland*, 2134-6, *Jourdain de Blaye*, 1606; these are almost at random, such phrases occur constantly throughout this literature.

15. *Chevalerie Vivien*, 807, cf. Frappier *op. cit.*, vol.1, 22-5, 286-7; cf. below, 113-14; Gerard: *Chanson de Guillaume*, laisse 92. Cf. Guiscard in laisse 94. Note that Gerard is alive in the second or cobbled part of the song.

16. *Chanson de Guillaume*, laisses 126-9, 136; *Floovant*, 2486; *Gormont*, 473; cf. *Enfances Ogier*, 790-1, 'François sont gent de grant hardement' and *Moniage Guillaume* (2) 3936-7 and *Gui de Bourgogne*, 2397, 'paiens ne puet pas vers François durer'.

17. *Roland*, 1724-5; 3870-1. So too *Couronnement* stresses Guillaume as a warrior when he weeps: *de pitié plore Guillelmes li guerriers*, AB 1317, C 1011.

18. *Aspremont* (1) 2212-9; cf. (2) 2763-73; *Couronnement* (1) 1938, AB 1919, C 1705.

19. *Blancandin*, 21-2, another late idealistic view, *Entrée*, 23-5.

20. *Escoufle* (Renart), 1630-1; 1632-6.

21. Antoine Oudin, *Curiositez françoises pour supplément aux
    dictionnaires*, Rouen and Paris, s.v. *vilain*, reprinted by La Curne
    de la Pelaye, Niort and Paris, 1882 (*Dictionnaire historique
    de l'ancien langage françois*, vol.x). See also in La Curne and
    in F. Godefroy, *Dictionnaire de l'ancienne langue française
    du IXe au XVe siècle*, Paris, 1880.

22. Eugène Vinaver, *Malory*, Oxford, 1929, 1.

23. *Roland*, 1117-8; *Jourdain*, 536-711; *Daurel et Beton*, 994-1033.

24. *Coilyear*, 744-5.

25. *Amadas*, 1419-26; for theory see also *L'Ordene de Chevalerie*
    and *L'Act de Chevalerie*; *Li Abrejance de l'ordre de chevalerie*
    (ed. U. Robert, Paris, 1897) is less relevant in some ways.

26. *Charroi*, 1351; 1372-85.

27. *Aspremont* (w), 2220, (2) 2774; cf. n.18 above.

28. *Moniage Guillaume*, 2e réd. 312-3, 347-79. (Young men,
    escüier et garchon.)

29. *Moniage Guillaume*, (2) 6451-97, Louis fulfils Guillaume's
    wish.

30. *Chanson de Guillaume*, laisses 8, 15, ll.346-8, 463-4. *Voyage*,
    469ff. *Roland*, laisse 86.

31. Thus Floire and Blanchflor's daughter Berte is the mother
    of Charlemagne.

32. *Moniage Guillaume*, (2) 6139-41 and 2275-7; *Barbastre*, 403-4;
    Chanson de Guillaume, 1325-6, 1431-2, cf. 2413. Cf. *Couronne-
    ment*, (1) 788-9, A B 791-3, C 537-8.

33. *Orange*, 1488, 1746.

34. *Otinel* 231-46; *Aspremont* (w) 9034-7; *Roland* 3172, cf. *Orson*
    1415; *Chevalier Ogier* 1540; *Entrée d'Espagne* 12130-2, cf. 11920;
    Aliscans 7356-8, 4013ff., 4382ff.; cf. *Chanson de Guillaume*
    3503ff. Cf. also *La Fille du Comte*, where the sultan recognises
    her nobility: 'il veoit en li qe ele estoit haute feme' (1.275-6)
    'ke ele estoit haute femme et de gentil lignage' (ll.355);
    cf. *Moniage Guillaume* (2) 3425.

35. *Daurel* 1253-5, 1545-50 (cf. 60-1), 1853; cf. Vivien's merchant
    upbringing, though the wife was *preux et nobile*; *Enfances*,
    laisses xxi-xxxviii, esp. 667-8, 685.

36. *Chanson de Guillaume* 1993-5; cf. 2014-5; *Maugis* 3138
    (Froberge) and see below, ch.4, n.19.

37. *Fierabras* 708-11, cf. 79-83, 96, 369, 413, 438-9, 458-63, 578,
    581-4.

38. *La Bataille Loquifer* 604, 706, 1008-9.

39. *Barbastre* 578, 580, 589, 868, 5602; *Fierabras* 2251; *Orange* 258-61. Cf. *Faucon*, 1571, "assez fu gente s'ele fu baptiziee'.

40. *Cordres* 1117; *Commarcis* 3304; *Aspremont* (w) 2963 (not in (2)); 6022 ((2): cf. 5984); 6029 ((2): cf. 5999); 10220; 2214 ((2): cf. 2765); w is notably more liberal in praise of Saracens. *Blancandin*, Sadoine, passim, and n.2297; *Daire* 3318; *Narbonne* 977; *Elie* 460-1; *Moniage Renoart* (1) fo.192v, col.1; *Aye d'Avignon* 1834; cf. 3794, 4077; 3817, 3829, 1437; *Gui de Nanteuil* M 50-2, V 49-50; *Chanson de Guillaume* 2134-5; cf. *Maugis*, where the father, Aquillant, unconverted, 3268, and son, Brandoine, converted (below 210), are praised alike. Cf. also *Roland* 894-9 (Balaguez) and *Loquifer* (1) 3416-9, also *Gormont* 346, 355, 533 and *CCGB* 6965; cf. Bédier, *lég. ép.* IV, 21ff.

41. *Fierabras* 737-42; 991-6; 1120-38, and see below, 198-9; *Otinel* 184-5.

42. *Loquifer* 1769-85, 2034-43.

43. *Moniage Guillaume* 4638; *Aspremont* (w) 10311; *Nanteuil* (1) 2397; (M) 2285, (V) 2478; *Entrée* 854-5; *Barbastre* 5886.

44. *Saladin* 128.51; 169.29; 109.55; *Fille du Comte* I 621, II 822, 825.

45. *Aspremont* (w) 2209-23; (2) 2760-76.

46. *Foucon* 9883-9904 and 12494-12515.

47. *Roland* 1471-6; 955-83; 1311-18; 1335; 3172-81. Cf. modern French *sembler*, and the phrase used of a Christian hero, *Elie* 2189. Cf. 'he looks every inch a king' or 'a soldier' etc. Cf. 36 and references at n.34 above.

48. *Haumtone* 395-6; *Elie* 375-6, 2175-6; *Entrée* 2021-3; *Enf. Ogier* 4700-2; *Andrenas* 910-3; *Commarcis* 2941; *Loquifer* 2157-9, 2716-7, 2816-8, 2908, 3213-5; *4 Fils Aymon* 3998; cf. *Orange* 1487 and *Foucon* 1646 and *Raoul* 7926, 'crestiens frere, molt iers preux gentis'.

49. *Orange* 1189; cf. Guillaume echoing this in the presence of Orable, 1357; *Simon* 1082-3; *Blancandin*, index s.v. Subien; *Gadifer*, passim, see Runeberg, *Etudes* 53ff.; *Roland* 3748; *Gui de Warewic* 3365-6, 8799ff., 8837-8; *La Mort Aymery* 1389, cf. 1635.

50. *Pampelune* 641-4; 976-80; *Anseis* 1846ff. and see below 191.

51. *Chevalerie Ogier* 1629; cf. 1540: 'de grant nobilité'. *Enfances*

Ogier 7086ff., 7113-14, 7139ff., 7549ff., 'le nobile guerrier' 7072, 'qui moult fist a louer' 4101, 'cortois et endoctrinés' 7274.

52. The most striking case is *Roland* itself, cf. Rychner 39-40: *B*alignant as counterpoise to Charlemagne. Possibly the test that Charlemagne imposes on Huon de Bordeaux in the form of a mission to the amir has the same implication (2315ff.). But in *Moniage Renoart* (1) fo.184r1 there are 14 emirs to 4 crowned Kings. See also *mulainne*, ch.3, n.54 below.

CHAPTER THREE
Courtly Pastimes

1. *Orange* 51, 55-64, 86-95. Guibourg in *Chanson de Guillaume*, *Aliscans* and *Moniage Renoart*, and Ermenjart in *La Mort Aymery* are examples of ladies who hold their husbands' castles successfully.

2. P. Meter, introduction to *Daurel* xiii, n.2.

3. *Roland* 111-3; *Aspremont* (w) 10581-2.

4. *Chanson de Guillaume* 2396-7; *l'Escoufle* 870; *Orange* 558; *Loquifer* 1242, 242; *Andrenas* 1977; *Aspremont* 2215; *Foucon* 9898, 12507; *Fille du Comte* 1.358, 386-7, 11.470, 500; *Aiol* 5420-3; *Gaufrey* 1795; *Moniage Renoart* (1) fo.184r1. Another case of references taken almost at random, there are many such scattered throughout the songs.

5. *Gui de Warewic* 3235, 3249, 4467-72; 7974-8008; *Bâtard* 3849-59.

6. *Fierabras* 4017ff.; *Gui de Warewic* 3217-9; cf. *Orange* 247, 410; *Blancandin* 42; *Loquifer* 243-4; *Aspremont* (w) 136 (2) 843, (w) 2216-7 (2) 2769-71; *Couronnement* (1) 2224 A B 2198 (C) 2027; *Aye* 1864; *Foucon* 9900, 12507-9.

7. *Maugis* 3886. In *Entrée*, pursuit of game and girls seems all one, 104-7.

8. In most cases quoted at n.6 above. The animals at sea in *Orange* 1313-17, are unexpectedly convincing.

9. The *faucon mué* is the bird in prime condition after the adolescent moult which brings it to maturity. I am much obliged for instruction on this subject to Mr Mark Allen.

10. *Orange* 852-5, 1083-9, 1631-2; *Simon* 1480.

11. *Orange* 1308; *Aspremont* (w) 10743, 10797, 10235; *Moniage Guillaume*, Iere réd. 920; *4 Fils* 15941-2; *Fierabras* 5891-2;

Gaufrey 8732.

12. *Commarcis* 3685; *Cordres* 1015-35, 1040-59, 944; cf. 912, 1108, 1224; *Godin* 8615, 8717.

13. Joinville 369; Vitry, cap.6 *de pessima doctrina* (see ch.4, n.4).

14. *Roland*, Turpin 1490-6, Roland's blows 1374, 1538, 1649; (*R*enoart's and in general, below, 108ff.) Veillantif 2160-1, 2167-8. See also n.18 below.

15. *Chanson de Guillaume*, laisses 127, 128; 138, 139; *Aliscans* 1350-8; 1366-74 (Folatille 56). Partial recapitulation in *Moniage Renoart* (1) fo.186r1 ('Aerofle le tyrant').

16. *Gadifer*, Boulogne MS fo.193, from Runeberg 56; *Moniage Guillaume*, 2e réd. 5277-95, 6536.

17. *Aiol* 581, 624ff., 919ff., 925ff., 1037ff., 1941, 4179, 5232, 5292. Another horse of character, almost a hero in his own right, is Arundel, in *Bueves de Hamtoune*. There is also Broiefort in *Enfances Ogier*, but he plays a smaller part (4073, 4094). See also n.23.

18. *Fierabras* 1119-38.

19. *Couronnement* (W) 644-58; 1096-8; 1147-50.

20. *Cordres* 2861-3.

21. *Loquifer* 2770-1, 2828-9; *Gui de Warewic* 3895; *Antioche* 3041-7.

22. *Roland* 1535; cf. 1572.

23. *Elie* 395-9, 480, 495-500; later in this poem Lubien has a terrible horse called Prinsart, reminiscent of *F*ierabras' horse (1827-8ff.).

24. E. Faral, *op. cit.*, passim but esp. App. 111.

25. *Destruction* 359-65; *Fierabras* 1997.

26. This is especially relevant to the Aymerid cycle and applies also for example to *Fierabras*, but hardly to the Guillaume poems; it is Guillaume himself who falls in love with a reputation in *Orange*: he is certainly not in love with the city only (as in the case of Nîmes).

27. *Loquifer* 28.

28. *op. cit.* 13.

29. *4 Fils* 16040; *Cordres* 2293; *Orange* 327-8, 721; *Aye* 1632, cf. *Blancandin* 2247.

30. *Barbastre* 512, 5470, 6268; *Simon* 1806, 1990; *Aliscans* 1376-8, 1422, 2066; *Chanson de Guillaume* 2170-1 ('Salomoneis'); cf. Moniage Renoart (1) fo.184r2; *Blancandin* 39-40; cf. *Fille*

du Comte 1.273, 11.352.

31. *Blancandin* 35-50; *Daurel* 1273-7, 1564-9, 1578-9; *Godin* 8743-8803; *Mainet*, reference at ch.2, n.9.

32. *Simon* 966-8; *Aiol* 5420-3; *Gaufrey* 1791-1800.

33. *Simon* 1124ff., 1139ff., 1229-1238 – the French are dazed in a manner more reminiscent of 'The Tempest' than of 'A Midsummer Night's Dream'. *La Fille du Comte* 11.542-3, cf. 1.427; *Maugis* 2537-45; *Chanson de Guillaume* 2591-4.

34. *Floovant* 739-45. Cf. *Foucon* 1117-8.

35. In *Le Bâtard* the episode of Arthurian magic over the Red Sea is no more than an episode; for the Huon group, see *Le Roman d'Auberon*, *Huon de Bordeaux* itself, *Esclarmonde*, *Clarisse*, *Yde et Olive*, *Godin*; Picolet in *La Bataille Loquifer*, passim killed in *Gadifer*, see Runeberg, *op. cit.* 54; Renoart in Avalon, *Loquifer* (2) laisses 73-7. In *Elie*, Galopin (the heroine's second choice, 83 below) has magic powers, 1890ff.

36. *Li Nerbonois* 3983-97, 7893-7902; *Conquête de Jérusalem*, VII.6402-8.

37. *Doon de Mayence* 10851ff. *Roland* 487.

38. *Orange* 336-9; they stain their skins 377-81, but the 'Saracens' recognise them at sight as 'African' 452-57. *Charroi* 890-4, 990-4, 1036-46, 1063-9; *Chanson de Guillaume* and *Aliscans*, as above, n.31; *Cordres* 1905-08.

39. *Li Nerbonois*, Cornuafer, laisses 89-99 (nota 3468-70), Danebru, long continued theme, cf. 6121-2; Clargis, laisses 158-62; *Simon* 1805-7; *Blancandin* 2245-50, cf. *Orange* 377-81, cited above, n.39. A girl in male disguise darkens her skin, *Floovant* 1777, 2177-8; but Saracens may include 'des blons et des noirs', *Foucon* 839.

40. *Fierabras* 2896-2940.

41. *Entrée d'Espagne* 13976.

42. *Gormont* 33.

43. *Aymery de Narbonne* 1046; *Gui de Warewic* 3603-4; *l'Escoufle* 1070-3; *Saladin* 114.41-2 (XVII); cf. *Aspremont* (W) 3593-4, 'plus sot de gerre que nule home carnal.'

44. *Entrée* 2779-93; cf. introduction, xxxviii.

45. *Aspremont* (W) 630 (2) 1567; *Moniage Guillaume* 4675-90.

46. *Orange* 1119, 1129, 1610; *Loquifer* 2, 6, 1558; *Commarcis* 3578; *Couronnement* (1) 756 (AB) 760 (C) 506; *Cordres* 1064, 1467ff.; cf. *Moniage Renoart* (1) fo.184r1, 'sale de vieil antiquité'.

Barbastre 583; *Narbonne* 3576; *Andrenas* 1920.

47. *Aspremont* (W) 3203; *Maugis* 2690-1; *Loquifer* 6.

48. *Roland* 3220ff.; *Chanson de Guillaume* 1709-1715, cf. 2058-63 and also 2137-9.

49. To take one example, the index to *Aspremont* (W) has 2 entries for beduins, 2 for *Mors*, 6 for *Arrabis*, 14 for Persians, 23 for Turks, and many more for Saracens. The *Esclers* (Slavs) may be a dim reflection of the Hungarians who, unlike the Slavs, did savage France for a time, but if so, any conscious memory has faded completely (cf. 243).

50. *Bâtard:* Mecca on the (navigable) river Jordan 2909-10; *Entrée* 11842-7; cf. *Elie*, where the copses and meadows as well as precipices are more plausibly Levantine.

51. *Gormont* 472, 443-4. The Vikings are Saracens also in *King Horn*, (1) 38 and 607; and (2) seven references, see index, s.v. *Saraʒin*; these people are 'ledlike and blake', suggesting a confusion of more than names. Saracens in Brittany, *Aquin* and *Elie* (where some come from Ireland). Bédier discusses much of this, *Légendes épiques* IV.41-8.

52. *Berte* 1506-16 and see Bédier, *op. cit.* IV.47ff.

53. *Otinel* 138-53; *Elie* 885-90; *Foucon* 12667-704, 12988-13000; cf. *Sebourc* XII.889-XIII.123.

54. Guillaume's journeys in the *Chanson* remain remarkable even when we allow for the spatchcocking of two poems together; the underground passage is in *Narbonne* 1003, 1005. Yet the songs are unreliable even in unreliability; the Bâtard wholly fantastic in all ways but this, has the Saracen title *mulainne* which can only surely be *Mawlāna*.

CHAPTER FOUR
The Family, Women and the Sexes

1. See ch.1, n.24.

2. The earliest Latin source is Eulogius, *Liber Apologeticus Martyrum*, MPL 115, coll. 859-60. Early sources translated into Latin later are the *Risāla* of the pseudonymous al-Kindi, which is much the most important of the books translated by Peter the Venerable's team; and the *Contrarietas Elfolica*, of doubtful origin, translated early in the thirteenth century by Mark of Toledo. For al-Kindi see Kritzeck, *op. cit.*; *Contrarietas*, unpublished, see M. d'Alverny, *Marc de Tolède*,

ch.1, n.18.

3. Norman Daniel, *Islam and the West, the Making of an Image*, Edinburgh, reprinted 1980.

4. Vitry: Iacobi de Vitriaco *liber orientalis*, Douai 1597, 27, 29-30, 26; Humbert of Romans, *opus tripartitum*, I.vi in *Fasciculus Rerum expetendarum et fugiendarum*, vol.2, Edward Brown, London, 1690.

5. *Quadruplex reprobatio*, printed as Ioannis Galensis *de origine et progressu et fine Machometis . . . et quadruplici reprobatione prophetiae ejus liber* (erroneously attributed) W. Drechsler, Strasburg 1550, cap.viii, 23ff. Accessible MSS are Cambridge University Library Dd.1.17 and Bibliothèque nationale Lat. 4230.

6. Peter of Poitiers in Kritzeck, *op. cit.* 215, *epistola*, followed by *capitula* 2.v and vi; Aquinas, *opusculum de rationibus fidei ad cantorem Antiochenum*, cap.1 (Fretté, *opera omnia*, volumen 27; *opuscula varia*, Paris, 1875, 129ff.).

7. *Orange* 85-91, 129-30.

8. *La Mort Aymery* (laisses 65, 66) 1649-53, 1675-80.

9. *Aspremont* (W) 3674-87 (2) 4027-40; *Orange* 1083-9 (cited above, ch.3, n.10); cf. Pérès, *op. cit.*

10. *Roland* 957-60.

11. *Foucon* 13165-9, 9899, 12510-12.

12. *Aspremont* (W) 2223-4 (2) omitted.

13. *Barbastre* 5626-8, 5654-5 (she is undismayed).

14. *Orange* 619-29. This poem assumes (528) that Saracen visitors will expect to call on the Queen.

15. *Chanson de Guillaume* 2603-10.

16. *Saisnes* 1431-43.

17. Lateran IV, canon 68, entered c. jur. can. lib.iv tit.vi *de judaeis et saracenis* cap.15: 'damnatae commixtionis excessus' (special clothing to remove the excuse of ignorance). Héfélé (Leclercq) v.2, 1386-7. *Bâtard*, laisses 93-6, esp. ll.2569-74 and 2591.

18. *Maugis* 3878, 3885-92, 3912-3; 3319-24, 3332-3, 3368-9, 3382-3, 3413.

19. *Maugis* 3129-40. Variants *arrement destrempe* MSS C and M, note on 92 at 341; cf. the nurse in *Loquifer* (1) 3740-2 (2) 4063-5.

20. *Aye* 1473-80, 3840-2.

21. *Aspremont* (w) 7833-46; 7916-30, 7993-8015.

22. *Fille du Comte* 1.278-80, 11.357-8 (sultan unmarried 11 only).

23. *Floire* 2059-88, 2713-35, 3057-78.

24. *Loquifer* 624-30.

25. *Antioche* 5325-8.

26. Tarbé, *Notice sur Herbert Leduc de Dammartin*, Rheims, 1860, lxi.

27. Constant use as crony: random examples, *Aspremont* (w) 622, 628, 782; *Narbonne* 4355; *Fierabras* 763, 1227; *Moniage Guillaume* 5157; *Cordres* 1807; *Enfances Guillaume* 1551 (30 kings!). Cf. Aebischer, *Voyage* 91.

28. Pepys: random examples again, vol.i (1660), entries for Feb. 25, Aug. 5, June 21, Sept. 2, Oct. 22; vol.vi (1665), entries for 31 July, 3 Aug. 'I went to bed with Mr Sheply in his Chamber, but could hardly get any sleep all night, the bed being ill-made and he a bad bedfellow'. (Ed. R. Latham and W. Matthews, London, 1970 and 1972.) Still common in the writer's lifetime at a social level where beds were few.

29. Mézières, *Vieil Pelerin*, vol.2, 229-30 (fo.248v1-249r2), a discussion of *mahommets*, i.e. of the rights and wrongs of advisers who are not the 'natural' feudal advisers, much unfavourable, but 'Le conte de Provence, par le grant gouvernment du dit pelerin, bon mahommet, devint riche et puissant a merveilles at bien aime de tous ses voisins' and this 'aussi comme il fu fait de Joseph en Egypte'. 249v2, 231 (Le Tiers Livre). Godefroy just gives the sense 'mignon, favori', as also La Curne de la Sainte-Palaye.

30. 'Amoureuse et compatissante', in 'La composition de la chanson de Fierabras', *Romania* 1888, 22-51.

31. *Orange* 256-7 cf. 204-5 and 277-80; 284-9 cf. 353-8; 290-1 cf. 359-60; 665-8, 204; ancient Egypt, for example the statues of Rehotep and Nofret in the Cairo Museum, husband brown, wife white.

32. *Orange* 371-5; 684-8; 910-22; 733; 931; 941-53; 1322-3, 265; 1374-8; 1400; 1477-81.

33. Anseis: Marsile recognises the abduction of his daughter as a French act: 'Et Franchois ont ma fille gaagnie', 6670.

34. *Cordres* 707-12; 731 cf. 1922 etc.; 715-18 (and see 50-1, above); 1932-43, 1949-66, 2032-41; 2059-73.

35. Not at all an inclusive or exhaustive survey.

36. *Saragosse* 627. Cf. the episode of Naime and Queen Anfélise

in *Aspremont* (w) 2   620-78 (2) 3125-76.

37. *Elie*, Gaston Raynaud's introduction, xx; *Elie* text, 2162-9, 2180-5. Elie in any case does not get the kingdom; he is compensated by Charlemagne for the inheritance he has lost with his bride. Probably it goes to Galopin, the new groom. Earlier, just between Saracens, *L*ubien had demanded that *M*acabré surrender his daughter and his Kingdom to him.

38. *Bâtard* 5436-9, 5931-2, 5936-7, 5961-3, 6245. Cf. ch.3, n.55.

39. Gui: e.g. Laurette, the emperor's daughter; his employer, *T*riamor, does not offer the usual daughter, but instead the release of Christian prisoners, at Gui's request. 'La fille al soldain' (3128) is not a serious runner. Bueves: the incredibly complex plot shows Josaine, daughter of King Hermine, to be far from lacking in resources, and she defends her virginity with great ingenuity; but she is more a victim than a plotter, and lacks the classic initiative. On the other hand, her son inherits her father's kingdom. Bueves' Jerusalem 'confession' early in his career, already sounds like a mercenary's c.v., 1346-56. Dynastic marriage in general, see G. Duby, *Medieval Marriage*, Baltimore and London, 1978, and *Le chevalier, la femme et le prêtre* (Paris, 1981).

40. For Carahuel see also 45, for la Fille du Comte, 41, 58-9, for Brandoine, 186.

41. *Maugis* 4328. Cf. *Foucon* 3697-8.

42. *Destruction* 252-62.

43. *Fierabras* 2007-2041, 5999-6006. Cf. *Gaufrey* 9146-59.

44. *ibid* 3075-81 (her father has sent the thief to steal her magic belt!); 2191-8; 2933-40.

45. *ibid* 5917-8; 5955-65ff. Roland persuades Gui to take *F*loripas, 2810.

46. *Loquifer* 2819-20, 2945, 3029-30, 3170-3, 3199, 3210-5, 3220-2, 3238-9, 3244-6, 3992-3.

47. *Aspremont* (w) 6751.

48. Thus *O*rable continues throughout *Orange* to be given these reminders, e.g. 1323, 1460, 1851; Ermenjart, mother of fighting sons, e.g. in *Li Nerbonois* 5137, in *Couronnement* A B 822 C 568, *G*uibourg still beautiful in *Loquifer*, 3193, 3492; Aye d'Avignon in *Gui de Nanteuil* 1, 34; *G*loriande, *Enfances Ogier* 7604. Again, the list of examples could be almost indefinitely extended. Even St Mary Magdalen receives the common

description 'qui tant ot de biauté' (*Moniage Renoart* (2) fo.197v).

49. *Gaufrey* 1682-3; cf. *Fierabras* 2810 (above, n.45).

50. *Ogier* 7622-31.

51. *Simon:* Jeanne Baroin's introduction 16.

52. *Blancandin* 1396-8, 3487-93, 5434-45, 5490-5, 8545-8.

53. *Loquifer. T*ibaut tries to carry *G*uibourg off 2634-48, 2688-90, but it is *D*esramé who tries to avenge his honour, 2816-23, 2906-10, wants *R*enoart to help him as his son and her brother, and who fights Guillaume.

54. See below 100, 102.

55. See below 106.

56. See below 183.

CHAPTER FIVE
Violence: Hatred, Suffering and War

1. 'Tu namque doctor es non coactor' (Q. sura 88, 21-2) Ketton MSS Azoara 97, e.g. Oxford, Corpus Christi College MS 184, Arsenal 1162, no note; Bibliander printed text 98, 185, l.1, annotation p.227. (*Machumetis ... alcoran*, Basle 1550). Cf. d'Alverny, *Deux Traductions* 98.

2. Peter the Venerable, *liber contra sectam* 1, Kritzeck *op. cit.* 241, ll.19-22. Vitry, *op. cit.* 26. Qur'ān wrongly cited.

3. Tripoli, *de statu saracenorum* in H. Prutz, *Kulturgeschichte der Kreuzzüge*, Berlin, 1883, cap.xxiv, opening sentence; Ricoldo da Monte Croce, *Itinerarius*, ed. cit., xxxv, 139 and *Antialcoran* V; XII; (*Refutatio*), in MS e.g. BL Royal 13.E.ix and BN lat. 4230 and cf. Daniel, *Islam and the West* 155 et alibi.

4. *Itinerarius* XXIX, 134 (and see above 12-13 and below 271).

5. Peter the Venerable, *contra sectam*, Kritzeck, 226. Humbert, *op. cit.* VI.3 and *de predicatione Sancte Crucis* 3 and cap.XVI, Nuremberg (?) 1490 and *Opus Tripartitum*, ed. cit., lib.1, cap.vi, and many quite disparate authors.

6. N. Daniel 'Holy War in Islam and Christendom' in *Blackfriars* September 1958 and *Arabs and Medieval Europe* (London, 1979) index s.v. jihād, for my views on this.

7. Holkot, *In librum Sapientie*, Basle, 1560, v lect lxv; Humbert, *Opus Tripartitum*, VI.i.

8. *Couronnement* (1) 1938 AB 1919 C 1705; *Roland* 1355-6; *Orange* 121-3, 822-3, 1603-6; *Maugis* 2652, cf. 3276. *Orange* is rich in these phrases, it is a light-hearted song, but they are

found almost everywhere. *Doon de Mayence* 10792-8.

9. Renoart's first blow at the Archamp battle kills 300, *Chanson de Guillaume* 2989; 3021-2, 3046, 3072-4, 3097, 3117-8, 3148-9, 3161-2, 3270-1, 3313-5; 3100-13.

10. P. G. Wodehouse, *Cocktail Time*, London, 1958, ch.2 and 25.

11. See also Bédier, *op. cit.* III.355-6. Another theme is the violence of Maillefer as a baby, provoking the dangers that threaten him, *Loquifer* (1) 3745-7 (2) 4070-2. For the theme of modern parallels see also ch.12, p.265ff. The references to *The Mikado* are one to each act.

12. *Moniage Guillaume* (2) 1513-14; 1699-1704 (1) 661-3.

13. *ibid* (1) 715-96; (2) 1920-2008; *Moniage Renoarrt*, (1) fo.182r1, 187v1 and 2, 193r3 and v1; (2) fo.169v-170, 183r-v, 207r-v. These are striking examples of a recurrent theme of the two poems.

14. *Moniage Guillaume* (2) 4358-9.

15. There is a striking similarity of tone, and I am not the first to feel it, cf. Frappier, *op. cit.* vol.1, 227. The Gospel itself uses exaggeration humour to make a point, e.g. Matthew 7.3 and 18.24.

16. Rychner *op. cit.* 47; *Chanson de Guillaume* 3360-2ff., 3474-5.

17. *ibid*. 1651-4, cf. 1465.

18. *Enfances Vivien* 24-6 (MS 1448) xi-xii. Vivien and his father, laisses xvi-xx, especially 603-4, 473-85.

19. *Chevalerie Vivien* 78-80, 103-13; cf. Renoart in *La Bataille Loquifer* (1) 126 v, (2) 733-44, and his *Moniage* (1) fo.183v1-184r1; cf. Runeberg, *Etudes* 50.

20. *Chanson de Guillaume* 587-8, 809-11, 884-93, 909-12, 920-5, 2011-52; cf. *Aliscans* 394-417, 693-7ff. Cf. 31 above.

21. Godin 12182-89.

22. *Aspremont* (W) 2951-72 (2) 3399-3405. *Destruction* 1369-74, 1379-80, 1248-53. *Fierabras* 56-69, 130-3, 371-81.

23. *Charroi* 566-79; *Moniage Guillaume* (2) 4646-59, 4691-4704 cf. 4710-2. Rape scenes, e.g. *Chev. Ogier* 11955-60, *Floovant* 268, 278, 302.

24. 'Uns povres hom' – *Aliscans* 7374-7488. In *Charroi* Guillaume's knights threaten peasants (presumed Saracen) who grumble when their carts and their goods are requisitioned that their eyes will be put out before they are hanged, but in the event they are not treated badly, and are even compensated: 961-3,

1474-81.

25. Women and children killed, *Chev. Vivien* 63. Saracen women fear rape: *Aquin* 2932-3, *Aye* 1724, *Aspremont* 10906. Cf. *Moniage Guillaume* (2) 3950, 4640-1, *Aliscans* 1050-6, *Barbastre* 5635-6, *Loquifer* 3369. The rape in *Antioche* 6413 is reproved in the following line 'de cel pesa Jhesus le roi de Paradis'. See also below 183. More often implied than stated.

26. *Gui de Bourgogne* 3417-20.

27. *La Mort Aymery* 1322ff. *Li Nerbonois* 4952ff. Threats, *Doon de Mayence* 10454, *Mon Guillaume* (2) 3967-8, *Couronnement* A B 545, C 296.

28. *A*umons, cited for his chivalry above (39) is responsible for the cruelties. So too with *A*golant.

29. *Gaufrey* 8658-65, 8742-5, 8716-32.

30. E.g. *Gaufrey* 1671. Orson de Beauvais, Bueves de Hamtoune, Guillaume by Synagon in his Moniage (2), see next note.

31. *Chanson de Guillaume*, 3529ff, *Moniage Guillaume* (2) 3267-71.

32. *Chanson de G.*, laisse 122 (in the first or original part of the existing text), l.1858.

33. *Roland* 3217, 19.

34. Almost equally exaggerated numbers of Christians are quoted, and the numbers generally are part of the exaggeration game; but the spirit of the hopeless fight against odds of Germanic verse often affects the general tone. Another device is the listing of monstrosities among the enemy, a fantastic expression of a simple sentiment. See 262 below.

35. *Doon de Maïence* 6339; Aymery at beginning of *Guibert d'Andrenas* 11-31 (cf. 27) and compare the closing lines of *Aymery de Narbonne* 4508ff.

36. *Loquifer* 3369; *Barbastre* 5635; *Moniage Guillaume* (2) 4640-1, 4643; *Otinel* 788-91 and cf. 243-4. Cf. *Couronnement* A B 834-5 C 577-8.

37. *Otinel* 148-58; *Roland* 1985, 3579; *Moniage G.* (2) 4671. For relics, see ch.10, n.1.

38. *Roland* 1015 cf. 3367.

39. *Chanson de G.* 540-4, *Gui de Warewic* 3475-82, 3895-3910.

40. *Chanson de G.* 1963-77; *Moniage Guillaume* (2) 3966-9, 4444-9; cf. 3277-8, 4144-6.

41. *Couronnement* 522-43.

42. *Roland* 1132-8, 1140, 2364-5, 2369-72, 2374, 2387-8, 2393-6.
    Ch. de G. 2042-4 (second part of poem); see also ch.10, n.25.
    Another battling archbishop, Renier in *Mon. Guillaume* (2)
    absolves the French from their sins, 4192. Cf. *Aspremont* (2)
    5501-6.

43. *Ch. de G.* 545-6. Frappier (*op. cit.* vol.1, 191-7) sees Vivien's
    death as a self-immolation which the poet assimilates to
    Christ's. This is one way to understand his reproving himself
    for praying not to die, because he is asking better treatment
    than Christ himself received, but it is not the only way.
    See 813-24.

44. *Roland* 1166 cf. 1467, *Loquifer* 3311 *Aspremont* (W) 10705;
    used by Saracens to mean torments, *Barbastre* 537, *Orange*
    1170, *Charroi* 1383.

45. *Couronnement* 387-96, A B 390-9 C 159-68.

46. *ed. cit.* vol.2, 259 cf. 217; lines 2987-94, 4041-54, 6412-4
    (text in vol.1).

47. *ibid.* 172-6, 205-13, 220-3.

48. *Aliscans* 1050-61, *Ch. de G.* 2111-20.

49. My views in Norman Daniel, *The Arabs and Medieval Europe*,
    London and Beirut, 1979, ch.3. Menendez Pidal, *Chanson
    de Roland*, ed. cit., 243 rightly argues that *Roland* is not about
    a holy war in the sense prevailing from the eleventh century,
    proclaimed by the Pope and supported by indulgences; it is a
    war for France, not for religion.

50. Perhaps the best examples are Simon de Pouille, Bueve de
    Hamtoune, Gui de Warewic and Blancandin.

51. *Voyage de Charlemagne* 15, 'un ris et un gabet'.

52. Cf. ch.4, n.17 and 182-3.

53. Gautier: *Les Epopées françaises*, 4 vols, Paris, 1878-92,
    in capitals at the end of vol.IV. Borg, *op. cit.* 161. *Roland* is epic
    in the same way as *Maldon*, see 262 below. Rychner, *op. cit.*
    39-40.

CHAPTER SIX
Why the Gods? Introductory

1. *Encyclopaedia of Islam*, s.v. *shirk*.

2. The articles which I have chiefly taken into account are:
   René Basset, 'Hercule et Mahomet' in *Journal des Savants*,
   n.s. 1 (July 1903); Henri Grégoire, 'Des Dieux Cahu,

Baraton, Tervagant . . . et de maints autres dieux non moins extravagants' in *Annuaire de l'Institut de philologie et d'histoire orientales et slaves*, VII (1939-44) and 'L'Etymologie de Tervagant (Trivigant)' in *Mélanges d'histoire et de théatre offerts à Gustave Cohen*, Paris, 1950; A. Eckhardt, 'Le Cercueil flottant de Mahomet' in *Mélanges de philologie romane et de la littérature mediévale offerts à Ernest Hoepffner*, Paris, 1949; and C. Pellat, 'Mahom, Tervagan, Apollin', in *Actas del primer congreso de estudios arabes*, Madrid, 1964, and Y. and C. Pellat, 'L'Idée de Dieu chez les "Sarrasins" des chansons de geste' in *Studia Islamica*, XXII (1965). See also A. d'Ancona, 'La leggenda di Maometto in Occidente' in *Giornale storico della litteratura italiana*, XIII, reprinted Bologna, 1912; and A. Mancini, *Per lo Studio della leggende di Maometto in Occidente*, Rome, 1935; D. Ziolecki, tr. C. Pellat, 'La Légende de Mahomet au moyen âge', in *En Terre d'Islam*, III (1943).

3. E.g. *Aspremont* (W) 2159 (2) 2721; *Moniage Guillaume* (2) 4657-8 and see 229, with references at n.44 (ch.10).

4. Contrast 222.

5. *Quadruplex reprobatio*, ed. cit., cap.1. I am paraphrasing slightly to avoid giving offence.

6. Psalm 100, v.6, AV 101; Vulgate 18 v.8, AV 19, v.8.

7. Above 71, ch.4, n.6.

8. Vincent de Beauvais, *Speculum Historiale* 23.40; Gerald of Wales, *de principis instructione* 157-8 (RS 21).

9. Ch.4, n.2 above.

10. These are cited in the Latin text recognisably and identifiably.

11. *Sobre el seta mahometana*, *Obras*, ed. P. Armengol Valenzuela, Rome, 1905-8.

12. *Itinerarius*, ed. cit., cap.XXX-XXXV.

13. Lull was perhaps the theologian most insistent that he could 'prove' the Trinity by 'conclusive arguments': see Daniel, *Islam and the West*, ch.VI.3, 175ff. See also below, 145, 151-2 but as corrective see D. Urvoy, *Penser l'Islam*, Paris, 1980.

14. E.g. Guibert de Nogent, MPL 156, *Gesta Dei per Francos*, lib I cap.iii, col.689.

15. Embricon de Mayence, *La vie de Mahomet*, ed. G. Cambier, Brussels, 1961; *Le Roman de Mahomet de Alexandre du Pont*, ed. Y. G. Lepage, with *Otia de Machomete de Gautier de*

Compiègne, ed. R. B. C. Huygens, Paris, 1977.

16. Y. and C. Pellat, 'L'Idée de Dieu' 12-14.

17. *Couronnement* (w) 845-53, AB 849-54, C 591-7; *Aiol* 10085-92
    Entrée d'Espagne 2444-64; also *Li Nerbonois* 5762-8.

18. *Turpinus* xii; *Entrée* 3627, 2149, 12415.

19. Eulogius, *loc. cit.* (col.860).

20. *Doon de Mayence* 10467; *Gaufrey* 3581-2; *Floovant* 374 cf. 745
    'si con il vint an terre pour lou pouple sauver'.

21. E.g. *Floovant* 559; *Fierabras* 1325 and cf. 173ff, 176 below.

22. Daniel, *Islam and the West*, index s.v. dove.

23. St Bernard, *de laude novae militiae ad milites templi liber* in
    opera omnia, ed. J. Mabillon, MPL 182 col.921ff. See however,
    Georges Duby, 'La noblesse dans la France médiévale',
    Hommes et Structures 158-9.

24. *La Queste del Saint Graal*, roman du XIIe siècle, ed. Albert
    Pauphilet, Paris, 1949.

25. Matthew Paris, *Cronica Majora* (RS 57) vol.2 (pseudo-Vitry);
    see 145 and ch.7, n.37, 38.

26. Daniel, *Islam and the West*, VI.4, 184ff., and see p.140.

27. *Popeliquant* occurs for example in *La Mort Aymery* 2714,
    Aliscans 2101; *der Festländische Bueve de Hautone* 4313, 9922;
    cf. ch.7, n.22.

28. Canonists especially were inclined to assimilate Saracens, not
    only to Jews ('de judaeis et saracenis'), so as to isolate them
    from any Christian community, but also to apply to them the
    rules that obtained before the secular power was Christian,
    for example, Raymund of Penaforte, *summa canonum*, Verona,
    1744, I.iv.2; see also ch.4, n.17 above.

29. Faral, above, 6.

30. Etienne Gilson, *Les Idées et les Lettres*, Paris, 1932, 219ff.
    Bacchic masses and other parodies: *Parodistische Texte*,
    Biespiele zur lateinischen Parodie im Mittelalter. Paul Lehmann
    (Munich) 1933.

CHAPTER SEVEN
Who are the Gods?

1. *Roland* 868, 1906; *Aspremont* 2520; *Barbastre* 4542 cf. 592;
   Aspremont (w) 2492, 3276-7 cf. 3374, 4421, 7694, 7827, 8228;
   Simon 882, 1130; *Aye* 1658; *Gui de Warewic* 8625.

2. *Aspremont* (w) 1110, 7896; *Aye* 7273; *Gui de Nanteuil* M 2550;

Orange 672; *Godin* 8946; *Orson* 1538; *Loquifer* 137, 2813, 2957; *Enf. Ogier* 4288, 4694, 3178; *Otinel* 144-5; *Elie* 385; *Narbonne* 3858; *Maugis* 2943, 2994, 3661.

3. *Charroi* 1097-8.

4. *Anseis* 939, 4590-1. There is also Nero, *Gaufrey* 8697.

5. *Aspremont* (w) 5886; *Mort Aymery* 1308. Invocations to Tervagant or Apollin alone are fairly common. In *Godin*, Margot takes precedence over Jupiter, and Apollin over Tervagant 8626-7, and elsewhere Margot over both Apollin and Mahon 9635-6; Mahomet is the last of four in *Renier* 11122-4, but there are constant rearrangements. *Charroi* 1097-8 conceivably distinguishes between Mahon and Tervagant in function but there is no reason not to consider the distinction haphazard.

6. *Enfances Renier* 11320-21, 17733.

7. *Raoul* 7674.

8. *Elie* 440-41.

9. *Orson* 1636 and comment on this line.

10. E.g. *Barbastre* 472, 5468; *Bueves de Commarcis* 3154, 3709; *Aspremont* (w) 2099; *Cordres* 1106 et alibi; *Quatre Fils* 16313; *Couronnement* A B 384, C 153; *Enfances Guillaume* 1516 'la pute gent salvage'; also *Antioche* 415 and *Moniage Renoart* (1) fo.184r2 cf. 185v2. Cf. p.108 above.

11. *Exhortation to the Greeks*, 11 (Loeb 53); *Book of Wisdom* 12.23-15.19.

12. *Sinica Franciscana* (thirteenth century) vol.1 *Itinera et relationes saeculi* XIII and XIV, ed. A. van den Wyngaert, Quaracchi, 1929; Roger Bacon, *Moralis Philosophia*, ed. F. Delorme, Zûrich, 1953, 213 (III.2.6) and see index s.v. Tartari, Saraceni; Vincent de Beauvais, *op. cit.* 31.2ff., 29, 49ff. Cf. C. Dawson, *The Mongol Mission*, London, 1955 and A. T'Serstevens, *Les Précurseurs de Marco Polo*, Paris, 1959.

13. Celtic folklore: J. Runeberg, *Etudes sur la geste Rainouart*, Helsingfors, 1905. Pagan survivals in Arthurian legend are too large a subject to review; for Oberon, refer commentaries on *A Midsummer Night's Dream*, and introductions to editions of the Huon cycle.

14. *Amadas* 1102-3.

15. *Pampelune* 1298-1300; *Godin* 12194 cf. 16673.

16. *Anseis* and *Enfances Renier* are particularly free with Jupiter

forms, but there are variants in many poems.

17. *Blancandin* 2619-20, 3132-72.

18. *Li Nerbonois* 5762-8; *Raoul* 7672-4; *Gaufrey* 8703, 8731-2, 9037; *Simon* 987, 1972; *Huon* 6308-9; *Chevalier du Cygne* 4600; *Aquin* 1264; *Saisnes* 7381; *Charroi* 897-8 cf. 892.

19. *Chanson de Guillaume* 2118; *Antioche* 5311-2; *Saisnes* 4105.

20. *Elie* 385-7; and 440-1 as at n.8.

21. *Couronnement* (1) 522-40, A B 525-43, C 279-94.

22. Frappier, *op. cit.* vol.2, 127, citing Meredith Jones ('Conventional Saracen' q.v.); but the sources quoted are only those that class Islam as a heresy in itself, and, though these compare it with other heresies, they do not suspect Catharism. See ch.6, nn.26 to 28 above, and cf. Peter the Venerable, *summa*, Kritzeck, *op. cit.*, p.204ff.

23. *Pampelune* 4119.

24. Bédier, *Les légendes épiques*, vol.1, 434.

25. *Rousillon* 9043.

26. Roger Bacon, *Opus Majus*, J. M. Bridges, Oxford, 1897, pars 2a, vol.3, 54-5, 64-6.

27. See s.v. Sarrasin (-azin) in Godefroy and La Curne de Sainte-Palaye.

28. *Le Roman de Troie*, vol.4, 348. *Le Roman de Thèbes*, 65-78. *Le Roy Advenir*, Mahon, 11, 654, Apollin 342, 3051, Tervagant 3000, 4856, Jupiter le grant 3049. *Eneas* has Jupiter, Mars, Venus, Juno, Pallas, but no Mahon or Tervagant; cf. *Auberon*, with its single invocation of Jupiter, 2340, and cf. ch.11 below, 253. *La Clef d'Amors*, otherwise very like *Blancardin*, has only classical gods and personifications.

29. *Couronnement* (1) 461-9 A B 465-72 C 224-9; *Auberon*, introduction lxix and lxviii and see preceding note and see p.65 above.

30. See *Turpinus* iv; for other references, see ch.6, n.2.

31. *ibid.*

32. *ibid.*

33. *Couronnement* 986-7 A B 987-8.

34. Lull, *Disputatio Raymundi Christiani et Hamar Saraceni*, in *Opera Omnia* (1; Salzinger) Mainz 1721, and in his work generally; see ch.6, n.14 above.

35. Alan of Lille, *de fide catholica contre haereticos*, lib.3, cap.1 and 2 (cf. lib.4, cap.1); *de arte seu articulis catholicae fidei*, lib.1, cap.xxv-xxx. Alexander III, *epistola ad soldanum Iconii*,

in MPL 207 ('instructio fidei catholica') and in Matthew Paris *Cronica Majora* s.a. 1169.

36. It may be that the theologians are simply uneasy with unitarianism and even a little aggressively defensive. It is normal to proceed straight from acknowledging Muslim monotheism to reproving anti-Trinitarianism, as do both Guibert and Alan, *loc. cit.*; so too does Peter the Venerable in his *summa totius haeresis* – 'although they confess God with the mouth they know nothing really about him'. He goes on to complain at the Quranic use of the first person plural when God speaks. *loc. cit.*

37. In the ninth century, Alvarus of Cordova tried to assimulate Islam to Old Testament idolatry, but he seems to be thinking of the call to prayer (cf. p.145 below), not of an actual idol (Migne, *Patrologia Latina* cxxi, 537-540). Among early Eastern writers St John of Damascus (attribution disputed, *Patrologia Graeca* xciv, 764) and George the Monk (*ibid.* cx, 873-874) refer to Aphrodite worship, and Nicetas of Byzantium (*ibid.* cv, 776-777) makes more general charges of animism; it is not clear how serious they are, what they say bears no resemblance to our authors' ideas, and even a putative influence on Latin theologians must be very remote.

38. See *de predicatione* xi. Humbert then compares the story of Jehu and the statue in Baal (Vulgate 4 Kings x.26, AV 2 Kings, RSV 'pillar'). Idolum may well be figurative, cf. imago (*ibid.*, at incipit): 'haec . . . deberent sufficere omni corde humano ad eum vitandum et imaginem suam post mortem stercoribus lapidandum'. If Humbert did think there was a real image, he thought it the statue of a human lawgiver, as it might be that of a saint. See also my *Arabs and Medieval Europe*. Index s.v. idolatry, and see n.57 below.

39. *Dialogi*, titulus V, MPL 157, col.603; the account is very confused, especially about buried idols of Saturn and Mars (also 'Amon et Moab'); and the most that can be said for it is that there was a pre-Islamic cult which Muslims would agree needed to be purified.

40. Cf. M. Eliade, *Traité d'histoire des religions*.

41. A not uncommon phrase, which occurs also reversed: both in *Aye* 1600 and 2236 (*Mahonmet de Meques*).

42. *Gui de Bourgogne* 1279-80, 1337-8, cf. *Simon* 1916.

43. Meredith Jones, *op. cit.* 217-8.

44. *Orange* 477; *Simon* 1595; *Pampelune* 4119-20; *Blancandin* 3627; *L'Escoufle* 1189; *Loquifer* 3933 (Renoart's 'praise God'); *Mon. Guillaume* (2) 4645.

45. At a relatively early date in the history of Arab Spain, Alvaro of Cordova witnesses angrily to the Arab acculturation of Christians, *Indiculus Luminosus* MPL 121, begins col.513

46. Turpinus xii. Cf. Sebourc XI, 611ff. esp. col. 523, 554.

47. *Elie* 440-1, already cited.

48. *Roland* 3490-3.

49. Either of the type 'qui tout a en baillie' (e.g. *Godin* 8946) or that of 'que ge doi aorer' (Cordres 576).

50. Jérusalem 6, 5583, cf. p.167ff. below; see also *Turpinus* xii, cf. vi.

51. *Aspremont* 6201-4.

52. *Otinel* 1296-8; *Aspremont* 8033-9.

53. Cf. ch.9, *Disputes and Reasons*.

54. Gods as standards, *Aspremont* (W) 2980; For fleet identification, *Hugues Capet* 6222; with shield, *Entrée* 8540, 12624; army standards proper, *Galiens li Restorés* 258.46-8; painted with images of the gods, *ibid.* 55.1.6; earlier than this group of late poems, *Roland* also has a standard of Tervagant and Mahon, as well as an image of Apollin: 3266-8, cf. *Aspremont* 9229; cf. also *Barbastre* 6110 (Mahon 'desus l'estendart'); and the image of Apollin on the *boucles*, *Fierabras* 668.

55. *Antioche* 5281; *Barbastre* 1474-6; in *Simon* Mahon is angry at being moved from Babylon, thus giving Duke Simon the chance to have a go at him, for which he had always longed, *Simon* (2) fo.41r-v. The Saracens think Mahon suffers; see p.168ff. above.

56. *Roland* 2580-91, the gods still lost 2695-9, their images 3266-8, images and gods distinguished (and functioning) 3490-4, broken up in town 3662-5; *Aspremont* (W) 3444ff., 7827-8, 7833, 7918, 7996, 8162-5, 8180, 8228-31, 8279-90; cursing the gods 8611-6; challenge to prove the true god 8033-9; prayer in spite of disillusion 7976-7; and see ch.8 on disillusion.

57. Balan: see 168ff. Gadifer, Runeberg 57. For gods as *simulacra* of the devil, *Turpinus* xii. Cf. Eulogius, MPL 115, col.862 (ps.96.7).

58. Vulgate/AV concordance: Psalm 113=115; 134=135; 111 Kings=1 Kings.

59. E.g. *Floovant* 559-61, cf. *Loquifer* 1626.

60. Note 36 above.

61. Bernard of Angers: *liber miraculorum Sancte Fidis* I.xiii, 48, ed. A. Bouillet, Paris, 1897.

62. 176.

63. *Loquifer* 185, cf. *Cordres* 1848; *Pampelune*, n.44 above.

CHAPTER EIGHT
The Cult of the Gods

1. *Gadifer*, text in Runeberg, *op. cit.* 57; *Gui de Warewic* 8444; *Barbastre* 1012-21.

2. *Floovant* 725-8; *Elie* 906-12; *Andrenas* 1411-19; *Cordres* 2809; *Aspremont* (w) 2983, 3408.

3. *Simon* 1548-9; *Enfances Guillaume* 1537-42; *Barbastre* 991-1004, 1474-92; *Antioche* 5301-05; *Fierabras* 3157-73; *Elie* 1773-6; *Simon* 1531-2; *Jérusalem* 7.6462-4; *Gaufrey* 8735; *Aspremont* (w) 2982 and 3376 cf. (2) 3690-5 'd'ors sont flamboiant'. There is a resemblance to the description of the idols in Lucian's *Syrian Goddess*, but a literary source is hardly likely, and least of all a Greek one.

4. See cases cited in last note. *Voute* in *Andrenas*, *loc. cit.*

5. As 'temple of Venus' in *Pampelune*, *loc. cit.*, classic instance of town, *Roland* 2580; *Barbastre* 970; another town mahommerie in Bueves de Hamboune, n.55 below.

6. See examples above; *Roland* 2580; *Godin* 12194.

7. *Cronica Adefonsi Imperatoris* ed. L. Sanchez Beld, Madrid, 1950, para.131ff.

8. Implicit in the offerings; nn.11 and 17 below and 160 cf. *Barbastre* 7118-9, *Blaye* 2763-6.

9. Gadifer (1) fo.231r-v; cf. *Fierabras* 3827.

10. *Cordres* 1154.

11. E.g. *Enfances Guillaume* 1519-20, 1558-60; *Barbastre* 1486-8; *Roland* 3492-3; *Loquifer* 985-6; *Antioche* 5298.

12. In the satirical passage (*Anseis*, *Turpin*), 189, the point against the Christian clergy is their *rentes*.

13. For St Baudime cf. Georges Duby, *St Bernard et l'art cistercien*, Paris, 1976. I owe this reference to M. Albert Prévos.

14. *Liber miraculorum*, *loc. cit.* 47.

15. See p.229. *Moniage Guillaume* (2) 4657 for example.
16. *Antioche* 5279-95.
17. *Loquifer* 982-6 cf. *Elie*, as cited, 911.
18. *Jérusalem* v.xiii.6466. Other examples of Christian rituals transposed, 'de Mahon se seigna', *Moniage Renoart* (1) fo.190v3; marriage before Mahon's altar, *Gaufrey* 8543.
19. *Aiol* 9703. In *Simon* the ventriloquised god says 'come and join your hands' to worship; but this is not the normal position of the hands in prayer for either Muslims or oriental Christians. Saracens kneel to pray to Apollin in *Barbastre* 4855, but standing is the usual position for prayer apart from *sujūd*. In all these cases the model is clearly Western Christian.
20. *Enfances Guillaume* 1563-4.
21. Psalms: Vulgate 67.26 AV 68.25; 113 (2).4 and 134.15 AV and 135.15. Cf. *Elie* 927: 'Il nen a ame el cors ne parolle ne vie'.
22. Jagannath, *The Times* 6 July 1981.
23. *Aspremont* (W) 4422-4 (2) 4755-59.
24. *Roland* 853-4 and *loc. cit.* (3492) cf. also *Simon* 2077-81.
25. *Fierabras* 668.
26. See above ch.7, n.54.
27. Blancandin 2763-6.
28. Cf. L. A. Meyer, *Saracenic Heraldry*, Oxford, 1933.
29. *Floovant* 730-53; *Antioche* 5306-20; *Simon* 1528-50. The gibberish spoken by the statue of Tervagant in the *Jeu de Saint Nicolas* 1517-20, is perhaps meant to be oracular, but is unexplained. See also *Enfances Guillaume* 1546-7 and cf. *Bâtard* 2767-8.
30. *Narbonne* 3505-29; *Cordres* 2807-8, cf. 2591; *Antioche* 4884-91; *Bâtard* 2755-66; *Roland* 3665.
31. See Eckhardt, *op. cit.* above ch.6, n.3, and cf. Lepage, introduction to the *Roman de Mahomet*, ed. cit. pp.46-9. Lucian (*Syrian Goddess*) claims to have seen an enthroned idol rise in the air, but he does not claim that it was magnetised. As a magnet cannot hold an object stable in the air, Pliny, Rufinas of Aquilea and Suidas, claiming that this was done at the Alexandria Serapeum, cannot be telling the truth, and it is anyway most unlikely that our poets had a literary source. This is probably one of those popular fancies that circulate over the centuries among those more credulous than the devout congregations they conceive to be duped.

In the songs they are part of the game.

32. *Roland* 609-11; *Aye* 1524 cf. 1772; *Barbastre* 6268-9; *Roland* 3637; *Floovant* 739-41; *Orange* 1140-2; *Charroi* 1099-1100.

33. *Doon de Mayence* 10467; *Entrée* 11855 cf. 12090.

34. *Roland* 3641-3. Cf. *Huon* 5924, 'Mahoms ait s'ame par la soie pité'.

35. *Barbastre* 4493.

36. *Narbonne* 3496-3504, 3594-5.

37. Above, p.146 and n.41 (ch.7).

38. *Entrée* 11868.

39. *Entrée* 13629-32; *Fierabras* 4017ff.; *Esclarmonde* – Saracens come from all parts for the feast 'de Mahomet a cui lors lois apent': 1466-9.

40. 'great feast' *Cordres* 998ff.; Easter, e.g. *Moniage Guillaume* (2) 4659; *Gaufrey* 1566-7; *Chevalerie Vivien* 88, Pentecost.

41. *Barbastre* 437 cf. 466; *Aye* 2241-2 cf. *Huon* 5507ff. and 5429; *Blancandin* 3242; *Narbonne* 3632; *Gui de Warewic* 8571-2; *Aiol* 10317.

42. In fact this is a very remote example; it is naturally found only in the English version and in one MS branch at that. *Sir Beues de Hamtoun* 461.

43. Cf. ch.10, 225-6.

44. *Fierabras* 3827-37, 5146-51, 5157-61, 5311-24.

45. *Aspremont* (W) 3661 cf. 7976-7; *Quatre Fils* 16125; *Otinel* 1525; *Maugis* 3587; *Roland* 2714-8; *Loquifer* 826, 850; ('sleeping'), *Aspremont* 8629; *Gaufrey* 3577. Cf. also *Roland* 3514, *Antioche* 4897-9; *Couronnement* 1282 A B 1264; *Barbastre* 1485 'que demores tu tant?'; *Jeu de Saint Nicolas* 134-5.

46. *Blancandin* 3177-80; *Orson* 1500-2; *Enfances Guillaume* 1565-89; *Elie* 940-1, 977-1002.

47. *Gui de Warewic* 3644-64.

48. *Aspremont* (W) 8149-66.

49. *Fierabras* 3178; *Loquifer* 826-7.

50. *Roland* 3661-4, 2580-91 cf. 3338. The mahommeries sacked in *Barbastre* might reflect the actual events of the two captures of the town of Barbastro.

51. *Orson* 1755-9; *Barbastre*, see n.5 above.

52. *Aspremont* 3661 cf. 8615 and 8180; 3335, 3451 (W) 3433-8, (2) 3738-47.

53. *Andrenas* 1415-19; *Fierabras* 5288-94.

54. *Enfances Guillaume* 1566-74; *Aiol* 9710-12.
55. *Simon* 1575-6, 1587-9, 1605-11; *Simon* (2), *loc. cit.* (fo.41v, col.1). Cf. also *Bueves de Haumtone* 877-84, where Bueves in Damascus hears a large number of priests praying, enters the mahommerie and attacks the idols; the Saracens under-react. In the English version (1159, 68) they are offering sacrifice, but this does not seem to be in the original.
56. *Loquifer*, see ch.4, 87-8 above and ch.9, 203 below. *Gadifer* (1), fo.231r-v and 232r, also perhaps a stereotype, cf. *Simon, si los a compissez les boches et les nez*, 1611. For the noise made by banging Mahon about, compare *Simon* (2), *loc. cit.*
57. See Runeberg, *Etudes* 57.
58. *Moniage Renoart* (1) fo.182r1 and 2 and (2) fo.170v-171r.
59. V. S. Naipaul, *The Overcrowded Barracoon*, London, 1972, 'The Middle Passage', Martinique, 226-30.
60. Joinville, paras 161, 162.

CHAPTER NINE
Conversion

1. *archy and mehitabel* (sic) by don marquis, 71; London, 1931.
2. *Roland* 651-2, cf. 635-40 and Runeberg, *Etudes* 147-8.
3. *Gadifer* (1) fo.218r. The abbot gives an additional reason (not a motive): 'so I believe in Mahon and his commandment, because he gives us the storm and the wind' (*ibid.*), but this is presented as the consequence rather than the cause of the act of belief.
4. See above, ch.4, 70.
5. See ch.1, 13, and ch.10, 255.
6. *Simon* 1460-2; later in the same poem Simon makes much the same offer to the 'Turk' Sorbaré (who accepts), 1747-9.
7. *Anseis* 1495-1511; *Gui de Bourgogne* 1711.
8. *Loquifer* 1617-26.
9. *Moniage Guillaume* (2) 3954-69.
10. *Elie* 899-901 (and -904).
11. *La Mort Aymery* 1363-4, 1405-9.
12. *Jourdain* 1251-5, 1615-19.
13. *Galiens* 260 44-6; *Saisnes* 7371-8.
14. Note 7 above.
15. *Aspremont* (w) 5822-7 (2) 5876-80; (w) 5851 (2) 5898. The Saracen war aim in this poem is to impose conversion or

death, another indication if it were needed that the poets are not thinking of the Islamic jihād, with its special alternative for Peoples of the Book. Neither is this a reminiscence of Viking raids. It is one kind of Christianity. (2) 3411-12.

16. *Narbonne* 1172-1225.

17. *Orson* 1732-4.

18. *Pampelune* 1288-90, 1294-6. Cf. *Barbastre* and *Bueves de Commarcis*, 1385-95.

19. *Aiol* 10908-10.

20. *Aye* 4094-5.

21. *Moniage Renoart* (1) fo.192v col.3, 192r col.3. See also *Bueve de Hamtoune* 15444-8, *Doon* 11304-309, *Barbastre* 7140-1, *Bueves de Commarcis* 1380-95, *Foucon* 4402 and cf. *Aspremont* (2) 3411-2.

22. See pp.161 and 166 above.

23. *Elie* 919-23, 927-34.

24. *Otinel* 509-30, 574-7, 595, 611-13, 648-50, 1260-4; Saracen king Clarel thinks he must be 'enchanté', 1267, but roundly calls him a forsworn renegade, 1434.

25. *Blancandin*, conversion passage, 3164-76.

26. *Simon*, principal conversion passages are 347-9, 530-3, Licoride 1000-4. Licoride does listen to Synados' brief theology of redemption; she is less romantic than Sadoine's unnamed lover in *Blancandin* and she has a shadow of a reason for conversion.

27. *Maugis* 3659-60, 3669-73, 3803-07, 3827-30.

28. *Aye*, 3839-42.

29. *Gui de Nanteuil* M 20-1, F 20-1, 1000; V omitted.

30. Ellen May Woods, 73-100, *op. cit.*

31. *Gui de Nanteuil* 2876-7.

32. *Andrenas* 892-912, 916ff., 2180-6, 2280-1.

33. *Cordres* 2361-78.

34. *ibid.* 1625-40.

35. *Barbastre* 592-5, 848-9, 868-9.

36. *Anseis* 1846-56, 1943-5-8.

37. *Pampelune* 637-44, 978-80.

38. *Anseis* 11476-11520.

39. *Turpinus* xiii.

40. *Chanson de Guillaume* 1189-1200, 1218. Other cases, Balan in *Fierabras*, p.189 above, and Obrant in *Charroi* 1448-51,

1455-62.

41. *Raoul* 8059-94.

42. *Aiol*: Macaire in this poem is, like Ganelon, an ambitious and disappointed feudatory, 10502-4 and he finishes like Ganelon 10901-6. Godin 8577. Maillefer, see 202 below; Maillefer, when he fights his father, is commanding a Saracen army harassed by Renoart and finally destroyed.

43. *Gormont* 658.

44. *Coilyear* 807, 892, 939-41.

45. E.g. Gaiete in *Andrenas*; Nubie in *Cordres* on sight of Bertran 713, and by line 752 is ready for baptism. Fleurdepine in *Gaufrey* 1682-5, 1801, and compare the effect of physical presence, 9100-1; and *Foucon* 1048-51, 1922-50, 2094 for Anfélise.

46. *Bueves* 2935-8, 3240-4 (3242 quoted in text); cf. *Barbastre*.

47. *Bueves de Commarcis* is a rewrite of *Barbastre* in a later taste that extends to the manners and customs of the characters. *Barbastre* 7149-54, 7247 and see n.49 below. *Roland* 3671-4, 3978-87, 3990.

48. A short statement of my views in *Arabs and Medieval Europe*, ch.9, section 5.

49. *Cordres*: Baufumé 770-7, 793-6, 1720-1; four baptisms, and Baufumé dubbed, 2078-81; Nubie offers her Christian faith and Bertran his personal faith, 871-4, 878; for pressure on the aumaçor see 81-2, 92 above; his appeal to Aymery 1962. *Barbastre* 7185-90.

50. *Floovant*: Maugalie in love, 437, announces conversion, 1556-7, publicly, 1576-80, baptised 2183-4, preferred by Floovant 2203-7, 2222-9.

51. *Anseis* 6637, 1076, 11555; *Aspremont* 11270-8; *Elie* 2682-6 and see ch.5, n.25.

52. Cf. Bernard the Wise, in T. Tobler, *Descriptiones Terrae Sanctae*, Leipzig, 1874, and English translation in Palestine Pilgrims Text Society, vol.3, London, 1897, ch.3ff.; *Chronicon Novaliciense*, v.9, *Monumenta Germaniae Historica,* Scriptores VII, 112-13.

53. Ysané, *Maugis, loc. cit.*; *Loquifer* 627; *Aye, loc. cit.*, *Saisnes* 2384.

54. *Daurel* 1850-70. Beton immediately promises the support of 3,000 men, apparently to honour his engagement (in both

senses).

55. See above, 74, and ch.4, n.17 above.

56. *Huon* 6688-7700 (6760-4, 6780-5).

57. *Aiol* 5357-8, 5376-80, 5407-12, 9702-5, 9706-7, 9715-6; *Enfances Renier* 11307-19; *Cordres* 2725-7, 2751-3, 2816-20.

58. *Fierabras* 2237-8, 2245; 1250-1, 1314-29; 1500-5, 1511-13, 1797, 1800-16.

59. *Orange* 1338-9; cf. above, 79-80.

60. *Chanson de Guillaume* 3351-72 and following laisses, 182, 185-7.

61. *Loquifer* 1008, 1484-9, 2194-5, 2235-43.

62. *Moniage Renoart* (1) 191v1 (Maillefer 'Mahon a doucement reclamé' 191r3); 191v2 and 192r2.

63. *Loquifer* 3236-9, 3366-74; the Arsenal/Boulogne version published by Runeberg diverges at laisse LXVII, 61, ll.3361-3, 'Lors quida bien que le roi ocis a, Mais Desr. de mort garde n'ara ...' *Fierabras* 5782-7, 5908, 5914-18, 5955-60, 5975-7, 5982-9.

64. *Cordres* and *Anseis* above, *Andrenas* 2236-55.

65. *Aquin* 367-70.

66. *Couronnement* 841-3, AB 842-4, C 585-7.

67. See above, 127-8.

68. *Couronnement* AB 845.

69. *ibid.* (1) and AB 1085-9, C 781-3.

70. *Gaufrey* 3448-53, 3460-4, 3493, 3543-7. In this poem the supposed Saracen claim that Mahon engenders the fertility of the crops is put forward by Garin in a mock debate in which he is pretending to be a Saracen convert. Cf. p.138; the occasion is the fight, p.104.

71. *Turpin*, cap.xvii (*de optima disputatione Rotholandi et Ferracuti*). *Entrée* 2129, 2160ff., 2440ff., 2470, 2489, 2957, 3255, 3613-4, 3620, 3627, 3633-65, 3725, 3758-9, 3769, 3770, 3794, 3804-5, cf. 3906, 3959-65, 3967, 3988-9. Qur'ān 19.16-22, 66.12, 21.91.

72. *Aspremont* (w) 481-540, 2612-3, 3752-8, (2) 1415-84, 3125-6, 4070-6, 5736-42; (w) 5734-48, 7072-5 and see Mandach, pp.205 and 320, note on 6107.

73. *Enfances Ogier* 7086-98, 7113-20.

74. Qur'ān, III.73, IV.169, V; 75, 116-7.

CHAPTER TEN
Christianity

1. *Fierabras* 737ff. *Loquifer* 159ff., 1797. *Gadifer*, text in Runeberg, *Etudes* 58. *Moniage Renoart* (1) 190v col.2-3. Relics throw the enemy down, *Fierabras* 5240-80. Fierabras fades a good deal out of the story, although we are told he was revered as saint Florent de Roie after his death, 1850-1. In this chapter I have benefited in different ways from Dom Jean Leclercq, *L'Amour des lettres et le désir de Dieu*, Paris, 1957 and 'Recherches sur d'anciens sermons monastiques', *Revue Mabillon*, 1946, and 'Prédicateurs bénédictins aux XIe et XIIe siècles', *ibid.*, 1943; A. J. Dickmann, *Le Rôle du Surnaturel dans le chanson de geste*, Paris, 1926; I have not been able to consult M. P. Koch, *Analysis of the Long Prayers in Old French Literature*, Washington, 1940, or M. Gildea, *Expression of Religious Thought*, Washington, 1943, both catalogued by BL but mislaid. The great period for relics of the Passion was the first half of the thirteenth century, with the sack of Constantinople, the impecunious condition of the Latin empire in the East, and the construction of the Sainte Chapelle in Paris. Charlemagne also was on record as having received relics of the Passion from the Patriarch of Jerusalem, so that the idea is not in itself anachronistic; needless to say, there was never any balm. Cf. Petits Bollandistes s. 3 mai (see n.9 below).

2. E.g. *Destruction* 1271, 1445; *Moniage Guillaume* (1) 812; *Fierabras* 5975; *Couronnement* AB 787 C 532; other phrases, *Cordres* 2816, *Bueves de Commarcis* 3376, and see above, 133-5.

3. *La Mort Aymery* 1445-1477.

4. E. R. Labande, 'Le "credo" épique à propos des prières dans les chansons de geste' in *Recueil de travaux offerts à M. Clovis Brunel*, Paris, 1955, vol.2, 68.

5. See *Dictionnaire d'Archéologie Chrétienne et de Liturgie* (F. Cabrol and H. Leclercq), vol.8.2, s.v. Lazare (IV).

6. *loc. cit.* 1482.

7. *Couronnement* AB 699-793 C 445-538 (1) 695-789.

8. An infancy miracle: see Lepage's note on ll.730-32.

9. Longinus: cf. Les Petits Bollandistes, *Vies des saints* (Bar-le-duc, 1872), vol.3, s. 15 Mars.

10. *loc. cit.* (w) 490-536, (2) 425-74; but *B*alan has already been so impressed by the splendour of Charlemagne's court as to forswear his gods privately. Another success reason: (w) 437-40, (2) 1364-6.

11. *Fierabras* 5898-5904.

12. Cf. Labande, *loc. cit.*

13. 11717-63.

14. *op. cit.* 70-8.

15. *Missale Romanum*: Tridentine most obviously but surviving the reforms.

16. *Roland* 2384-8.

17. Labande, *op. cit.* 67-8.

18. *ibid.* 63 – D. Scheludko, *Neues über das Couronnement Louis*, discussed by Frappier, *op. cit.* vol.2, 138, as well as other works cited by Labande 64.

19. Frappier, Labande, *op. cit.*

20. *Blancandin* 3217-22.

21. *loc. cit.* 70.

22. *Otinel* 522, *Gaufrey* 3455 (and see p.205 above); cf. *Aliseans* (2) 7885-98 and *Aiol* 830-1; but *F*ierabras is well impressed, 969-70.

23. *Maugis* 3716, 3723; *Orange* 859; *Loquifer* 185.

24. *Elie* 460-2.

25. *Roland* 2365, 2369-70, 2374, 2383, 2393-4; *Chanson de Guillaume* 2042-52. However superior the literary qualities of the first part of the latter poem, it is poorer Christianity: Vivien is concerned with his vow, not his sins. *Gui de Warewic* 11460-72, 11863-4. *Moniage Guillaume* and *Moniage Renoart*, see below, 229ff.

26. *Doon de Mayence* 10496-7.

27. Labande, *op. cit.* 64, n.1.

28. Ricoldo, *Epistolae commentatoriae de perditione Acconis*, 295-6 in *Archives de l'Orient Latin*, vol.II, ed. R. Röhricht, Paris, 1884. Job, 33.14, Gregory, *Moralia*, 23.18.

29. See below, 267-8.

30. The intrusion of Maccabees (as in *Auberon*) into fiction, in however fictional a guise, blurs the distinction between history and romance. On the other hand, the rise of Islam came to be formulated in almost ritual phrases ('vi armata maximas Asiae partes tota Africa ac parte Hispaniae paulatim

occupans . . .', Peter the Venerable, *summa totius haeresis*, Kritzeck 208); a more elaborate form woven into the argument in Joachim of Flora, *Expositio in Apocalypsim* (Venice, 1527, reprinted Frankfurt a.M. 1964), 165r1, and 'turn by turn Asia, Africa and some of Spain overwhelmed' is characteristic of this recurring episode of 'sacred history' in many authors; see also 63-4; cf. 95 and ch.5, n.5.

31. The saints carried the position of the kings and prophets into the new dispensation. The story of Charlemagne, like the Maccabees a figure of history, though not of Scripture as they were, fitted very easily into the perspective, and the assimilation of fiction to history is taken furthest, perhaps, by Philippe Mouskes' *Chronique Rimée*.

32. The prophetic character of Islam was well-known, even beyond the theologians, cf. Daniel, *Islam* ch.1, 17-27 and 'Il fu prophete' passages in the songs, pp.127-8 above; the Quranic treatment of Jesus, which does not occur in the songs, was even better known, *op. cit.* ch.6, 166-175.

33. Examples at *Chanson de Guillaume* 2106, *Fierabras* 3167, *Doon de Mayence* 7843, *Aspremont* 5405 and 5976; *R*enoart in *Loquifer* 3933, straddles this case and the case at ch.7, n.44; *Moniage Guillaume* (2) 4063, 6070.

34. E.g. 193 and 194 above.

35. Common phrase, e.g. *Fierabras* 5975.

36. Note 1 above.

37. *Destruction* 1281.

38. *Entrée* (and introduction), *loc. cit.*, or *Enfances Ogier* 7635ff.

39. *Roland* 2246-8.

40. *Couronnement* 391.

41. See pp.162-3.

42. *vespres*: see Godefroy and La Curne. *Cordres* refers unambiguously to the office: vespers and compline, 958, prime, 2087, compline, 2604; cf *Destruction*, 'hour of compline' 359. Even in the satirical passage where the Saracen captive rejects Christianity because it does not care for Christ's poor, the monks in the case of *Anseis* are simply described as praying for Christians at matins early; *Turpinus* says 'invoke the Lord's majesty for us' (i.e. for Charlemagne, who is speaking). It is the clerks 'qui ont les rentes' but the monks are inevitably classed among the wealthy (ch.9, nn.38-9).

43. Cluny, e.g. *Foucon* 22476, *Gui de Nanteuil* M 324; *Huon féerie* 201v18, 96; *Huon de Bordeaux* 612-27, 1666-27, 1953-2058 (Ruelle); but mentions of St Denis even further outrun the value of listing them here, whether serious, as at *Enfances Ogier* 7635, *Voyage* 1, 863; *Floovant* 11-13; *Enfances Guillaume* 3, or just in passing or even as an oath, e.g. *Charroi* 1308, *Moniage Renoart* (1) 18113. General cases: *Cordres* 2843; *Aspremont* 845, 914, 937, 2159, 3820; *Galien* 201.10-13; *Loquifer* (2) 668; many more, however casual, witness to the constant influence of St Denis.

44. E.g. references in last note, *Galien* and *Aspremont*, *Moniage Guillaume* (2) 4657, etc.

45. See Cloetta's introduction to *Moniage Guillaume* and Runeberg's *Etudes*.

46. Aiol puts up for the night at a monastery, and it is attacked by robbers, whom he challenges and who tell him to stay where he is and sing matins and compline, 775-6, 830-2 (and see n.22 above). On the other hand, Guillaume entrusts Louis to the abbot of St Martin of Tours for safekeeping: he shall be 'as well guarded as the relics of the saints', the abbot promises, *Couronnement* 1994-5, AB 1974-5, C 1762. It is the height of *démesure* in Raoul de Cambrai to burn the nuns and their abbey.

47. *Moniage Guillaume* (1) 125-135, (2) 305-20, 794-6, 811-6; the angel is at 821-4.

48. (2) 347-78.

49. (2) 2193-2207 (1) 854-79 (2) 2472-99, 1509-10, 2763-4, 6509-10. It must be relevant that in another poem both Guillaume and Guibourg are shown as thinking of entering religion; just possibly this is the source of his vocation in the later poem: *Chanson de Guillaume*, laisse 148.

50. *Moniage Guillaume* (1) 492-505, cf. *Aliscans*, ed. Hartnacke *et al.*, pp.213-4, ll.54-63 and p.212, l.3721.

51. *op. cit.* 153-4.

52. *Moniage Renoart* (1) 18112 (2) fo.167r; *Aliscans* 7536, 7539-40; *Gadifer*, Runeberg p.58 and Arsenal 6562, fo.231v; *Loquifer*, see above.

53. *Moniage Renoart* (1) fo.182v3, (2) 171v.

54. Despoiled peasant, *Aliscans* 7374-7491.

55. *ibid.* (1) fo.18311, (2) 174r. (in the same general sense the two

versions nevertheless diverge in wording). Renoart has been taken for a folk hero in a more drastic sense than mine, even for a quasi-revolutionary, cf. Frappier, *op. cit.*, vol.1, 227ff., who does not endorse this view as his own. He does, however, accept the principle of the humorous element in epic forms.

56. *Moniage Renoart* (1) 182v1, (2) 172r-v. Cf. *Simon* (2) fo.41v1.
57. *Moniage Renoart* (2) fo.167r.
58. *loc. cit.* (*Roland* 1015).
59. *loc. cit.* ch.5, n.24.
60. *Iste confessor*: *Repertorium Hymnologicum*, U. Chevalier, Louvain, 1892, vol.1, p.547; *Analecta Hymnica Medii Aevi*, G. M. Dreves, C. Blume and H. M. Bannister, Berne and Munich, 1978, Band Erster, Halbband A-J, 14093, 2, 77/51, 134.
61. *Roland* 1879-82; a Guillaume or Renoart is not quite like life, an Herluin (the founder of Bec) or an Odo Arpin (the hero of Orderic Vitalis, vol.v, book x, who became a Cluniac). See bibliography, and ch.11, n.58 below. For the 'canonisation' of heroes, see Frappier, *op. cit.* vol.1, p.232.
62. Faral, *op. cit.* 25ff.

CHAPTER ELEVEN
Corroboration

1. *Chronicon Salernitanum, ed. cit.* 530, ch.113; but written by a monk of Salerno (cf. above, ch.2, n.3).
2. *Antapodosis* 1.4, *Mon. Germ. Hist.* Ss. III.
3. Ch.9, n.52 above.
4. *Antapodosis* 2.46.
5. *Gesta Francorum* 50-1 (4.9).
6. *ibid.* and 52-3.
7. *ibid.* 70-1 (5.12), 164-5 (10.30).
8. *ibid.* 202-3 (10.38).
9. *Conquête* 4467-71 and ff. Relation of *Gesta* to *Antioche* see Duparc-Quioc, pp.208-11. *Gesta*: see Bréhier's index, s.v. *conversion au christianisme*.
10. *Gesta*, text, pp.118-9, Karbuqa='Courbaram', his mother 9.22, and Bréhier n.1, p.119; Fatimid amir, pp.216-7, 10.39: 'o deorum spiritus' and 'omnia deorum numina'.
11. Text, 122-3, Bréhier, 123-4.
12. *Cantar de mio Cid* 53-63 (*passim*); 88-90ff.
13. E.g. (23), l.448; there are some fifty such references to loot.

14. *ibid.* (90), l.1643.
15. *ibid.* (66) 1102 (b).
16. *ibid.* (114) 2315-5.
17. As usury, *ibid.* (9) 130; as booty, *passim* (e.g. as n.13 above).
18. Cf. (24) 501 and (119) 2453.
19. (72) 1174-9.
20. (31) 619-22, (26) 541, (46) 852-6.
21. (83) 1464, 1517-9, (84) 1528, 1551, (127) 2671.
22. (118) 2409-25.
23. (36) 730.
24. (18) Dona Ximena, 330-65; lucky hour, (4) 41, (5) 71 etc. In this case also there are some 50 examples.
25. (86) 1573, 1585-91.
26. (94) 1704-9, cf. (116) 2370-9, 2382, (117) 2385-6, (95) 1795-6.
27. (152) 3727-8.
28. Above, ch.1, p.11.
29. *Partonopeus de Blois* 93, ll.2661-4; cf. English version, 3375-9.
30. *ibid.* (French text) 2381-6, 2853-6, 2089-90.
31. *ibid.* 7335-42, 7813-4; 9485-40.
32. *ibid.* 2853, 2856.
33. *Flamenca* 684-5.
34. *Floire et Blancheflor*, see bibliography, is only a fragment beside most epics; *alf layla wa layla*, see above, p.6.
35. Dorothee Metlitzki, *The Matter of Araby in Medieval England*, New Haven and London, 1977, 249-50.
36. *op. cit.* 13.
37. 1392-6; Babiloine, 1799ff.; 2931-2, 2991ff.
38. *ibid.* 450.
39. *ibid.* 163, 3053; 1435, 1630, 3180.
40. 1965 etc., 304, 1804, 2697.
41. 3321-3326.
42. 9-12.
43. *Aucassin*, chantefable du xiie siècle, viii; another cousin german to *alf layla wa layla*.
44. *ibid.* III.10; and see index s.v. *Saisnes, Sarrasins*.
45. *ibid.* XXXVI.2-3.
46. *ibid.* xii.
47. *Fouke*, 74-26-78.19.
48. *ibid.* 75.29-30, 76.24-5.
49. *Comte d'Artois* xxxv, J. C. Seignerat.

50. 91.60, 91.50.

51. Jehan de Saintré: 'ce tressaint passaige de Prusse qui hastivement contre les Sarrazins se faisoit', 189, 22-3ff.

52. Malory, *Works*, ed. by Eugene Vinaver, printing from the manuscript, book 11; but in Caxton, still perhaps the more familiar, Book v; I am quoting from Vinaver.

53. Cf. p.65 above; but there is nothing like the amorphous elaboration reached by *Amadis de Gaula*.

54. Malory, 130, 5; 132, 2-3; cf. 134, 40-3.

55. *Morte Arthure* 2199-2200 and 2276-7.

56. *Lancelot du Lac*, part 2, fo.xlv.

57. *Ecclesiastical History of Orderic Vitalis*, Vol.v, Bk.x, 358ff. See also ch.10, n.62.

58. *ibid*. 350-2.

59. *ibid*. 374, cf. 370.

60. for *Deus* by false analogy, cf. 129 above.

61. Orderic, 344-6; cf. Marjorie Chibnall (editor), *ibid*. xviii.

62. *Vie de Saint Louis*, 162.

63. *ibid*. 52-3.

64. Guillaume de Saint Pathus, ch.19, 151; ch.3, 21.

65. Joinville, 394-6.

66. Guillaume de Saint Pathus, ch.19, 152.

67. Joinville, 530-8.

68. *La Mort Aymery* 1405ff. *Li Nerbonois* 4928ff.

69. Joinville, 537, 198, 282, 174.

70. *ibid*. 548-9.

71. *ibid*. 457, 418.

72. *ibid*. 172, 201, 529.

73. *Lettre a Nicolas Arrode*, xi, 6.

74. Joinville, 199 (the names are confused: 'Secedin le filz Seic'; King Philip, *ibid*. 560.

75. *ibid*. 367; examples of curiosity, 248-9, 459-63, 543, 584-7.

76. *ibid*. 735.

77. *Opus Tripartitum*, lib.I, cap.vi-xvi; he contrasts the ancients, *de predicatione, loc. cit.*

78. Rutebeuf, *Disputizon* xx, xxv.

79. For my views, my *Arabs and Medieval Europe*, 312, but much more fully Terry Jones, *Chaucer's Knight, The Portrait of a Medieval Mercenary*, London, 1980; the critical review by Maurice Keen (*History*, vol.66, no.218, Oct. 1981) seems rather

to extend the scope of the argument. I owe this reference to Mr Peter Daniel.

80. See e.g. William of Adam, *de modo Saracenos extirpandi*, in *Recueil des Historians des Croisades*, documents arméniens, vol.2, 523-5; cf. my *Arabs*, 221ff.

81. *Songe du Vieil Pelerin*, Premier livre, 13, vol.1, 231.

82. *ibid.*, *et seq.*

83. Rubruck, *op. cit.*; 137 above and ch.7, n.12.

84. Bertrandon de la Brocquière, *Le Voyage d'Outremer*, ed. Ch. Schefer, Paris, 1892, reprinted Farnborough 1972, pp.97 and 121.

85. *The Battle of Maldon*, 312-3.

CHAPTER TWELVE
Conclusions

1. Konrad Lorenz, *Das Sogenannte Böse*, Vienna, 1963, English translation *On Aggression*, London, 1966, 216, 232, 234.

2. Cf. the break-up of the gods, above 156-7, 173ff., with the Cid's frank pre-occupation with *ganancia*, 245.

3. My mother noticed that when, in the course of the Forsyte Saga series, Soames Forsyte died, she had the impression that an actual acquaintance of hers had died.

4. Cf. my *Islam*, 244-60, 288-301.

5. Tripoli, *op. cit.* (ch.5, n.3), cap.xxi.

6. Ricoldo, *Itinerarius*, cited above, 12-13 and 95.

7. Rubruck's Tatars and la Brocquière's mamelukes could easily have formed the basis on which to elaborate new fantasies, and fourteenth and fifteenth century descriptions of oriental courts likewise.

8. Barbastro, which changed hands three times, contributed its name and its repute, but not the authentic details of the action.

9. This comes out most clearly in the brilliant edition of *Antioche* by Suzanne Duparc-Quioc; see bibliography.

10. Most recently de Mandach, *op. cit.*; in the nineteenth century for example Tarbé's *Folques de Candie* (see bibliography). The editor of *Li Nerbonois*, Hermann Suchier (1898), suggests knowledge of Spanish Arab events, reflected not always very clearly.

11. Guibert, *Gesta Dei per Francos*, MPL 156, lib.I, cap.III, col.689; Alanus, *de fide catholica*, MPL 210, lib.4, cap.I, col.421. The

learned themselves were not of one mind. Peter the Venerable, in no sense *plebeius*, hesitated between *heretici*, *pagani* and *ethnici* (*summa*, Kritzeck 208). Others (as Abelard, *Historia Calamitatum*, ed. J. Monfrin, Paris, 1962, 97-1223) prefer *gentes*; Alvarus, *op. cit.*, 555, *gentilicia*; St Thomas, *contra gentiles*.

LIST ONE
*Sources that observe the convention of pagan gods
(some closely connected poems included)*

Advenir: *Le Mystère du Roy Advenir par Jehan du Prier dit le Prieur.*
A. Meiller, ed., Geneva, 1970.

Aiol, chanson de geste. J. Normand and Gaston Raynaud, eds,
Paris, 1877.

Aliscans:
1) F. Guessard and A. de Montaiglon, eds, Paris, 1870.
2) E. Wienbeck, W. Hartnacke and P. Rasch, eds, Halle, 1903.

Andrena: see Guibert d'Andrenas.

Anseis von Karthago. Johann Alton, ed., Tübingen, 1892.

Antioche: *La Chanson d'Antioche*
1) Suzanne Duparc-Quioc, ed., 2 vols, Paris, 1976-8.
2) P. Paris, ed., Paris, 1848.

Aquin: *Le roman d'Aquin ou La Conquête de la Bretaigne.* F. Joüon
des Longrais, ed., Nantes, 1880.

Aspremont:
1) *La Chanson d'Aspremont, chanson de geste du XIIe siècle.*
Louis Brandin, ed., 2 vols, Paris, 1924 (Wollaston MS and
referred to in the notes as w).
2) *La Naissance et Développement des chansons de geste en
Europe by André de Mandach.* 4 vols, vols III and IV, La
Chanson d'Aspremont. Geneva, 1975, 1980. (To line 6107,
equivalent to (w) 6154.)

Auberon: *Le Roman d'Auberon.* Jean Subrenat, ed., Geneva, 1973.

Aye d'Avignon, chanson de geste anonyme. S. J. Borg, ed., Geneva,
1967.

Aymery:
Aymery de Narbonne, chanson de geste. Louis Demaison, ed.,
2 vols, Paris, 1887.
La Mort Aymery. J. Couraye du Parc, ed., 2 vols, Paris, 1884.

Aymon: see Quatre Fils.

Barbastre: *Le Siège de Barbastre, chanson de geste du XIIe siècle.*
J. L. Perrier, ed., Paris, 1974.

✳ There are more recent & authoritative editions

Le Bâtard de Bouillon, chanson de geste. R. F. Cook, ed., Geneva, 1972.

Baudouin: *Le Romans de Baudouin de Sebourc.* L. Napoléon Boca, ed., Valenciennes, 1841.

Blancandin et l'Orgueilleuse d'Amour, roman d'aventure du XIIIe siècle. Franklin P. Sweetser, ed., Geneva/Paris, 1964.

Bodel, Jean: see Saisnes; Saint Nicolas.

Bueves de Commarcis par Adenes le Rois. Aug. Scheler, ed., Brussels, 1874.

Bueves de Haumtone:

    Der anglonormannische Bueves de Haumtone. Albert Stimming, ed., Halle, 1899.

    Der Festlandische Bueve de Hautone. *Gesellschaft für romanische literatur,* Fassung 1 band 25, II.30, III.34, III.ii.42, Dresden, 1911, 1912, 1914, 1920.

    The Romance of Beves de Hamtoun. E. Kölbing, ed., London, 1885, 1886, 1894.

Le Charroi de Nîmes. J. L. Perrier, ed., Paris, 1972.

Charlemagne: see Mainet; Voyage.

Chétifs: *La chanson des chétifs,* with *Jérusalem,* below.

Chevalier (CCGB): Le Chevalier au Cygne et Godefroid de Bouillon. F. de Reiffenberg and A. Borgnet, eds., in *Monuments pour Servir,* vols 4, 5 and 6, Brussels, 1846-59.

Clarisse et Florent: see Esclarmonde.

Coilyear: *The Taill of Rauf Coilyear.* S. J. H. Herrtage, ed., Oxford, 1882.

Commarcis: see Bueves.

Cordres: *La Prise de Cordres et de Sebille, chanson de geste du XIIe siècle.*

Couronnement:

    1) *Le Couronnement de Louis, chanson de geste du XIIe siècle.* Ernest Langlois, ed., Paris, 1925.

    2) *Les rédactions en vers du Couronnement de Louis.* Yvan G. Lepage, ed., Geneva, 1978.

Croissant: see Huon.

Daurel et Beton, chanson de geste Provençale. P. Meyer, ed., Paris, 1880.

La Destruction de Rome. G. Groeber, ed., in *Romania,* 2nd year, Paris, 1873.

Doon de Maience. M. A. Pey, ed., Paris, 1859.

Elie de St Gilles, chanson de geste. Gaston Raynaud, ed., Paris, 1879.

Enfances: see Guillaume; Ogier; Renier; Vivien.

L'Entree d'Espagne, chanson de geste franco-italienne par Antoine Thomas. Paris, 1913.

Esclarmonde, Clarisse et Florent, Yde et Olive. *Ausgaben und Abhandlungen aus dem Gebiete der Romanischen Philologie,* LXXXIII, Marburg, 1889.

L'Escoufle, roman d'aventure par Jean Renart. Franklin Sweetser, ed., Geneva, 1974.

Fierabras, chanson de geste. M. A. Kroeber and G. Servois, eds, Paris, 1860.

La Fille du Comte: see Pontieu.

Floovant:

    1) *Floovant, chanson de geste du XIIe siècle.* S. Andolf, ed., Uppsala, 1941.

    2) *La chanson de Floovant.* F. H. Bateson, ed., Loughborough, 1938.

Foucon de Candie:

    1) *Folque de Candie.* O. Schultz-Gova, ed., *Gesellschaft für Romanische Literatur,* Band 21, 38, Dresden, 1909, 1915.

    2) *Foulque de Candie.* Prosper Tarbé, ed., Rheims, 1860.

Gadifer:

    1) MS Arsenal 6562.

    2) Extracts. J. Runeberg, *Etudes sur la Geste Rainouart,* Helsingfors, 1905.

Galiens li Restorés. Edmund Stengel, ed., *Ausgaben und Abhandlungen aus dem Gebiete der Romanischen Philologie,* LXXXIV, Marburg, 1890.

Garin de Montglane in BL MS Royal 20 D xi.

Gaufrey, Chanson de geste. F. Guessard and P. Chabaille, eds, Paris, 1859.

Girart de Vienne, chanson de geste. F. G. Yeandle, ed., New York, 1930.

Godin: *La chanson de Godin, chanson de geste inédite.* Françoise Meunier, ed., Louvain, 1958.

Gormont et Isembart, fragment de chanson de geste du XIIe siècle. Alphonse Bayot, ed., Paris, 1921.

Gui de Bourgogne, chanson de geste. F. Guessard and H. Michelant, eds, Paris, 1858.

Gui de Nanteuil:

1) *Gui de Nanteuil*. P. Meyer, ed., Paris, 1861.

2) *Gui de Nanteuil, chanson de geste*. James R. McCormack, ed., Geneva/Paris, 1970.

Gui de Warewic, roman du XIIIe siècle. Alfred Ewert, ed., 2 vols, Paris, 1932-3.

Guibert d'Andrenas, chanson de geste:

1) J. Melander, ed., Paris, 1922.

2) J. Crosland, ed., Manchester, 1923.

Guillaume:

La Chanson de Guillaume ('La Chancun de Willame').
D. McMillan, ed., 2 vols, Paris, 1949-50.

Les Enfances Guillaume. Patrice Henry, ed., Paris, 1935.

Le Moniage Guillaume, chanson de geste du XIIe siècle.
Wilhelm Cloetta, ed., 2 vols, Paris, 1906-11.

(see also Couronnement, Charroi, Orange, Loquifer, etc.)

Huon de Bordeaux:

1) *Huon de Bordeaux*. F. Guessard and C. Grandmaison, eds., Paris, 1860.

2) *Huon de Bordeaux*. P. Ruelle, ed., Brussels and Paris, 1960.

Huon et Calisse: see below, following item.

Huon roi de féerie: Über die Pariser HSS 1451 und 2255 der Huon de Bordeaux-Sage beziehung der HS 1451 zur 'Chanson de Croissant'; die 'Chanson de Huon et Calisse'; die 'Chanson de Huon roi de féerie'. Hermann Schäfer, ed., *Ausgaben und Abhandlungen aus dem Gebiete der Romanische Philologie*, XC, Marburg, 1892.

Jehan le Prieur: see Advenir.

Jérusalem: *La Conquête de Jérusalem*. C. Hippeau, ed., Paris, 1868.

Jourdain: *Amis et Amiles und Jourdains de Blaivies*. C. Hofmann, ed., Erlangen, 1852.

Loquifer: *La Bataille Loquifer*

1) J. Runeberg, ed., *Acta Societatis Scientiarum Fennicae Tom.*, XXXVIII, Helsingfors, 1913.

2) Monica Barnett, ed., *Medium Aevum Monographs* NS vi, Oxford, 1975.

Mainet, fragments d'une chanson de geste du XIIe siècle. G. Paris, ed., *Romania*, IV, 1875.

Maugis d'Aigremont. F. Castets, ed., *Revue des Langues Romanes*, série 4, tom. 6, Montpellier, 1892.

Moniage: see Guillaume; Renoart.

Li Nerbonois: *Les Narbonnais, chanson de geste.* Hermann Suchier, ed., 2 vols, Brussels, 1898.

Ogier:

    Les Enfances Ogier par Adenés li Rois. Aug. Scheler, ed., Brussels, 1874.

    La Chevalerie Ogier de Danemarche . . . poème du XIIe siècle. Joseph Barrois, ed., Paris, 1842.

Orange: *La Prise d'Orange, chanson de geste de la fin du XIIe siècle.* Claude Régnier, ed., Paris, 1972.

Otinel, chanson de geste. F. Guessard and H. Michelant, eds, Paris, 1858.

Pampelune: *La Prise de Pampelune, ein franzozische gedicht.* Adolf Mussafia, ed., Vienna, 1864.

Pontieu: *La Fille du Comte de Pontieu.* Clovis Brunel, ed., Paris, 1926.

Quatre Fils: *La chanson des Quatre Fils Aymon.* Ferdinand Castets, ed., Montpellier, 1909 (also in *Revue des Langues Romanes*, série 5, tom. 9 and série 6, tom. 2, 1906 and 1909.

Raoul de Cambrai, chanson de geste. P. Meyer and A. Longnon, eds., Paris, 1882.

Rauf Coilyear: see Coilyear.

Renart, Jean: see l'Escoufle.

Renier: *Enfances Renier, canzone di gesta inedita del secolo XIII.* Carla Cremonesi, ed., Milan, 1957.

Renoart: *Moniage Renoart*

    1) BL MS Royal 20 D xi.

    2) Arsenal MS 6562.

    3) Extracts in Runeberg, *Etudes*, see Gadifer.

    (see also Gadifer, Loquifer)

Roland: *Chanson de Roland.* Joseph Bédier, ed., Paris, 1922; 6th edition, 1937.

Roland à Saragosse: poème épique méridional du XIVe siècle. Mario Roques, ed., Paris, 1956.

Le Roy Advenir: see Advenir.

Runeberg (J): see Gadifer.

Saint Nicolas: *Le Jeu de Saint Nicolas, by Jean Bodel.* F. J. Warne, ed., Oxford, 1972.

Saisnes: *Jean Bodels Saxenlied.* F. Menzel and E. Stengel, eds, Marburg, 1906.

Saladin: suite et fin du deuzieme cycle de la Croisade. L. S. Crist, ed., Geneva, 1972.

Sebourc: see Baudouin.

Simon de Pouille, chanson de geste
1) Jeanne Baroin, ed., Geneva, 1968.
2) BL MS Royal 15 E vi.

Thèbes: *Le Roman de Thèbes.* L. Constant, ed., 2 vols, Paris, 1890.

Turpinus:
1) *Turpini Historia Karoli Magni et Rotholandi.* C. Meredith Jones, ed., Paris, 1936.
2) *The Pseudo-Turpin (Bib. nat. fonds lat. 1765-6).* H. M. Smyser, ed., Cambridge, Mass., 1937.
3) *Der Pseudo-Turpin von Compostela* (introduction by Andre de Mandach). Munich, 1965 (Bayerische Akademie der Wissenschaften).

Vivien:
La Chevalerie Vivien, chanson de geste. A. L. Terrachier, ed., Paris, 1923.
Enfances Vivien. C. Wahland and H. von Feilitzen, eds, Uppsala/Paris, 1895.

Voyage de Charlemagne. Paul Aebischer, ed., Geneva, 1965.

Yde et Olive: see Esclarmonde.

LIST TWO

Other sources that observe the pagan/Saracen convention

Amadas et Ydoine, roman du XIIIe siècle. J. R. Reinhard, ed., Paris, 1874.

Amadis de Gaula: *Le huitième livre d'Amadis de Gaule.* French translation by des Essarts and de Brissac, Antwerp, 1561.

Artois: *Le Roman du Comte d'Artois.* J. C. Seigneuret, ed., Geneva/Paris, 1966.

Aucassin et Nicolette, chantefable du XIIIe siècle. Mario Roques, ed., Paris, 1936.

Berte: *Li Romans de Berte aus grans pies.* Aug. Scheler, ed., Brussels, 1874.

Bertrandon de la Brocquière. Le voyage d'Outremer. Ch. Schefer, ed., Paris, 1892 (see ch.11).

Busone da Gubbio, L'Aventuroso Ciciliano, with *l'Ordene de Chevalerie.* George F. Nott, ed., Florence, 1832.

Capet: see Hugues.

Chevalerie: *L'Art de Chevalerie, traduit du de re militari de Végèce, par Jean de Meun.* U. Robert, ed., Paris, 1897. See also with Busone, above.

Cid: *Cantar de mio Cid.* R. Menendez Pidal, ed., Madrid, 1913.

Chronicon Salernitanum: see ch.2, n.3.

Cronica: see Primera Cronica.

La Clef d'Amors. A. Doutrepont, ed., Halle, 1890.

Eneas: *Le Roman d'Eneas, texte critique.* J. Salverda de Grave, ed., Halle, 1891.

Flamenca: *Le Roman de Flamenca.* P. Meyer, ed., Paris, 1865.

Floire: *Le Conte de Floire et Blancheflor.* J-L. Leclanche, ed., Paris, 1980.

Florence de Rome, chanson d'aventure. A. Wallensköld, ed., 2 vols, Paris, 1907-9.

Fouke Fitz Warin, roman du XIVe siècle. Louis Brandin, ed., Paris, 1930.

Gaydon, chanson de geste. F. Guessard and S. Luce, ed., Paris, 1862.

Gesta Franorum: Histoire anonyme de la première croisade. L. Bréhier, ed., Paris, 1924 (see ch.11).

Girard de Rousillon. E. Boehmer, ed., in *Romanischen Studien,* XVII (Fünfster Bandes Erstes Heft), Bonn, 1880.

Guillaume de Saint Pathus, Vie de St Louis. H. Francois Delaborde, ed., Paris, 1899.

Horn: King Horn.

   1) *Specimens of Early English.* R. Morris and W. W. Skeat, eds, Oxford, 1935.

   2) *King Horn, Floris and Blauncheflur, The Assumption of Our Lady.* J. R. Lumby and G. H. McKnight, eds, London, 1866/1901.

Hugues Capet, chanson de geste. F. Guessard, ed., Paris, 1859.

Joinville, Vie de Saint Louis. Noel L. Corbett, ed., Quebec, 1977.

La Sale, Antoine de: see Saintré.

Lancelot du Lac. Paris, 1533.

Liutprand of Cremona. Antapodosis. *Monumenta Germaniae Historica,* Scriptores III.

Maldon: *The Battle of Maldon.* E. V. Gordon, ed., London, 1937.

Malory:

   1) *Works.* Eugene Vinaver, ed., Oxford, 1971 (reprint).

   2) *Morte d'Arthur.* William Caxton, ed. (many reprints).

Mezières: *Philippe de Mezières, Le Songe du Vieil Pèlerin.* G. W.

Coopland, ed., 2 vols, Cambridge, 1969.

Morte Arthure:

1) E. Brook, ed., London, 1865.

2) G. G. Perry, ed., London, 1865.

Mouské: *Chronique Rimée de Philippe Mouskés.* Baron de
Reissenberg, ed., 2 vols, Brussels, 1836-8.

Orderic: *The Ecclesiastical History of Ordericus Vitalis.* Marjorie
Chibnall, ed., Vol. v, bks ix and x, Oxford, 1975.

Partonopeus de Blois:

Partonopeus de Blois. A. Crapelet, ed., Paris, 1834.

The Middle English Versions of Partonope of Blois. A. T.
Bödtker, ed., London, 1912.

Primera Cronica General de España. R. Menendez Pidal, ed.,
Madrid, 1955.

Roussillon: see Girart.

Rutebeuf: *Oeuvres completes de Rutebeuf.* Edmond Faral and Julia
Basta, eds, vol. 1; 2 vols, Paris, 1959.

Saintré: *Jehand de Saintré by Antoine de la Sale.* J. Misrahi and
C. A. Knudson, eds, Geneva, 1978.

Sarrasin: *Lettre à Nicolas Arrode de Jean Sarrasin.* A. L. Foulet,
ed., Paris, 1924.

Troie: *Le Roman de Troie par Benoit de Ste Maure.* C. Constans,
ed., 6 vols, Paris, 1904.

PLOT SUMMARIES

Advenir: *Le Mystère du Roy Advenir*. A fifteenth-century play based on a
Buddhist legend and set in a pagan India early A D.

Aiol. Aiol sets out with his father's old horse and arms to recover his
father's lands, but he also inherits his father's enemy, Macaire of
Lausanne. He is sent on a mission to *M*ibrien, Saracen ruler of
Pampluna, whose daughter *M*irabel he carries off and marries. The
pair are captured by Macaire, Aiol imprisoned, their children
thrown into the Rhône (but saved) and *M*irabel returned to her
father. Aiol escapes, Pampluna is captured and Macaire dis-
embowelled.

Aliscans. The story of the great battle by the sea where many French
heroes and especially Vivien are killed; Guillaume d'Orange comes
to their help but cannot turn the tide of battle; he seeks help first at
Orange, where *G*uibourg his wife keeps the castle against the
invaders, and then from King Louis, who sends *R*enoart, kitchen
servant, born a Saracen prince, a giant club-wielder who performs
prodigies and brings victory out of defeat. (And see *Chevalerie
Vivien, Chanson de Guillaume, Prise d'Orange*.)

Anseis de Cartage (= Cartagena = Spain). Anseis is left to rule Spain by
Charlemagne, with Ysoré as counsellor. Anseis is seduced by
Ysoré's daughter Lutisse and dishonours her, causing Ysoré to
change sides, and religion, and join the Saracen King *M*arsile.
Anseis is reduced to the last extremity (although he has had time to
seduce, baptise and marry *M*arsile's daughter *G*audisse), but Charlemagne returns, wins, beheads *M*arsile and hangs Ysoré.

Antioche: *La Chanson d'Antioche*. This is the story of the First Crusade
to the capture of Antioch and the framework is historical.

Aquin. The amir Aquin and his Norwegians invade Britanny, Duke
Naime fights him and converts his beautiful Queen, whom all
Christendom honours, and after bitter struggles Aquin is defeated
and killed.

Aspremont. The invasion of Italy by King *A*umon and his father King
*A*golant in turn, with an interchange of defiant embassies (the
Saracen *B*alan to Charlemagne and Duke Naime to *A*umon);
Charlemagne, in close-won battles, and finally with the help of
Girart de Fraite, defeats them both.

Auberon. The son of Caesarius, emperor of Rome, is Julius Caesar, who
marries Brunehaut, the fairy daughter of Judas Maccabeus, an

enemy of Saracens, by a Saracen princess; he saves Hungary from being ravaged and extends his empire, but he has a son, Auberon, king of fairy, by Morgan le Fay whose twin, St George, seduces the King of Persia's daughter, is succoured by, and serves, the Holy Family in Egypt, and he too becomes emperor.

Aye d'Avignon, wife to Duke Garnier, is carried off by Berenger, son of Ganelon, who wants to marry her, and she becomes the prisoner of the Saracen King Ganor of Aigremore, who also loves her but treats her honourably. Garnier rescues her in Ganor's absence and Ganor carries off their son Gui, whom he brings up honourably. When Garnier has been killed by his French enemies, Ganor becomes Christian, marries Aye and takes on Garnier's other responsibilities.

Aymery. *Aymery de Narbonne.* Aymery, returning with Charlemagne's army from Roncesvaux, takes Narbonne from the Saracens. He goes to Pavia to fetch his bride Hermengarde, and spies send to King Desramé in Orange, who sends to the amir of Babylon, to say that there is a good chance to take Narbonne back. Aymery, with the help of Girard de Vienne, his uncle, defeats and destroys the besiegers.

Aymery. *La Mort Aymery de Narbonne.* Aged and all but senile, Aymery is besieged in Narbonne by the Saracen Corsolt, and captured, tortured and nearly burned to death; while Hermengarde stands siege in the castle keep, Guibert returns in time to save his father, with the help of some of his brothers and King Louis. The French capture an army of women from Femenie, friends to Corstolt, and disguise themselves as the women, recapture the city of Narbonne and kill Corstolt. The women are captured by Sagittaires, a legendary race of centaurs, who are destroyed in their turn, but Aymery is killed in the fighting. (See also *Les Narbonnais*.)

Barbastre. Bueve de Commarcis, one of the sons of Aymery, is captured by Saracens during an attack on Narbonne, and taken prisoner with his sons Gorart and Guielin to Barbastro; they escape with the help of a dissident Saracen, Clarion, and capture the town, where they stand siege till the arrival of Louis and some of the brothers.

Le Bâtard de Bouillon. Baudouin of Bouillon invades Arabia and captures Mecca, where the amir's daughter seduces him; the resulting Bastard grows up and, helped by his friend Hugh of Tabarie, forces Ludie, daughter of Hugh's enemy the amulainne of Orbrie, to marry him, but she is faithful in her heart to her own lover Corsabrin (and hates her father's murderer) and the two manage to take the Bastard prisoner; but he is rescued by Hugh and Ludie is burned.

Baudouin de Sebourc. An adventure story set in Flanders and the Holy land, in which the wicked Gaufroi de Frise is ultimately foiled in his treacheries, is remotely based on the career of Baldwin II of Jerusalem (Baudouin du Bourg).

Blancandin, brought up as a prince should be (except that he is not taught to bear arms) runs away to become a knight and seek adventure. He snatches three kisses from l'Orgueilleuse, female ruler of Tormadai, who is furious, but soon loves him. He joins battle with her Saracen enemy King *A*limodés who also loves her. Blancandin is captured, but escapes in a shipwreck to Saracen Athens (in India), and becomes the friend of the king's son, *S*adoine, who, in the course of a joint expedition, becomes Christian, and together they rescue the daughter of *A*limodés who loves *S*adoine. *S*adoine is captured and l'Orgueilleuse is betrayed by her seneschal, but both are rescued, *A*limodés is captured and *S*adoine succeeds to the rule of his father-in-law's city.

Bueve de Commarcis by Adenet le Rois is *Barbastre*, which is assonanced (q.v.), rewritten in the rhyme fashionable in Adenet's time.

Bueve de Hamtoune. A story of wandering adventure of great complexity and obscure structure: Bueve falls in love with *J*osian, daughter of the pagan king *E*rmin, on whose behalf he fights. A series of battles are interwoven with *J*osian's struggle not to marry other men (one she hangs at the marriage bed, and she has finally to disguise herself as a leper). The lovers are first served and then betrayed by the monstrous *A*scopard. *Y*vorin, a principal villain, refuses conversion and is killed by Bueve, who marries *J*osian, one of their sons succeeding to the throne of England, and the other to that of Ermine.

Le Charroi de Nîmes. Guillaume d'Orange (q.v.), young and fiefless, is granted Nîmes by King Louis, if he can take it from the Saracens, and he does so by masquerading as a merchant, and bringing his knights in hidden in barrels on a train of wagons.

Les Chétifs. A First Crusade fragment.

Le Chevalier au Cygne et Godefrois de Bouillon. This is a highly fictionalised version of the First Crusade and of the romantic rise of the family of the protagonist in Flanders.

Clarisse et Florent, see *Esclarmonde.*

Coilyear: *The Taill of Rauf Coilyear.* Charlemagne is separated from his court by a storm in the wild moors round Paris, and he receives rough but generous hospitality from Rauf, a churl and a collier. He tells him to bring a load of his fuel to the court to sell, and only when he gets there does he discover that his guest was the King, who knights him. When he fights a strange knight on the moors he is gratified that his opponent should turn out to be a Saracen. Ostensibly in France, the scene is unmistakably Scottish.

Cordres. *La Prise de Cordres et de Sebille.* The events take place after those recounted in *Guibert d'Andrenas* (q.v.), but King *J*udas is still alive, and attacks Andrena at the wedding of Guibert and *G*aiete, takes Guibert prisoner to Seville, and Bertrand and others of the kin to Cordova, where *N*ubie, the aumaçor's daughter, loves Bertrand and secures their release; battles end in Christian victory and the recovery of Guibert and his reunion to *G*aiete in Andrena. Bertrand and *N*ubie succeed to Cordova.

Le Couronnement de Louis. Guillaume defends Charlemagne's son and successor as king and emperor, Louis, from various dangers (some from Christians) but principally from the attack on Rome by the Saracen King *G*alafre, and his giant champion, *C*orsolt.

Daurel et Beton. One of the stories of a traitor with Charlemagne's ear, from whom the jongleur Daurel saves the baby Beton, innocent heir to a feud, by sacrificing his own baby son, in whose place he takes Beton to the court of the amir of Babylon; there Beton proves his noble blood as he grows up, by the way he behaves, saves Babylon from the attack of the Saracen King *G*ormont, is lent an army by the amir with which to establish his rights against his enemies in France.

La Destruction de Rome. An attack on Rome which is sacked (reminiscent of the Arab attack of 846 which did not break into Rome but did pillage St Peter's which was *extra muros*) but saved and avenged by Charlemagne.

Doon de Mayence demands from Charlemagne, as a fief, not Nevers or Laon, but Vauclerc in pagan country, among Saxons, Saracens, Turks and Danes. He loves *F*landrine, daughter of the pagan King *A*bigant and his Christian wife Helissant. He forces Charles to help him. The Christians offer to support *A*bigant against his Danish enemies, but he refuses this alliance. He shuts Helissant and *F*landrine up, although by now *F*landrine has managed to marry Doon. They are able to join forces with Antequin, the sergeant who originally brought the Queen from Flanders, but his wife betrays them. Doon breaks in to save *F*landrine. He is helped throughout by the formidable Robastre. Finally Charlemagne arrives in force and *A*bigant is killed.

Elie de St Gilles rescues Christian knights (including Guillaume d'Orange) who have been captured fighting Saracens in Brittany; the prisoners escape but Elie himself is carried off to a Saracen country (Sobrie); he steals a horse and escapes and falls in with robbers who include a dwarf called Galopin, who joins him. He is wounded and taken by the Saracens under their king *M*acabré, whose daughter, *R*osamonde, tends him and falls in love with him. He defends her when *M*acabré is attacked by another Saracen, *L*ubien, who wants his daughter and his kingdom. A Christian victory follows the killing of *L*ubien by Elie and of *M*acabré by Galopin, who marries *R*osamonde when Elie is not allowed to do so after the victory.

L'Entrée d'Espagne. Roland, bored by a peaceful phase, persuades Charlemagne to take an expedition to save Compostela. He has an epic fight with the giant Feragu, but at the siege of Pampluna a quarrel with Charlemagne drives him away from the Christian army, and on his travels he takes service with the King of Persia and distinguishes himself in the war against *M*alcuidant, who is after the King's lands and his daughter. *M*alcuidant is killed and the King and his daughter are converted to Christianity. Meantime the war in Spain makes no progress and Roland returns to Spain and the siege of Pamplune, and is reconciled to Charles. (v. *La Prise de Pamplune*)

Esclarmonde, wife of Huon de Bordeaux (q.v.) is loved by Raoul, emperor of Germany, who tries to carry her off; Huon sails for the East, where he has a number of enchanted adventures, but Bordeaux (and *E*sclarmonde) are saved by Auberon, who is succeeded as King of fairy by Huon. In *Clarisse et Florent*, Clarisse, daughter of Huon and *E*sclarmonde, is persecuted by a number of suitors but loves and is married to Florent of Aragon. Ide, in *Ide et Olive*, is the daughter of Clarisse and Florent, who makes incestuous advances to her. Ide, dressed as a man, is married to the daughter of the German emperor, but these psychological deviations are straightened out. See also *Godin*.

L'Escoufle is a roman d'aventure of which only the first section, describing the rather dull adventures of Richard of Normandy among the Saracens, is relevant. (He is the father of the protagonist.)

Fierabras. A related account of the *Destruction of Rome* (q.v.) with sequels; the aggressor, *B*alan, is accompanied by his son *F*ierabras and his daughter, *F*loripas; *F*ierabras fights a duel with Oliver and is converted; *B*alan goes to Spain with his loot, which includes relics of the Passion. Oliver and others of the 12 peers are taken prisoner, among them Gui de Bourgogne, with whom *F*loripas falls in love. She allows no one to stand in the way of an escape. After the usual battles, Charlemagne captures *B*alan and executes him.

Floovant is exiled by his father Clovis and is loved by two heroines, also heiresses, and he is involved in the wars of their fathers. Working with Richier his squire, he defeats the giant *F*erragu and captures the Saracen amir's daughter, *M*augalie, who quarrels with Florete, daughter of Floovant's ally, King Flore. Her brothers betray him to *M*augalie's father. Finally Floovant is reconciled with Clovis, whom he succeeds in rescuing from his enemies.

Foucon de Candie is a divergent form from the *R*enoart poems (q.v.) of events after the battle of *Aliscans* (q.v.). Foucon, a nephew of Vivien, takes the lead, and *A*nfelise, sister of *T*ibaut, the cuckolded first husband of *G*uibourg, loves him, and her friend *F*ausete loves

Foucon's cousin Gui; they betray the Spanish town of Candie to the Christians. Povre-Veu, bastard of the latter pair, steps into the role of hero in the middle phase of this long poem, but, brought up Saracen, he is finally converted. In the last phase of the plot, *T*ibaut changes character and himself becomes preux; he and the Christians together, when he relinquishes his claim to Candie, advance against Eastern Saracen kingdoms.

Gadifer is the continuation of *Moniage Renoart* (q.v.); *R*enoart's abbot becomes so keen to get rid of his embarrassing *conversus* that he sells out – monastery and monastic profession alike – to the Saracen *T*ibaut, here still a villain doomed to disaster. *R*enoart and the good monks are besieged in the town of Aiete and reduced to the extremity of starvation, but are rescued by his son *M*aillefer, with Guillaume, and *R*enoart fights the monstrous Gadifer in another combat of classical type. He wins.

Galien le Restoré, bastard son of Oliver and Jacqueline, daughter of the emperor of Constantinople (v. *Voyage*), sets out to find his father, but succeeds only on the field of Roncesvaux itself (v. *Roland*) where Oliver, dying, is proud to recognise him. Galien has in the meantime overthrown the Saracen *M*auprin in a fight, and after that, with his help, and that of *G*uinarde, daughter of the Saracen King *M*arsile, who has fallen in love with him, he captures Montfusain, and frees Christian prisoners captured by the amir *B*aligant besieging Montfusain. He pursues *B*aligant who attacks Constantinople; his mother is in trouble, but he rescues her and becomes emperor. Returning to Spain to rescue *G*uinarde, again under siege, he makes her his empress.

Garin de Montglane, a series of haphazard adventures not much to our purpose, but interesting as the first in the Aymery group in fictional chronology.

Gaufrey is seeking to rescue his father Doon and Garin de Montglane, who are both prisoners of the Saracen *M*acabré. His daughter *F*leurdepine, in love with Berart de Montdidier (by repute) will help them, if they will help her to get Berart. Gaufrey meets Passerose, loves her, marries her, engenders Ogier, but has sworn not to remain more than one night in any place till he has rescued his father. Doon and his fellow prisoners meantime keep things lively for their captors. *M*acabré decides to set his two principal prisoners to fight each other, and Garin pretends to turn Saracen to encourage this. *M*acabré's plan is to starve them into weakness but of course Doon manages to kill him. The remaining prisoners are armed and, led by Berart, seize the palace, but the war – and the song – end with a series of conversions.

Girard de Vienne is one of the sons of Garin and uncle of Aymery who comes to join him at his court at Vienne. Girard does homage to Charlemagne, who is in bed, and the empress tricks Girard into kissing her foot instead of the King's. The insult arouses the fury of the kin who get Charlemagne at their mercy, but are reconciled, Aymery the most reluctantly.

Godin, the son of Huon de Bordeaux and *E*sclarmonde (q.v.) is carried off by Auberon and brought up at the court of the amir of Babylon, his mother's city (v. *Huon*); in the course of a series of wars in which magic is used to transport armies, Godin rediscovers his religion and his birth and the Saracens are discomforted.

Gormont et Isembart. Only a fragment survives of the song, although more is known of the story. King Louis persecutes Isembart maliciously and without cause and drives him to join the Saracen King *G*ormont and to change his religion. *G*ormont with Isembart invades France, and all are killed (King Louis dies of his wounds); Isembart repents his apostasy.

Gui de Bourgogne. The sons of Charlemagne and his companions grow up during the 27 years that their fathers are warring with little success in Spain, and elect Gui as their own king, and set off for Spain to find the lost army of their fathers. The armies meet and operate with affectionate rivalry; they besiege and capture the city of Luiserne, the honour being disputed between Gui and Roland, so that Charlemagne orders the city evacuated, and prays God to destroy it, which he does; it becomes a lake.

Gui de Nanteuil is the sequel to *Aye d'Avignon* (q.v.). Although Gui has settled well into *G*anor's kingdom and helped convert the people, he has to take on his father's feuds. He wages war on Charlemagne, who favours his enemies. At the siege of Nanteuil he is only saved by the arrival of *G*anor, and of his step-brothers by Aye and *G*anor, and the amir of Iconium ('Coine'), a friend of *G*anor's, called *G*randoine. *G*randoine and Gui fight side by side in the ensuing battle, also described as a tourney, and *G*randoine and Flandrine, niece to Charlemagne, fall in love, and he turns Christian to marry her. There is a general reconciliation and Gui marries his lover Ayglentine, from whom the war has separated him.

Gui de Warewic. The unstructured adventures (as so often in the later poems) of a muscular Christian who at the end of a long life of excitement and endurance is fetched away by the archangel Michael; two episodes interest us, his war in defence of Constantinople against the amir of Babylon, and his service with King *T*riamor of Alexandria against the giant *A*morant.

Guibert d'Andrenas. Hermengarde wants the aged Aymery, now 140 years old (v. *Aymery*), to endow his youngest son, Guibert, with his own fief of Narbonne, but he leaves it instead to his godson; Guibert, like the other sons, must earn his fief from the Saracens, but the family go in force to help him, they take Balaguer and invest Andrena, where Aymery is captured by the Saracens. *G*aiete, daughter of the Saracen King *J*udas, is in love with Guibert from his reputation, and helps the French to storm the city.

Guillaume: *La Chanson de Guillaume*, of which the only manuscript was discovered in 1901, combines the plot of the end of *Chevalerie Vivien* (q.v.) with that of *Aliscans* (q.v.), which begins with Vivien's death and goes on to the victory of *R*enoart that follows the defeat of Guillaume. This version links a first half of high tragedy, modified by the usual note of unreal exaggeration, with a carelessly joined continuation of near knock-about.

Guillaume: *Enfances Guillaume*. Adventures against Saracens who attack Narbonne; in the course of these Guillaume first meets *O*rable, who marries *T*ibaut, but loves Guillaume (but v. *Orange*). The Saracens capture Aymery, but Guillaume rescues him and wounds *T*ibaut, and the Saracens are thrown back to the sea.

Guillaume: *Moniage Guillaume*. There are two versions; the basic story of both, and the only one in the first, is Guillaume's vocation to end his days in monastic repentance, when his wife and family are dead. He cannot adjust his way of life to that of the monks, and he so embarrasses them that they plot to get him killed by bandits; when this fails there is a reconciliation, but all agree that he should become a hermit. There are minor variations in the second version, but there is also a long interlude when he is kidnapped by *S*ynagon, Saracen King of Sicily, and escapes as an army of rescue arrives, he saves Paris in single combat with King *Y*soré, who is campaigning to avenge his uncle *S*ynagon, and then returns to his hermitage.

Huon de Bordeaux, in trouble with Charlemagne for killing his son 'Charlot' under provocation, is sent by him to the court of the amir of Babylon to kiss his daughter, bring back a hair of his beard and four teeth, and to kill the chief guest present. The amir's daughter, *E*sclarmonde (q.v.), befriends him, they fall in love and escape together under the presiding influence of Auberon (q.v.), King of fairies, and experience increasingly magical and enchanted adventures, and return to further struggles in France, before Huon is settled in his inheritance.

Jérusalem, the story, as in *Antioche*, fantastic in detail but historical in framework, of the First Crusade (after the capture of Antioch).

Jourdain as a baby is saved by the sacrifice of his liege's child from his feudal enemy (like Beton, v. *Daurel*) and as he grows up experiences various adventures against Saracens before he recovers his rights.

Loquifer. Renoart and his wife Aelis are kidnapped by *D*esramé's men and taken to sea, but *R*enoart saves them himself. *D*esramé,

*R*enoart's and *G*uibourg's father, then sends his monstrous ally *L*oquifer against them, and *R*enoart kills him at the end of a protracted battle. *D*esramé, with *G*uibourg's former husband, *T*ibaut, kidnaps her to wipe out her shame (v. *Orange*); *R*enoart does not intervene, but she is rescued by her present husband, Guillaume; he fights *D*esramé, who in one version is killed, in another, escapes death, though apparently dead. Picolet, Auberon's brother, is *L*oquifer's envoy, interferes constantly, and in both versions kidnaps Maillefer, *R*enoart's baby son, after *R*enoart experiences aberrant enchantments. *M*aillefer is saved by Picolet from death, but left to be brought up by *T*ibaut (v. *Moniage Renoart*).

Mainet (fragment). Charlemagne's youth, as a refugee from a usurper, at the court of the Saracen King *G*alafre of Toledo, whose daughter, *G*allienne, he marries; his further adventures; how he saves Rome; his restoration to the French throne; the death of *G*allienne. (The story is known from a number of sources.)

Maugis d'Aigremont. The adventures of the skilled enchanter and amorous cousin of the Quatre Fils Aymon (q.v.) in Saracen service.

Les Narbonnais. Aymery (q.v.) has plans for his seven sons, who scatter in different pursuits, four of them at the royal court. The Saracens besiege Narbonne, but the sons and the king save the city and destroy them.

Ogier: *Chevalerie Ogier*. Charlemagne's son Charlot has killed Ogier's son with a chess-board, and a vendetta ensues; Ogier is captured and imprisoned, and Charlemagne thinks starved to death, but he is saved by Archbishop Turpin by a trick. The Saracens invade France successfully, and all the paladins agree that only Ogier can save them. He does so, on condition that he is given the right to kill Charlot, but at the last moment an angel intervenes to forbid it and he is quit for a blow.

Ogier: *Enfances Ogier*. Another attack on Rome, under the leadership of the Saracen *C*orsuble; Ogier fights with *C*arahuel, lover and accepted suitor of the amir's daughter, *G*loriande. Ogier is captured by treachery which so horrifies the honourable *C*arahuel that he gives himself up to Charlemagne. *C*orsuble wants to give *G*loriande to a new lover, but she helps Ogier to escape, the lovers are united, and *C*arahuel helps the (honourable) Christians to defeat the (dishonourable) Saracens, but he refuses baptism.

Orange. An escaped Christian prisoner's account of Orange and *O*rable its queen excites Guillaume's cupidity; he and his nephew Guielin go in disguise to Orange, and with the help of *O*rable, and after the usual battles, they take it from *A*rragon, her stepson, who is holding it for his absent father, *T*ibaut. She is baptised under the name of *G*uibourg, and marries Guillaume.

Otinel, ambassador from the Saracen Marsile to Charlemagne, wants to fight Roland, who has killed his uncle; he does so, but the fight is interrupted by the descent of the Holy Ghost, and the consequent conversion of Otinel, who is rewarded with the hand of Belissant, daughter of Charlemagne; he becomes one of the paladins, accompanying Charlemagne in his campaign against the Saracens in Italy, and taking his share of the fighting.

Pampelune (continuation of *l'Entrée d'Espagne,* q.v.). Charlemagne conquers Pampluna, and its king, Malceris, becomes Christian, with his son Ysoré, but is refused the honour of being numbered among the 12 peers, and goes back to his allegiance to the Saracen King Marsile; Ysoré, however, remains Christian and advises and fights for the French; after embassies, treasons and battles, the French win the usual victories.

Pontieu. The countess of Pontieu is captured by Saracens and marries the sultan; later her original husband, the count, is also captured, and she devises their escape together, but her child by the sultan gives birth to the line of Saladin.

Quatre Fils Aymon is in the classic form of the feud with Charlemagne, whose son is killed by Aymon's brother, killed in turn by Charlemagne's agent; Renaud, eldest of the sons, quarrels with Charlemagne, and kills his nephew with a chess-board (cf. *Ogier*). The rest of a long poem is about their wars with the emperor. Two episodes chiefly concern Saracens, the aid they give to the King of Gascony against the Saracen Bege; and their pilgrimage to the Holy Land, where they take part in a war against the Saracens, and, returning home, another war, in Sicily, against the amir of Persia. In the end they make their peace with Charlemagne, but Renaud, working as a pilgrim mason in Cologne, is martyred by jealous fellow-workmen.

Raoul de Cambrai, disinherited by Louis, he takes arms against inoffensive neighbours on a moral quibble, and attracts his own mother's curse. He threatens every sacrilege against a convent of nuns, whose abbess is his squire Bernier's mother, and does in fact burn her and her nuns in their convent; finally he is killed in battle by Bernier who after great heart-searching has renounced his allegiance. In a patched on section Bernier's son, Julien, carried off and brought up a Saracen, is surrendered to his father, in return for services rendered to King Corsuble the Saracen.

Enfances Renier. This is a final flicker of the Renoart sub-cycle (Renier is Maillefer's son, for Maillefer see Renoart), set in Sicily and Greece, and a complex series of adventures. Ydoine, daughter of the Saracen Brunamont, loves Renier. Their son will be Tancred (de Hauteville: Hauteville propaganda).

Renoart: Moniage Renoart. Just as Renoart decides to become a monk to

repent his sins of violence, he sees one coming, robs him of his habit
and presents himself at the monastery, where he gains entry by
killing the porter. He tries to join in singing the office, but the monks
do not want him, he cannot fast because he must be strong to fight,
and he is always distracted by the need to search for Saracens and
destroy them. He encounters an army of them under his own son
Maillefer, kidnapped when he was a baby (v. *Loquifer*). A ding-dong
battle between father and son ends when they realise each who the
other is, and Maillefer and his Saracens are converted. *R*enoart
returns to his monastery; but see the sequel in *Gadifer*.

Roland. An exchange of embassies (this is the prototype of the embassy
challenge) between *M*arsile of Spain and Charlemagne leads to the
treason of the latter's envoy, Ganelon. The rear-guard of Charlemagne's army returning to France is caught at Roncesvaux, where
Roland's obstinate refusal to sound the oliphant until too late ensures
their death, but warns Charlemagne to return and avenge them. In
his turn the amir *B*aligant comes from Babylon to turn the tide again,
but the Frenchmen win the final victory.

Roland à Saragosse (Provençale). Roland wants to keep an assignation
with Queen *B*raslimonde (though they have never met) in Saracen-
held Saragossa. Oliver is offended because Roland wants to enter
the town alone, as he in fact does. He meets the Queen in public, and
she gives him her cloak, which he will wear for love of her. King
*M*arsile sends troops to capture him; he fights them off, but is very
hard-pressed. It is long before Oliver finally comes to his rescue and
their quarrel is not made up immediately.

St Nicolas: *Le Jeu de St Nicolas*. The saint's miraculous intervention to
protect treasure entrusted to his care, to defend his own image and
resist Saracen invasion ends in the conversion of some but not all of
the Saracen amirs.

Saisnes: *Chanson des Saxons*. Guiteclin, Saxon king commanding an
army of pagan nations and Saracens, makes war on the Franks, and
massacres Christians at Cologne. Charlemagne takes the field, the
two armies are separated by the Rhine, and Sebille, Guiteclin's wife,
makes love to a Frankish extrovert hero called Baudouin, who, when
Guiteclin is killed, marries Sebille and succeeds to the kingdom; but
Guiteclin's sons avenge him, and Charlemagne has to conquer the
Saxons over again.

*S*aladin. A legendary account of *S*aladin's rise and entry into Cairo, and
an entirely legendary visit to Europe, his tourneyings and gallantries
there, his brief invasion of England and return to his own country
and his death.

Simon de Pouille. Charlemagne sends his counts to Jerusalem where a
rumour is circulating that *J*onas, amir of Persia, plans to invade

France. When they investigate they are taken prisoner but, led by Simon, they escape, and meet *S*ynados, *J*onas' seneschal, whom they defeat and convert. They shut themselves up in a tower, *S*ynados is captured, but escapes with the help of *L*icoride, daughter of the amir, who loves him. Simon is captured, but overturns the gods, tricks the amir, and rescues *L*icoride; in another version the lovers are captured, but an attempt to ambush Simon fails, and in both cases the armies of Charlemagne arrive in time to save them all.

Thèbes. The story of Oedipus.

Turpinus. Legends of Charlemagne dressed up as history; his youth (cf. *Mainet*) and campaigns in Spain supposedly told by his archbishop Turpin of Rheims. In one expedition the French sweep successfully across Spain; in the next, the African invader *A*golant is defeated after an interesting argument, and in a new campaign all Spain submits. Charlemagne's death is revealed to Turpin in Vienne and Calixtus II adds the death of Turpin.

Vivien: *Chevalerie Vivien*. Vivien, Guillaume's nephew swears at his dubbing never to retreat a foot of land before Saracens; Guillaume warns him against imprudence. Vivien leads an army into Spain and after some success mutilates horribly a shipful of Saracen merchants who are sheltering in port; *D*esramé swears vengeance, his huge army invades France at the Archamp (Aliscans), Vivien, outnumbered, shelters in an old tower at night and sends to Guillaume for help. As he arrives, Vivien is terribly wounded, and the poem ends; it is here that *Aliscans* takes it up (q.v.).

Enfances Vivien. Garin is a prisoner of the Saracens, freed against the surrender of his 7-year-old son Vivien as hostage. Sold into slavery and brought up by a kindly merchant and his wife, he breaks away at the head of a band of adventurers, captures Luiserne and holds it until relieved.

Voyage de Charlemagne. Charlemagne, whose wife has said that Emperor Hugo of Constantinople is his better, tours Jerusalem with the 12 peers, and then calls on Hugo; in their excitement they rival each other in making absurd boasts. Oliver's night with the emperor's daughter is ambiguous. Heavenly intervention makes some of the silly boasts good on condition there shall be no more.

INDEX

841.
103
2
DAN